THE DEMON
IN
THE WIZARD

R. THOMAS RODGERS

Note for Librarians: A cataloguing record for this book is available from Library
and Archives Canada at www.collectionscanada.ca/amicus/index-e.html

Printed in Victoria, BC, Canada.

ISBN: 978-1-4269-0177-5 (soft)
ISBN: 978-1-4269-0179-9 (e-book)

*Our mission is to efficiently provide the world's finest, most comprehensive
book publishing service, enabling every author to experience success.
To find out how to publish your book, your way, and have it available
worldwide, visit us online at www.trafford.com*

Trafford rev. 10/1/09

 **www.trafford.com**

North America & international
toll-free: 1 888 232 4444 (USA & Canada)
phone: 250 383 6864 ♦ fax: 812 355 4082

PART ONE

ALONE, MISERABLE, AND ANXIOUS, sixteen-year-old Rhiannon dropped to her knees in the snow and wept. After the episode passed, she pulled herself together and sat back on her heels. "Come on, Rhi," she said to herself, "you can do this, I know you can." After taking a deep breath, she opened her eyes and stood up again, her back against the relentless wind.

High above, the moon called Titan moved sluggishly through the clear night sky, escorted by her sisters, Eden and Chaos. Their reflected light illuminated the ice on the escarpment wall, casting shadows across the jagged rocks below. The southern face of the Wizard's Escarpment was still covered with ice and snow, completely indifferent to the spring breeze that was scouring away the winter in the valley beyond the shadows.

Rhiannon now stood on the edge of those shadows facing the steep vertical wall of the escarpment. If she was going to look for her friend, Breandan, she'd have to move fast, for once winter released its grip on the frozen face of the rock, climbing would be all but impossible as the rock face of the escarpment wall became too brittle to support any weight.

Rhiannon closed her eyes and pictured Breandan on that evening two years past. The fond image brought a smile to her pretty face. They had been friends since they were five years old, and had spent nearly all of their free time together, but as they grew older, family responsibilities had prevented them from being together as much as they would have liked. While Breandan's father had kept him busy working in his tavern – The Yellow Dog Inn, Rhiannon's father kept her busy tending his flocks of sheep in the meadows and glens around their small village. However, whereas Rhiannon was content with the simple life of a shepherdess, Breandan had a more restless spirit. He thoroughly enjoyed listening to the fascinating tales told by some of the old-timers who frequented the tavern. He never grew tired of hearing about the colorful wizards who had once inhabited the land. It did not trouble him for a moment that no one else believed the old legends for he had seen something in the eyes of those old storytellers that had made a believer out of him.

Breandan was only sixteen when he finally decided to climb the escarpment in his quest for the elusive wizard that supposedly lived there, and Rhiannon had not tried to talk him out of it. She knew that it would've been a waste of time. Instead, she took him to see the one person who might be able to help him accomplish his mission – the village shaman.

Sihir was a sorcerer of minor magic. He was a kind old man who did his best to heal the sick, but his mind was no longer as sharp as it once had been, and his memories could no longer be trusted. All the same, he was the only person alive that could still claim to have climbed the escarpment and met the wizard who lived there.

"Sihir, can you tell us how *you* managed to climb the escarpment?" Rhiannon asked as the fragrant aroma of freshly brewed tea filled her nostrils.

"There's nothing much to tell, I'm afraid. I just started climbing until I reached the top. It was easy at first, but it became more difficult by the yard. I was a young man in those days...and much thinner. Much, much thinner," he added, patting his thick paunch. "I could never do it again. Never, never."

"Is there any advice you can give me?" Breandan asked hopefully. "Anything at all?"

Sihir sighed and closed his eyes. "Oh dear, let me think. It was very dangerous, you understand. Very, very dangerous. You must watch your step every foot of the way. Don't try to rush."

"That's it?" Rhiannon asked, a troubled frown distorting her face. "That's all you can tell us?"

"Oh my, oh dear. I wish I could do more to help you," the old sage replied, "however, my memory is not as good as it once was."

"I understand," Breandan said sympathetically.

"I have good days and bad days, you see. Today is not so good, no, no. Not so good. Even if I could remember more, it wouldn't matter," Sihir added with a frown as he moved to the small stove in the corner where he started pouring tea into cups. "Would either of you care for some tea? I just brewed it."

"Why wouldn't it matter?" Rhiannon asked, accepting the cup of tea with a nod.

"Because, lass, if Breandan is supposed to succeed, he will succeed. If he is supposed to fail, he will fail. It is as simple as that. It's really up to the wizard, you see."

"Wizard? What does the wizard, supposing there really *is* a wizard; have to do with climbing the escarpment?" Rhiannon asked.

"Oh my, oh dear. There is a wizard, all right, yes, yes. That I can promise you. Yes, yes."

"Right," said Rhiannon, skeptically. "But like I said, what does a wizard have to do with it, anyway?"

"Well...it *is* his escarpment after all," Sihir stated with some mild amusement as he handed Breandan a cup of steaming hot tea.

"So?"

Sihir sighed. "The escarpment is a test, lassie. And believe you me when I say, it is a very difficult test. Not just anyone can accomplish it. If you slip and fall---"

"Splat!" Rhiannon finished for him, looking at Breandan with an 'I told you so' smirk.

"Yes, yes," Sihir agreed as he sipped tea from his own cup. "Quite."

"All right, we all agree that the climb is dangerous. So what?" Rhiannon continued.

"If Breandan really intends to climb the escarpment, he will need an extraordinary amount of courage and determination. As well as some common sense."

Rhiannon looked at Breandan. "Breandan is very brave. He also has more common sense than anyone I know."

"I hope you're right," Sihir said. "For there's much more to climbing the escarpment than meets the eye. There are other... obstacles you know."

"Obstacles? Like what?" Breandan asked, suddenly more interested than he had been.

"Oh dear. I'm afraid I can't quite remember," Sihir said unhappily.

"Because---" Rhiannon began.

"Because I'm not supposed to remember," Sihir finished.

"Thank you, Sihir," Breandan said as he stood to leave. "You've been very helpful."

"I have?" Sihir asked, somewhat surprised.

"He has?" Rhiannon asked, just as puzzled and disappointed.

"Yes...of course you have," Breandan smiled, shaking the

old shaman's hand. "Now, I know for certain that I will find a wizard at the top of that escarpment, for you have seen him with your own eyes."

"Thanks for the advice, Sihir," Rhiannon said, taking Breandan by the arm as she pulled him out the door. "And thank you for the tea," she called, towing Breandan halfway across the street before she spoke again. "You don't really believe all this nonsense about a wizard, do you?"

Breandan nodded.

"Listen, just because Sihir says he climbed the escarpment, doesn't mean that he actually climbed the escarpment," Rhiannon whispered. "And even if he did, it doesn't mean that he really met a wizard up there. You know he's not quite right in the head. He said so himself."

"He was right about this," Breandan insisted. "Besides, you're the one who brought me here to see him," he added with a grin.

"Okay...all right...but even if he did meet a wizard up on the escarpment, that was a long time ago. Maybe he's dead by now."

"Wizards don't die."

"How do you know?"

"I just know."

"But Breandan---"

"I'm gonna do it, Rhi. I've made up my mind."

Rhiannon shrugged. It was no use. She could talk until she was blue in the face and it wouldn't change Breandan's mind. All she could do now was hope that he would survive the climb. "If you don't find your wizard, will you return to me?"

"Yes, of course. If I don't find the wizard, I'll return. I promise."

And so, on that poignant day two years earlier, Breandan had gone in search of his destiny leaving Rhiannon behind to ponder his fate. She had patiently waited for two years as she had promised. Now it was her turn.

With one more look up at the thousand-foot ascent, Rhiannon stepped into the shadows, took a deep breath, and began making her way up the rock wall. She assumed that the first hundred feet of the climb would be simple and straight forward, the footholds and handholds were fairly abundant, but she wasn't sure what to expect after that. She would just have to follow Sihir's advice and take her time.

Rhiannon never cared much for Breandan's talk of wizards and magic. When she tried to picture Breandan as a wizard she couldn't help but smile. Although she loved him with all her heart, she simply could not see it. He was just too mild mannered for such a grand label.

Rhiannon sighed and shook her head to rid herself of the images flowing through her mind. She didn't have time to reflect. She needed to concentrate on her climbing. She had elected not to wear any restrictive clothing. She wore only a pair of woolen breeches, and a heavy woolen sweater to keep her warm. She had no specialized climbing gear to assist her, just a pair of soft leather boots that Breandan's mother had made for her. She also carried the bed-warming pan that Sihir had given her. Before leaving home, she had followed Sihir's instructions and filled the bed-warmer with hot coals from the hearth in her parent's cottage and placed it inside her small backpack. It seemed to be working. It was keeping the cold at bay.

Just as Rhiannon had guessed, the first hundred feet of the climb had been relatively easy, not that much different from climbing the narrow hayloft ladder in her father's barn. However, by the time she had ascended the first four hundred feet, she found the climb becoming increasingly difficult. The cold was starting to get to her, too. Her hands and feet felt half-frozen. She needed to stop for a rest and warm up a little.

Before heading out on her search, Rhiannon had paid another visit to the old shaman. Fortunately, this time Sihir was a little more cognizant, and he was able to recall more about his own quest for the truth. In addition to this new information, he gave her two unusual gifts to help make the climb a little more bearable.

The first gift was a bundle of special twigs upon which he had cast a 'lasting' spell. The 'lasting' spell would allow the twigs to burn much longer than ordinary twigs. These special twigs could come in handy, providing she had the chance to use them; otherwise, they were just useless baggage.

The second gift was much stranger. "It's a bed-warmer," Sihir had said as he held out the strange object. It was made of brass and shaped like two small shallow bowls placed together rim-on-rim with a long wooden handle sticking out of one end.

"A what?" Rhiannon had asked.

"A bed-warmer," Sihir laughed. "Here, let me show how it works. First, you open the lid like this," he continued as he lifted one end of the contraption. "It opens on a hinge much like a claim-shell. Once you've opened it, you fill it with some hot coals from the fireplace. The coals will heat up the brass casing. Normally, you'd place the bed-warmer between the sheets of your bed and move it around to warm up the cold mattress before climbing in to sleep. It can make a chilly night much more pleasant."

"I see," Rhiannon said. "But how is a bed-warmer going to help me climb the escarpment? You don't really expect me to carry that thing up the escarpment wall on my back with that long pole sticking out of it, do you?"

"No, no, lassie, look here. You see...the handle is removable," the shaman said as he twisted the handle out from the brass casing. "See! Now all you have left is the pan."

Rhiannon nodded.

"You fill the pan with the hot coals and close the lid. Wrap some old rags around it before you put it in your pack. Make certain that you use clean rags, not greasy ones. The heat from the pan will radiate out from your backpack and help keep your body warm. I'm afraid it won't do much for your hands and feet. You'll have to stop from time-to-time to warm them."

"Can I actually do that? Stop from time-to-time?" Rhiannon asked.

"Yes...well...there are a few narrow ledges on the escarpment wall where you can rest. Some are narrower than others. However, if you're lucky, you'll find one where you can sit and build a little fire. Make sure that you take some food with you as well. You may need it."

"Is that thing heavy?"

"The bed-warmer? Not at all. The brass is thin but very sturdy. However, regular coals will not last very long. When you stop to rest, you can replace the used coals with some fresh ones from your fire. If you use the special twigs I gave you, and you are a little conservative, they should last until you reach the top of the escarpment."

As the old shaman was bending over to close the lid on the bed-warmer, Rhiannon noticed a small blue star tattooed on top of his bald head, but she was too polite to question him about it. Besides, she already knew that many of the men from her village bore one kind of tattoo or the other.

"Thank you for your help, Sihir," Rhiannon said. "I will not forget your kindness to me."

"Don't worry, lass," Sihir said as he walked Rhiannon to the door. "You will find Breandan. He is safe. I can sense it. Later tonight after vespers, I will light a few prayer-candles for you."

———•———

Looking around, Rhiannon spied a narrow ledge about thirty-five feet above her, slightly to the right. It took several minutes and most of her remaining strength, but she managed to reach it. She used a sharp-edged stone to chip away the ice directly above the ledge. It took nearly an hour, but at last she had a small, reasonable shelter where she could sit to escape the persistent wind that assailed the escarpment. Exhausted, she leaned back into the shallow spoon-shaped nook and gazed out at the land that stretched away far below.

Rhiannon was shocked at how quickly the time had passed. From the position of the sun, it was somewhere already well past midday. That meant that she had been climbing for nearly twelve hours. The sun was hiding behind a thick layer of dark nimbostratus clouds, and the shadows in the valley were merging into a patchwork of gray. In the dusky gloom, she could barely make out the smoke rising from the village chimneys just beyond the hills.

Exhausted, Rhiannon closed her eyes against the chill and fell into a deep and restless sleep.

———•———

Five hours later, Rhiannon awoke with a start. Her entire body ached and her neck was stiff. She felt as if she had been beaten with a wooden club. She stretched her neck this way and that, turning her head from side-to-side in an attempt to work out some of the stiffness.

High above, the clouds had finally dissipated. In the west, the sun was about to kiss the horizon goodnight. In the east, Titan and her sisters were peeping out at the retreating sun from behind a curtain of low clouds before taking the stage.

Rhiannon knew that she had to get moving again, except she dared not climb in the dark for fear of losing her footing and falling to the merciless rocks far below. She decided to wait until the moons were ready to lend their phosphoric light to her cause. It was also a good opportunity to address another issue. She was very hungry. She would have to eat before she could go any further.

Not wanting to burden herself with a heavy pack, Rhiannon carried her meager provisions in a small canvas sack strapped to her back. Apart from the bed-warmer pan, it contained a fresh loaf of her mother's bread, some dried beef, and a small tin drinking cup. She had also brought a flint stone with which to light a fire, and the tightly bound bundle of 'special' twigs Sihir had given her.

Rhiannon cleared a space on the ledge beside her and stacked half of her twigs into a neat little pile. She then built a barrier around it using some of the small stones she had chipped away from the rock face. The twigs were dry and took only a moment to catch the spark from her flint.

As Rhiannon's twigs began to burn, she scooped some snow into her cup and held it over the small fire. Within seconds, the snow had melted and she held the cup to her lips and drank. After warming her hands and feet, she leaned back into her niche and began to nibble on a piece of bread. She relished the taste of the plump juicy raisins that her mother had added just for her. Her meal was modest, but it sated her hunger and helped soothe the growing anxiety that gnawed away at her confidence. After some time, her humble little fire had completely devoured its fuel, so Rhiannon added the rest of the twigs Sihir had given her. They popped and snapped as what little remained of their moisture evaporated in the flames. They lasted longer than she expected.

Leaning back into her niche again, she closed her eyes and thought about the village shaman. She remembered his gentle, chubby hands patting hers as he handed her the enchanted bundle of sticks. Addlebrained or not, old Sihir was certainly the best-educated man in the entire village, and he had been the only one willing to help her.

Like most people in her community, Rhiannon had never received any kind of formal education. She had taught herself how to read and write, but she knew very little of the world beyond her village. Yet, when it came to understanding animals, Rhiannon was a natural. She felt a genuine empathy for them. She loved them all and treated them as if they were her own children. This was evident in the flock of sheep she tended. Not once in all her years of service had she lost a lamb, ewe, or ram to the relentless wolf packs that so often stalked the flocks in winter. Rhiannon had also given every animal under her care a name, and if she called to them, they would come running to her with their little tails wagging behind them.

It was not just sheep that loved her. It seemed as if every animal in the village had been bewitched to one degree or the other, and it was not unusual to see Rhiannon strolling along the street with a number of love-struck animals tagging along behind her.

As Rhiannon grew older and lovelier with time, her natural charms and magnetic personality captivated the hearts of the local lads as well, but Rhiannon was only interested in one boy – Breandan.

Breandan loved Rhiannon as well, but in the end, the lure of wizards and magic had been too strong to resist.

On the morning of his departure, he had kissed her lightly on the corner of her mouth and said, "Rhi, I don't know exactly what I'll find up there, but I want you to promise me one thing."

"Anything, Breandan," she had replied.

"Promise me that you'll wait two years before you try to follow me."

"And what makes you think I'd want to follow you?"

Breandan had not replied. Instead, he had just waited.

"Oh...all right," Rhiannon finally said. "I'll wait. But two years, that's all. No more, no less."

"Okay."

"But, Breandan, how will I know if you make it?"

"Rhi, if they don't find my body among the rocks, you'll know I made it."

"All right, but what will you do if you can't find this wizard of yours?"

"I'll find him, Rhi. I know without a doubt that I will find him."

"Okay...so, barring death by fall, what's the worse that could happen? You reach the top of the escarpment, but there's no wizard. Then you get hurt. You break your leg or something serious like that. Then what will you do?"

"Don't worry. I'm not going to get hurt. And if by some chance I do, I know that you'll come looking for me when the time comes."

"Two years is a long time to wait for help."

"I'll be fine, Rhi, and so will you."

Rhiannon tilted her head back and looked up at the escarpment towering high above them. "How do you know that I'll even be able to climb this thing?"

"If I can do it, you can do it. You know that you've always been better than me at everything," Breandan said with a smile.

Rhiannon blushed, but it was true. "If you do find this wizard, what'll you do if he refuses to acknowledge you? I mean, what if he's sick, or...or too busy to bother with you?"

"Rhi---"

"Okay, okay. You win. Go then. I'll follow in two years, not before. I promise. Except I'd better not climb all the way up that rock just to find out that you're dead," she said, only half in jest. "I love you, Breandan," she said with a hug.

Breandan smiled and kissed her lightly on the cheek. "I love you, too." Then he had turned away and walked into the shadow of the escarpment.

Rhiannon fell asleep, but her little fire burned on and on into the night. This time she slept more soundly.

———•———

When Rhiannon opened her eyes again, the three moons of Nox had returned to light her way. She stretched her aching arms and legs to help get the blood flowing again. All of the twigs the old shaman had given her were gone, having finally burned up during her slumber. However, the ashes were still hot. She quickly swept them into the shallow compartment of the bed-warmer, wrapped it up in an old chemise, and carefully placed it back inside her backpack along with her cup and the vestiges of her meal. To quench her thirst, she broke off a small icicle from the overhanging ledge and placed it on her tongue.

Rhiannon surveyed the valley far below. Here and there in the distance she could make out lights, perhaps those of some isolated farmhouse, or maybe the campfire of some lonely traveler like herself.

Rhiannon felt a sudden tug at her heart as the realization of what she was doing finally struck her. She was risking her life for love. *If Breandan really loves me, would he have run off in search of a silly dream? If he truly loves me, would he not have attempted to contact me after all this time? Two years have past and not a single word from him. Maybe the villagers are right. Maybe he is dead. Maybe he made it to the top of the escarpment only to meet with his death at the hands of something unexpected. The old shaman is the only one who still insists that Breandan is alive. But Sihir is a silly addlebrained old fool.* She considered turning back, but if she went back now, she knew that she would never see Breandan again.

"Okay, Rhi," she said aloud, "let's get this over with."

Rhiannon bent down and retied her boots straps, then stood up straight and adjusted her backpack. With one last look at the valley below, she began to climb again.

The sleep had done her some good, and she found herself making excellent time. During the night, the temperature had dropped well below freezing, refreezing the face of the wall and giving her the slight advantage she needed. She was worried that she might have misjudged her timing and waited too long to begin the climb. If only she had started a week earlier, her chances of reaching the top would have been better. Rhiannon also realized that once the sun caressed the frozen face of the rock wall, the ice would start to melt and the climb would become more dangerous than it already was. Any misstep could easily be her last. If she lost her footing now, she would tumble to the rocks below.

By sunrise, she had scaled an additional three hundred feet, putting her more than halfway to the summit. She was beginning to tire but stopped just long enough to finish the little bread and dried beef left over from her earlier meal.

Resuming the climb, she munched on ice crystals to ease her thirst.

The climb was becoming more difficult by the minute, and Rhiannon had slowed to a snail's pace. Several times she lost her footing on the crumbly rock and slid back several feet. Her body was covered with dozens of painful cuts and bruises. Nevertheless, she struggled on until darkness forced her to halt once again. This time there was no place to sit and no way to get out of the wind. In fact, the ledge on which she stood, was so narrow, she barely had room to stand.

Frightened and cold, without food or a place to rest, Rhiannon turned and pressed herself against the wall as tightly as possible. A thick mist now shrouded the top third of the escarpment, making it impossible to see more than a few feet in any direction. She didn't know how high she had climbed, or how much farther she had to go.

She was exhausted. She fought to remain awake, but she was losing the battle. Her battered body was growing numb with cold, and her eyelids felt as if the weight of the world rested upon them.

She fell asleep.

Her subconscious mind soon began to entertain her with lovely visions of home – her pleasant little village with familiar smiling faces, the peaceful valleys with their lazy rivers, rolling green hills, and lush green pastures where she tended her sheep. All at once, she was walking through a familiar field, surrounded by her flock, heading back to the little cottage and another of her mother's delicious meals. She could even smell the beef stew simmering on the stovetop.

As she drifted deeper and deeper into the dreamscape, her unconscious body began to slip forward until she was leaning out over the abyss.

Suddenly, Breandan was there in her dream. His dark brown eyes, his unruly hair, and his warm smile filled with love. It caused a tear of joy to run down her cheek. Then, the smile on his face fell away as his expression changed to one of alarm. Silently he called out to her, *"Wake up, Rhi...wake up!"* The unexpected change jolted the dreaming girl awake and back into reality just as she was about to slip over the ledge. In a frantic attempt to regain her balance, she windmilled her arms backwards. Just before her feet slipped out from under her, her left hand grasped the branch of some unseen plant or tree growing out of the rock directly above her head. Rhiannon found herself dangling hundreds of feet above the rocks below. In desperation, she reached up and grabbed the branch with her other hand and slowly dragged her feet back onto the narrow ledge.

Pressing herself against the rock wall, she untied the leather strap that she wore around her waist and slipped it over the branch until it was secured. Then, taking a deep breath, Rhiannon leaned back and gave the branch a hard tug. It held. She tried again, only this time she pulled as hard as she could. Still it held.

Relief flooded through her. She felt confident that the tree, or whatever it was, would hold her weight. With a deep sigh, Rhiannon released her grip on the strap. No longer able to fight it, Rhiannon closed her eyes and fell into another deep and dreamless sleep.

Around mid-morning, Rhiannon awoke to the clamor of angry birds. As soon as her eyes adjusted to the gray winter light, she looked around. The mist had dissipated somewhat allowing her to see more than she had during the night, and what she saw amazed her. She was surrounded by dozens of birds, birds of all kinds, pecking and clawing at one another in a frenzy of down and feathers.

At first, she thought they were fighting over her, and then she saw the real object of their contention – heart-berries. The rocks around and above her were literally carpeted with heart-berry bushes. In the mist enshrouded darkness, she had climbed right into their midst without realizing it. It was a heart-berry bush to which she had tethered herself. Unrestrained tears of joy and relief poured down her cheeks. The sound of her happy sobbing alarmed the quarrelsome birds into taking flight, only to return several seconds later to stare at her suspiciously. Within moments, they were quarreling again, but Rhiannon ignored their noisy company. She was more interested in filling her own empty stomach with the nourishing fruit.

Heart-berries were one of the most precious natural resources her world had to offer. Their bright red color was always a welcome sight to any wearisome traveler. Heart-berries were much more than mere food, for they had the power to rejuvenate one's body and spirit. Their juice could also be used to heal superficial wounds and bruises, and ease the pain of aching muscles and joints.

Rhiannon reached up, grabbed a large cluster of the sweet

berries, and began eating them whole. The plump, succulent fruit tasted heavenly, and she continued to stuff her mouth full.

Heart-berries took their name from their large heart-shaped seeds found within their centers. The seeds are also eatable, and many taverns and other drinking establishments generously served the seeds, lightly salted of course, to their regular customers to help prevent hangovers.

As the tasty juice ran out the corners of her mouth, it dripped down onto her scratched hands and forearms, promptly reminding her of the berry's medicinal uses. Grasping another handful of fruit, Rhiannon squeezed the healing juice onto her battered body and rubbed it into the tender scrapes and contusions. Immediately her fresh wounds began to sting terribly, but within seconds the pain began to fade leaving her cuts and scrapes clean and disinfected. As the tangy-sweet berries digested in her stomach, a sense of well-being spread throughout her entire body, giving her the renewed strength and confidence she needed to continue her endeavor.

With her belly full, her appetite sated, Rhiannon felt it was time to start again. Taking hold of the strap for security, she leaned out over the ledge, and looked down. It was difficult to determine exactly how high she had climbed. She estimated that she was approximately two hundred feet from the top of the escarpment. It was this last two hundred feet that would be the most difficult. She only hoped that she could reach the summit before the next sunset. Taking a deep breath to clear her head, she carefully unfastened her strap from the over-hanging heart-berry bush.

The hungry birds ignored her for the most part. They seemed to have settled their dispute over territory and were busy stuffing themselves with as many berries as they could eat.

Carefully, Rhiannon turned herself around to face the wall

again. She reached up, grabbed hold of the bush and hoisted herself onto the overhanging ledge. Then, using the heart-berry bushes as a sort of ladder, she continued up the rock wall. Suddenly one of the feasting birds attacked her, snatching a few strands of hair from her head with its beak.

Rhiannon was startled by the suddenness of the assault and almost lost her grip on the bush. Then, two more birds dove at her. The first darted in and scratched her right forearm while the second managed to snare a few more strands of her hair.

Within seconds, a score of birds were darting in and out, scratching, biting, and pecking.

"Stop it!" Rhi shouted.

The birds ignored her. They were determined to protect their territory.

Then Rhiannon saw the true cause of their concern. The heart-berry bushes were full of nests, and the nests were crammed full of eggs. She knew that she had to get out of there as quickly as possible or the birds would continue to attack her until they had torn her to shreds.

Keeping her head low, Rhiannon pulled herself up the escarpment wall one bush at a time. She moved as quickly as possible, although it was impossible to avoid the angry birds completely. They struck at her repeatedly. She tried her best not to damage any of their eggs, but it was unavoidable. At last, her living ladder ended and she emerged from the bushes scratched and bloodied in at least two dozens places, but at least the birds had stopped attacking.

Rhiannon sighed in frustration as she gazed upward. From here, the wall above was completely smooth. There was not a single handhold anywhere to be seen. There was no place to rest, no place to recuperate. Her only option now was to move horizontally and hope that she could find a way up the escarpment wall at some other location.

Despite the painful wounds on her arms and hands,

Rhiannon laughed, for once the infuriated birds had abandoned their assault, the bleeding stopped, thanks in part to the heart-berries she had just consumed.

"Why did the old shaman send me this way?" she wondered aloud. "Surely he knew I'd come to this dead end. There must be a way up somewhere."

Abruptly, a small sparrow hawk alighted on a small branch near her right shoulder. Cocking his head, he gazed at her with beady avian eyes.

Rhiannon managed a weak smile. "Well, little friend," she said, "are you going to attack me as well?"

The little hawk gave Rhiannon another inquisitive look and then hopped away a few feet to the right.

Not yet understanding the hawk's purpose, she watched in silent amusement.

Hopping back to her, the odd little bird bobbed its head a few times and then skipped off again to the right.

Rhiannon wrinkled her nose. "Are you trying to tell me something, little one?" she asked. "Or is it just wishful thinking on my part? Do you know a way out of here?"

Bobbing its head again, the hawk skipped away a few more feet. Then it turned back to stare at the girl.

"You want me to follow you?" Rhiannon asked with a sigh. "Wait a minute. You wouldn't be trying to lead me into another ambush, would you?"

The little hawk fanned its wings as if to say, "Who? Me?"

"Well...all right then...what do I have to lose? Lead away my little friend."

The sparrow hawk led Rhiannon on a treacherous, but manageable route horizontally along the face of the rock wall. The going was slow but steady. From time to time, Rhiannon would have to stop and rest. Each time, the sparrow hawk waited patiently until she was ready to move again.

After several hours, the little hawk glanced back at

Rhiannon one more time and then suddenly sprang up and flew away into the newly developing mist.

Well, Rhiannon thought, *it looks like I've been abandoned. I guess the little hawk got tired of waiting for me.* She put her face to the rock. She sighed. She felt like crying. Then she realized that the rock was surprisingly warm. Much warmer than it should have been. She looked up. Above her, only a foot away, the mist had parted to reveal a stairway carved into a narrow crevice. It looked like a tunnel with light showing through at the other end. The top edge of the escarpment was only a hundred feet away. Warm tears of joy flooded down her face as she hauled herself up onto the lower landing at the foot of the steps. For the first time in over twenty-four hours, she could stand without clutching at the rock. However, before she could go any further her trembling legs gave out and she sank to the floor in relief. Warm air drifted down from above driving away the chill and warming her face.

Exhausted, Rhiannon fell asleep.

Deep inside the planet, another life form – an entity of uncommon intelligence and completely alien to the outer world, had grown restless. It dreamt of only one thing – escape. Escape to where or what it did not know or care. It only wanted freedom. Yet, only once before in the long history of its underground world had any of its nature ever escaped from their prison. Very few of its kind knew or even considered the possibility that a different world outside of their own existed. But the entity was determined to try and escape even if it meant that its life might be forever extinguished in the process.

The entity, whose strange name was Neraka, waited until it was alone. It had waited a very long time. Only then did it begin to make its way up and out of the bleakness.

It slipped and slithered through molten rock and solid

stone unharmed, as its essence was indestructible to such things as heat and fire. For ages it climbed. Yet it knew no age. It knew no time. It had existed forever. It knew neither pain nor pleasure, felt no grief or joy. Only need, desire, and a deep longing for something else, anything else. At last Neraka reached the outer world. It poured out onto the surface of a cold flat stone like an invisible viscous liquid, invisible to the eyes of man. High above, a bright globe of fire burned in an endless expanse of a gray vapor. *Curious,* it thought. *What is this place?* It lay there for days pondering its next move. Occasionally there were sounds. Strange creatures moved through the open space above it. Suddenly, an even stranger creature crawled onto the rock beside it. Whatever it was, it seemed to be able to move about with ease. Whatever it was, it suddenly dropped down and stopped moving. *It is not dead. I can sense the life within it. Perhaps this creature will make a good host.* Neraka slipped inside the still creature and patiently waited to see what would happen next.

When Rhiannon awoke, she looked up and saw stars twinkling in the opening at the top of the stairway. She didn't care. All she wanted for the moment was to go back to sleep. Snow and ice that had collected on either side of the stairway was melting so rapidly that it was running down the stairway in little rivulets. She opened her mouth to catch some of the drops as they trickled past her face.

Out of the corner of her eye, she caught a flash of feathers as the sparrow hawk landed on a step at eye level only a foot from her head. In his beak was a cluster of heart-berries that he laid near her shoulder.

"There you are," Rhiannon said. "And here I was thinking that you had gone off and left me here for the buzzards."

The hawk nudged the cluster of heart-berries closer to the girl.

Rhiannon gratefully accepted the offering and stared at the hawk, who stared back at her while she ate. In no time, the berries had worked their special magic and Rhiannon was ready to climb the stairway.

The hawk, his work done, fanned his wings and prepared to fly away.

"Wait," Rhiannon called as she removed a thin silver chain from around her neck. "This once belonged to my grandmother. I want you to have it," she added as she held out the chain. "You saved my life. Please except it as a token of my gratitude."

The visceral creature flew to Rhiannon and landed upon her wrist. His talons gently gripped her arm. He bowed his head and allowed the girl to place the silver chain around his neck. That's when Rhiannon first noticed the small blue star on the top of his head.

Rhiannon's eyes widened in surprise. Then she smiled. *Sihir? Is that you?* The sparrow hawk did not reply, but went flying off into the night.

Filled with emotion, Rhiannon sighed and began to crawl up the stony stairway. Her legs felt like lead. She was shaking with both excitement and fear of the unknown. Her mind was a flurry of thoughts. A warm breeze drifted down from above, enveloping her with the scent of pine and wildflowers. When she neared the top of the staircase, she hesitated before taking the last few steps. Then, with her heart pounding against her ribs like a drum, she climbed the last few steps and set foot upon the legendary plateau.

The substantial differences between the plateau and the valley below were astonishing. A thousand feet below, winter clung stubbornly to the valley. Here, high above the land in which she had grown up, an enchanted summer spread out before her like a thick carpet. To the west she could see rolling green hills smothered with wild flowers that bloomed even in the twilight. To the north she could see lush green forests rich with flora and fauna of all descriptions. There were gently flowing streams and vast lakes full of fish and waterfowl. It was a garden of plenty. A paradise much like the one in the story from her people's holy book.

Then a weariness overcame her. Perhaps it was due to the time of night or perhaps it was because the anxiety was finally draining out of her. Whichever the case, Rhiannon crawled under a stately old willow tree and removed her small pack. Then she stretched out her limbs in the thick green grass and went promptly back to sleep.

The parasitic entity inside of her relaxed, too. The human senses – sight, taste, hearing, smell, and touch – were all completely new, and it was beginning to enjoy the sensations. It would learn. It would adapt. It would wait.

Meanwhile, Rhiannon slept on, completely unaware that her body and mind had been invaded by something so strange and utterly alien.

Petamor found her just as he knew he would, fast asleep. He gazed down upon her for several moments before reaching down to brush aside the hair that had fallen over her eyes. At that very moment, the late-morning sun burst through the clouds. Petamor could now see her clearly. He could see beyond the cuts and bruises that covered her pretty face to the beautiful woman she would eventually become.

Rhiannon was a petite girl, standing only four feet ten inches tall and weighing around a hundred pounds. Being from a northern climate, Rhiannon's skin was naturally fair. Her medium length hair was dark brown and tended to be unruly, giving her a somewhat wild appearance. She had a small heart-shaped face, with eyes the color of the northern sea – deep blue-grey. Her nose was neither small nor overly large, but it added a lot of character to her face. When Rhiannon awoke with the bright sun in her face, she looked up to see the silhouette of a mysterious figure looming over her. With a slight gasp she quickly drew away from the tall stranger. As her eyes adjusted to the light and her mind cleared away the remnants of the weird dream she had been having, she finally realized that she was looking up into the face of an old man.

The wizard stepped to one side, effectively blocking the sunlight that had been shining directly in Rhiannon's eyes. He smiled down at her; his kind gray eyes twinkled even though his face was turned away from the light. Using his wooden staff for support, he leaned down and offered her his hand.

Rhiannon tried to smile back and took the wizard's hand as he pulled her to her feet.

Petamor immediately noticed the cuts and scratches that covered Rhiannon's arms but decided not to mention it. Apparently, her climb had been more traumatic than he had anticipated.

"Welcome, Rhiannon. My name is Petamor and this," he continued as he gestured towards the expansive of land, "is my plateau. Breandan and I have been expecting you."

"Breandan?" Rhiannon asked hopefully.

"Yes," replied the old man with a warm smile. "Worry no longer. He is here, and he is alive and well."

Rhiannon looked around expectantly, hoping to spy her friend.

"Breandan's told me a great many things about you," the old man continued. "He's back at the tower now, preparing dinner. He wanted to come himself, but I insisted on coming alone. You and I have a couple of important matters to discuss first. We can talk while we return to the tower. It's not very far. Will you walk with me?"

Rhiannon nodded. "Are you...the wizard?" she asked.

"Yes, I am."

"And Breandan? Is he---?"

"A wizard? Well...no. Not yet at least. However, he has only one more year in which to complete his studies, and then we'll see. Now, my dear, the tower is this way." Without another word, Petamor turned and headed into the pine forest.

Rhiannon followed, nearly running to keep up with the long-legged wizard.

Impossibly tall trees towered majestically above them as they made their way through the cool sylvan shadows. Along the way, Rhiannon saw many strange animals, most of which she had never seen before. One of them was a tiny winged creature that resembled a dragonfly from a distance, but up close, it actually appeared to have a human face. Whatever it was; it was not the least bit alarmed by her presence and made no effort to fly away.

After some time, the forest gave way to gentle rolling hills laced with wild lavender. Rhiannon glanced up at the sky and then, for the first time since entering the forest, she shyly looked up and made eye contact with the old wizard.

Petamor's eyes were bright and clear; his smile was warm and sincere, and although his face was lined with age, it had a healthy glow.

"What is it you wanted to talk to me about?" Rhiannon asked.

"Well my dear, by climbing the escarpment you passed the first test. Now, I am obligated to offer you an apprenticeship."

"Apprenticeship? You mean...to a wizard?"

"Exactly. Of course, you would have to work very hard and---"

Rhiannon was no longer listening. She was in too great a state of shock.

"Rhiannon?" Petamor asked.

"Yes? Oh, I'm sorry. I...I---"

"If you accept the apprenticeship, you would also be the first human woman to do so. Well? What do you say? Do you wish to accept my offer?"

"Yes. I mean...yes, sir. I would very much like to be your apprentice." Rhiannon could not believe that those words had come out of her mouth. She had no real desire to be a wizard.

Petamor smiled. "Good. Breandan will be very excited."

At the mention of Breandan's name again, Rhiannon smiled.

"Don't worry, my dear," Petamor said. "It's not much farther. In fact, we're almost there. Then you can get yourself washed up, and we can treat those injuries of yours before we eat. I understand Breandan is preparing your favorite meal. While we dine, you can help Breandan get caught up on all the latest gossip."

Rhiannon smiled and nodded. She liked this old wizard. He seemed friendly and down to earth, not at all what she had been expecting.

Petamor stood more than six feet tall. He wore a lightweight woolen caftan, which was a deep chocolate brown in color, and matched perfectly the color of his hair and coarse beard. Despite his age, there was not a gray hair anywhere on his head.

In his right hand, he carried a slender staff of white oak equal in length to his height. The staff was carved with delicate, leafy vines that wove their way around strange runic symbols, set here and there between bands of polished copper.

"My staff," he said when he noticed her gaze. "Every wizard has one. Each one is different, and each one has unique properties related to the specific powers of the wizard who carries it."

"May I touch it?" Rhiannon asked.

"You may," Petamor replied.

Rhiannon reached out and gingerly ran her fingers over the intricately carved runes. It seemed to hum beneath her fingertips.

"What do these letters mean?"

"It is an ancient language. It is the language of my people. It will all be explained to you in good time. And if you successfully complete all of the curriculum I give you, you will have a staff of your own someday."

As Rhiannon gazed up at the wizard, her attention was suddenly drawn by something that flew past high in the sky. She stared in disbelief as a number of small winged horses disappeared into a dense bank of low drifting clouds.

Petamor glance back over his shoulder and said, "Is this the first time you have seen them?"

"Yes, but one of the men in my village claimed to have seen such a creature, and no one believed him. What do you call them? Have you ever seen one up close?"

"Yes, as a matter of fact I have. Many times. They are called rock hoppers."

"Really? They're so beautiful!" Rhiannon exclaimed. "Can they be ridden?"

"Ridden? Oh no, my dear, I'm afraid not. They may resemble horses, but they're not horses. They are wild animals, proud and free. They would never tolerate being ridden. However, I do have an arrangement with their leader. In return for protecting them from predators and poachers, he helps me transport my supplies from one of the local villages below the northern wall of the escarpment."

"They are truly a remarkable sight, don't you agree?"

"Yes, they are."

"What village do you go to for your supplies?"

"It is called Lorelei."

"That's odd. I have never heard of a village called Lorelei? Where is it?"

"Yes, well not many people on the southern side of the escarpment have," Petamor replied.

"Oh," Rhiannon replied, suddenly full of questions. But before she could ask any of them, they reached the crest of a broad hill. The old wizard stopped and pointed across a large lake at the bottom of the hill.

"There it is, my dear. That is what we call the Wizard's Keep."

Rhiannon followed Petamor's gaze. There, rising up from the center of the lake was a cylindrical stone tower roughly one hundred and twenty feet high by thirty-five feet in diameter. It was built out of dark gray granite, which presented a rather sinister, unwelcoming appearance, more like a prison than the abode of a friendly wizard.

Upon seeing the expression on Rhiannon's face, Petamor laughed aloud. "Oh, I realize that it doesn't look like much from the outside, but I can assure you that it is very cozy and accommodating on the inside."

"It looks a little like a jail house," Rhiannon stated honestly, "and I don't see any windows, either."

Petamor laughed again. "Well, I suppose it does look a little like a prison. The wizard who built it was called Allacor. He wanted a fortress that could withstand the passage of time; accordingly he built it strong enough to handle almost anything."

"Oh, I see. It's a little like a castle."

"Well...a little. However, the keep could not withstand a real siege by a determined enemy if it was not protected by my magic. And if you look a little closer, my dear, you'll see that there are, indeed, windows. They're just a little hard to see because they are covered with shutters that match the color of the stone."

Narrowing her eyes, Rhiannon stared across the lake towards the keep. With a little effort, she could make out several tall narrow windows spaced at various points in the tower wall. She also noticed that the top rim of the structure included an overhanging parapet supported by a corbel. "Yes, I can see them now," Rhiannon admitted.

———•———

Despite the cool breeze coming in off the lake, by the time they reached the southern shore Rhiannon was perspiring heavily. Obviously, Petamor was in better condition than she was, for he had not even broken a sweat. She looked down at the sparkling water of the lake. It looked so cool and inviting, she wanted to tear off her clothes and jump right in. Only modesty prevented her from doing so.

Then Rhiannon saw a lone figure standing at the base of the tower. He was waving. It was Breandan. For the first time in two years, Rhiannon felt that everything was going to be all right. She lifted her right hand and waved back.

"I don't see a boat anywhere. How do we get across?" she asked anxiously.

"No need for a boat," Petamor answered.

The old wizard stepped up to the pebbly shore of the lake and held out his oaken staff. Slowly, he lowered it until the tip broke the surface of the lake. Speaking aloud in a language that Rhiannon did not recognize, Petamor stirred the water from side-to-side using the symbol for infinity – a lazy eight. Within seconds, a faint blue glow began to spread out from the spot where the staff touched the water. Then the eerie blue light shot across the surface of the lake to the base of the tower. The water began to bubble and churn, followed by the sound of heavy stones rubbing together. Suddenly, a flagstone walkway appeared, rising up from the lake bottom like a prehistoric crocodile. It extended all the way from the shore at their feet to the base of the tower.

"Come, my dear. We can cross now," Petamor said with a smile.

"Is it safe?" Rhiannon asked anxiously.

"It's safe enough for the moment," Petamor replied, slightly amused at the look on Rhiannon's face. "Do not fear. The stones will remain in place until we reach the other side. But they will not wait forever. We must cross immediately."

Rhiannon did not need any further encouragement, nor did she wait for the wizard. In a flash, she was running to meet Breandan.

Petamor followed Rhiannon, although at a more dignified pace. As he went, the stone walkway fell away behind him, settling back to the bottom of the lake stone by stone.

"Breandan!" Rhiannon cried as she reached the base of the tower and ran into his arms.

"Rhi," he began, "I knew you'd make it. I never doubted it for a moment," he added, tenderly kissing her forehead.

Rhiannon looked up, her eyes wet with tears of joy. "When did you get so tall?"

"When did you get so short?" he teased, hugging her gently.

"Pardon me, Breandan," Petamor said. "I hate to interrupt this glad reunion, but I do believe that our guest would like to freshen up before we eat. Could you get her some fresh clothing and then escort her to the bathing chamber?"

"Right away, Grandfather," Breandan answered with a slight nod. Then he turned back to Rhiannon. "Follow me, Rhi. I'll get you some fresh clothing, and then I'll take you to the bathing chamber. It's very relaxing. I think you'll enjoy it," he added as he turned, and walked right through the tower wall.

Rhiannon gaped.

Petamor laughed. "It's just an optical illusion. You see, the door is surrounded by a force field, which reflects the stonewall like a mirror. It's all but invisible to the naked eye."

Rhiannon tentatively reached out and put her hand to touch the stonework, but it passed right through.

"Ah, now watch this," the old wizard said. He bent down, picked up a small stone, and tossed it at the invisible door. The stone bounced off as if the wall were solid. "You see. The force field will only allow us to pass through. No one else can enter without my permission."

"Wow!" Rhiannon responded.

"Ah...yes. Wow!" Petamor responded, as if using the word for the first time. "Wow, indeed! If I do say so myself. Now, if you will allow me," he added, offering Rhiannon his arm.

Rhiannon took it shyly.

Petamor led Rhiannon through the force field and into the great tower.

Rhiannon was certain that her eyes had deceived her. From the outside, the tower appeared no more than thirty-five feet across. However, the inside appeared to be twice that and more. Mystified, she followed Breandan through the main hall and into the study where a huge wardrobe stood against the wall. He opened the doors and reached inside. "Ah, here we are," he said. "This should fit you. It's very soft and very warm."

Rhiannon took the garment. It was a white cotton caftan, just her size. Next, he opened a drawer and found a new pair of sandals that also fit her perfectly. Then he took another slightly heavier garment from a hook. "This is a nightgown. It's made of wool and lined with rabbit fur to help keep you warm after sundown. This old tower can get quite chilly at night this time of year."

Rhiannon crossed her arms over her chest and shivered. For the first time since she'd entered the ancient edifice, she realized that it was at least fifteen or twenty degrees cooler inside the tower than outside. "I don't get it," she said. "It's just like summer outside, so why's it so cold in here?"

"Long story," Breandan answered with a smile. "I think I'll let Petamor explain it to you."

Rhiannon shrugged. "All right."

"Don't worry. The bathing chamber is quite warm, as you'll see. Now, if you'll bring your things along and follow me, I'll take you down there," Breandan added as he started down the great spiral staircase in the center of the tower. He led the way down into the very bowels of the tower keep.

The deep chamber had been carved directly into the ancient granite and extended far below the level of the lake, yet it displayed no signs of water leakage. In the heart of the circular room, set level with the floor, was a large circular pool of steamy water. In the center of the pool, fresh water cascaded down over a pile of smooth stones.

Breandan crossed the room to a large wooden chest set against the wall. He removed several candles and went around the chamber placing them in the graves of their predecessors. "What do you think of our bathing pool?" he asked, once he had lit the candles one by one.

"It's wonderful!" Rhiannon exclaimed as she began removing her climbing boots. "How deep is it?"

"The far end's about five feet deep, give or take an inch. The shallow end here is about three feet deep. Warm water from an underground hot-spring is forced up through those rocks in the center of the pool, constantly replenishing the pool with a supply of fresh clean water," Breandan explained as he opened the chest and took out two clean bath towels and a small wooden box.

Without thinking, Rhiannon began to remove her soiled clothing, but stopped when she saw the concerned look on Breandan's face. "Is something wrong?" she asked.

Breandan pretended not to hear the question. Instead, he hurriedly laid the towels on a low bench beside the pool and handed the box to Rhiannon. "This box contains some cleaning grit for bathing."

"Cleaning grit?"

"Yes. It's a mixture of powdered soap and very fine volcanic pumice," Breandan added as he opened the chest. "You see? Just scoop a little into the palm of your hand and rub it on the skin with a little water. You can also use it to wash your hair."

"Ummmmm...okay," Rhiannon said.

"Well then...enjoy your bath. And don't worry. You can take your time. I'll keep the food warm until you're ready. When you're done, you can join us back in the main dinning chamber. Just follow the stairs back up to the next level."

"Okay."

"Good. I'll see you in a little while," Breandan said, turning towards the stairs.

The entity inside Rhiannon stirred eagerly, wanting to exploit Rhiannon's physical urges. Her reaction was uncharacteristic. "Breandan! Wait a moment," she called. "Where're you going? Don't you want to join me? We can wash each other's backs like we used to do when we were children."

Breandan stopped but did not turn around. "Can't," he said, "I still have work to do."

"But Breandan...it's been so long since we spent any time together alone. I...I thought that you would be happy to see me. Can't you at least---"

"I am happy to see you, Rhi. Except things are different now. I'm not the same person I was two years ago."

"What're you saying? Don't you love me anymore?"

"Of course, I still love you, Rhi. But we're not children anymore. Look, I have to go. We can talk about this later. I'll see you after your bath."

"But---"

"I really have to go."

"Okay," she said, but Breandan didn't hear her. He was already gone.

Rhiannon sighed. Breandan was right. He had changed. But then again, so had she. He still loved her, of that she was certain, nevertheless two years was a long time to be apart. *I'm not going to worry about this now. I'm too excited. Perhaps in time, Breandan's feelings for me will resurface. I'll just have to be patient.*

Rhiannon felt strange. She looked around. For some reason, she had the impression that she was not alone. And sometimes her thoughts were so bizarre; they felt as if they were coming from someone else. *Perhaps it's just the altitude, she told herself. I've heard that the lack of oxygen can have strange effects on the brain, and the air up here is much thinner than it is in my valley. Hey! I bet that's it. That could also explain Breandan's behavior as well.*

⸻

Breandan hurried up the spiral staircase. He was troubled by Rhiannon's cheekiness. She had always been a very modest girl, valuing her honor and her virginity as her mother had always taught her. *Has she changed so much in two years?* He supposed it was possible. And there was something else, too. Something in her eyes. Something he'd never seen there before. It was a strange inner light that seemed to be watching him even when Rhiannon was not looking directly at him. On the other hand, maybe he had just imagined the whole thing.

⸻

Rhiannon removed her dirty clothing and ran her hands over her naked body. The heart-berries had done wonders, but there were still a few scratches and tender bruises. *Could this be the reason Breandan ran away from me just now? Am I so hideous? Maybe he isn't attracted to me any longer. Maybe there's someone else. Perhaps he's met someone new – someone in that village that the wizard mentioned. A shopkeeper's daughter or the like.*

Rhiannon sighed, lowered herself to the edge of the pool, and tested the temperature of the water with her toe. Finding the water temperature satisfactory, she slid into the pool until her shoulders were below the surface. Leaning back, she wet her hair. The warm water felt great, very relaxing. She could already feel some of her aches and pains dissipating. She took a deep breath and gazed around the room. It was one of the most unusual rooms she had ever seen.

The solid granite wall was dark-brown in color, in contrast

to the dark-gray of the rest of the structure, and it had been painstakingly polished to a high-gloss shine. As a result, it reflected the candlelight like a mirror. Its surface reminded her of the rolling waves of the sea. And even though the room was well below the surface of the lake, thick glass windows set into the wall allowed the lake-filtered light to penetrate even at this depth. She could actually see lake fish swimming past the windows.

Rhiannon reached for the cleaning grit and began to scrub her face and hair. The soap lathered nicely and had a pleasant lavender scent. The cleaning grit worked well on her skin, although it still took several washings to cleanse all of the dust out of her hair. Then she climbed up onto the edge of the pool to soap up the rest of her body and scrubbed away until her skin was as fresh and pink as that of a newborn babe's.

While she bathed, the water in the pool became cloudy with dirt and soap scum. Within minutes, however, the water had cleared up on its own. Curious, Rhiannon slipped back into the water and felt around with her foot until she found a small drainage grate about the size of a dinner plate near the center of the pool. She could feel the water being sucked out through the opening.

Rhiannon swam over to the middle of the pool where water cascaded down a mound of rocks that had been carefully arranged to resemble a natural waterfall. She reached out and let the soothing water run over her fingertips. *This is wonderful,* she thought with a smile. *I think I could learn to enjoy this lifestyle.* From somewhere deep within the very core of her being, her uninvited guest agreed with her.

At last, Rhiannon felt clean again. She climbed out of the pool and wrapped a dry towel around her body. She used her fingers to brush the tangles out of her hair as best she could, but there was no mirror in the room. In fact, she had not seen a mirror anywhere in the tower. She would have to ask

Breandan to try to find her one. In the meantime, the polished rock wall would have to do.

While she was attending to her outward appearance, her stomach began to growl. She suddenly had a ferocious appetite. Nevertheless, she must remember not to make a pig out of herself in front of Petamor and Breandan.

Despite her rumbling stomach, Rhiannon took the time to drape the damp towel over the bench to dry. Then she returned the unused towel and the remaining cleaning grit to the large wooden chest where Breandan had found it. She laced up her new sandals and slipped into the clean caftan.

While she was getting dressed, the water in the pool had cleared itself completely. She hoped that someday she could learn how it worked, so she could teach the people of her village how to build one. However, the idea stole away from her as her impatient stomach let loose with a fresh tirade of complaints. Hence, without further delay, Petamor's newest and youngest apprentice blew out all of the candles and hurried up the winding stairs to the main dinning chamber.

———•———

"Grandfather," called Breandan from somewhere within the great hall, "are we having wine with our meal?"

"Yes, of course we are, Breandan. After all, this is a special occasion. You do enjoy wine, don't you, my dear?" Petamor asked Rhiannon as she joined him at the table.

"I've only tasted it once or twice in my entire life," Rhiannon answered. "But it seemed very nice."

"Excellent. Well then, tonight, I think we'll have the heartberry wine, Breandan. It'll help Rhiannon's body heal from the inside out."

A moment later, Breandan emerged from somewhere behind the winding staircase carrying a tray of food.

"I take it the kitchen is back there," Rhiannon said.

"You take it correctly," Petamor replied. "Later this evening,

I'll have Breandan give you a complete tour of the place. I'd do it myself, but I know that you two want to spend a little time together."

"Can I go and look around a little now?" Rhiannon asked.

"Of course. You go right ahead," Petamor said.

While Breandan was busy setting the table, Rhiannon took a few moments to explore the kitchen that was hidden behind the great spiral staircase. It was unlike any kitchen she had ever seen before, and it would be the envy of any eating-place in the land. There were ovens, grills, iceboxes, and butcher-block tables. There were pots, pans, bottles, barrels, jars of spices, and fresh herbs drying from hooks. In addition, there was every type of cooking utensil imaginable.

To the left of the central staircase was a sitting room or den. It contained a fireplace, as well as several large overstuffed armchairs. There were also several enormous bookcases full of books and other unusual items, as well as a huge globe of the world that could turn on its own axis.

In both the sitting room and the dining room, the walls were adorned with ancient and elaborate tapestries depicting scenes of events that Rhiannon did not recognize. The dining room contained one massive dining table and two smaller tables set at each end of the larger table to form a short-sided U. All of the furniture was old and exquisitely made. Their warm colors abruptly reminded Rhiannon of the chill in the air and she shivered again.

"Are you cold, my dear? Would you like me to get you a warm cloak?" Petamor asked. "No, I'm fine. I just caught a cold draft," Rhiannon replied. "I don't need a cloak right now. But I don't get it. Why is it so cold in here when it's so warm outside?"

"Ah, yes. I was wondering when you would ask that question. Well, you see, many years ago when the original enchantment was placed on this escarpment; this tower was not yet built. Some time later, when the wizard Allacor finally constructed this tower with his own hands, it was still summer in the valley. He never placed the tower under the same spell as the plateau because he forgot to include the tower in the enchantment. Now the tower experiences the same weather conditions as the valley below. When it's winter in the valley, it is winter in the tower. Subsequently, when it's summer in the valley, it is summer in the tower. When he realized his error, he decided to leave it the way it was as a reminder that no one, not even a wizard, is infallible."

Rhiannon smiled as she took her seat at the table. "I don't mind the cold. I've always liked the winter season, sitting in front of a cozy fireplace. It's one of my favorite times of year." Breandan was filling large ceramic bowls with a savory beef stew. "That really smells wonderful," Rhiannon exclaimed.

"I should hope so. It's your favorite," Breandan said. "Bite-sized chunks of beef with lots of onions, potatoes, and carrots smothered in gravy."

"Beef?" said Petamor a bit surprised. "I would think that your favorite dish would be lamb, since your father raises sheep for a living."

"Rhiannon hates lamb," Breandan answered for her.

"Interesting," said the old wizard. "However, I think I understand. You become so emotionally attached to your animals that you can't tolerate the thought of eating one of them."

"That's part of it," Rhiannon admitted. "I'd never eat an animal from my own flock. But the truth is I just don't like the taste of it. My father's the same way. We both prefer beef when we can get it."

"How do you feel about chicken?" Petamor asked.

"I like chicken fried in butter, but my mother hates it. She claims that chickens are one of the filthiest animals that ever lived. She refuses to touch one, much less eat it. Mostly we eat vegetables because we're too poor to eat meat everyday."

Breandan turned and headed back into the kitchen. "I almost forgot the bread," he said.

"You know how to bake bread, too?" Rhiannon asked, amazed.

"Of course. I learned how to do a lot of things when I was working in my father's tavern," Breandan replied as he headed for the kitchen, "including baking bread."

"How come you never offered to cook for me before?"

"You never asked," Breandan replied.

Petamor winked at Rhiannon. "He's a fine lad and a good apprentice. And if he's as good at magic as he is in the kitchen, he'll make an excellent wizard one day."

Rhiannon was somewhat surprised by the old wizard's remark.

"Yes," Petamor continued. "Breandan's done very well. He studies hard, and he has learned all that I've taught him. I have no doubt that the league will approve of him when the time comes. Yet...there are times when he seems distracted. It's as if something is preventing him from realizing his full potential. He needs a little more time to learn how to focus his energy, I think. I'm hoping that your presence here will help anchor him more fully to his studies."

Rhiannon felt herself blushing. She was sure that Petamor was referring to her when he said that Breandan was distracted. *Is this old wizard blaming me for Breandan's shortcomings,* she wondered.

As if reading her thoughts, Petamor replied, "I know Breandan cares a great deal for you, my dear. He has not stopped talking about you since the day he arrived. If you are the reason for his lack of concentration, it's not your fault. A wizard must learn to deal with a great many emotional issues, lest of all the opposite sex."

Rhiannon wanted to say something in Breandan's defense, but before she could speak, Breandan returned with the bread.

"Grandfather, have you told Rhi about the league?" Breandan asked.

"League?" Rhiannon asked. "What is the league?"

"The League of Wizards," replied Petamor.

"You mean there's more than one of you?" Rhiannon asked although she was not completely surprised.

"Oh yes, my dear, there are still a few of us left. Not as many as in the old days, of course, although we can still hold our own if we need to."

"I don't understand," Rhiannon began. "If there're so many of you, why do you remain so... secretive? Most people don't even believe that you exist."

"We do what we can, but our powers are beginning to fade. The time has come for humans to take responsibility for their own world. But if you like, you can ask the other wizards that question in about a year, when they come here for Breandan's final test."

"What is the final test?"

"It's called the Lamp of Life ceremony. It is a test given to the apprentice by the members of the league to help them determine whether the apprentice, in this case Breandan, has mastered his studies and can be trusted with the powers that he will wield."

"I see, "Rhiannon said.

Breandan, however, seemed unconcerned. He looked at Petamor and asked, "Would you like some wine, Grandfather?"

Petamor nodded as he held out his wine glass.

Breandan poured some wine into the wizard's glass and then finished ladling the chunks of steaming hot stew into his bowl. Then he quickly and efficiently cut the bread into thick slices, and placed them on a platter beside a saucer of freshly whipped butter in the middle of the table.

"At home we only eat like this on special occasions, like papa's birthday," Rhiannon said. "If we have enough food, that is."

"Well...you'll find no shortage of good food here, my dear," the old wizard replied. "I like to keep my pantry well-stocked. And you are welcome to help yourself to anything you like anytime you like."

Petamor took a bit of beef and tasted it. "You have outdone yourself, my lad," he said. "This stew is delicious. You sure know your way into an old man's heart."

"You mean stomach, don't you, Grandfather?" asked Breandan as he filled his and Rhiannon's glasses with heart-berry wine.

Rhiannon smiled and tried to stifle a yawn. She took a sip of her wine. It was cool and sweet and went straight to her head making her feel sleepy again. She looked at her hand as she lifted her glass. Most of the scratches and bruises were already fading. Her scraped knuckles were all but healed.

"Raw heart-berry juice has great healing powers," Petamor said. "Except heart-berry wine works much faster. The alcohol helps speed up the healing process. By morning those scratches of yours will have all but disappeared."

"How *did* you get so cut up, Rhi?" Breandan finally asked. "Surely it wasn't from the rocks alone."

"No, it was just one of Petamor's obstacles," Rhiannon replied with a shy smile.

"Obstacles?" Petamor asked with raised eyebrows.

"Well...yes," Rhiannon answered. "You know...the obstacles you placed there to make the climb more difficult."

Petamor looked at Breandan. Breandan looked at Petamor. Neither one seemed to comprehend what she was talking about.

"You know...the soft, crumble rock...the birds---"

"Rhiannon, I didn't place any obstacles in your path. The climb, itself, is difficult enough as it is. Where did you get the idea that I would do such a thing?"

"The shaman told me."

"Sihir?" Petamor said with raised eyebrows. "Ah...Sihir is an addlebrained old fool."

"I realize that now, Grandfather. I apologize. I...I didn't mean to offend you."

"I'm not offended, my dear," Petamor replied with a sincere smile.

"You know how Sihir is," Breandan added. "He doesn't know if he is coming or going most of the time."

"That's true," she admitted. "But you're right, Grandfather," she added hastily in an attempt to change the subject. "This heart-berry wine is amazing. I was sure that it would take months for some of these scratches to heal completely."

"Yes," added Breandan. "Did you know that in some cases, heart-berry wine can even prevent death? Providing, of course, that the wine is administered immediately after the fatal injury."

"Really?" asked Rhiannon, surprised. "You mean heart-berry wine can bring the dead back to life?"

"No, no," interrupted Petamor quickly. "Breandan didn't mean that. No one, not even a wizard, can bring the dead back to life. However, if the wine is administered before death occurs, the wine can often begin to heal a serious wound in time to prevent the loss of life. But such a thing must not be taken lightly. In some cases, it is better to allow the victim to die rather than experience the rest of their life as an invalid."

Rhiannon looked at the old wizard questioningly.

Petamor continued. "Take a serious head wound for example. Heart-berry wine, if administered in time, could begin the healing process quickly enough to prevent death. However, the wine cannot repair the function of the brain that was damaged by the injury. In other words, the person may live, but may never be able to remember who they are or even how to feed themselves. Are you following me?"

"I think so," Rhiannon admitted, pushing her half-eaten meal away.

"I'm so sorry, my dear. I didn't intend to ruin your appetite. Please forgive me," Petamor said.

"No, it's not that," Rhiannon said. "I'm full. I don't think I could eat another bite. The meal was very delicious, though. Thank you, Breandan."

Breandan smiled. "Would you care for more wine, Rhi?" he asked, picking up the bottle.

"No, thank you. Maybe later. I do have a question, though," she said looking at the wizard. "Why does Breandan keep calling you, Grandfather?"

"It's just an old tradition, my dear," Petamor answered. "I don't care to be addressed as 'sir' or 'master', and since I'm old enough to be Breandan's grandfather, it seems appropriate enough. I hope that you, too, will address me as grandfather. Is that too much to ask?"

"No, sir...I mean, no...Grandfather," Rhiannon said.

"It can also be very useful to have a grandfather that can turn your enemies into toads," Breandan jested.

Petamor shook his head. "I do not turn people into toads," he said gruffly. "At least not anymore."

Petamor and Breandan looked at each other and laughed. Rhiannon wasn't sure if they were joking or not.

Breandan offered more wine to Petamor who accepted another glassful. Then he collected the empty ceramic bowls and placed them into a heavy wicker basket that was attached to a rope above a small trapdoor in the stone floor.

Rhiannon remained silent, but Petamor had seen the look of curiosity in her eyes. "Rhiannon, don't be shy. When you wish to know something, please ask. How else do you expect to learn? I may be a wizard, but I am not a mind reader after all, although there are some of my kind who can read the thoughts of others."

"Yes, Grandfather. Why is Breandan putting the dirty dishes in that basket?"

"I'm glad you asked me that question," Petamor said with a twinkle in his eye. "Do you see that trapdoor in the floor?"

Rhiannon nodded.

"Beneath that door is a shaft that reaches all the way to the bottom of the lake. If you place the dirty dinnerware into the basket, you can lower the basket down into the lake where the natural current of the lake will rinse the dinnerware clean until they are needed again."

Rhiannon didn't want to comment and hurt anyone's feelings, but she couldn't stop herself. "Seems like more trouble than it's worth," she said. "I mean…how long does it take to wash a few dishes by hand?"

Breandan just smiled.

Petamor said, "Ah…yes. Well…umm…that's true. Still, I hope you'll learn to take advantage of my little time saving inventions in the future. I do try to invent useful gadgets that can make life a little easier."

Breandan sat back down on the bench beside Rhiannon. He poured himself another glass of wine. "Actually, Rhiannon, you're right. It would only take a minute or two to clean the dishes. Grandfather is just showing off. He insisted that I use his little invention to clean the bowls so that you could see how clever he is. However, he really does enjoy designing his little contraptions," Breandan said with a wink and a smile.

"I think that I've had just about enough of your insolence, laddie buck," Petamor said in mock anger. "Humans," he added, shaking his head sadly. "No wonder your world is in such a sorry state."

Rhiannon could not help but wonder what he had meant by that, but decided that she was not ready to get into that conversation just yet. The wine had given her a warm fuzzy feeling and she was beginning to relax and enjoy herself.

"May I have another glass of wine, Breandan?"

As Breandan filled her glass, he said, "I want to hear all about my family and friends. Don't leave out a single detail. I can't tell you how much I've missed them."

Rhiannon began to answer all of Breandan's questions, filling him in on past and current events regarding his family and friends, though not all of her news was good. When she mentioned the ever-increasing number of Horrans in the valley, Petamor's face darkened, but he remained inscrutable. After several hours and two more bottles of wine, Rhiannon had run out of things to say. Her eyelids were heavy, her lips were numb, and her tongue felt a little thick. "I think I've had too much wine," she said groggily.

Petamor nodded, "Yes, but at least the heart-berry wine will have a much more positive effect on your body than grape wine. Breandan, will you kindly assist Rhiannon to her room?"

"Yes, Grandfather," Breandan answered. As Breandan stood up from his chair, he realized that he was going to have to carry Rhiannon to her room. The exhausted girl had already fallen asleep.

The next morning, as the sun rose on the little village of Ravenwood, a lone eagle landed gracefully upon the roof of a badly weathered barn. The eagle carefully scanned the small yard behind the nearby cottage. A light was on in the back window and wood smoke drifted from the chimney. A moment later, Petamor walked up to the door and knocked softly.

A middle-aged man opened the door. He took one look at Petamor and nearly slammed the door in his face. "What'd you want, huh? Food? Fine, you can come in for a little bit to warm up, and I'll be more than happy to give you something to eat, but then you'll have to move on. I'm not running a homeless shelter here."

Rhiannon's father stepped aside to allow Petamor to enter.

"I didn't come here for food. I came here about your daughter, Rhiannon."

"Our daughter?" said a middle-aged woman who was ob-

R. THOMAS RODGERS

viously Rhiannon's mother. "What do you know about our Rhiannon?"

"First, allow me to introduce myself. My name is Petamor, and I live on the escarpment. I came here to tell you not to worry about your daughter. She is alive and well. She's staying with me and Breandan in my tower," the old wizard said.

"What?" asked Rhiannon's father angrily. "What'd you know about this? Are you telling me you have her? Are you holding her for ransom?"

"Yes...I mean, no. What I'm trying to say is, Rhiannon reached the top of the escarpment. She's safe. You no longer need to worry about her. I was also hoping that perhaps you might be able to give me something of hers that I could take back to her to prove that I was here. Something personal but useful, perhaps."

Rhiannon's mother was near tears. She took a small, wooden box off a shelf and held it out to Petamor. "This was hers," she said. "She's had it since she was a little girl."

"Momma, don't give that to him. He'll just sell it for some cheap wine. Look at him. He's a con man. He doesn't know anything about our little girl. He's just an old bum that's heard about our little Rhiannon running off, and now he's trying to make a profit out of our grief."

"Why not give it to him, Papa? Maybe he's telling the truth. Besides, it breaks my heart just to look at it. Let him have it. I can't bear to look at it no more."

Petamor took the box. "Thank you, my lady. But please, don't be upset. Rhiannon really is fine. And I'll see that she gets this."

"I don't know what game you're playing, you old scallywag," Rhiannon's father spat, "but you won't be making a fool out of us."

"I assure you, sir, I do not play games."

"Fine! Take the bloody box then and get the hell out of my

house! Go buy your wine or your rum! Can't you see that we
are grieving for our daughter?"

Petamor could see no point in arguing with these people.
They were going to believe what they wanted to believe no
matter how hard he tried to convince them otherwise. Before
he could say another word, Rhiannon's father grabbed him
roughly by the collar of his robe and shoved him out the door.
"There," he said, almost bursting into tears himself, "now get
out of here before I call for the constable."

Petamor stood with his back to the slammed door. He was
not completely surprised by the manner in which he had been
greeted. He knew that most village people were leery of strangers. He sincerely hoped that once Rhiannon's folks came to
their senses, they would realize that he had been telling them
the truth, and that he had brought them good news.

Wasting no more time, Petamor quickly transformed the
box Rhiannon's mother had given him into a smaller version
of itself so that he could carry it back to the tower. Then he
transformed himself back into an eagle and flew back home
to the keep.

———•———

When Rhiannon awoke, she found herself in a strange bed,
in a strange room. Judging from the amount of moonlight
that filtered in through the narrow slats in the window screen
above her bed, the hour was well after midnight. She did not
remember how she came to be in this room. The last thing she
did remember was sitting at the dining table and talking with
Petamor and Breandan. Her head hurt. She rolled over and
went back to sleep.

Several hours later she sat up on the side of the big down-
filled mattress and placed her bare feet on the cold flagstone
floor. Stretching and yawning, she caught a glimpse of a
braided cord dangling down from the shuttered window above
her bed. She needed to stand on her bed to reach it. She gave

it a gentle tug and the wooden shutter slid into a slot in the wall, allowing the morning sunlight to brighten the wedge-shaped room.

The sound of movement outside her door caught her attention. Rhiannon hopped down off the bed and quietly tiptoed over to the door. She placed her ear against it, listening. When she did not hear any further sound, she drew back the bolt and yanked open the heavy door.

Outside, the spiral staircase wound its way past her door. Without thinking, she jumped out onto the landing and nearly knocked Breandan off his feet. He had been in a rush, running down the steps from an upper level carrying a heavy sack of potatoes under each arm. Judging by the sweat on his brow, he had been working for some time.

Rhiannon smiled and quickly apologized for having drunk so much wine the night before.

Breandan leaned forward and kissed Rhiannon on the cheek. "You don't need to apologize," he said. "Petamor said that the heart-berry wine would do you more good than harm. And look here," he continued as he gently took her arm, "the scratches have already faded. By tomorrow they'll be completely healed."

"I can see that. But my head feels like it's stuffed with cotton," Rhiannon replied.

"It's just a little hangover. You'll be fine in an hour or two. If you go down to the kitchen, you'll find a jar of heart-berry seeds on the counter next to the spice rack. A small handful of them should fix you right up. And I made you some breakfast, too. It's in the oven keeping warm. Right now, I have to get the rest of these supplies put away. I'll come and find you when I'm done and give you a guided tour of the place." Then, without another word, he hurried on down the steps to disappear around the next turn.

As the sound of Breandan's footsteps faded below, Rhiannon heard the sound of Petamor's voice drifting down from somewhere above. She gazed up into the dimly lighted stairwell.

As far as she could tell, the staircase wound its way up along a central stone column. The living quarters and other rooms were all placed around the outer wall where the narrow windows would allow in the light. There were niches placed at regular intervals along the supporting column where candles shed their humble light on the stone risers. The candles barely provided enough light to make one's way without stumbling, but as Rhiannon's eyes adjusted to the gloom, she became more confident, and she bounded up the stairs two at a time.

As she followed the foot-worn steps, the old wizard's voice grew increasingly louder and clearer. It soon became obvious that he was speaking to someone on top of the tower.

Rhiannon continued to thread her way up the steps until she came to an open hatch in the roof at the end of the stairs. Cautiously she poked her head up for a quick peek.

At first, all she saw in the bright sunshine were a few sacks and baskets heaped alongside a stack of boxes and wooden crates. Then her eyes were drawn towards the strange and beautiful mountains in the near distance to the north. They were unlike any mountains she had ever seen. Instead of the typical pyramidal shapes of majestic weathered rock, these mountains resemble giant segmented columns of gray stone. *Fingers,* Rhiannon thought, *those mountains look just like fingers.* It was true. It appeared as if a battalion of giants had thrust their pudgy fingers up through the earth in a desperate attempt to claw their way out of their subterranean world. Rhiannon could see dense patches of green mosses and yellow-brown lichens growing across the surface of the ancient granite, as well as what appeared to be some large birds flying between the snow-capped peaks.

The astonished shepherd girl climbed the last remaining steps and found herself standing on the top deck of the tower. No longer aware of her surroundings, she started towards the parapet to get a better view of the extraordinary mountains when a strange, yet somehow familiar sound came from behind her. She waited, listening. She felt dizzy and her head began to spin.

Then the sound came again, the distinctive neighing of a horse, a small horse by the sound of it. Rhiannon spun around and froze. Before her stood one of the most strikingly beautiful and extraordinary animals that she had ever beheld. Of course, it wasn't a horse at all. It was a rock hopper, and it had wings – great furry wings.

The rock hopper was actually smaller than an average horse but somewhat larger than a pony. It had a muscular body and a mane of thick shaggy hair. Its coat was as black as coal. The wondrous creature was staring back at her with the biggest, most beautiful blue eyes she had ever seen.

Petamor was standing beside the splendid beast, speaking to it in a gentle, soothing voice. "Don't be frightened, my dear," Petamor whispered. "He won't harm you. He's the one I told you about. He's our friend. Why don't you come over and say hello."

For a long time Rhiannon and the rock hopper faced one another without moving. Then the winged creature tentatively advanced toward the young girl. When they were but a foot apart, hand and muzzle reached out simultaneously. It was love at first sight. It almost seemed as if both beast and girl were under a spell.

Rhiannon's unquestionable appeal to all warm-blooded creatures was uncanny, to say the least, but to Petamor *this* encounter was nothing short of a miracle. To the best of his knowledge, no rock hopper, unless under the spell of a wizard, had ever allowed a human being to get close enough to touch it. Even under Petamor's enchantment, it had taken several months just to coax the creature onto the roof of the tower.

It had taken even longer before the rock hopper would allow the two shopkeepers from the nearby village of Lorelei to load supplies onto its back for transport back to the tower.

"Amazing!" Petamor exclaimed. "Simply amazing! I have to admit, my dear, I am truly impressed. Breandan has told me about your extraordinary ability to charm *domesticated* animals. But I never expected this!"

Rhiannon barely heard Petamor's comment. She was too enamored by her new friend.

The rock hopper snorted softly and nudged Rhiannon's shoulder with his muzzle. Rhiannon exhaled softly into his nostrils to help him assimilate and remember her personal scent.

Meanwhile, the uninvited entity hiding within Rhiannon's body was very satisfied. The winged creature had not been able to detect his presence, as Neraka had first feared. Neraka decided there and then that the strange beast might be useful when the time came to make his move. As for now, Neraka still had much to learn about the surface world.

Breandan, who was yet unaware of what was taking place on the upper deck of the tower, emerged through the hatch and eyed the remaining crates and sacks of food with a frown. Reaching into a pocket of his tunic, he pulled out a rag and began to mop the sweat from his brow. When he turned around and saw Rhiannon standing beside the rock hopper, his mouth dropped open in shock. As the full implications of what he was seeing began to sink in, he looked, saw the expression of bewilderment on the old wizard's face, and doubled over with laughter. His laughter was enough to bring both Rhiannon and the rock hopper out of their trance.

Breandan's laughter had also startled the temperamental rock hopper. He reared up and spread his wings. Rhiannon stepped back just as the winged horse leaped into the air and headed off in the direction of the finger-shaped mountains that she had been admiring moments earlier.

"Oh, I'm sorry," Breandan said. "I didn't mean to frighten him away...it's just that...that look on grandfather's face...I mean...it is priceless."

"Yes. Well, enough of this for now," Petamor said as he waved away Breandan's apology. "No need to apologize. He'll come back when I summon him," he added as he stared at his newest pupil in amazement.

The old wizard's stare caused Rhiannon to blush, but Breandan was grinning from ear-to-ear. "Rhiannon, if you don't mind, I want you to help Breandan finish the morning chores. After you two have finished putting away the supplies, the three of us will meet in my study and go over the lesson plans I have designed for you." Petamor turned and with a flurry of his robe, stepped through the hatch and disappeared into the tower.

Rhiannon looked questioningly at Breandan. "Did I do something wrong?"

"No, no, not at all," Breandan answered. "I informed Petamor that you had a gift with animals. I think he was just a little surprised by how quickly you befriended the rock hopper. No one's ever done that before. At least not without using a magic spell. I guess you gave grandfather something to think about. But I wouldn't worry about it if I were you."

Rhiannon couldn't help but smile, and she turned to hide her blushing face from Breandan.

Breandan returned her smile. In the bright daylight, Rhiannon noticed for the first time how much Breandan's face had changed over the past two years. He was even more handsome now than he had been two years earlier.

Tears began to flow from her eyes.

"There, there," Breandan comforted, misreading Rhiannon's mood, "everything will be fine. You're going to love it here. You just need a little time to adjust, that's all."

Petamor was already seated at the table. He smiled and nodded as Breandan and Rhiannon entered the study.

Rhiannon's eyes immediately shot to the middle of the table which was set with a variety of fruits, nuts, and cheeses, many of which she had never tasted before. They all looked inviting, and it was difficult for her to decide which fruit to try first.

Breandan lifted a pitcher of fresh goat's milk and filled her cup.

Rhiannon looked to Petamor who was quietly studying her with his kind, gray eyes.

"Don't be shy, my dear," he said. "Please help yourself. You'll need all the energy you can muster once we begin your lessons."

Rhiannon smiled at the old wizard and reached for a plump purple fruit glistening with condensation. The fruit was cold to the touch because it sat on a bed of crushed ice.

"Go ahead, Rhi," Breandan said with a wink. "Try it. We never had such a fruit in our village, but it is delicious."

Rhiannon examined the egg-shaped fruit and then took a cautious bite. Her eyes opened wide as her mouth filled with the sweet taste.

"Mmmmm...it's wonderful! What's it called?"

"It's called a plum," Breandan said enthusiastically as he chose one of the purple fruits for himself. "And here," he added holding out a long sausage-shaped yellow-skinned fruit, "try this one next. It's called a banana. It comes from the land far to the south where it never snows and you never have any need for mittens."

Rhiannon took the banana and started to take a bite.

"Wait!" Breandan exclaimed. "You have to remove the peel first...like this," he added peeling the skin off the banana in long strips. "Here, now try it."

Rhiannon tasted the fruit. "This is very nice," she said. "Is there really such a place where it doesn't snow?"

"There are many places on this world where it never snows,

Rhiannon," answered the old wizard. "And there are places where it never stops snowing. You'll learn all of this in time. First, I want to give you this," he added holding out the small wooden box that Rhiannon's mother had given him.

Rhiannon did not recognize the object at first, for it was wrapped in a piece of sealskin cloth. She removed the cloth and carefully examined the box. It was the one that her father had carved for her when she was still a young child. Inside, she found the ivory comb and brush that had once belonged to her grandmother as well as a small hand-held mirror.

Once again, Rhiannon's thoughts turned to home. The comb and brush brought back so many happy memories of quiet evenings when she and her mother would sit and talk about the day's events while they brushed each other's hair. Neither one of them had ever dreamed that someday she would climb the escarpment to become an apprentice to a wizard.

Rhiannon took the mirror and held it up so that she could see her reflection. She was not too shocked to see that her hair was sticking out in all directions. She picked up the brush and brushed her hair until it was reasonably tidy. When she looked up again, the wizard was smiling at her. "Sorry," she said.

"No need to keep apologizing, my dear," Petamor replied. "This is your home now. I want you to feel comfortable here. You must learn to think of us as a family."

"I will," Rhiannon answered sincerely. "Thank you for your kindness, Grandfather. I only hope that I do not disappoint you. But how...where...did you get this?"

"I paid a brief visit to your parent's cottage," Petamor replied.

"A very brief visit," Breandan winked. "Apparently your father thought that he was just a beggar or a con man. He ran him off."

"Oh, no!" Rhiannon exclaimed.

"Breandan, please," Petamor said.

"Well, it's true, isn't it?"

"Many people do tend to take me for a common street dweller at first, I'm afraid. But you see, my dear, with the situation being what it is in the valley, I try to keep a low profile whenever I have business to attend to there. After all, I just can't go strolling around in fancy garments doing magic tricks and such."

"I...I suppose not," Rhiannon said, for she didn't know what else to say.

"But don't worry. I did try and explain to them that you were alive and well."

"What did they say?" Rhiannon asked.

"Ah...I'm afraid that your father didn't believe me. However, I'm certain that once he takes the time to think about it, he'll realize that I was telling them the truth."

"My father's a good man," Rhiannon said. "But he's the type who must see things for himself before he believes them. But thank you for trying, Grandfather."

"Yes...well...all right, let's move on, shall we? We have other things to discuss. While you two finish your little snack, I will try to explain what you can expect over the next three years. All right?"

Rhiannon nodded.

Breandan reached for a piece of cheese and handed it to Rhiannon. "Here," he said, "try this with a bit of apple. They go perfectly together."

"Just like the two of us," Rhiannon said.

This time it was Breandan's turn to blush.

While Breandan and Rhiannon ate, Petamor sat quietly sipping wine and explaining the syllabus of his educational program to Rhiannon.

"Aren't you going to eat anything?" Rhiannon finally asked.

"No, I'm content to sip my wine."

"But this cheese is so delicious. Are you sure you won't have some?"

"As much as I once loved cheese, I'm afraid it no longer loves me. It's bad for the digestion."

Rhiannon suddenly stared at the platter of cheese as if it were a poisonous snake.

"No, no, my dear," Petamor recanted quickly, "you need not worry. I meant to say that at my age, cheese is bad for the digestion. You're young and in good health. You have nothing to be concerned about."

"But I would have thought that wizards never---" Rhiannon began to say.

"Became ill?" Petamor finished for her.

"Yes...or die," Rhiannon finished for herself.

"Well, as far as death is concerned, we will discuss that later. As far as illness is concerned, I'm afraid that even wizards are susceptible to the ailments of old age. We suffer like everyone else."

"Can't you use your powers to heal yourself?"

"I could use my powers to ease some of the pain in my joints; however, the pain would only be worse the next time. You see, every time we use our powers, it drains a little more of our energy, which in turn, makes us physically weaker. At your young age, you possess an abundant amount of energy, more than you really need. However, at my advanced years, it is a different story entirely. I need to try and be a little more conservative."

"Don't let him fool you, Rhi," Breandan said. "He gets around pretty well for a man of his advanced years."

"If you don't mind my asking," Rhiannon asked innocently, "how old are you, Grandfather?"

"You wouldn't believe me even if I were to tell you, which I will not. At least not today. Now, we have already wasted enough time," the wizard said, standing up from the table. "Rhiannon, you will begin each day by helping Breandan with the morning chores. You two can take turns doing whatever needs to be done. I will let the two of you work out the details yourselves. After all, a healthy body leads to a healthy mind."

"Yes, Grandfather," Rhiannon replied.

"Very well. Now please follow me to the library so that we can go over some of the books you will be using."

⸻

Petamor sat at a low table near the center of the room. On the table in front of him rested a large thick book. It was the biggest book Rhiannon had ever seen. As Breandan and Rhiannon seated themselves on floor cushions opposite Petamor, he opened the great book and let his fingers float over the strange pictures and symbols on the yellowed pages. He looked like a sightless man reading from a book for the blind.

The room was deftly quiet and lighted by the late afternoon light that now filtered in through a row of narrow windows in the outer wall of the tower. Rhiannon had noticed upon entering that this room was different from the other rooms in the tower. Whereas the other rooms were either circular or wedge-shaped, this chamber was eight-sided – a perfect octagon. Two of the walls were hidden behind a dark-green velvet curtain. The other six walls contained bookshelves from floor to ceiling. As might be expected, not a single space upon those shelves was empty. Not only were there books, there were ancient scrolls by the hundreds; as well as collections of unusual rocks, seashells, insects, and arachnids. There were butterflies mounted in frames, and dried flowers and leaves. And most interesting of all, glass jars containing a variety of small animals floating in some sort of preserving fluid.

"Ahem," Petamor said clearing his throat to gain Rhiannon's attention.

Rhiannon turned to face him.

"Rhiannon," Petamor said softly as he waved his hand towards the vast collection of books, "over the next three years, I will teach a great many subjects. You will study astrology, biology, chemistry, geography, mathematics, medicine, physics, as well as the history of both your world and the known universe."

Rhiannon swallowed hard. "Wow," she said, "that sounds like a lot of information to try and memorize."

"Indeed it is. And that is just the tip of the iceberg," Petamor stated. "There's much more. Including anthropology, philosophy---"

"When do I learn how to do the magic?" Rhiannon interrupted suddenly. "Oh, I'm sorry, Grandfather, although you did tell me that it was okay to ask questions."

"Knowledge *is* the magic, my dear. Science *is* the magic. Your brain *is* the magic. But don't worry. You'll learn plenty of magic tricks that you will be able to use to impress your friends, if that's what you wish."

Rhiannon was silent. Again, she didn't know what to say. This was quickly becoming a habit.

When Rhiannon had no further comments, Petamor continued. "The three years that you will spend here with me is only the first phase of your education. You will learn a general knowledge of all of the subjects that I have mentioned. Later, once you have completed your studies here, you will be free to decide which field of study appeals to you the most. Then you can focus your attention there. The rest you will learn your own through research and experimentation. You'll never know all there is to know. No one does, except of course for our Creator."

"But I've never even heard of most of the subjects you mentioned. How am I going to learn all of this stuff?"

"That's why you are here. To learn. And learn you will. My own field of study is earth lore. I will be your teacher, your guide, as well as your mentor. A long time ago, my mentor Allacor, nominated me to be his successor. The League of

Wizards accepted my nomination and elected me to be the teacher. Since that time, my purpose has been to seek out and find worthy students among the human population of this planet. After many years of searching, along with a great many disappointments, I decided that I was wasting my time. I had nearly given up hope of ever finding a worthy apprentice until Breandan came along.

"Now I find myself with not only one very capable student, but two very capable students. You passed the first test by scaling the escarpment wall alone. Now it is my responsibility to train you in the wizardly craft. For several centuries now I have gathered the knowledge of this world and placed them upon the shelves in this room. There is more information here in this small room than anywhere else on this planet. There is more knowledge here than any one person, including myself, has ever been able to assimilate."

"If I should fail, will I become an outcast, or will I become a shaman like the one in my village?"

"Ah, Sihir. Yes...well, he *was* once one of my students, and although he did manage to climb the escarpment, he failed to master the craft. He became lazy. He found other distractions to waste his valuable time. As a result, he failed the Lamp of Life test and became a shaman, not a wizard. He possesses no real power. He is limited to a small number of spells and incantations which can be helpful to him when he needs to heal the people of your village. And, if truly necessary, he may be able to transform himself into small animals."

"B...b...but sir, I...I mean, Grandfather," Rhiannon stammered, "I can't learn from these great books. I barely know how to read and write."

"I am well aware of your shortcomings, my dear. But I can see within you the potential for greatness. Therefore, I will begin your lessons by teaching you how to read and write in your own language and others as well. You will also learn the ancient language of my kind – the old race. By the time we are done, you will be able to assimilate any language you hear in less than a minute."

"What do you mean by the old race?" Rhiannon asked.

"My kind came here to this world many eons ago from a distant star."

"A distant star?" Rhiannon asked. "Are you telling me that you were not born here on this world?"

"Exactly. We came here from another galaxy, thousands of light years away."

"But how? How can anyone travel between stars? What kind of transport did you use?"

"Ah! If you and Breandan would be good enough to join me later tonight on the roof, I can show you, weather permitting of course, exactly how we came here to this world."

"Yes, Grandfather," Breandan assented. "We'll be there."

"However, if I show you the ship in which we traversed the stars, I expect both of you to devote yourself to your studies."

"Yes," Rhiannon said. "Thank you, Grandfather! I promise to work very hard. I only hope that I don't let you down!"

"Yes…of course, my dear," Petamor smiled. "There are two things I want you to understand. First, let me congratulate you. You have already accomplished a great deal. Only a handful of people have been brave enough to try and climb the escarpment. You are also the first woman to have accomplished it."

"Does that mean that anyone who manages to climb the escarpment is a potential wizard?"

"No. Many people could climb the escarpment if they only tried, but fear and superstition prevent them from ever trying. Fear is understandable. The climb is very dangerous as you already know, and most people are not willing to risk their lives in such an endeavor. It is superstition that clouds the mind. Those clouds can also block one's ability to learn the proper skills needed to wield the power of a wizard."

Rhiannon looked to Breandan who only smiled and nodded.

"You said that I am the only woman who has ever climbed the escarpment, does that mean that there are no women in the league?"

"No. There is one woman in the league. Her name is Eeowyn. However, she is of the old race and came here to this world, as did I, in our starship. What I meant to say was that you are the first human woman of this world to be accepted as apprentice."

Rhiannon nodded and said, "Are you...I mean...your kind... the old race...is not human?"

"Genetically, there are some minor differences. But a rose is a rose after all."

"Pardon? What is that supposed to mean?"

"Ah, it is just an expression. One of our great poets first said it. It simply means that whatever differences we have, they are so insignificant that no one would be able to tell us apart just by comparing us."

"I see," Rhiannon said.

"Excellent. Now let me see. Where was I? Oh, yes. The books. There are some books upon these shelves, ancient tomes that contain information that is so dangerous, no wizard, regardless of their abilities or status has ever been allowed to access them without the unanimous consent of the league. To open any one of these forbidden books without the league's consent would condemn the perpetrator, whether they are of the new race or of the old, to a life of confinement here within these walls – forever. Do you understand, Rhiannon?"

Rhiannon did not reply. For some reason unknown to her, she had to force herself to stifle a laugh.

"Do you wish to think it over before we continue?" Petamor asked.

Rhiannon shook her head.

"Speak up, child," the old wizard said. "This is not the time for indecisiveness."

"No, Grandfather," Rhiannon answered, recalling her first impression of the tower. "I understand. I don't need to think it over."

"Excellent."

"May I ask exactly how many wizards there are?"

"Including myself, there are currently nine of us," Petamor replied.

"How many wizards came here...from that other star?"

Petamor flinched. Clearly he had not expected this question. "When we arrived on this world there were hundreds of us, my dear," he said sadly. "Hundreds."

Rhiannon sighed and looked down at her hands in her lap. "I don't feel worthy of this honor, Grandfather," she said before Neraka could stop her.

"I must tell you again, my dear, I can sense a great power within you. I think that you're one of the most promising apprentices that I've ever had. Present company accepted," he added with a kind little wink at Breandan.

"I'm well aware of Rhiannon's potential," Breandan said without a hint of jealousy. "That's why I did not try to discourage her from following me here. I've always known that she was destined for greatness."

Rhiannon ignored the compliments. She held up her fingers and wiggled them as if to make a point. "So, why are there so few wizards now? After what you just told me, I should think that there would be scores and scores of them."

"As I was saying, there were many of us at one time. Although as time passed, some of them grew weary of helping the new race, while others became frustrated. Eventually they abandoned their mortal bodies and moved on to the spirit world."

"They died?" Rhiannon said, shocked by the unexpected news. "I thought wizards could live forever, at least...that's what I was led to believe," she added with a quick glance at Breandan.

"Forever is a long time, Rhiannon. Even a wizard can get tired of living in the physical world."

"How long *can* a wizard live?" Rhiannon asked.

"No one really knows the answer to that question. You must also remember, the people of my race live much longer than the people of your race, or as we now call it – the new race."

"So, even if I become a wizard, I will still die someday?"

"Yes, death is inevitable for all members of your race. But you must also remember that once you've mastered the skills I teach you, you may be able to extend your own life for many, many years."

"Like ten...or twenty?"

"More like two or three thousand."

"If I become a wizard, can I be killed?"

"Ordinary mortals will not be able to harm you. Only a wizard can kill another wizard. And even then...it is no easy task."

"Has a wizard ever killed another wizard?"

"Unfortunately...yes."

"Has any of the wizards who moved into the spirit world ever returned?"

"What a strange question," Petamor said. "But the answer is no. None have ever returned."

"Could they return if they wanted to?"

"Well, I suppose they could return if they still had a body to return to. But once they leave their body, the body dies and begins to corrupt."

Rhiannon nodded. "Has the league always worked together?"

"The league did not exist in the beginning. It only came about many years after a divergence split my people into two factions. You see, shortly after we arrived here on this world, there was a serious disagreement as to what role we should play in the evolution of the human race. Most of us wanted to guide them in a positive direction, but a small percentage of my people wanted to dominate and subjugate the indigenous peoples. A split occurred in our order and the two factions went their separate ways. The majority eventually formed a brotherhood which eventually evolved into the league, while the minority was corrupted by their own greed and cruelty. They evolved into a completely different species now known as ogres. The word ogre means 'fallen ones' in our language. They became so greedy and corrupted that they lost nearly all of the wizardly powers."

"Ogres? I've heard of them. My grandmother once told me that she actually saw an ogre when she was a young girl. She had been sent to live with her aunt in the coastal village of Clearwater when some pirates attacked their ship. The pirate captain was an ogre. She said that he was big and ugly; and had a face like a pig."

"Ah, yes...I have heard of such an ogre. I believe his name is Hog Face."

"Yes!" Rhiannon exclaimed. "That's it! I remember my grandmother telling me how he had introduced himself. He'd said his name was Hog Face."

Rhiannon suddenly felt as if her head was about to explode. She was dizzy – disoriented. Neraka was getting excited, but quickly receded back into the girl's subconscious mind where it could not be detected.

"What's wrong, my dear? Are you ill?" asked the great wizard.

"No. I'm fine. I just felt a little strange there for a moment. But I'm fine now, really."

"All right, then. Enough of this talk of starships and ogres. Let's continue with our discussion. Now, I expect you to study for a minimum of ten hours a day. You'll spend most of your time reading the books and other materials I assign you. Then you will report to me what you have learned. As we go, I will teach you how to control some of the mental powers you never knew you had. Once you master those techniques, you will be able to assimilate information much faster than you ever thought possible."

"I have mental powers?" she asked, somewhat surprised.

"Yes, everyone has them. The main difference between the old race and the new race is the ability to master those powers."

"It's true, Rhi," Breandan said. "We humans only use a small percentage of our brain power. Petamor can teach you how to use one-hundred percent."

"Yes, well...one-hundred percent may be expecting too much. Although in time, Rhiannon, it is quite possible that you will learn to use most of your brain. The mind is an extraordinary tool. With it, you can travel great distances in the blink of an eye. You will also be able to temporarily transform yourself into an animal or one of the forces of nature such as lightning or whirlwinds."

"Could I learn to fly like Topaz?"

"Topaz?" Petamor said with a slight frown. He looked at Breandan who shrugged.

"Oh!" Rhiannon exclaimed, her pretty face reddening. "I mean the rock hopper. I named him Topaz. He...he...has such beautiful blue eyes...the color of Topaz. He told me he liked the name."

"He told you? He actually spoke to you?" Petamor asked, his frown replaced with a look of wonder.

Rhiannon nodded and looked to Breandan for support.

"I told you she could communicate with animals, Grandfather," Breandan whispered.

"Did I do something wrong?"

"No. But tell me...how exactly did he communicate?" Petamor asked.

"I don't know what it's called," Rhiannon said. "All I know is that some animals can talk to me inside my head. Then

I think-talk back at them. I know they can hear me because sometimes they answer me."

"Sometimes?" Petamor asked.

"Yes. But sometimes, if the animal is upset or frightened, they don't pay attention, or maybe they misunderstand me...I don't really know. Mostly I just listen and respond by helping them as best I can."

"I see. Fascinating. Absolutely fascinating. Do you think that you could teach me how to communicate with animals?"

"I thought that you already knew how to talk to animals," Rhiannon said. "You said that you could communicate with the rock hopper."

"Yes, but I need to use my wizardly powers. You accomplished it without the use of magic."

Rhiannon shrugged.

"Well, no matter," Petamor assured her. "We can discuss this again later. Now let's see...where were we? Oh, yes. As for now, there are a great many wonderful concepts for you to learn. Just try to remember that each one can be as dangerous as it is helpful. The power can get away from you and destroy your mind. That is how some of my race became ogres. Therefore, before we begin, you must take an oath to never abuse these powers once you acquire them and to use them only for the good of your people."

"Grandfather, this is all very intimidating to me. I am a simple shepherd girl with very little education. Do you really think I can learn all these things you wish to teach me?"

"Rhiannon," Petamor began, "if I had any doubts before, you laid them all to rest with your remarkable ability to communicate with the rock hopper. That is already a great achievement."

Rhiannon smiled at Breandan. Breandan smiled at Petamor.

"Very well. I promise that I will only use the powers I obtain here to help the people of this world," Rhiannon avowed.

"Very well, then. Let's begin," the old wizard said.

———•———

It was a warm balmy night on the escarpment and the northern breeze carried with it the smell of the salty sea. The sky was filled with stars, and the sister moons were dressed in their usual butter-yellow gowns. Petamor was already waiting when Breandan and Rhiannon arrived. He was standing in the center of the roof beside a long cylindrical object atop a wooden tripod.

"Good evening, Rhiannon. Good evening, Breandan. Thank you for joining me. It's a perfect night for stargazing."

"I thought you were going to show us your starship," Rhiannon said.

"Yes, but first things first. Do either one of you know what this is?" Petamor asked as he lovingly patted the long gray cylinder.

"I have no idea," Rhiannon said, shaking her head.

"I've seen something very similar," Breandan admitted. "But the one I saw was much smaller. It was about four years ago, an old sailor came into my father's tavern. He traded one of those things for a hot meal and a flagon of wine. He called it a telescope. He said that it was used at sea to help spot ships and land on the horizon. Right?"

"Yes, that's correct. A smaller version of this one is often used by sailors at sea to help them spot land or other vessels. This one, however, is for looking at heavenly bodies such as stars, planets, and moons."

"How does it work, Grandfather?" Rhiannon asked.

"How it works is a lesson for another day. Tonight, I want to show you an amazing sight which will help prove that what I have told you about my race is true."

"I have never doubted you, Grandfather," Breandan insisted.

Petamor smiled warmly. "Thank you for that, Breandan. However, I realize how difficult it is for you to accept all of the things I've revealed to you. I mean...ogres and starships that can travel through outer space? Who in their right mind would believe such a thing? Most people would think that I was ready for the loony bin if they heard me talk of such things."

Rhiannon giggled. It was the sweet laugh of an innocent young girl. "That's true," she admitted. "The people in our village already think that Breandan and I are crazy just for believing in you, Grandfather. They don't believe that wizards exist at all, much less something as strange as a starship."

"I am aware of that fact. I'm afraid that the league has been inactive for so long, that many people doubt our existence. But never mind that for now. I have been waiting all day to show you this. Breandan, if you don't mind, I'd like Rhiannon to have the first look."

"Not at all, Grandfather," Breandan replied.

"Rhiannon, if you will put your eye here and look through this tiny lens, you will see a close-up view of the moon, Titan."

Rhiannon stepped up to the big telescope and carefully placed her eye to the viewfinder. "Wow! It that what the moon really looks like?"

"Yes. As you can see, there are craters and mountains and other features on the surface, which you cannot see very well with the naked eye."

"It's so beautiful. Breandan, come here and take a look. You have to see this."

Breandan looked through the telescope and smiled. "You're right, Rhiannon. It's beautiful. Have you ever been there, Grandfather?" Breandan asked.

"To the moon? No. I'm afraid there's no atmosphere on

Titan. If you went there, you would die within seconds due to a lack of oxygen. And humans need oxygen to breathe."

Breandan and Rhiannon nodded while taking turns looking through the lens.

"All right, let's move on," Petamor said as he adjusted the telescope and aimed it at the moon called Eden.

"Have a look," he said.

Rhiannon and Breandan took turns again looking through the lens.

"Looks pretty much the same," Rhiannon said. "Only a little smaller."

"Yes. Now, just give me a moment and you can have a look at Chaos," Petamor said as he fiddled with the adjustment knobs. "There, I think that has it. Now take a look."

Rhiannon stepped up to the telescope again and looked through the viewfinder.

"See any difference?" Petamor asked.

"That's odd," Rhiannon said. "I can't see any craters...or mountains. It...it's smooth, except for a few lines here and there. The color is different, too. I don't get it. How can Chaos look so different from the other two moons?"

"Because Chaos is not a moon at all. It is the starship I told you about."

Rhiannon's mouth hung open as she stared through the lens. "Breandan," she said, stepping away from the telescope, "have a look."

Breandan took his turn and said, "Grandfather, you mean that Chaos is really a starship, not a moon! But it's so big! How can something that big fly through space?"

"When it travels through space, it is reminiscent of a stone skipping across the surface of a pond, or a ball bouncing along the ground. And since there is no atmosphere in space and no gravity to hold it down, it can move quite quickly."

"Although from the way you described it earlier," Breandan

said, "I thought that the ship had crashed when you came here."

"I never said we crashed. I only said that the ship was so badly damaged from its trek through space that it became unstable. We parked it in orbit around the planet on the chance that we might find a way to repair it someday, but the element we need is not found here on this world."

"Some people call Chaos the chameleon moon because it often turns red for no apparent reason. Is it because of the ship?" Breandan asked.

"Yes. You see, although most of the ship's principal operating systems are shut down to help conserve energy, the guidance systems which keep the ship in the proper orbit must be checked from time to time to make certain that the ship is where it should be. The faint red glow you often see comes when the propulsion system comes on long enough to adjust its orbit."

"How does the ship know when to adjust its orbit? Is it alive?" Rhiannon asked.

"No. The ship is not a living entity. It's just a ship. However it does have a computer that keeps a close watch on all its operations."

"A what?"

"A computer. An artificial brain."

"The ship's not alive, but it has a brain, and it can think?" Rhiannon asked.

"In a way, yes. The computer depends on a wizard called Thoradal for all of its commands. He was one of the original pilots of the ship, you see."

Rhiannon started massaging her temples.

"I know that most of what I'm telling you is...unfamiliar to your way of thinking, but someday you will understand it all."

Rhiannon nodded. "Can you show us the star you came from, Grandfather?" Rhiannon asked excitedly.

"Yes," Petamor answered with a smile, pleased that someone

was interested in his history. He took the telescope, pointed it to the northeastern part of the sky, and began searching the heavens.

Petamor, Breandan, and Rhiannon spent a good deal of the night gazing at the stars and planets. By dawn, they were tired and hungry, and they were wondering where the time had gone.

Rhiannon spent the next few months in constant study. Petamor was deeply impressed by Rhiannon's commitment to her lessons. Even Rhiannon, herself, was a little surprised by her increasing hunger for information. She often felt as if some other force deep within herself was compelling her onward. More often than not, she would continue to read long after her required study time had elapsed.

Breandan was also a bit bewildered by Rhiannon's intensity. As long as he had known her, he had never seen her so completely absorbed in her work. There were days when Petamor had to remind her to eat and sleep. It seemed that the only things that could pry her away from the books were the increasingly frequent visits from the rock hopper she had named Topaz.

Although the old wizard was pleased with Rhiannon's dedication and remarkable progress, he too, was a little concerned with her obsession when it came to her studies. However, when faced with the girl's wide-eyed enthusiasm, not even his wizardly skills could prevent him from resisting her. She had him wrapped around her little finger, and they both knew it. As a result, Petamor spent more time with her than he had with Breandan, and Rhiannon was able to master the basic skills of wizardry much faster. Whereas it had taken Breandan three months to learn how to read and write, it had only taken Rhiannon a few weeks.

Breandan was neither jealous nor upset by Petamor's commitment to Rhiannon. He had expected as much, because Rhiannon had the same effect on nearly everyone. His own apprenticeship was nearing completion. He had done well, and Petamor was confident that he would pass the final test.

Because Breandan and Rhiannon were often at different levels of their instruction, they found themselves spending less and less time together. Both were so deeply involved in their studies that they had hardly noticed the physical changes that had taken place in each other.

Breandan had grown an inch or two taller since Rhiannon's arrival, and thanks to all of the physical labor that Petamor demanded of him, he was leaner and stronger than ever before. However, it was Rhiannon's appearance that had changed the most. Her hair was much longer and her fair skin was practically flawless. And although she had not grown a single inch taller, her body had developed a much more womanly shape.

It was only her eyes that occasionally betrayed the unwanted presence within her, for therein could be seen an alien light, the light of a greedy child-like entity with a growing desire for sensory input and an unquenchable thirst for power.

Rhiannon was full of other surprises as well. She had so charmed the wild rock hopper that it now allowed her to ride upon its back, and it was not unusual to see the two of them soaring through the air high above the keep.

When not hitting the books, Rhiannon loved to explore the region around the lake. Sometimes, she and Topaz would roam the nearby forests for hours on foot, picking wild flowers, and making friends with the unusual and peculiar animals that lived there. When the original enchantment had been placed over the plateau, nearly all of the wild animals that had been living there had been affected by the change. They had slowly evolved into creatures never before seen outside the range of fantasy and magic.

As the weeks passed, Petamor was growing increasingly concerned with Rhiannon's restless and often reckless behavior. Nevertheless, he was reluctant to intervene, fearing that he might disrupt the girl's momentum. He was also impressed with the speed and accuracy with which she was completing her assignments. As improbably as it seemed, Rhiannon had already surpassed Breandan in every subject. Soon, the league would assemble to oversee Breandan's final test and decide whether or not he was ready to move forward. Perhaps it was time for Rhiannon to move forward as well. He would leave it to the league to decide. But in his mind, Rhiannon already possessed all of the skills she needed to be accepted into the league.

Petamor stood atop the Wizard's Tower and stared up into the clear night sky. The three moons of Nox were once again in their full glory with Chaos, as always, in the foreground. A slight chill ran up his old wizard's spine as he looked at her, and he sensed the presence of something evil in the air around him. Whatever it was, it vanished after a moment.

Shaking off the sudden chill, Petamor raised his oaken staff into the air, closed his eyes, and began the summoning. One-by-one, bolts of blue lightning erupted from the top of the shaft and shot away across the starlit sky. Eight bolts in all left his mighty staff, each on a mission to seek out and deliver a personal message to the wizards of the league.

Once the last bolt of lightning was on its way, Petamor lowered his staff to the stonework beneath his feet and leaned back against the battlements completely drained. The summoning always sapped his strength and left him feeling weak and weary. After a few moments, some of his strength returned and he felt strong enough to move again. He had to be strong. This was an important event and there was still much work to be done. It had been fifty-three years since the League of Wizards had assembled in the council chamber. He only hoped that everything would go well.

Petamor had decided not to tell Rhiannon of his intentions. He didn't want her to be disappointed should the league decide to veto his recommendation. He walked to the open hatch and descended the staircase and entered the study. The great wooden door was ajar, revealing the candlelit faces of Breandan and Rhiannon, their noses stuck in their books. When the old wizard entered the room, Rhiannon looked up with uncharacteristic apprehension until she realized that his attention was focused on Breandan.

"Breandan," Petamor said softly, "go to your room and prepare for the arrival of the league. I will send Rhiannon to fetch you once we are ready to begin the ceremony."

"Yes, Grandfather," Breandan said, getting up from his seat. He picked up the heavy book he had been reading and placed it back in its slot on the shelf. Before leaving the study he embraced his old mentor.

The old wizard now turned his attention upon Rhiannon, who was pretending to read. "Rhiannon," he said as he placed his hand on her shoulder, "I hate to interrupt your studies, but I think it would be a good idea if you readied yourself as well."

Rhiannon looked up anxiously. "Grandfather?"

"I could use your help greeting the other wizards as they arrive. I have a feeling that they'll be very anxious to meet you. Would you mind?"

Rhiannon tried to appear serious, but shortly her face brightened as all her efforts to conceal her delight completely vanished. "Not at all, Grandfather," she answered.

"Very good. Go on now, my dear," Petamor chuckled, shaking his head. "I want you to look your best."

Rhiannon eagerly jumped up from the table and started for the chamber door. Then she stopped halfway, spun around; and ran back to Petamor. She hugged the old wizard with genuine affection before turning and darting from the room.

Petamor laughed again, although his heart was heavy. "I'm really going to miss that girl," he said to the empty room.

From the study, Petamor headed straight to the council chamber one floor below. On one side of the octagonal room stood a large half-round table that conformed perfectly to the shape of the outer wall. Between the table and the wall stood twelve solidly made and ornately carved wooden chairs. Behind each chair was a domed niche built directly into the stonework. Nine of the stone niches contained small lamps, each of which burned brightly with a different colored flame. The remaining three niches were currently empty and cold, but Petamor solemnly hoped that at least one of those empty spaces would be occupied before the meeting ended later that night.

He recalled the first time he had seen this chamber. He had been a young lad, not much older than Rhiannon. It was here where he had first sworn allegiance to the wizards of the old race. And it was here, in this very room, where he had taken the final test to prove himself worthy. That had been well over five hundred years ago, yet his lamp still burned as brightly as it had the moment he had lighted it. In fact, all of the lamps were burning brightly, a positive sign that all of the remaining wizards were alive and well.

Petamor walked over to the niche in the wall that held his lamp, which was the color of polished amber, and carefully picked it up by the handle. It brought a smile to his face as he recalled that long ago day.

To successfully complete one's apprenticeship, every would-be wizard was required to make and light their own lamp without the aide of anything other than a few basic materials and their mental powers. The ceremony was simply titled 'the Lamp of Life.' It was one of the most important and difficult tests given to the apprentice. To be successful, a great deal of concentration was required, as well as the knowledge of the three main elements: earth, water, and fire.

An old wizard by the name of Allacor had been Petamor's mentor, the very same Allacor who had built the keep and placed the original enchantment on the plateau. Petamor recalled how, on that fateful day, Allacor had carefully explained each step of the ceremony to him. "First, lad, you must use a pound of raw clay from the planet on which you were born, and mix it with water from a nearby spring or lake. Next, you must add a drop or two of your own blood to the mix. The blood is the link between you and your lamp and it is vital. Then you mix all of these elements together with the broken fragments of a small seashell that has been ground into a course powder. Form the mixture into a lamp in any design you like. You must then cure the clay using the power of your mind and the heat from your hands. If you have learned anything at all, the clay should harden within a few seconds as if it had been curing in a kiln for several hours.

"Once your lamp is completed, a member of the league will give you one ounce of a special oil that will burn cleanly once lit. This oil has magical properties that are known only to me and the other members of the league, so that no fraud can be perpetrated. Add another drop of your blood to the oil, so that the oil and the clay will bond. And finally, my young friend, you must once again use the power of your mind to light the lamp. This is the most crucial step. Are you following me thus far?"

"Yes, Grandfather," the young Petamor had responded. "But how can I use clay from the world upon which I was born when it is thousands of light years away?"

"Don't worry, lad. Our starship incorporated gardens for growing fresh vegetables and herbs. Many of those gardens contained actual soil from our home planet. I have already collected enough clay for your ceremony."

"Thank you, Grandfather."

"You're welcome, lad. Now listen carefully, for this last step will require you to focus all of your attention on the lamp. When you can feel and see nothing but the lamp, you must speak the correct words as you expel your breath into it. If you have learned and remember all of the knowledge I have taught you during your apprenticeship, and the universe believes you to be worthy, the oil in the spout of the lamp will light and you will go forth into the world as a man of science – a wizard. If, however, the lamp remains unlit for any reason, you will be returned to the village from whence you came and you will assume the role of a shaman."

By this time, Petamor's confidence had begun to slip.

"There is no need to be frightened, Petamor. I know you can do it. You have been an excellent student these past three years," Allacor said as he patted Petamor on the back. "You'll do just fine. Now...where was I? Oh, yes...the color of your flame will match the color of your aura, which in your case happens to be a lovely shade of amber. Once lit, your flame will continue to burn for as long as you remain in your mortal body. Do you understand?"

Petamor nodded. "What will become of the lamp when I cease to exist in this mortal form?"

"In that event," Allacor said solemnly, "the flame would extinguish itself and the lamp would crumble into dust."

Old Petamor breathed a heavy sigh and placed his lamp back into its niche. Allacor had chosen to return to the spiritual world over two centuries earlier. It had been a sad day when Petamor had learned that his mentor had left the physical world. Allacor had been like a father to him – the father he had never known.

Along with the news of Allacor's transcendence, Petamor had also learned that his old teacher had designated him as his replacement. The league had accepted Allacor's nomination, and Petamor was given the responsibility of finding and training new candidates.

What am I doing? Petamor wondered. *I have too many*

things to do to be daydreaming about the past. I must get moving.

He began by lighting the candles in the chamber and dusting off the table and chairs. As he was sweeping the dust-bunnies up off the floor, Rhiannon strolled into the room wearing a turquoise-blue cashmere caftan, which clung to her body like a second skin. Her dark brown hair glistened like silk in the candlelight.

In that moment, Petamor thought he detected a slight rose-colored aura surrounding the girl, although it could have been a trick of the candlelight. There was, however, one thing about which he was absolutely certain. Rhiannon had never looked so lovely. If beauty alone mattered, she would be certain to win over the hearts of the league as quickly as she had won over his.

The hand-made lamps, burning in their respective niches, immediately captured Rhiannon's attention. To her eyes, the room appeared to be occupied by a beautiful rainbow. She had known, of course, of the lamps existence through her studies, and although she had been in this chamber many times, the wall holding the lamps had always been concealed by a velvet curtain. This was the first time that she had actually been allowed to see them. She quickly realized that the lamps radiated much more than light, they radiated incredible power. She could feel it in the air. She was just about to move in closer for a better look when Petamor interrupted her reverie by placing his hand upon her shoulder. Startled, she looked up into the kind grey eyes of her mentor.

"Rhiannon," Petamor said, "please go no closer to the lamps. It's a privilege given only to the wizards themselves. However," he added quickly once he saw the disappointment on her face, "since I did ask you for your help tonight, I suppose I can make an exception this one time. You may take a closer look. Just don't touch them."

Rhiannon's smile returned. She said, "They're so beautiful.

I've never seen such light before. It's almost as if each flame is alive."

"In a sense, they are alive, my dear, as long as the wizards who brought them to life are alive. Now, come along. We must go up and greet the other wizards. They will be arriving within the hour."

The old wizard and his youngest apprentice stood atop the Wizard's Tower, Petamor gazing up into the night sky, Rhiannon gazing up at Petamor.

"Do you remember your promise to me?" Rhiannon asked.

"What promise was that?"

"You promised to tell me about the old race...about your people."

"Oh, yes. I did promise to tell you, didn't I?"

"Well?"

"I have already told you that we came here from a distant star system."

Rhiannon nodded and pointed to the night sky. "That one there," Rhiannon said. "In my village those stars are known as the six sisters."

"Yes, although there are actually seven stars, and there are many worlds around those stars, only one held intelligent life. It is from that world that my people first came here to your world."

"Why, Grandfather? Why did you come here in the first place?"

"The people of my world had been around for many thousands of years. Their technology was very advanced. But there were those among my kind that were greedy and selfish. They were never satisfied with what they had. They always wanted more. Eventually, those in power began to fight among themselves. There were wars and more wars until at last, almost everything had been destroyed. Nearly all of the natural resources of my world had been exhausted or rendered useless because of the wars.

"A few of the most brilliant of our scientists, or wizards as you know them, came up with a plan of their own. They convinced our most powerful leader to build a starship that he could use to conquer other worlds in search of a fresh supply of natural resources. However, the true purpose of their mission was not to look for new worlds to conquer, but to escape our used up world and search for a new home where we would be free of war and destruction. A vast starship was constructed, the very one you saw through the telescope the other night."

"Chaos," Rhiannon said.

"Yes, Chaos. It was large enough to hold more than fifty-thousand people. It had comfortable living quarters, gardens for growing crops, parks for recreation. We had libraries, theaters, and much more. In reality, however, it was nothing more than a very well armed cargo ship, but the scientists never intended to activate any of the weapon systems. As soon as the ship was completed, the scientists...ah...I mean, the wizards, smuggled their families and friends on board. They were then hidden in a specially designed section of the ship. Then the leader and his handpicked crew of military personnel were brought aboard the ship for a demonstration. Once underway, the section of the ship carrying the leader and his army, along with their weapons of mass destruction, was jettisoned into deep space. The leader's section of the ship had no propulsion unit of its own. It was set adrift in the emptiness of space, full of the most ruthless and bloodthirsty men that had ever lived."

"What ever happened to them?"

"No one knows for certain. All we do know is that they were left behind."

"How long has it been?"

"Well over ten thousand of your years," Petamor replied.

"It seems so far to travel. Were there no suitable worlds closer to the one you left?"

"There are many inhabitable worlds within this galaxy, although most of them are inhabited by incompatible and hostile life forms."

"So you chose this world because it was already inhabited by people similar to yourselves."

"That was one reason, yes. However, when we first arrived here, your race was still in its primitive form, a hunter-gatherer society living in caves. We gave them fire. We introduced simple tools. We introduced the wheel. We introduced agriculture. We taught them how to use certain plants and herbs to help cure diseases and ease pain. This led to other small technological advances such as the lever, and the bow and arrow. That gave your people the spare time for other activities such as arts and games."

"And war?"

"Unfortunately. It seems that your people were as predisposed to greed and war as were my own people."

"But you traveled here in that ship?"

"Yes. The wizards of our world developed a type of warp drive that allowed us to skip across the galaxy the way a stone can skip across the surface of a pond. It still took many years to reach this world."

"How was the ship damaged?"

"In deep space, there are many objects, big and small, floating around, debris left over from the creation. Comets, meteors, asteroids. Yet something as tiny as a grain of sand can damage or even destroy a space ship when you are traveling at such speeds. Our ship suffered a great deal of damage during the voyage. Even though the ship was made from a special nearly indestructible element not found on your world, the outer hull deteriorated and the ship could not be repaired. We could go no farther. Like it or not, we were here to stay."

Suddenly, Petamor raised his right hand and pointed towards the eastern horizon. Rhiannon turned just in time to see a bolt of bright green lightning flashing towards them. Before she could budge, the bolt struck the roof in a blinding flash of emerald-green sparks.

Rhiannon blinked and rubbed her eyes with the back of her hands. When she opened them again, she was standing face-to-face with a strange man.

The man was dressed in a wizard's robe of sparkling emerald green. Tall and slender in build, the wizard had a lean handsome face that immediately gave Rhiannon the impression of nobility. His long silver hair and great bushy beard surrounded his face like a lion's main. His eyes, also silver in color, seemed ablaze with light.

In his left hand, he held a staff carved from the blackest ebony wood that Rhiannon had ever seen. It was banded with silver rings and inlaid with fine silver runes. The top of the staff was capped with an emerald the size of a goose egg.

When Rhiannon looked up into the regal face of the new arrival, she felt a chill run up her spine. His silver eyes were fixed upon hers. Unable to meet his unnatural stare, Rhiannon quickly looked down at her feet.

"Welcome Rimahorn," Petamor began, "as usual, you are the first to arrive. I hope---"

"Yes, yes, my trip was wonderful, simply wonderful, and I am just peachy. Enough with the formalities, old friend," Rimahorn interrupted impatiently. "First tell me, who is this charming creature? Surely, this is not the apprentice, Breandan, for whom you have summoned me out of my warm bed on this chilly night."

At the mention of Breandan's name, Rhiannon looked up in surprise. *This Rimahorn must be jesting. Surely, he can see that I am not a boy. Only a blind person would ---"* Rhiannon froze at the thought. *Of course, that's it! Rimahorn is blind! That explains the silver eyes and the icy stare.*

"Petamor," Rimahorn croaked, "what the devil are you

waiting for? Introduce us so I can get out of this night air. I hope you have my room prepared. I need to freshen up."

Petamor winked at Rhiannon. "Rimahorn, I would like you to meet my newest apprentice, Rhiannon of the village of Ravenwood."

Rimahorn bowed slightly and said, "It is a pleasure to meet you, my dear. I do hope you will forgive my mistaking you for Breandan, however no one bothered to inform me that your mentor had taken a second apprentice."

"I do apologize, Rimahorn," Petamor said before Rhiannon could respond, "but I wanted to surprise everyone."

"Old friend," Rimahorn frowned, "exactly how would I be surprised by you? I have been on to your tricks for many years now."

"Well," Petamor began, "Rhiannon is the first human woman---"

"I may be blind, but I can still tell the difference between a man and a woman," Rimahorn continued holding out his hand. "Rhiannon, I can feel the power radiating off you like heat from a sun-baked stone. We must have a long talk later. I find you very intriguing. I have a feeling that you will become a very powerful wizard someday. Yet...there is something else. Something...oh well, it will come to me sooner or later."

Rhiannon took Rimahorn's hand. "It's very nice to meet you too, sir," she said with a quick but graceful curtsy. "I look forward to talking with you."

"Please, my dear, address me as grandfather," Rimahorn said, patting her hand.

"You may address all of the members of the league as grandfather, Rhiannon," Petamor interjected. "Or grandmother in Eeowyn's case."

"Yes, Grandfather," Rhiannon said somewhat confused. "But if I address each of you as grandfather, how will you know which of you I am addressing?"

"Don't worry, Rhiannon," Rimahorn smiled kindly, "we will know. We *are* wizards after all."

Rhiannon smiled and then remembered that Rimahorn could not see her face and said, "Yes, Grandfather."

"May I touch your face, my dear?" Rimahorn asked.

Rhiannon glanced at Petamor who nodded.

"Yes, Grandfather," she replied.

Despite his silver hair, Rimahorn appeared much younger than Petamor, yet he was the eldest member of the league and the highest-ranking member. He rested his staff against his left shoulder and reached out with both hands. His touch was as light as a feather as he carefully explored the contours of Rhiannon's face. He nodded with approval until his fingertips focused on her eyes. At that moment, he winced and stepped back as if struck.

For the next few moments the night air was filled with an awkward silence. Petamor was not sure what had happened. Rhiannon wasn't sure what had happened either and she was embarrassed. However, Neraka knew exactly what had happened and he was greatly displeased with Rhiannon for allowing the old wizard to touch her face and betray his presence.

"What is it, old friend?" Petamor asked, mildly alarmed. "Tell me, what's wrong?"

Rimahorn was much more troubled than he let on. He felt as if he had been stung by an angry hornet. *How in the world can this young girl be so powerful in such a short time?* he wondered silently. *What is going on here?* "It's nothing, really," he lied. "I was just overwhelmed by Rhiannon's incredible aura. Old men like me rarely come into contact with such extraordinary beauty."

Neraka was angry. It sensed that Rimahorn was upset and concerned. It would need to find a way to make amends before the old wizard became too suspicious.

Another sudden crackle of thunder brought the three of them back to the moment as an intense flash of orange lightning struck the tower. When Rhiannon's eyes readjusted after the blinding flash and stinging smoke, she found herself standing face-to-face with another member of the league.

He was a tall burly man with a curly, black beard and dark hair that hung down to his shoulders. He was grinning ear-to-ear and his teeth appear whiter than white beneath his dark complexion. His bright orange cloak swirled as he turned to survey the tower roof. "What is this we have here?" he said with a smile. "Have I wasted my grand entrance on two crusty old wizards and a slip of a girl? I must be getting old. My timing needs some serious work."

Rimahorn, ignoring the newcomer, shuffled towards the open hatch shaking his head. "Please excuse this crusty old wizard," he spat sarcastically, "but I for one prefer the heat of a fireplace to the hot air blowing around up here."

The orange wizard's smile did not waver. He was used to the senile old wizard's cantankerous manners. He and Petamor embraced for a moment, and then Petamor introduced him to Rhiannon.

"Cinaran, this is one of the most outstanding students I have ever had the pleasure of training. This is Rhiannon."

Cinaran bowed and graciously kissed Rhiannon's hand.

Rhiannon instantly liked him. She had learned about him in one of her earlier readings. He ranked fourth in the league and was by far the most flamboyant of all the wizards, including Rimahorn, which might explain why Rimahorn acted the way he had.

Like Rhiannon, Cinaran was fond of animals. He looked like a big bear, himself. He put his arm around Rhiannon's shoulders and said, "We must have a long chat before I leave. I want to hear all about your adventures with this rock hopper of yours. I must admit, I am simply amazed by your achievement. What was that name you chose for him?"

"Topaz," Rhiannon responded brightly, surprised that the wizard knew about the rock hopper.

"Ah yes, Topaz...very nice name. Because of the eyes, I take it? Did you pick the name or did he?"

"Thank you, and yes, Grandfather, I chose the name."

"Excellent, excellent. Now if you will excuse me, my dear, I must go and find Rimahorn. We have a lot of news to catch up on."

"Yes, Grandfather," Rhiannon answered.

Cinaran nodded to Petamor and disappeared down into the hatchway.

Petamor looked at Rhiannon.

"Wow!" Rhiannon exclaimed, "The wizards are nothing at all as I anticipated."

Petamor laughed, "Yes, they do enjoy putting on a good show for occasions like this one. Ordinarily they dress no differently than anyone else."

Before Rhiannon could ask another question, another flash lit the tower, but this time it was not due to a bolt of lightning.

Salaran, the lowest ranking member of the league, had arrived. Unlike the others who preferred a more dramatic entrance, he appeared in the form of a great white owl and landed so quietly on the nearby wall, that neither Rhiannon nor Petamor noticed him at first. Nevertheless, Rhiannon regarded his transformation from owl into his human form as nothing short of spectacular. She also noticed that after the transformation, he still had a few downy feathers sticking out of his hair and beard.

He greeted Rhiannon with a slight smile and a nod of his head and despite the icy blue color of his eyes, Rhiannon saw nothing but warmth and compassion within them. He appeared to be a lot younger than her mentor, Petamor. In fact, if her memory was correct, he was currently the youngest member of the league. His robe was made of white silk and embroidered with an elaborate design of silver stars and crescent moons. His wizard's staff was made of ebony wood, inlaid with strips of solid silver; and engraved with all manner of complicated symbols and letters.

Immediately after their introduction, Petamor quickly ushered Salaran to the hatchway door.

Seconds after Salaran disappeared below, a sparkling mist of violet-blue appeared and hovered directly above the tower. Slowly, the dazzling vapor settled to the roof and took the shape of a man. It was Boradal, the water wizard. His hair and beard were such a vivid red that at first they appeared to be on fire. Then his big smile split the illusion in two, causing Rhiannon to smile back into his mischievous brown eyes. His wizardly robe was the color of the sea and matched Rhiannon's eyes exactly. His simple staff was carved from a single piece of sun-bleached teakwood decorated with pieces of blue and purple coral that had been carved into runic symbols.

Thoradal was the next member of the league to materialize. He arrived in the form of a whirling dust devil, but after the dust settled he appeared to be the least remarkable of the lot. His hair and beard were a tawny brown in color and looked wild and unkempt. His sunken eyes were the color of jasper. His robe, a faded shade of midnight blue, was tattered and frayed around the edges. Even his unadorned staff had been crudely carved from a simple piece of knotty pine. Overall, he did not impress Rhiannon one bit.

By midnight, the three remaining wizards: Salahorn, Zalamar, and Eeowyn [the only female member of the league] had arrived, and Rhiannon had managed to impress each one with a certain degree of confidence.

When Petamor approached them and explained Rhiannon's extraordinary progress, all of them, with the exception of Rimahorn, agreed to accept his recommendation and allow her to take the final test. And since the league was a democratic society, majority ruled. Rhiannon would be allowed to take the test.

For the first time in over fifty years, the wizards of Nox gathered in the council chamber of the ancient stone tower. Rhiannon, still unaware of the league's unprecedented and controversial decision to allow her to take the final test, waited nervously outside the chamber door, lost in thought. When the door opened, Petamor's tall figure stood silhouetted by the brightly illuminated room behind him, and even though his facial features were barely discernable on the darkened stairway, Rhiannon sensed he was smiling.

"Rhiannon," he said calmly, "Breandan has passed the final test. He has lit the Lamp of Life and is now officially a wizard and a member of the league."

Rhiannon tried to hold back her joy but could not; she let out a yelp and jumped into the air clapping her hands.

"I am also very pleased to inform you," he continued, "that based on the results of your accelerated studies; the league has decided to offer you the opportunity to take the test tonight as well. Would you like to accept or decline this offer?"

Rhiannon plopped back down onto the bench on which she had been sitting as if her legs had given out.

"But Grandfather," she said, "I've only been here for one year. I still have two more years of study to go."

"That is true, Rhiannon. But, you have worked harder than any apprentice before you. Furthermore, you have managed to complete all three years worth of study in that one year."

"But this is Breandan's night. This is his ceremony."

"I have already spoken to Breandan, and he said that he would be very pleased to share this moment with you."

"Do you really think that I'm ready?"

"If I didn't think so, my dear, I would never have recommended it to the league. Still, it is your choice. Will you take the test?"

Rhiannon stood up, once again the humble and innocent daughter of a poor sheep rancher. "Yes, Grandfather," she answered, "I will take the test."

"Very good," he responded solemnly, "you may enter the council chamber now."

Rhiannon slipped past him into the well-lighted chamber, but stopped just inside the door in complete wonder of the sight before her.

Each one of the wizards was seated at the table with their backs to their lamps, which burned in a rainbow of colors.

Breandan appeared from her right and took her by the hand. He led her to a chair near the center of the room directly in front of the council table. He then placed a small writing table in front of her. There were several items on the desk, including a pound of raw gray clay, a vial of spring water, a long thin needle, and a bowl of a powdery substance that glittered like pearls. Then Breandan went to join the other wizards already seated at the table. After Petamor took his seat, Rhiannon found herself staring at the ten most powerful individuals in the world, otherwise known as the League of Wizards.

Rimahorn was the first to speak. "Rhiannon, despite the fact that you have only been a student here for one year, your friend and mentor, Petamor, has convinced us that you are ready to take the final test. This is a remarkable accomplishment. In fact, this has never happened before in the history of the league. You are indeed an amazing young woman. Therefore, it has been decided that you are eligible to take the finale test tonight. If you pass the test, you will have earned the title of wizard. You will also become a member of our league. On the other hand, should you fail the test for any reason, you must return to your village and lead a less demanding life as a shaman or a healer. That choice will be yours.

"On the table before you are the components needed to fashion a simple oil lamp. Once you have fashioned your lamp, a single ounce of rare oil will be provided to you. You must complete the test by the time Chaos disappears from the window above my head," Rimahorn added.

"Yes, Grandfather."

"Very well. Are you are ready to begin?"

"Yes, Grandfather. I am ready."

"Then you may begin."

Rhiannon had often helped her mother make pottery pieces for their home, especially the kitchen. She looked down again at the objects on the table. A pound of clay, a vial of water, a small bowl of finely powdered seashell, and a needle with a very sharp point. She took a deep breath and began by pricking the tip of her thumb with the needle. Immediately, a bright crimson drop of blood appeared. She squeezed the drop onto the lump of clay and kneaded it in. Then she divided the raw clay into five separate pieces. The first she formed into a ball a little larger than a goose egg. Using her thumbs, she made one hole in the top of the clay egg and carefully hollowed it out until it was large enough to hold an ounce or two of oil. Next, she used another piece of clay to fashion the spout. She used the third piece to form a handle and the forth piece to make a lid. To create a base for the lamp Rhiannon flattened the last piece of the raw clay into a small, oval-shaped saucer.

Finally, she decided to add a feminine touch. She removed the finely carved ivory barrette from her hair and used its hand-carved pattern of tiny grape leaves, vines, and clusters to stamp a decorative boarder around the lamp's rim and lid.

When she was satisfied with her work, Rhiannon held the lamp up for the wizards to see. Petamor nodded and Breandan smiled. The first part of the three-part test had been accomplished. Now the wizards waited for Rhiannon to complete the second part of the test. The lamp still had to be cured before it could be lit.

Rhiannon lowered the lamp and cradled it gently between her small hands. She closed her eyes and began to speak softly to herself. No one could quite hear her words, although the wizards knew exactly what she was saying. It seemed like forever, although in reality, only six minutes had passed when the clay began to glow. It was a soft light at first, much like the sun on a winter's day when it is hidden behind a thin layer of grey clouds. The color grew brighter, changing first from a pale white to orange, then from orange to red, followed immediately by a brilliant almost blinding white. Then the light blinked out with a sound like a cork popping out of a champagne bottle.

An eerie silence filled the chamber and was broken only when Breandan cleared his throat. Rhiannon, who was still holding her lamp, looked up startled. The lamp had been cured and was now as hard as a rock. Part two of the test had been a success.

Breandan turned and looked up at the window. Chaos was now framed there in full view.

"Hurry, Rhi," he said. "You only have a couple of minutes left. You must light the lamp now."

Rhiannon did not answer. Time was too precious to waste. She quickly removed the lid as Rimahorn handed her a small vial of the special oil. Once again, she used the needle to puncture the tip of her left index finger and allowed several drops of her blood to mix with the oil. She poured the mixture into the belly of the lamp and closed the lid. Then, holding the lamp in front of her face, she gently exhaled into the spout. She closed her eyes and concentrated on the proper incantation. Almost immediately a small red flame about the size of a fingernail appeared at the tip of the spout, nearly singeing the tip of her nose.

Outside the tower, in the stillness of the warm clear night, Titan and her smaller sister Eden joined hands to bathe Rhiannon's face with a golden buttery light.

At that exact moment, Rhiannon's flame sprouted to life. Suddenly, Chaos's light began to waver. All eyes in the tower turned in time to see the pygmy moon change from pale yellow to a ghastly crimson, which flooded the council chamber with a gruesome light.

The alien presence within Rhiannon began to writhe in pain like a wounded centipede. Whimpering, Rhiannon collapsed upon the floor, and her breathing became labored.

Thoradal, who had risen to his feet behind the table, felt a chill scurry up his spine like a poisonous spider chasing a fly. For the first time in his long life he actually experienced fear, for he had foreseen his own death in the face of that tiny moon.

The council chamber suddenly became as cold as ice. Rhiannon's unconscious body immediately began to cover over with frost, which in the eerie light of the moon, took on the appearance of coagulating blood. Then Chaos passed from view, and the temperature in the council chamber returned to normal. The frost on Rhiannon's body began to melt away, and her breathing returned to normal.

Breandan knelt down beside her and helped her into a sitting position. He gently brushed away the frost that stubbornly clung to her eyelashes, and placed his warm hand on her brow.

When Rhiannon opened her eyes again, the first thing she saw was the worried faces of the wizards gathered around her.

"Help me up," she said to Breandan, who then helped her to her feet. She looked to the window again as if to reassure herself that the evil, or whatever it was, had passed and noticed that Thoradal too, was gazing up at the heavens. "What just happened?" she asked. "What was that?"

Breandan shook his head. "I don't know. But whatever it was, it was very powerful."

"It is a sign," Thoradal said, turning away from the window finally.

"What?" Petamor responded.

"Yes," Rimahorn chimed in, "what do you mean by a sign? Can you be a little more specific?"

"No...not yet at least," Thoradal replied, slowly shaking his head. "However, I fear that some terrible evil has been unfettered upon the land."

Everyone looked at Rhiannon.

"What?" she said defensively. "You certainly don't think that I had anything to do with this...whatever it is?"

"No, no, of course not, my dear," Petamor replied. "It may be nothing more than a malfunction in the ship."

"The ship did not malfunction," Thoradal said. "I checked all of its systems earlier today and they are functioning normally."

"Perhaps one of the backup systems came up on its own," Petamor suggested.

"If that is the case," Rimahorn said, "then one of us should go up to the ship and check it out, just to be certain. After all, if the ship is unable to maintain its orbit and comes crashing down on the planet, the results could be devastating."

"And just how are we supposed to get there, brother," Cinaran asked. "Despite all of our powers, none of us has the capability of traveling through space without a ship."

"What about the shuttles. They still function, do they not?" Rimahorn asked.

"Yes," Petamor admitted, "but they are parked on the bottom of the lake and it would take months to prepare them for space flight again."

"Well then?" asked Rimahorn.

"Well what? I just told you that it had nothing at all to do with the systems on our old ship," Thoradal said angrily. "This was an omen...a message."

"If that is true, then we need to find out who sent it and why. We need to find out as soon as possible," Eeowyn said.

"Perhaps Rhiannon *is* responsible for this untimely event," suggested Thoradal.

"That's ridiculous," Petamor spat.

"Do not be so certain, Petamor."

Rhiannon was horrified. *Thoradal actually believes that I had something to do with this... whatever it was. And, no doubt, Rimahorn believes it, too.*

Neraka was horrified as well. It knew that the reddening of the moon had been a warning, a warning sent by Rhiannon's subconscious mind. *Even after all this time, this silly creature still tries to fight me,* Neraka wondered, amazed. *This is unacceptable. I cannot allow her to do this ever again.* Neraka immediately began to tighten his grip on Rhiannon's mind, so that she would never try to betray his presence again.

The council chamber was very quiet while the wizards considered the possibility of a future encounter with the architect of this premonition.

"I know that Rhiannon is anxious to leave the keep. However, I think that perhaps it would be in her best interest if she were to remain here for a few more days, at least until we are able to discover what actually happened here tonight," Rimahorn suggested.

"Rhiannon has done nothing wrong," Petamor was quick to say. "We have no right to hold her here as if she were a convicted criminal."

"That's true," Eeowyn admitted. "Rhiannon has passed the test, and she can now claim the title of wizard. We must treat her with the same respect that we all demand. We cannot hold her here or anywhere against her will. She is free to pursue her place amongst us. Nonetheless, I must agree with Rimahorn. It may be in Rhiannon's best interest if she chose to stay here in the keep for a few more days. Otherwise, she may be placing herself and the league in unnecessary danger. Are there any objections?"

Everyone was silent.

Outside, far above the planet, Chaos flickered once more and returned to its normal buttery hue.

Inside Rhiannon's body the unwelcome parasite was not happy. It quickly devised a scheme to defuse some of the tension in the air. Rhiannon would continue to play innocent. Pretend to be the victim, not the threat. She would have to create a diversion somehow.

Suddenly, and despite the fact that she had eaten supper before the ceremony, Rhiannon felt hungry again. Her stomach rumbled loudly enough to break the uncomfortable silence, reminding everyone that a splendid feast awaited them downstairs in the dinning chamber. The entity – or demon, for that is what it truly was – was pleased that his little ruse had worked. It had made a near fatal mistake by allowing Rhiannon's subconscious mind to regain control long enough to attempt suicide. *Nevertheless, these silly sentimental old fools who call themselves wizards have, for now at least, failed to see the truth of it,* Neraka thought. *More's the pity.*

"Well, we can discuss this anomaly later. For now, let's not let it spoil our celebration feast. This is, after all, quite a special occasion. Tonight for the first time in our history we have welcomed not just one new wizard into the league, but two." Petamor said.

Cinaran broke the apprehensive mood with a jovial laugh. "Petamor, my brother, you are a man after my own heart. Of course, let us feast and celebrate this momentous occasion, as is our custom. I must admit, I am hungry enough to eat Rhiannon's flying horse, wings and all."

At the image of Cinaran feasting upon her beloved Topaz, Rhiannon's facial expression turned sour, causing everyone, with the exception of Thoradal and Rimahorn, to join in the laughter.

"Oh, don't worry, young lady," Cinaran said good-naturedly as he put his arm around Rhiannon's slender shoulders. "I promise to limit my repast to that which our good host has provided. Now if only he would be kind enough to lead the way to the table before I die of starvation, I for one would be very grateful." Then he winked and playfully began to slap out a little song on his amble belly.

———•·———

The somber mood of the group softened immediately once they got a whiff of the bountiful feast that Breandan and Rhiannon had prepared. It was indeed a mouth-watering banquet consisting of roasted beef tenderloin, smoked turkey, braised pheasant, and char-grilled lobster, not to mention a wide variety of fresh baked breads, cheeses, ripe fruits, steamed vegetables, and enough chilled wine and ice-cold ale to float a small armada.

The great feast continued well into the wee hours of the morning and no one, except for Rhiannon, noticed that Thoradal ate very little and drank even less.

The feast finally came to an amiable end when Petamor caught Rhiannon trying to stifle a yawn. He insisted that she go straight to bed, forgetting for the moment at least, that he was no longer her mentor or guardian.

Rhiannon thanked the wizards for their support by kissing each one lightly on the cheek. She expressed her desire to spend some time with each of them so that they could all get to know her better. It was all a pack of lies, of course. The demon had no intention of allowing Rhiannon anywhere near the wizards once she was completely free of them. Until then, however, she would continue to play along.

Knowing that she would be leaving soon, old Petamor could not help but feel heavy hearted as he escorted Rhiannon back to her room. "Rhiannon, I know that you are eager to be on your way," he said, "but it would please me and the others if you decided to stay here a few days longer."

"If that's what you wish, Grandfather," Rhiannon agreed with a sleepy smile. "I'll stay for a few more days. This night, I mean the ceremony and all, happened so unexpectedly. I can use the next few days to decide what I want to do next."

"Excellent," Petamor said with a sigh of relief. "If there's anything I can do to help, don't hesitate---"

Before Petamor could finish, Rhiannon hugged him and pulled him tight. "You have already done so much for me. I...I don't know how I can ever repay you."

"There's no need. You know that I will always think of you as my own granddaughter."

"Grandfather," she began, "do you still believe that the starship malfunctioned? Or do you think that it was my...that... that I---"

"No! I don't believe for a moment that you had anything to do with what happened here tonight, my dear," he answered before she could ask the question.

---·---

Upon learning that Rhiannon had agreed to remain at the tower a few days longer, Breandan also decided to extend his stay. He was more concerned over the incident than he had let on, and he wanted to discuss it with Rhiannon in private.

---·---

The next morning, Rimahorn and five of the other wizards returned to their own fortresses and their own clans. It was time to reestablish contact with the people of Pega. This resulted in a celebration throughout the land, as the astonished and overjoyed people discovered that the League of Wizards had not just been a fanciful tale after all. The wizards were real and were prepared to help the people deal with the latest threat to their land.

As to be expected, however, not all of the current inhabitants of the valley were thrilled with the news.

The Horrans of the Far Reaches beyond the Western Sea were not at all pleased with the information as it placed their well-guarded invasion plans in jeopardy. Unlike the humans in the valley, their emperor had always known of the wizards' existence and understood the potential threat therein. Now, their unexpected reemergence at this crucial time in his campaign was not welcomed. He understood just how potent and deadly these adversaries could be.

The Horrans were a ruthless and bloodthirsty race. Although primarily human in appearance, a mutation in their primordial evolution had left them with a distinctively reptilian appearance. A few of the genetic differences between humans and Horrans included thick scaly skin, cold reptilian eyes, as well as an insatiable hunger for fresh meat. They also possessed lizard-like jaws, sharp pointed teeth; and a long narrow tongue that caused them to speak with a distinctive hiss.

To help protect their thick scaly hides, Horranian soldiers always wore heavy armor of steel plates and chain mail that made them very difficult to kill in hand-to-hand combat. In ancient times they had often hired themselves out as mercenaries to anyone willing to pay their fee. Their biggest weakness was an unbridled lust for human females whom they often forced into slavery.

In that last war so long ago – known as the War of the Worms – the evil Horranian emperor, Ko-Kahn the Terrible, had nearly defeated his long-time rival, Taj-ru-Kat. At the last moment, the Wizards of Nox had stepped in and provided support to Taj-ru-Kat's forces. As a result of their intervention the war had ended in a draw, and Ko-Kahn was forced to return to his palace in humiliation. Ko-Kahn the Terrible was no longer so terrible. He never forgave or forgot the wizards for their meddling and shortly before he died at the age of two hundred and six, he vowed revenge by conquering and enslaving the entire human population of Pega. After his death, his dream of world conquest was passed on to his heirs.

It had been over eight-hundred years since the last major war took place between humans and the Horrans, and there had been a continuing unbroken peace in the land ever since.

In the Wizard's Keep, high above the valley, while Breandan admired the new staff that Petamor had made for him, a small band of Horranian horse soldiers was entering his home village of Ravenwood in search of a little entertainment. They stopped at the Yellow Dog Tavern to drink a few tankards of grog.

Breandan smiled as he looked out over the edge of the plateau. Ordinarily the mist surrounding the top of the escarpment would have made it difficult to see his village far below. However, his wizardly eyes were sharper than normal human eyes, and as a result, he could see the village quite clearly. In his left hand, he held his new staff. Beneath his dark-brown winter cloak, he wore the new robe that Rhiannon had made for him.

Petamor was beaming brightly. He was very pleased with the staff he had made for Breandan. He had carved it out of a piece of golden maple and ringed it with bands of rare red gold.

Both Petamor and Rhiannon were there to see Breandan off. It had been a week since the Lamp of Life ceremony and there was no reason to delay his departure any longer. He had spoken to Rhiannon privately about the strange occurrence on the night of the ceremony, and he had ascertained that she was not responsible.

Secretly Rhiannon was sad to see him go, however, the demon within her was anxious to be rid of him, seeing as he posed a potential threat. Nevertheless, she kissed him softly on the lips and embraced him one last time. There was no need for words. This was supposed to have been a beginning, not an end.

Breandan embraced Petamor one more time and then

lifted his newly fashioned wizard's staff into the air. In a flash of reddish-gold light he was gone.

———•———

Breandan was happy to be home again and could hardly wait to see his mother and younger sister. But out of respect for his parents' privacy, he stood outside the door to the cottage and knocked. Only when no one answered the door did he enter unbidden. What he saw shocked him to the core.

Breandan's mother lay prostrate on the floor weeping and moaning as if the world was about to end. The joy within his heart dissipated instantly, replaced by a sense of dire dread. When she saw him standing there, his mother exclaimed, "It is a miracle! My son has returned at the very moment he is needed most!" With that, the hysterical woman jumped to her feet and ran to Breandan.

"Mother," Breandan said softly. "Why are you crying? What's happened?"

"It's your sister, Breandan. She's in terrible danger!"

"What do you mean? Where is she? Where's Heather, mother?"

"She's down at the tavern. She been working there since you went off in search of your wizards and magic. It was all fine until they started coming around actin' like they own the place."

"What do you mean by *they*? Who are they?"

"The Horrans...the Horrans are down at the Yellow Dog. They been there all morning. They're drunk...and...you know what they do to pretty womenfolk."

For a moment, Breandan felt a wave of utter hopelessness wash over him. The shock had momentarily caused him to forget who and what he was. However, there was no time to waste; he had to get to the tavern as quickly as possible before the Horrans carried his sister away.

As he turned to rush out the door, his mother yelled,

"Breandan, wait! If you try to interfere, they'll kill you as well."

Breandan heard his mother's warning but had no time to try to explain himself. He had to rescue Heather. He ran all the way to the tavern.

───•───

The Horranian horse soldiers were sitting at a corner table, eating and drinking themselves drunk. One of them, a young and inexperienced cavalier, had been licking his cruel lizard-like lips as he watched the pretty young barmaid serve drinks to her human customers.

Breandan's sister was aware of the danger she was in, although she pretended not to notice, hoping against hope that if she ignored them, the Horranian soldiers would go away and leave her alone. Breandan's father could do nothing but hope as well, for if he made any attempt to interfere, the Horranian soldiers might decide to kill everyone in the tavern. Meanwhile, his other male patrons were growing more nervous by the minute. They realized that if trouble started, the women present would expect them to stand up and fight. They also knew that, unarmed as they were, they didn't stand a chance against the Horranian warriors.

Every head turned as Breandan entered the tavern, but they promptly turned back to their ale when they failed to recognize the young man in the brown cloak who resembled any other traveler passing through the village.

Breandan quickly surveyed the room and assessed the situation. As a wizard, he could read some of the villagers' thoughts and sense their fear. He could not prevent the feeling of loathing that crept into his soul when he realized how unwilling these men were to protect a defenseless young woman. "Cowards," he whispered sharply under his breath.

The Horranian soldiers, who were still seated in the corner, were pounding on the table and laughing at their comrade who was clutching Breandan's sister. And with the exception of their captain, who was eyeing Breandan with silent suspicion, none of the Horrans seemed to notice that a tall dark-cloaked stranger had entered the establishment.

The drunken and grotesquely ugly cavalier moved to the middle of the floor dragging Breandan's unwilling sister by the arm. Her blouse had already been torn exposing her small left breast. As the beastly creature licked its savage lips, a viscid string of saliva dripped down from its mouth onto its uniform. The obscenities that issued from its mouth were crude enough to cause a veteran sailor to blush.

Heather was traumatized with fear as the drunken soldier ripped away the rest of her blouse, but before his claw-like fingers could close around her exposed flesh, Breandan called out to him.

"Stop," he said. "Let my sister go, you Horranian buzzard; or you will leave me no choice but to kill you where you stand!"

Without releasing the girl, the Horranian cutthroat spun around to face his antagonist. His head was a little foggy from all of the grog he had guzzled, but he relished the idea of butchering another stupid human male even more than he desired the female. The Horranian soldier quickly sized Breandan up and then shoved the half-naked tavern girl aside. He drew his scimitar and started across the floor to kill the party crasher.

Breandan had changed a great deal in the past three years, so it was not difficult to understand why no one in the tavern, including his own father recognized him. Besides, it seemed that everyone was too busy pretending to ignore the Horrans to pay any notice to a stranger. However, the instant Heather heard Breandan's voice, she acknowledged him, and called out to him to be careful.

Now some of the men in the tavern began to recognize Breandan, and they began to stand. Suddenly Heather ran to Breandan, who removed his outer cloak and gently drew it around his sister's shoulders covering her nakedness. Until that moment, Breandan's staff had been partially hidden beneath his cloak.

The big cavalier's mind was too clouded with grog to notice the wizard's staff, not that he would have known what it was in the first place, for he was far too young to remember that long ago war. He had only one thing on his mind, to kill Breandan as quickly as possible. He boldly approached his challenger while his comrades, with the exception of his captain, cheered and applauded, urging him to butcher the interloper.

Breandan had never had to kill anyone before, but he would defend himself and his sister if necessary. He clutched his staff with confidence and felt the power surging through him. When he lightly tapped the lower tip of his staff on the floor, he and Heather were immediately surrounded by a protective force field.

The snarling Horran raised his scimitar and struck at the young wizard's head.

Breandan sidestepped and instinctively raised his arm to deflect the blow, a blow that would have killed a normal man instantly. The scimitar struck Breandan's invisible force field and glanced off as if hitting stone.

Meanwhile the Horranian captain sat calmly at his table sipping his grog. He no longer had any doubts. He now knew for certain that the tall dark stranger was a wizard. He had heard such rumors and now realized that they must be true. He would have to report this to his superior officer right away.

Breandan's opponent was as bewildered as were his comrades. He knew that his scimitar should have killed the human. He was just beginning to realize how drunk he was. Once again, he lifted his scimitar. This time he intended to cleave Breandan's skull in two and be done with it. He was anxious to get back to his grog and the pretty barmaid. He brought the scimitar down on the stranger's head with all of his might. This time as the scimitar hit the invisible barrier, it instantly vaporized into a fine silvery mist. At the exact same moment, the doomed cavalier's body shattered into thousands of tiny harmless fireflies that flew around the tavern room in confusion before fluttering out an open window, never to be seen again.

The silence that filled the tavern was so complete; you could have heard a mouse sneeze.

Breandan turned and faced the remaining Horrans.

Their captain muttered something and pointed towards the tavern door. As one, they stood up from the table. Several of them grabbed the hilts of their swords, although they were not sure what to do. They were afraid to pull them. One moment their friend had been standing there, and the next moment he was gone while the human he intended to kill just stood there glaring back at them, waiting for their next move.

Their leader eyed Breandan for a few moments and waited while the rest of his men filed out of the tavern one-by-one. They grumbled a little but wasted no time vacating the premises. Once they were gone, the captain stood and smiled at Breandan. He then took his right fist and slammed it against his chest, a salute to the victor. Without a word, he turned his back on the young wizard and casually walked out the front door.

The Yellow Dog's patrons were delighted and amazed. The cheer they raised was heard all over the village. A few of the less sober men ran out into the street to throw rocks at the retreating Horranian soldiers as they rode away. Now that the threat had been neutralized, it seemed that their courage had returned.

———•———

Rhiannon sat in the dimly lighted kitchen alone. The fire in the hearth was dying rapidly. She appeared to be watching the shadows dancing around the chamber walls, but she was actually so lost in thought that her eyes did not notice them.

What's wrong with me, she pondered. *I don't understand. I'm frightened and exhilarated all at the same time. It's almost as if I am two people. And I keep hearing a voice inside my head. Sometimes it tells me what to say and I say it. Sometimes it tells me what to do and I do it. What's wrong with me! I want to tell Petamor, but every time I try, I get sleepy and can barely hold my eyes open. This all started during the ceremony. No. No! It started before the ceremony! It started the day I arrived here! Maybe the wizards are right. Maybe someone is trying to send them a message through me. Breandan has been gone for nearly a week now. I wish he were here. I desperately need to talk to someone.*

She heard footsteps approaching, slowly descending on the stone steps outside the chamber. She glanced at the dying embers in the hearth and remembered that she was supposed to be tending the fire for the evening meal. With a slight nod of her head, she caused the dying flames to burst into life. The firelight lit up the entire room.

Rhiannon knew that she was forbidden to use magic to create fire unless in an extreme emergency, but she could not help herself. Something inside of her was taking over control of her thoughts and actions. She was terrified that soon she would disappear altogether.

Petamor entered the chamber and proceeded directly to the fire to warm his hands. He lifted the heavy cast-iron lid on the kettle that was hanging from a hook over the flames. The aroma pleased him. The kettle was filled with stewed beef and vegetables. Since Rhiannon's arrival it had become his favorite meal.

"Smells delicious," he said turning to Rhiannon.

Rhiannon nodded as she pretended to read a book while she stirred the stew with a long-handled spoon.

Petamor went to the trapdoor in the floor and hauled up the basket containing the dinnerware from last night's meal. They had been cleansed by the lake current. He carefully dried them off and carried them to the table. As he set the table, he frowned at the Rhiannon's hunched back. He knew that something was troubling her, but whatever it was, she was not willing to talk about it. He was also aware that she was no longer happy here although she pretended to be for his sake.

It was time for her to go out into the world and find her own place. Whatever it was that was troubling her, she would have to find a way to deal with it in her own time. So blinded was he by his love for Rhiannon, Petamor couldn't see the truth.

Petamor had other concerns as well. The news spreading throughout the land was not good. The Horrans were preparing to make war on the residents of Pega.

Petamor moved back to the hearth. The stew was already steaming hot and ready to be serve. He slipped a thick cotton mitten over his hand and used it to remove the kettle from the fire. He carried the kettle to the dinning table where Rhiannon was pouring chilled wine from a crystal carafe.

They ate in awkward silence.

The storm raged all during the night, and the thunder was preventing Rhiannon from getting any sleep. She decided to take a warm bath.

The tower was silent as she crept down to the bathing chamber in the base of the structure. Upon discovering that the water in the pool was not quite as warm as she liked, she spat out a simple spell that instantly heated the water into a boiling cauldron of steam. Rhiannon waved her hand and the tempest instantly subsided to a simmer. Neraka laughed, causing Rhiannon to wince in pain. If someone didn't help her soon, she would be unable to prevent the greedy monster from taking over completely. She would be lost forever.

An hour later Rhiannon dragged herself out of the pool.

She loved these long relaxing baths. They always left her feeling clean and refreshed. As she dried her body with a big fluffy towel, she contemplated all of the changes her body had gone through since the day she first set foot upon the escarpment. She had matured in both body and mind. Physically and emotionally she was a woman, although she remained pure and chaste, for she continued to obey the laws of her people's religion that forbid sexual relations with anyone other than a lawful spouse. Yet the desire to mate was escalating at an alarming rate.

Rhiannon examined her body in her small mirror. She was stunned by the changes; they had happened so fast, almost overnight. *I'm a woman now,* she told herself, *and I like what I see. I can't help but wonder if Breandan has bothered to notice.*

Rhiannon set the mirror aside and closed her eyes. Once again, images of home played back on the insides of her closed eyelids. But when she tried to picture her tiny village, the images appeared vague and weak, as if she was seeing them through a heavy fog. It was almost as if something was attempting to prevent those memories from resurfacing.

The demon had also enjoyed the warm sensations that Rhiannon's body experienced while bathing. In fact, Rhiannon's healthy young body was providing all sorts of new pleasures. But now, as the two completely different creatures began to meld into one being, Rhiannon's memories and thoughts flowed into her uninvited guest's mind, and Neraka was beginning to see a way in which it could put those memories to good use.

Rhiannon draped the damp towel across the wooden bench to dry, gathered up her things, and scampered back to her room. She didn't bother to dress; she was thrilled by the flow of the chilly air around her naked body. It reminded her of the long night rides she occasionally took on the back of the rock hopper.

It was not until she had reached the safety of her room that she considered the risk she had taken. If old Petamor had seen her, he would've been shocked and deeply troubled by her puerile behavior. For a moment, she was once again the brave young girl who had courageously climbed the escarpment despite the odds. For a moment, she was once again the innocent young girl who loved Breandan. And for a moment, she was once again Petamor's naïve young apprentice. Then a mischievous smile flashed across her face, and once again, she was the new Rhiannon – half-demon, half-human.

Going to her wardrobe, Rhiannon took out her favorite riding breeches and tunic. She had designed and made the outfit herself. She did not take her sandals. She had decided to ride barefoot.

The rain had stopped and dawn was breaking on a perfectly clear sky. A restless lacy fog was beginning to drift up from the lake, although the rest of the plateau, including the mountains where Topaz lived, was as clear and pellucid as a crystal raindrop.

Rhiannon used the telepathic link she had established with Topaz to summon him. A few moments later, she smiled when she saw him streaking towards her from the west.

When Topaz alit upon the tower roof, Rhiannon flung her arms around his muscular neck in greeting. He snorted, whinnied, and pranced in joy at seeing her while his warm breath plumbed from his nostrils into the cool morning air.

Rhiannon grabbed a handful of his black mane and swung herself up onto his back. Then they were airborne. As was customary, they headed straight towards the enchanted woods that hugged the northeastern shore of the lake and covered the entire northern half of the plateau. They landed in a clearing near the edge of the woods and headed into the forest. As they walked, Rhiannon removed her breeches and tunic and used her leather belt to secure them to Topaz's back. Rhiannon enjoyed being naked, and the woods gave her the freedom and the privacy she required.

Petamor awoke from an unremembered dream feeling as if he had not slept at all. He put on his robe and left his bedchamber listening for any sounds of activity. He really didn't expect to hear her. Rhiannon always moved as quietly as a cat. He hurried to the kitchen hoping to find her in the middle of preparing breakfast for the two of them, but the stone hearth was cold and silent. So, he prepared his own breakfast and ate alone for the first time in nearly three years.

When Petamor finished his morning meal, he went looking for Rhiannon. After a quick but thorough search of the tower, he went up onto the roof, but it appeared that she was already gone. He shook his head and sighed. Just as he was about to descend back through the hatchway a dark shadow passed overhead. It was Rhiannon and Topaz returning from their early morning romp.

No matter how many times Petamor witnessed this incredible sight, it never ceased to amaze him. Rhiannon's control over the animal was flawless. It was as if Topaz was not an animal at all, but an extension of her own body.

Rhiannon swung her leg over Topaz's back and dropped to the stone roof in her bare feet. She was a little embarrassed; she could feel her face blushing. She was thankful that she had remembered to get dressed again before returning to the keep. When she looked up, she was sure that Petamor would be displeased with her. Instead, he was smiling. Then he reached out, took her small hands between his big rough ones, and patted them reassuringly.

As for Neraka, his control over Rhiannon's movements was not yet complete. He was not yet able to quell her sudden and spontaneous reactions.

Rhiannon hugged the old wizard.

On any other day Topaz would have started back to his

home in the mountains by now. Today, however, he remained where he was and regarded Rhiannon with questioning eyes.

"I don't think he wants you to leave, my dear," Petamor stated.

"I'm taking him with me," Rhiannon declared boldly before Neraka could stop her. "He wants to come."

The old wizard sighed. "I expected as much," he said, wishing that he too could follow the girl to whatever part of the world she would wander. He reached out and gently scratched Topaz's ears. "When are you leaving?"

"Well, I really want to get an early start. Topaz and I have a very long journey ahead of us. And since we've already wasted so much daylight saying goodbye to our forest friends, I think that we'll wait until tomorrow morning at first light. That will give me a chance to study some of the old maps in your library."

"Do you still intend to visit your mother and father in the village?"

"Yes. I will go and visit my mother and father before I leave the valley. Then I think I'll go south, to the Southern Reaches. Maybe I can find the place where they grow bananas," she added with a grin.

"I thought you liked winter weather."

Rhiannon cocked her head in a strange way, as if she were listening to something far away. "I've changed a lot over the past year. Now, I think that it would be nice to live in a warmer climate for a while. It may do me some good."

Petamor laughed. "I didn't think you liked bananas that much."

Rhiannon shrugged. "It's not the bananas that appeals to me. It's the climate."

"I was actually hoping that you might stay in your home village for a while. After all, Breandan intends to remain there."

"I know, but my relationship with Breandan has changed as well, and I don't think Ravenwood needs two wizards."

"Your relationship with Breandan will restore itself if you give it time. If you remain in your village you could---"

"I want to be on my own for a while, Grandfather. I've been cooped up in this tower for too long as it is, and I really want to find that place where it never snows."

Petamor was a little hurt by Rhiannon's remark concerning the time she had spent at the tower, and when she realized what she had said, she quickly threw her arms around the old wizard's neck and hugged him tightly. "I didn't mean that the way it sounded," she said. "You know I love you more than anything."

Petamor felt a little better. He said, "Very well. You're right, Rhiannon. You have to find your own way in this world. I just hope that you'll come and visit me from time-to-time. And just in case you haven't noticed, it doesn't snow here, either."

Rhiannon giggled. "That's true, Grandfather. Perhaps you'll consider coming to visit me once I've found a place to settle."

"Of course I'll try. But I'm afraid that I'm getting too old to be traveling around the world. However, you must promise to come and visit me here as often as you can."

"I will," she lied.

"Perhaps you could visit during the winter solstice celebration," Petamor said hopefully. "That has always been my favorite time of year."

"Yes," Rhiannon agreed, "the winter solstice celebration is my favorite as well."

At that moment, Topaz's ears began to twitch. Suddenly, he spread his great furry wings and jumped into the air.

Petamor looked at Rhiannon puzzled.

"I sent him home to wait until I am ready to leave. He'll return when I summon him again," she said. "Will you escort me to the library?"

"Certainly," Petamor replied.

As they walked down the winding stairway, Rhiannon asked, "Are you still worried about the starship?"

Petamor was caught off guard by the question. "Well, we all are a little concerned. However, no one's blaming you. Moreover, there have been no more omens since the ceremony. All the same, Thoradal still insists that the starship is functioning properly."

"Thoradal still believes that I had something to do with it, doesn't he? He's been a little cold towards me ever since that night."

"That's just his way. If he didn't act like that, I'd be worried about *him*," Petamor said.

They were standing in front of the door to the library.

"You look tired, Grandfather. Are you going to be all right?" Rhiannon asked.

"The excitement of the past few days has prevented me from sleeping well. I spend most of my nights tossing and turning."

"Are you worrying about me?"

Petamor sighed. "You *and* Breandan. Sometimes I---"

Rhiannon put a finger to Petamor's lips. "Don't worry about us," she whispered. "Breandan and I will be fine. Now, Grandfather, if you will excuse me, I have some maps to go over." Then she turned and slipped quietly into the library chamber and gently closed the door behind her.

Petamor stood there in the dark stairwell for a long time staring at the closed door. *Tomorrow,* he thought, *Rhiannon will be gone, and I'll be alone again.* He didn't want to say anything to Rhiannon, but the true reason he was having trouble sleeping was, in fact, because of her. Thoradal was right. He had allowed his emotions cloud his judgment. As much as he hated to admit it, he was beginning to think that the incident with the starship had a stronger connection to Rhiannon than he had originally believed. He would have to figure out what that connection was before something terrible happened to her. Slowly he turned and walked down the winding stairs to the dinning chamber where he knew some serious conversation awaited him.

————•————

Petamor heard the heated debate long before he entered the dinning chamber where the discussion was taking place.

"---then why did it only affect the girl?" Cinaran was asking.

"Most likely because Rhiannon was the target," Thoradal answered. "Perhaps if it had happened a few moments sooner, it might've killed the girl before she could light her lamp."

"Well then, if that is the case, we must do everything we can to protect Rhiannon from harm," Cinaran said.

"Rhiannon doesn't need our protection," Thoradal stated. "Like it or not, she is a wizard now and quite capable of defending herself. Unless, of course, she was attacked by one of us."

"I seriously doubt if one of our own is responsible," Cinaran said. "Would we not have felt it?"

"Not necessarily," Thoradal added. "None of us has needed to use our full power in over eight-hundred years. We've gotten a bit rusty, you said so yourself. But there was a surge of power in the council chamber that night, and it came from Rhiannon, I am certain of it."

"Are you saying that Rhiannon used her own powers to try and kill herself?" Petamor asked astonished.

"Yes, I believe that it's possible," Thoradal admitted.

"Why? What possible reason could she have to want to kill herself?"

"Perhaps her subconscious is aware of a hidden flaw within her character," Thoradal said.

"A flaw?" Petamor asked. "We are all flawed, my brother. None of us is perfect."

"Yes, of course. Nevertheless, I cannot help but wonder if Rhiannon knows something we don't. Perhaps, deep down within the very essence of her being, she is aware that something is fatally wrong with her. It may be dormant at the moment. But, if it ever comes to light, she may prove to be a danger to both herself and to those around her."

"All right, then. The question is what can be done about it?" asked Cinaran.

The wizards sat there in silence, thinking. Finally Petamor spoke. "There is nothing we can do but let her go," he said. "Even if what Thoradal says is true, we have no proof. Even if Rhiannon did attempt to kill herself the other night subconsciously or by accident, we have no proof. And even if she is responsible for Chaos...I mean, the starship turning red...so what? It is not a crime. No damage was done. It was a light show at best. A magician's trick, like cutting a woman into two. No one was actually harmed."

"I am telling you, brother, I saw my own death on the face of that moon," Thoradal said.

"Did you? Are you certain that you did not imagine it? Do you want to punish Rhiannon to satisfy your own fear of mortality?"

Thoradal was shocked by Petamor's bitter defense of Rhiannon.

"You...*we* have no proof whatsoever that she's responsible. We have no reason to hold her here against her will. I'm not even sure if we *could* hold her against her will. She has grown very strong over the past few months." Petamor sighed heavily and added, "And...if she really wants to die, there's nothing we can do to prevent it."

"Very well," Thoradal said. "But do not forget, brother, that we have a responsibility to protect the people of this world, and if Rhiannon poses a threat, wizard or no, we will have to use any means at our disposal to deal with her."

Petamor only nodded.

"Petamor, my brother," Cinaran said, "Thoradal and I have decided to stay here in the tower for the time being. That is, if you will have us. We both feel that we can better analyze this situation more accurately if we stay close and work together."

"Very well," Petamor said. "You both are welcome to stay as long as you wish."

"Unfortunately, Rhiannon is not our only problem. Trouble is brewing in the valleys and the Horrans appear to be up to their old tricks," Cinaran said.

"Then we have our work cut out for us," Petamor stated.

"We may be in residence here for a long time," Thoradal added.

"Well, in that case I'll need a few extra hands. I will employ the two men from the village of Lorelei," Petamor said.

"That's fine with me," Thoradal said, "just be sure they are trustworthy."

"Topaz trusts them," Petamor added.

"He trusts them because he is under a spell," Thoradal interjected harshly.

"I trust them as well," Petamor said, trying hard to control his temper.

"What exactly are Rhiannon's plans?" Cinaran jumped in, wanting to defuse an argument between the two wizards. "Has she spoken to you of them?"

"First she intends to visit her mother and father in Ravenwood," Petamor replied.

"That's good, is it not?" Cinaran said. "Isn't Breandan there, in the village, too? He can help us keep an eye on her."

"Unfortunately," Petamor said, "Rhiannon doesn't intend to stay there more than a day or two. She's heading into the Southern Reaches to find a new home and continue her studies."

"The Southern Reaches?" responded Thoradal. "Not much there but a few islands."

"Yes, I know." Petamor said.

"Good. At least she'll be far enough away that she cannot cause us any problems while we are dealing with the

Horranian situation. We don't need her involvement in the impending crisis right now," Thoradal said.

"You talk as if Rhiannon is our enemy," Petamor stated angrily.

"You need to stop letting your personal feelings for the girl cloud your judgment, old friend. I've never said that she was our enemy. All I'm saying is that we need to be careful. We all care about her, and we all want what is best for her," Thoradal continued.

"Thoradal's right," Cinaran said. "We mean the girl no harm. We all find her sweet and charming, and we all can see that she possesses the potential to become a great and powerful wizard. And that is exactly why we must monitor her activities. We'll need to know what she's up to at all times. If the red moon incident had anything to do with the impending conflict with the Horrans, the power that sent that message may try and use Rhiannon to prevent us from interfering with their plans."

"So be it," Petamor said reluctantly.

———•———

Later that night Rhiannon had a rather uncomfortable dinner together with Petamor, Thoradal, and Cinaran. Afterwards, she returned to her room for what would be the last time. For reasons she could not comprehend, she felt vulnerable and restless, and she paced the floor like a nervous panther. After some time, however, Rhiannon climbed into bed and fell asleep, but Neraka remained alert and watchful throughout the night.

———•———

As the sun peeked over the eastern horizon from behind a blanket of pink and purple clouds, Rhiannon awoke from a dreamless sleep with a start. Neraka had forced her to be fully awake in order to facilitate a speedy departure. He could take control over Rhiannon's physical body at almost any time, and by reading her thoughts, could anticipate most of her moves. Yet, he had been unable to conquer her mind, and it was still impossible to predict every move the impulsive girl might make.

The demon did not fear Rhiannon; it had no reason to fear her. It was quite at home now in her body and did not want to leave. He did fear the power of the league. If there was anything that could betray his presence within the girl, it was within her eyes. For anyone who looked deeply enough into Rhiannon's eyes would know that something was wrong. However, the most difficult challenge, the lighting of the Lamp of Life, had already been accomplished. Sometime during that ceremony the demon had lost control for a brief moment, and during that momentary lapse, Rhiannon's subconscious had become aware of the intruder. At that moment she had attempted to warn the league and destroy both herself and her unwelcome guest. Neraka would never allow that to happen again. In the future it would only allow Rhiannon to take control of her own actions just for fun, just to see what the imaginative girl would do next.

As for Rhiannon, she had no choice. The demon's grip was too tight. She was trapped inside her own head. Although Neraka usually allowed her to move her own body, she often felt like a puppet on a string. What frightened her most was that her own thoughts were beginning to meld with those of the thing controlling her.

Thus far, the demon had not done any real harm. It hadn't hurt anyone or anything. It didn't appear to be evil, exactly. His attitude was more that of a selfish spoiled child. If only she could find a way to warn Petamor without alerting the intruder, perhaps he would know a way to cast out this demon menace. Right there and then, Rhiannon decided to face the problem head on. She would go straight to Petamor and explain the situation. What, after all, did she have to lose?

Throwing back the blanket, Rhiannon jumped out of bed,

but before she could take that first step a mischievous smile touched her lips. Neraka would never allow her to betray his presence again. He instantly crushed Rhiannon's feeble hope for freedom.

Instead, Rhiannon stepped up to the full-length mirror set against the wall next to the bed. Old Petamor had given her the mirror shortly after she had arrived at the keep. The demon forced her to examine the sensuous curves of her body. Her unblemished skin felt warm to the touch. It seemed to glow in the hazy golden light from the candles. Slowly her fingers traced a path along her silky skin. She admired her womanly curves.

Rhiannon heard laughter in her head. It was a wicked laughter, and the tower floor began to tremble beneath her feet.

———•———

Petamor awoke as a low moaning rumble filled his bedchamber. He stared wide-eyed as dust showered down from the wooden rafters overhead. He brushed the dust off his robe and quickly dressed. He stepped out onto the landing beside his door and looked around. A fine dust drifted through the air and covered the floor and stairs. He hurried to Rhiannon's room to see if she was all right. *It must have been an earthquake,* he decided.

Rhiannon wasn't in her room, but her footprints were easy to follow in the fresh dust. He followed them down to the dinning area where he found her preparing their meal as if nothing had happened.

"Ham and eggs sound good, Grandfather?" Rhiannon asked with a smile. "I've also squeezed some juice out of those orange colored fruits. What do you call them again?"

"Oranges," Petamor answered.

"Oh yes! Of course!" Rhiannon said brightly. "Oranges." She

laughed. I thought that it would be nice if we shared one last meal together. I hope you slept well."

"Yes, I slept like a baby," Petamor admitted. "Did you feel that vibration a little while ago?" he asked calmly.

"What? You mean that shaking? Yes, I felt it. Must have been an earthquake, don't you think? A very mild one. I don't think it did any damage to the keep. Dust everywhere, though. If you want, I can stay and clean it up before I go," Rhiannon added with another dazzling smile.

"No, no," Petamor said, beginning to relax again. He was pleased to see Rhiannon behaving more like her old self. "After you leave, I intend to engage a couple of servants to help out for a few weeks. A good thorough dusting will give them a chance to learn where everything is."

"Oh, you're taking on servants?"

"Yes, but only for a short time. Just until Thoradal and Cinaran get tired of my company. Personally, I think they enjoy being pampered."

"Don't we all?" Rhiannon continued to smile. She knew the real reason Thoradal and Cinaran were staying. They were still suspicious of her, and the old fools were not going to let it go that easily.

"Well, have a seat, Grandfather. Let us enjoy our last meal together."

Petamor's mood had darkened a little as Rhiannon's offhanded remark reminded him of the events of the past few days. He looked down at the dusty floor and remembered why he had come looking for her in the first place. He was beginning to suspect that it had not been an earthquake after all.

"Strange about the earthquake," he said. "I've lived on this plateau for hundreds of years, and not once in all that time have I ever experienced even the slightest tremor, not even a tiny vibration, much less an earthquake."

"Perhaps it was the thunder then," Rhiannon said quickly.

"From the look of those dark clouds rolling in, I'd say that we are in for a major thunderstorm, enchantment or no."

Petamor pondered that for a moment. "I suppose it could have been lightning striking the tower that caused the dust to fall." He moved over to one of the nearby windows and looked out across the lake. Sure enough, the swollen bellies of rain clouds swaggered low over the plateau nearly smothering the early morning sky.

Rhiannon continued to smile despite the old wizard's troubled expression. She could not even influence her own facial features. The demon was in complete control. She placed a plate full of streaming hickory-smoked ham and scrambled eggs on the table in front of him. As he sat down to eat, Rhiannon tried to read his thoughts. He was wondering whether she had conjured up the storm as a distraction from the real cause of the tremor.

In fact, Rhiannon *had* conjured up the storm in an effort to cover her unwanted guest's momentary loss of control. Neraka was pleased to know that Rhiannon possessed enough power to create such an earthquake, even if it was mild. Nevertheless, he would have to be more careful in the future.

"Grandfather, the time has come. I'm leaving just as soon as we finish our meal," Rhiannon said as she poured the old wizard a mug of hot coffee. "I'll miss you more than you can ever know."

Petamor could sense by her tone that she was sincere. He nodded and fought back the tears that attempted to conquer his eyes. "I only hope that I have given you as much as you have given me, my dear. I will miss you, although I have a feeling that we will be seeing each other again sooner than we expect."

Rhiannon was curious by Petamor's statement, but decided not to respond. Instead, she sat down and began to eat her breakfast. Petamor did likewise. His only further comment during their meal was on how delicious the food tasted.

By the time they had finished their meal the storm clouds Rhiannon had conjured up had started moving out over the southern half of the continent converting the heavy rain into a raging snowstorm.

Rhiannon returned to her room to collect the rest of her things: her small pack, the tin cup, the bone brush and comb, and lastly, her small mirror.

She tried once more to break free of the demon's grasp, but failed. The intruder's hold on her was too great. She was slowly becoming it, and it was slowly becoming her. And with every breath she took, her willingness to fight dissipated a little more.

The young wizard girl slipped on the scarred boots that she had worn during her climb up the escarpment. They were a little tight, and she realized how much her body had changed over the past several months. She cast a simple spell and suddenly the old boots fit perfectly. She wrapped some woolen leggings around her lower legs and held them in place with several strips of thin leather. Although it felt like summer on the plateau, it would be winter in her village near the foot of the escarpment.

Petamor stood atop the tower staring out between the battlements. The air was unusually cool, but he passed it off as being the result of the early morning storm. Behind him, Topaz nickered and snorted impatiently.

In the distance, on the far side of the lake, several of Topaz's kin romped happily among the rocks of their ancient mountain home. It was a sight few mortal men had ever witnessed or ever would witness. The old magic was beginning to fade.

It was just after dawn. Gleams of the orange sun were striking through the clouds that were hurrying towards the south to join the blizzard. A second later the brilliant star found a wider break in the clouds and burst through the haze to warm the face of the old wizard. The morning light revealed more age lines than had been there before. At that very moment, Rhiannon stepped through the hatch. Her new red robe billowed around her in the soft breeze.

The instant Rhiannon's foot touched the roof, Topaz was by her side. Petamor watched in silent admiration as the girl and the winged beast greeted each other affectionately. The rock hopper was devoted to Rhiannon, of that there was absolutely no doubt. What Petamor did not realize was that the creature was enchanted by a Rhiannon who was now more demon than human. Topaz *was* aware of the changes that had taken place in Rhiannon but was unable to understand the cause. His mind was uncertain, but his heart was bound to the girl forever. Preparing for flight, Topaz stretched his great furry wings as Rhiannon went to Petamor for one last goodbye.

Petamor looked down at her and smiled with those kind grey eyes of his, the same ones that had first welcomed her to the plateau just over a year earlier. Despite the presence of the cold-hearted demon inside her, real tears of sadness came to her eyes. Even Neraka could not control that reflex.

"I wanted to make you a staff as well, but---"

"It is all right, Grandfather. Once I have decided upon which field of knowledge to focus, I will come here again. Then, if you are still willing, you can make a staff for me."

"I would be honored, my dear," Petamor said as he fought to contain his own tears.

Rhiannon hugged him tightly for a few moments, and then she said, "Topaz has arranged for one of his siblings to take his place to help you with your supplies. You can call him when you need him and he will come to help you." Then she hopped up onto the back of her winged friend.

"Thank you," Petamor said. "And thank Topaz for me."

As Topaz lifted his mighty wings and took to the sky,

Petamor lifted his hand to wave goodbye, but Rhiannon did not turn to see it. Slowly he lowered his hand to his side. He watched them go until they disappeared into the clouds. With a heavy sigh and a heavier heart, the old wizard returned to the loneliness of the keep.

Now that both Breandan and Rhiannon had departed the escarpment, Petamor prepared to go down to the forested shore below the north side of the plateau to talk to the two shopkeepers who had been providing him with provisions for the keep. If Cinaran and Thoradal were serious about remaining in residence for a while, he was going to need some help with the daily chores. He was aware that it might take a little friendly persuasion to recruit the two men to the undertaking, and he had no time to waste on resistance. If they refused, he would be forced to resort to magic to convince them. Once they agreed, he would have to transport them back to the tower by air.

Eight hundred years had passed since the last major conflict involving humans and Horrans. At that time a man of the new race named Dillard had discovered that he possessed an uncommon power over other men. Dillard was an extremely intelligent and charismatic man, handsome, charming, but most importantly – persuasive. Using these abilities he had proclaimed himself king and began annexing as much territory into his realm as possible. For many years he had been very successful. All those who had attempted to hinder him were destroyed.

It was during this time the wizard Thoradal had discovered that Dillard was possessed by a high-ranking demon from the underworld named Norack. Thoradal knew that in order to stop Norack, he would need help, so he organized the League of Wizards. Together, they managed to defeat Dillard's army of men and Horranian mercenaries before it was too late.

In the end, the demon Norack managed to escape back into the fiery pit where he was mercilessly destroyed by his own kind. At that time, a new commandment was issued in the underworld stating that any demon that successfully managed to escape the confinement of the underworld and returned would also be put to death.

The history and legends of that war and others had been handed down to the people of Nox by oral tradition. Most of these stories, some true and some fictitious, were so terrifying that the mere possibility of another war could send the inhabitants into a blind panic. It was for that reason that these latest rumors of war were being kept quiet until a suitable plan could be devised to defeat the Horrans before things got out of hand.

Petamor had chosen the village of Lorelei on the northern coast of Pega because it was isolated from the rest of the continent by the plateau that split the land in two. Lorelei was also a self-sustaining isolated community untouched by the previous war. The residents of that community had never heard of the Horrans much less seen one.

In Lorelei, Petamor had established a relationship with two local shopkeepers. They provided him with his supplies and in return, he used his magic to acquire a wide variety of fresh tropical fruits and vegetables from the Southern Reaches that they could sell. It was an arrangement that suited both parties.

Petamor stood atop the tower as the morning sun climbed steadily into the sky. The old wizard closed his eyes and cast the necessary spell that would transform him into a bird of prey. Within the single beat of his heart, a great eagle with piercing grey eyes appeared perching on the very spot where Petamor had stood just seconds before. The eagle hopped onto the merlon and then flew through the warm morning air.

It circled the tower once and then turned north towards the coast.

———•———

As the grey-eyed eagle began its trip to the village of Lorelei, Rhiannon was arriving in her own village. As she and the rock hopper glided over the snow covered fields and hills, some of her nearly forgotten memories of her childhood began to resurface. For the unwelcome entity, these childhood memories were nothing more than entertainment, but to the young girl trapped within her own body, it was more painful than anything she had ever experienced. She now understood without a doubt that there was no way out for her. She was a hostage in her own body and only death would release her from her prison.

Neraka was completely aware of Rhiannon's pain, as it was aware of every emotion Rhiannon experienced. He was indifferent. He simply would never allow Rhiannon to kill herself. He would remain in his host's body for as long as possible. When and if the time came, when he had no other choice but to evacuate, then and only then would he choose another suitable host.

As Rhiannon flew over the village, the demon analyzed the visual images that flowed from her memory. Because the sleepy little hamlet below was covered with several inches of snow, it took her foggy mind a few minutes to locate her parent's cottage. Finally, Topaz descended to a small clearing behind Rhiannon's childhood home. The snow was deeper than Rhiannon had anticipated, but Topaz seemed untroubled. He trotted effortlessly to the back door of the stone dwelling.

The dogs that Rhiannon's father kept to tend his sheep came running to greet her. They recognized her the instant they saw her and were excited to see her again. However, when they were within a few feet of her, they suddenly came to a complete stop. They looked at her with their heads cocked to one side, whimpered pathetically and ran around in circles unsure of what to do next.

Rhiannon understood. The dogs could sense the presence of the unwelcome one. She dismounted and called to them reassuringly. "Bear! Zak! Boo! Come here and let me see you. I've missed you all so much," Rhiannon coaxed.

At the sound of their names, the dogs approached Rhiannon cautiously, tails tucked between their legs. They instinctively knew something was wrong, but their love for Rhiannon was simply too strong, and their resistance broke altogether. They rushed to her, tails wagging happily.

Rhiannon hugged them and rubbed their furry bellies as they wiggled and squirmed for her attention.

Bear, the only female of the pack, had always been Rhiannon's favorite. Rhiannon had named her Bear because she resembled a bear with her thick tawny-brown fur and stocky frame.

Zak and Boo were brothers. They looked like big balls of fur; only their long curly tails gave away the fact that they were dogs at all.

Wood smoke wafted from the chimney of the little cottage. A light burned behind the kitchen window. As Rhiannon trudged her way up to the back door through the snow, she could hear the sound of her mother's voice.

This was to be a crucial test. If Rhiannon's demon could deceive her own mother and father, it should be able to fool anyone. She opened the door and stepped into the warmth of her mother's kitchen. Rhiannon's mother and father were seated at the table. Her mother was busy mending a tear in her father's coat while her father was busy carving a new handle for his knife. They both looked up from their work at the same time.

"Rhiannon!" they cried in unison as they jumped up from the table.

Rhiannon's father came around the table so quickly that he

nearly knocked it over. As he pulled Rhiannon into his arms and placed her in a big bear hug, her mother dropped her sewing needle and began to cry tears of joy.

"Rhiannon," cried her father, "you're alive! You've come home at last! Your momma and I have prayed for your safe return. We've missed you so. I can't believe it's really you. Just look at you," he added as he finally held her out at arms length. "You've grown into a young woman. Look, Momma! Our Rhiannon's alive. She has returned to us at last!"

Rhiannon's mother was so overcome with emotion; she was unable to move. Rhiannon went around the table and kissed her cheek. "How did you get here, dear?" her mother asked. "Surely, you didn't walk here in the snow? Is there anyone with you?" she asked suspiciously, looking over Rhiannon's shoulder.

Before Rhiannon could answer, her father went to the open door to close it and saw the rock hopper standing outside in the yard.

"What in the world?" he said in amazement. "Is that what I think it is? Where did you find him, daughter?"

"He's a rock hopper, father, and he is my friend. I call him, Topaz. We flew here together from the plateau above the escarpment."

"Flew?" her mother responded, starting for the door to see for herself. She stopped beside her husband and stared with equal curiosity at the strange animal, her mouth agape.

Topaz, noticing all of the attention, nickered questioningly.

Rhiannon smiled. Then she took her parents by the hands and led them outside to meet her unusual friend.

"I don't see a saddle. How do you ride it without a saddle?" her father asked. "And no bridle?"

"I don't know. I just climb on and hold onto the fur between his wings. It doesn't hurt him. And I don't weigh enough to be much of a burden."

"Well, I guess I can put him up in the barn until we find a better place to keep him," Rhiannon's father said as he started towards the wide-eyed creature.

With a snort of defiance, Topaz backed away with wings raised.

"Hold on there, fella, I'm not going to hurt you," her father added as he reached out again to touch the animal.

Topaz jerked back away from his hand for a second time.

"It's all right, Papa," Rhiannon said. "He prefers the outdoors, and he'll not let anyone touch him but me."

"Maybe so," said her father, "but if we leave him out here, everyone in the village will be coming around to gawk at him. Best we keep him hidden away in the barn, least for the night."

"I'm sorry, Papa," Rhiannon said. "I hate to disappoint you and Mama, but I'm only here for a visit. I can't spend the night."

"What? First you run off after some boy who doesn't want to marry you. You're gone for over a year. Now you're too good to spend the night in our humble little cottage? Why?""I've grown a lot in the past year, Mama. I've worked and studied very hard to become a wizard," Rhiannon replied. "But I have still much to do. I wish I could stay longer, but I'll come back when I have more time to spend with you. I promise." Lying was getting easier all the time.

"Does this have anything to do with that old man, that... that...street dweller who claimed that you was living with him on the escarpment?"

"Are you talking about Petamor, Mama? Petamor's not a street dweller. I mean...I know he looks a little like a homeless person and all, but he's actually a wizard. And so am I. Look at me, will you! Look at my robe. Do you see? This is the robe of a wizard. I have passed all their tests, Mama. But most importantly, I passed the *final test*, the Lamp of Life. And so did Breandan. We're both wizards now. You and Papa should be happy for me, for me *and* for Breandan!"

"You can't just run off again, Rhiannon," her father said sternly, ignoring her request for a little understanding. He was both disappointed and concerned. "I need you here. Do you realize that after you ran away last year, I lost almost half of my sheep to the wolves? I swear, it's almost as if they can sense that you were gone and wanted revenge after all of the years that they spent afraid of you. I just know that if you go away again, I'll lose the rest of them. Do you understand? I'll lose them all! Your mama and I will end up as paupers, living on the streets for handouts. Is that what you want?"

"No, of course not, Papa, but I *can* still help you. I...I can place a spell on the sheep...or...the dogs...or both. I can cast a spell that will make the wolves afraid to go anywhere near your sheep again."

"Oh, do you hear that, Papa," responded her mother sarcastically. "Now our little Rhiannon is a fancy wizard and can do all kinds of magic tricks. Her in her fancy red robe and all." She turned to Rhiannon. "Do you really think a few little tricks can make up for all of the heartbreak you put us through?"

Rhiannon was in a partial state of shock. She had not expected this. Her parents were behaving like complete strangers. "I am so sorry, Mama," she cried. "I didn't know. I thought Petamor explained it all to you when he came here to visit."

"Is that what that old man calls himself? Petamor? That old man who came here told you he was a wizard?" her mother spat. "That was no wizard. He was just an old beggar...a common thief."

"A con artist," her father added.

"Yes, a con artist. He only said that he knew you so he could steal from us."

"Mama---"

"Did he touch you? Is that what this is all about? Did you let him touch you?" her father demanded to know.

"No, Papa. Petamor is a good man. A very kind and considerate man. He always treated me with the utmost respect. He was like a grandfather to me. He only came here to talk to you so that you would know that I was alive and wouldn't worry. How else would he have known about me?"

"How did he know about you?" questioned her mother. "Everyone within twenty miles of here had heard of you running off like some crazy person after a boy who had abandoned you."

Rhiannon was shocked to hear her mother talking like this. "Well, I don't care what any of the villagers said about it. What do they know? I'm your daughter, and I'm telling you that Petamor is a wizard, and a good man. He taught me many things. Things I never would have learned if I had stayed here in Ravenwood."

"Well, I guess we was wrong about him, Mama," her father said acerbically. "I guess that we misjudged him. Maybe stealing someone else's property is okay if you're a wizard. Maybe all these years we had it all wrong."

"I don't understand, Mama...Papa. If you didn't believe him, why did you give him the comb and brush that had belonged to grandmother...the ones in the little box that Papa had carved for me when I was a little girl?"

"Mama didn't give it to him," Rhiannon's father replied. "That old man stole it, didn't he Mama? Grabbed it right out of her hand."

"That's right. He took it right out of my hand he did. When he first came to the house, your papa felt sorry for him, offered him a warm meal. He even invited him in out of the cold so he could warm up a bit. Then, the old trickster asked to see something that had belonged to you. So mama showed him the box I had carved for you when you was a little girl. No sooner had I held it up for him to see, he snatched it up right out of your mama's hand."

"Petamor said that you gave him the box."

"Well, then he's a liar, too. Why would we give an old beggar something that had belonged to you? Oh, I would have given him something to eat if he was hungry. Yes. And I would have given him some warm clothes if he'd asked for them. It certainly looked as if he could have used them. But all he really wanted was to steal something that he could sell, probably so he could buy some cheap wine."

"No, Mama...Papa, you've got it all wrong. You must have misunderstood him. Petamor truly is a great and powerful wizard. He lives on the escarpment in a huge tower in the middle of a lake. It's so beautiful there, I wish you and Papa could see it. It's summer all of the time. And there are birds and flowers and trees the like of which you'd never seen before. And there are these mountains that look like giant fingers---"

"Yes, yes, I'm sure it's all wonderful," her father interrupted. "He's a great and powerful wizard. Well, he didn't look very great or powerful to me. He was dressed in a tattered old brown robe with little feathers stuck to it as if he'd been sleeping in a chicken coop somewhere. No coat...sandals instead of boots...and in this weather no less. He didn't even have a hat to keep his head warm. If that's what you have become, daughter, then I pities you."

Rhiannon could say no more. Her father had described Petamor pretty accurately. Actually, Petamor did look like a common street dweller. He was not one to be concerned about his personal appearance. But Rhiannon could not believe that Petamor would simply have taken the box unless he'd misinterpreted her parents' intent.

All the while, the demon was enjoying the bizarre conversation. Up until now, it hadn't known that humans could be so amusing.

Rhiannon made another effort to break free of the entity inside of her. Her will had never been stronger; nevertheless, the demon would not relinquish his grip on her. She collapsed onto the snow at her father's feet.

When Rhiannon awoke, she found herself in her old bed in a corner of the cottage. Her mother was seated beside her knitting a new pair of socks for her father.

"Mama?" Rhiannon said. "How long have I been here?"

"Not long, dear, less than an hour, I think. There, there, now," her mother said setting her work aside and patting her hand. "Everything's going to be all right."

"What happened?"

"You fell down. I think you need some rest. Papa and I are sorry for upsetting you the way we did. I don't know what came over us. We acted as if we was possessed. This has been a particularly bad winter, a hard winter with losing half of our sheep and all. Papa's been so worried about you. Can you find it in your heart to forgive us?"

"Of course, Mama. Where is Papa now?"

"He's outside with that creature of yours. He's trying to coax it into the barn and out of sight."

Rhiannon sat up placing her feet on the slate floor. "I already told him that Topaz would never allow anyone to put him inside a barn or any other structure for that matter. Why does he want Topaz out of sight, anyway? Is he ashamed of me, or is he just still angry because I left?"

"He is a little hurt that you don't want to follow in his footsteps, dear. You can understand that, can't you? After all, you are his only child. With no son to carry on the family business, he always hoped that you would take over someday."

Rhiannon looked down at her hands in her lap. "I don't want to disappoint, Papa. But I don't want to be a shepherd for the rest of my life."

"I know that, dear. Papa knows it too."

"I promised him that I would protect his flock. I can do it, Mama, I really can!"

"Yes, and that is another worry, all this talk of wizards and magic. And now, this winged horse. Do you understand what could happen if one of those lizard men was to come around and see your animal friend outside there? They'll start nosing around asking all kinds of questions. They might cause us trouble. Big trouble."

"The Horrans are here? In the village?"

"They don't stay here in the village, they come and go. But they're up to no good, that's for sure. And we don't need to give them a reason to stay any longer than they already have."

"I'd better leave right away, then. Just as soon as I take care of Papa's wolf problem."

"Rhiannon, dear, won't you please change your mind and stay here with us? This is where you belong. Breandan's back you know. Maybe the two of you can still work things out. If you two decide to be wedded, we could throw a big wedding feast. It would---"

"No, Mama. There's nothing between Breandan and I any longer. We're just friends, that's all. We are wizards now---"

"Please, Rhiannon...please! Stop all this talk of wizards. Just send that strange beast away. It'd make Papa so happy if would you stay and help him tend the sheep again."

Before Rhiannon could say another word, her father came in from outside. "I've tried everything I can think of to get that critter in the barn, but he's as stubborn as an old mule."

"Papa, I have to leave before the Horrans find out about the rock hopper," Rhiannon said quickly. "Will you take me to the sheepcote before I go? I want to put a protection spell over your flock."

"I would be obliged if you could do something," he responded doubtfully. He looked at his wife and added, "I don't think we can talk her into staying, Mama. We must let her go her own way. We'll just have to manage without her somehow. Come along, daughter," he continued. "The sheep are waiting.

They've been making a fuss ever since you arrived. I think they can sense your presence."

Rhiannon followed her father to the cote where the sheep greeted her with bleats of joy. She went to greet each one individually and used her newly acquired powers to ensure that each animal would remain healthy and safe from the wolves. She also ensured that all of the mature ewes would produce many lambs in the coming spring to help replace the animals her father had lost to the wolf pack.

"Why don't you use your magic to kill the damn wolves and we'd be rid of them once and for all?"

"The wolves belong here too, Papa. Besides, a new pack would just take over the territory, and your wolf problems would begin all over again."

Thirty minutes later, when they left the cote, large feathery snowflakes were drifting down from the blizzard that continued to push in from the northwest.

"It's been a hard winter, Rhiannon," her father commented. "And it doesn't look like it's going to let up anytime soon."

"Many of our neighbors say it's a bad omen," her mother added. "Some claim that it's a sign that there's evil afoot."

"That's true," her father said. "And if that ain't enough, those bloody lizard men have been snooping around again. They're starting to make everyone as jittery as a humming bird."

"Yes, Mama already told me about the Horrans."

"Maybe you can use some of your magic to frighten *them* off," her father said with a touch of scorn. "They're up to their old tricks again, stirring up trouble and scaring folks half to death. Breandan had a run in with one of them down at the Yellow Dog the other morning."

"What!" Rhiannon exclaimed. "When?"

"It was just a few days ago," her mother responded, "on the same morning he returned to the village. I hear tell that one of them was trying to molest his sister, Heather when Breandan walked through the front door. He told the filthy thing to leave her alone and well, you know. The Horran attacked Breandan and Breandan killed him."

"Killed him?" Rhiannon asked in surprise. "Killed him how?"

"Those that was there and saw it with their own eyes. They said Breandan turned the Horran into a swarm of fireflies."

"Fireflies? Ah, yes...I get it. Living energy into living energy. That sounds like Breandan," Rhiannon said.

"Yes. That Horranian bastard disappeared right there in the tavern. Right in front of Breandan's father and all of his customers, including his own comrades."

"What did the other Horrans do?"

"That's the odd thing. They didn't do anything. They just got up and walked out of the tavern just as pretty as you please, and rode out of the village on their horses. Must of scared 'em pretty good, and they ain't scared of much. They ain't been back since. But that don't mean they won't return. If Breandan wants to live, he'd best leave the village until things cool down a bit."

Rhiannon had never actually seen a real Horran herself, she *had* seen several illustrations of them in one of Petamor's old books, and she hadn't cared for the look of them very much.

Meanwhile, the blizzard was getting worse; the snow was falling heavier as they walked back to the cottage. Despite the fact that traveling in the middle of the storm would be difficult and uncomfortable for Topaz, Neraka was anxious to get started. First, however, Rhiannon's body would require a little nourishment.

"Come back in the house, daughter, and warm yourself by the fire," her mother said. "I'll fix you something warm to eat. I have a pot of potato soup heating up on the stove. It should be ready about now."

"What about this critter?" her father said, pointing to the rock hopper. "Is he hungry, too? What does he usually eat?"

"He eats the same thing horses eat, Papa. Oats, hay, fresh grass, that kind of thing."

"Well, I'll see what I find out in the barn. I reckon I'll have to bring it to him, seeing how his majesty is too good to set foot into my barn," he said as he stomped off through the snow shaking his head and muttering to himself.

"Thank you, Papa," Rhiannon said after him.

———•———

Sitting at the kitchen table, Rhiannon used a wooden spoon to eat from a bowl of her mother's potato soup, savoring the tiny chunks of flavorful ham. Outside, the wind howled at the eves of the small cottage while fat snowflakes tapped on the windowpanes like the bony fingertips of a restless ghoul.

"This soup is delicious, Mama," Rhiannon said, "I just hope it doesn't make me sleepy."

"Not to worry. I'm brewing you a pot of good strong coffee to take along with you. You can take a couple of Papa's old water pouches to carry it in. He won't mind. He doesn't use them anymore."

"Mama, why were you so cross with me earlier? You knew when I left here that I was going to try and find Breandan. You knew that I was going to try and climb the escarpment," Rhiannon said.

"Yes, but after you left everyone in the village started talking. They was saying that you was mad to go chasing after a boy who obviously didn't want you."

"But you knew that wasn't true, Mama. You and Papa knew how Breandan and I felt about each other. What changed your minds?"

"After you left, we began to have our doubts. People was saying that you was as crazy as Breandan to go chasing after fairy tales. We was worried about you. We didn't know what had happened to you. We thought that maybe you fell some-where among the rocks. Some of the children even went out to look for your body, but of course they never found it 'cause here you are. At that time, we was sick with fear. Fear is a kind of sickness, too, you know. It eats away at your soul day after day after day until all that's left is a bitter shell of what you once was."

"I'm sorry I put you through that, Mama. I...I didn't know. I...I didn't think---,"

"And what if Breandan hadn't been there...or...or suppose you had found him dead or dying. What would you have done? Would you have stayed up there on that rock for fear of being ridiculed if you returned to the village?"

"No, of course not, Mama."

"Then that old man came to our door trying to tell us that you was all right," her mother continued. "No one, not even Breandan's own father, believed it for a moment. We reck-oned that he must have heard about you when he was passing through and decided to try to cheat us out of money or some-thing. What else was we supposed to think?"

Suddenly the outer door swung open and Rhiannon's fa-ther reappeared. "I hope that beast of yours is happy," he said. "I gave him my finest hay. Mmmmm...that soup sure looks good, Mama. Save any for me?"

"Sit down, Papa," the old woman said. "I'll fetch you a bowl of soup and you can talk to your daughter for a while. I was just telling her why the entire village thought that she had gone mad."

Rhiannon was not in the mood to listen to her father's bel-lyaching. She didn't care one iota what the villagers thought. She attempted to change the subject.

"Is he eating, Papa?"

"Is he eating? I'll say he's eating. He acts as if he hasn't eaten in weeks. Won't let me get anywhere near him, mind you, but he sure doesn't mind eating my hay."

"He knows we have a long journey ahead of us. He's just stocking up," Rhiannon said.

"I was just telling your daughter, no one ever believed that story of a wizard that lived up there on that escarpment. If wizards ever was real, they died off ages ago," her mother continued.

"Listen to me, Mama. I've met them. They're as real as you and Papa. They are a wise and noble race. They'll help our people if the Horrans start any trouble."

"Wise and noble? That seedy old man who came to the house didn't appear very wise or noble to me or anyone else around these parts. Why he's lucky he wasn't run out of the village on a rail or stoned senseless. Especially after stealing from us," her father said.

"You misunderstood him, Papa. I know he doesn't look like what you would expect a wizard to look like, but he dresses like a vagabond so that he doesn't attract any unwanted attention."

"Well, Rhiannon," her mother started, "I have to admit one thing, you don't look like you've been starved. You look healthy enough. You lost most of your baby fat while you was away, too. Breandan said that you had grown some, but I didn't expect this. It's as is you become a woman overnight."

"You talked to Breandan?"

"Briefly," answered her mother.

"When? When did you talk to him?"

"I thought you didn't care about Breandan anymore. Isn't that what you said?"

"Oh, Mama. All I said was that our relationship has changed. We're still friends. Now, tell me please, what did Breandan say?"

"When I heard that he had returned, I went to see him seeking any news of you. It was just after that incident with the Horrans. I asked him if he knew what had happened to you. He told me that you and him had been living with that old man on the escarpment, and that you both had studied to become wizards. I didn't believe a word of it until you walked in that door."

"What else did he say?"

"He said that you would be coming home soon, but he didn't know when. He never said anything about you leaving again so soon."

"He didn't know," Rhiannon said.

Rhiannon's mother just looked at her.

Rhiannon stood up from the table. "I must go now, Mama," she said, "before the Horrans find out that I'm here."

Rhiannon's mother and father looked at one another and lowered their heads.

"When do you plan on coming home again?" her father asked solemnly.

"I don't know, Papa, but I will come and see you and Mama as often as I can." Rhiannon hugged them one more time, and even the demon could not stop her tears from flowing. "Walk me outside, Papa?" Rhiannon asked.

Her father nodded and took her hand, squeezing it gently between his big-callused ones. As they walked together side by side, Rhiannon – the real Rhiannon not the Rhiannon controlled by Neraka – began to daydream about her childhood again. The lazy quiet days she had tended her flock. The happy times she had spent with Breandan. Now all of that had changed forever. She had been possessed by something that was too strong for her to resist. Neraka laughed at her pain, for it could not feel her emotional anguish, it could only experience physical sensations. The laughter spilled out of Rhiannon's mouth into the cold winter morning.

"What's so funny, Rhiannon?" her father asked, surprised by the unexpected outburst. "Do you think it's funny that Mama and I worry about you?"

"No, Papa," Rhiannon lied. "I was just picturing how silly I must have looked clinging to the side of the escarpment wall. No wonder the villagers thought I was mad."

"Love can make a sane person do crazy things," her father replied kindly. "You did what you had to do, I reckon. You were very brave. I'm very proud of you, daughter. I love you."

Once again, the demon could not prevent the tears from flowing as Rhiannon turned and hugged her father tightly. "I love you too, Papa," she said sincerely.

The restless entity inside of her tightened his grip and forced Rhiannon to break the hug, fearful that any extended contact between her father and her might betray his existence.

"I have to be on my way," Rhiannon said grabbing hold of Topaz's mane.

"Tarnation, daughter," said her father, "don't you see that storm out there? How can you travel in that? That's a blizzard, you know! How can this...this critter of yours fly in that storm?" The old man looked at his wife, who had followed them outside. "Mama, talk some sense into this girl."

"Make up your mind, Papa. Do you want her to stay, or are we going to let her go?" her mother said. "I have a feeling that she can handle herself. She must have learned something from that wizard of hers. I don't think he would have let her go out on her own if he thought that she was in any danger."

"How can that old fool protect her? He isn't here," her father pointed out.

"I don't think she needs his protection. Do you, Rhiannon?"

Rhiannon shook her head. "No, Mama, I can protect myself. I just don't want the Horrans to hurt you or Papa after I'm gone."

"If our Rhiannon truly is a wizard, I don't think anyone can hurt her."

"I reckon you're right, Mama," he answered reluctantly, his shoulders slumping forward in resignation. "Still, it just doesn't seem natural to be running around in weather like this."

"It's *not* natural, Papa," Rhiannon answered.

He simply nodded realizing that Rhiannon's newly acquired skills were more than he could comprehend. "Well...be careful," he finally said. "No telling what kind of trouble might be lurking out there. Remember, those lizard men are---"

"I can handle the Horrans, Papa," Rhiannon replied before he could finish. "They can't hurt me." She kissed him on the cheek. Her head was spinning. The insipid manner in which her parents were behaving had given her a headache. "Now I really must go. But I'll return soon, I promise."

Topaz could sense that it was time to go. He moved to Rhiannon's father and neighed softly.

"Well," began Rhiannon's father, "Did you finally get your belly full?"

Topaz looked directly into his eyes and nodded.

"Did you see that, daughter?" he asked, incredulously. "I actually think he understood what I just said."

Rhiannon giggled. "Of course he did, Papa," she answered.

Rhiannon's father tentatively reached out his hand toward Topaz's muzzle. This time, Topaz did not flinch or pull away. He carefully brushed snowflakes away from the animal's eyelashes. "Does he talk as well?" he asked in jest.

Rhiannon giggled again. "Not yet," she answered with a smile, "but I'm working on it."

Rhiannon's father gave her a strange look and then pulled his hand away and scratched his head. Then he reached down and helped Rhiannon onto Topaz's back. Meanwhile, her mother handed her two water skins, one full of fresh water and the other full of hot coffee.

"Come home soon, Rhiannon. We love you. This will always be your home," her mother said as she struggled to hold back her tears.

There was nothing more to say. It would have done little

good anyway. Rhiannon said goodbye with a smile, although she felt like weeping, while Neraka was unmoved by Rhiannon's emotional distress.

Then Topaz leapt into the air and they were on their way.

Rhiannon's father put his strong arm around her mother and the two of them watched until Rhiannon disappeared into the white curtain of snow. Then they turned slowly around and walked back to the warmth of their little cottage, talking hopefully of their daughter's promise to return. However, deep down inside, they both knew that they would never see her again in this lifetime.

———•———

At first, Rhiannon found the swirling snow disorientating. She was constantly buffeted by strong winds while surrounded by a continuously changing pattern of grey and white. Yet Topaz continued to climb higher and higher until they broke through the canopy of clouds into the clear, where the late-morning sun cast a cold eerie light on a seemingly endless world of white. They flew south for hours with no break in the cloud cover below. As the day passed into night, the clouds finally began to thin. From time-to-time, Rhiannon could see the surface of a blue-green ocean far below through the ragged clouds. She guided Topaz down until they were practically skimming the waves that sparkled like a sea of diamonds on dark-blue velvet in the brilliant moonlight.

The coffee helped to keep her awake, but did little to keep her warm. Then the cold began to make way for warmer temperatures. Rhiannon, as well as her unwanted guest, welcomed the warmer air. Both were amazed at Topaz's endurance and apparent strength. Since leaving Rhiannon's home village, they had been flying for nearly twenty hours assisted only by a tail wind, yet the rock hopper showed no signs of weakening.

Once again, the eastern horizon began to glow as the sun

began its ascent. Along with the rising sun, the temperature was rising as well. At last, Topaz was beginning to tire. They had to find land soon or the two of them would end up in the water.

Rhiannon urged the weary beast to climb, hoping that the cooler air high above would revive him. The higher altitude also gave Rhiannon a wider view of the vast ocean before them.

Hours passed with still no sign of land.

With its strength rapidly fading, Topaz began to drop closer and closer to the waves. Then Rhiannon spotted something on the distant horizon. With the last of its strength the beast flew in the direction indicated by Rhiannon's gentle urging. As they drew closer to the tiny speck of hope, Rhiannon recognized the top of an ancient volcano surrounded by a lush tropical island. She had read about volcanoes in one of Petamor's books on geology.

Neraka was elated. This island just might be the ideal place to build his lair, the perfect paradise where it could begin to weave his diabolic scheme.

It was well past midday when they landed on the deserted beach on the northern end of the tropical island. Rhiannon slid off the exhausted animal and led him up to the shade of the palm trees that edged the beach. She untied her pack and poured fresh water into Topaz's parched mouth. She fed him the entire water skin saving only a few drops for herself. When the water was gone Rhiannon tossed the empty skin aside. She removed her leggings and used them to wipe down the heavily lathered animal.

Even in the shade, the temperature was unbearably hot. Before long, Rhiannon's heavy woolen robe was soaked with sweat. It would be useless in this climate. Knowing that her magic would protect her, she removed her robe exposing her bare skin to the scorching sun. Still Rhiannon hated to part with her fancy red robe. As with the rock hopper, Neraka decided that it might come in handy someday.

While Topaz rested, Rhiannon collected some cool sweet grasses for him to eat, all the while eyeing the waves rushing in on the beach. As Topaz began to regain his strength, she added more grass to the dwindling pile so that he could dine at his leisure.

Rhiannon had never seen a real beach before, never set foot in its salty water. Once she was certain that Topaz was comfortable, she was no longer able to resist the temptation of the placid waves rolling in on the sand. She ran into the gentle swells allowing the tepid water to refresh her own weary body.

As she splashed about in the water Rhiannon noticed assorted bits of coral and tiny seashells on the ocean floor. They reminded her of the staff carried by the wizard, Boradal. She was so impressed by the beauty at her feet she decided to make herself a new staff using the treasures of the deep to embellish and enhance its power. After all, few forces in nature were as powerful and enduring as the sea. Boradal or no Boradal, she would draw upon that force to enhance her own powers, for if she could learn to control the oceans, she could learn to harness the other forces of nature.

Neraka was delighted with the scheme, and Rhiannon's heart grew one shade darker.

Up on the beach, Topaz continued to rest while watching Rhiannon frolic about in the waves.

By early afternoon, Rhiannon had grown bored with the sand and the sea, and her stomach was growling as her insatiable appetite made another appearance. Utilizing her wizardly senses, she entered the tropical jungle in search of food. Topaz followed closely, never letting the girl out of his sight. Before long, she came to a crystal-clear pond complete with its own miniature waterfall. Both Rhiannon and the demon could appreciate the beauty of the setting. It was a veritable paradise of gorgeous flowers, verdant ferns, and succulent fruits. In some ways, it reminded her of the bathing pool back at the keep.

Rhiannon grabbed a handful of luscious looking wild grapes. She plucked one off its stem and popped it into her mouth. The taste was heavenly. Sweet nectar dribbled down her chin and onto her body. She greedily sampled every type of fruit she could find, and when she was full, she was covered from head to toe with the juice of over a dozen different fruits, including a tropical version of her personal favorite – heart-berries.

Rhiannon needed to rinse the sticky juice off her body before every insect on the island decided to have her for lunch. She slowly eased herself into the cool water of the pool and discovered that it was even more refreshing than the seawater. Standing waist deep in the pool, she scrubbed the sticky juices off her skin and rinsed the salt water out of her hair.

Meanwhile, Topaz had found his own supper and was grazing contentedly nearby.

Climbing out of the pool, Rhiannon yawned and stretched her arms. She was sleepy, so she decided to take a nap. Since she did not yet know if anyone lived on the island, so she instructed Topaz to stay nearby and not wander away. Then she cast a spell that would render them both invisible to anyone who might stumble upon them by accident. Confident that all was well, she curled up on a warm flat rock and went to sleep.

In the coastal village of Lorelei, a large eagle landed on the eave of a small log cabin on the seaward edge of the pine forest. It was the home of two brothers named Ragi and Nikulas. They were businessmen, entrepreneurs, who, with the help of Petamor's magic, imported such rare items as fresh fruit and vegetables from the Southern Reaches.

Both men were short and stocky in stature; however, that was where most similarities ended.

Ragi, the older of the two, possessed a crop of thick snow-white hair with matching eyebrows. He had clear intelligent blue eyes set in a face that looked as if it had been chiseled out of stone. He had a keen wit and a great desire for adventure.

Nikulas, on the other hand, was at least fifty pounds over-weight. He had thinning brown hair with a beard to match. His dark brown eyes were always glossy and rimmed with red from his love affair with cheap rum. He hated change and despised anything new.

Despite their differences, Petamor found the two men completely trustworthy when he required them to be. That is why he had chosen them to help him. Now all he had to do was convince them that they were needed on the escarpment.

Ragi and Nikulas had had a working relationship with the old wizard for several years prior to Rhiannon's arrival. They had kept their partnership with Petamor a secret from the rest of their clan, telling them instead, that Petamor was just a harmless old hermit who lived in a hidden cave somewhere along the base of the escarpment.

On this cold winter morning, Ragi and Nikulas were seated at their breakfast table when the old wizard arrived, but as usual, Petamor waited outside until he had a chance to observe the mood of the two men before making an entrance.

Still in the form of an eagle, Petamor flew to the closed window directly across from where Nikulas was seated. Nikulas was in the process of taking a swig of ale when he saw Petamor transform from eagle to man through the glass bottom of his pewter tankard. It nearly did him in. He choked on his ale until it was coming out of his nose.

Ragi, who was used to his brother's strange behavior, casually looked up from his meal. Upon seeing his brother's frozen angry stare, he turned and saw old Petamor standing in the door brushing tiny feathers off his robe. He smiled warmly at the old man. "Greetings, Mr. Petamor. We didn't expect to see you again so soon," he said. "What in the world brings you out in this terrible blizzard?"

Before Petamor could answer, Nikulas went into a mild tirade. "I wish ta hell you would stop doin' that," he shouted at Petamor. "Ya nearly caused me bloody heart ta stop! Just because yer a high-an-mighty wizard, don't give ya the right ta pop in-and-out of me house like a bloody jack-in-the-box, scaring the life out of us simple folk! And look here! Ya caused me ta spill me bloody ale!"

"It's good to see you too, Nikulas," Petamor said with a wink at Ragi.

Ignoring his disgruntled brother, Ragi said, "So what is it we can do for you today, old friend?"

Upon seeing that he was going to be ignored, Nikulas gestured to an empty chair. "Ya might as well sit yerself down, ya old fart and tell us why yer here." He looked at Ragi. "Well, this'd better be good. Can't wait for a decent hour like normal folk – no! Gotta come sneakin' in like a mouse, interruptin' a man's breakfast?"

"I need your help, gentlemen. Both of you," Petamor added, looking directly at Nikulas.

"What now?" asked Nikulas. "Are the mangos we sent ya not juicy enough? Or maybe some of them bananas were a little too bruised for yer sophisticated palate."

"Never mind him," Ragi said, continuing to ignore his brother's ravings. "What can we do to help you, Mr. Petamor, sir?"

"If ya don't like the way we do things around here," Nikulas continued with no regard for his brother's question, "why do ya even bother with us? Ya certainly don't need our help anyway, do ya? All ya gots ta do is wiggle yer nose or yer little finger, or whatever it is ya do, and whatever ya want appears right out of nowhere."

"Nikulas, that's enough," Ragi said. "No need to be rude to our guest."

"Oh...now I'm the one that's being rude, am I?"

"My dear Nikulas," began Petamor, "I do apologize for interrupting your meal. As for my supplies, you are correct. I could...ah...wiggle my nose, as you suggested and have all of the supplies I need. However, that would be selfish of me, wouldn't it? I prefer to share these provisions with your clan. This way, everyone can benefit. Do you not profit from our little arrangement? No need to answer. Of course you do. You make a tidy little profit. Moreover, your customers are happy, too. They get fresh fruit and vegetables that they could not get elsewhere, and you get money in your purse."

Nikulas shrugged without further complaint.

"Mr. Petamor's right, Nikulas," Ragi said. "We all benefit from our little arrangement, and best of all, our customers think that we're the wizards because we can provide them with fresh fruit from the Southern Reaches, and they can't figure out how we do it."

"It still doesn't make a bit of sense ta me," said Nikulas, addressing Ragi. "Why should he care if our clan gets fresh fruit or not? They don't even know that he exists. What does he get out of it?"

"I am a wizard, after all, and it is my job to care, Nikulas," Petamor replied. "These people, your clan, are my responsibility."

"Then why do ya not provide fresh fruit for the clans on the other side of the escarpment? Why just ours?"

"Your clan is isolated from the other clans on the southern side. If I provided tropical fruits for the villages below the southern rim of the escarpment, the Horrans would become suspicious. As for now, they are not even aware that *this* little strip of land is inhabited. As far as they are concerned, it has no strategic value, so they have ignored it. However, if they thought for a minute that there were people living here, they would start asking a lot of questions and eventually send soldiers here to investigate. Once they learn the truth, they would send a small invasion force here and...well. You can figure the rest out for yourself."

"He's right, Nikulas," Ragi agreed. "Business has been great since Petamor came along. Stop complaining. Remember that old adage – 'Don't look a gift horse in the mouth'."

Nikulas took another drink from his tankard. "What is it ya want with us, anyway?"

Petamor smiled. "Two members of the league are taking up temporary residence at the keep, and I'm going to need help attending to the daily chores. I was hoping that the two of you would come and stay with me at the keep and help out for a while. If you agree, I will pay you well, and compensate you for any financial loss which may occur while you are away from your business."

"Servants?" Nikulas said angrily. "It's servants he wants, brother. Ya want Ragi and meself ta be yer bloody servants, don't ya?"

"Shut up, Nikulas," Ragi said. He was becoming angry as well, but his anger was aimed at Nikulas. "Petamor, do you mean that you want Nikulas and me to come and live on the plateau? In the keep...with you...and all those other wizards?"

"Yes," Petamor answered simply.

"Yahoo!" Ragi cried, jumping for joy. "This is a dream come true! Ever since I was a wee lad, I have dreamt of just such an adventure, but father would not tolerate such talk. He had other plans for me. This is great! This is truly wonderful! Nikulas, can you imagine? The two of us living in the midst of all of those powerful wizards. Can you imagine all of the magic we'll get to see with our own eyes? No one else on the planet has ever been invited to reside with the league. Ain't that right, Mr. Petamor, sir?"

"Not exactly, but the only humans who have ever lived in the tower have been my apprentices."

"Wait a minute," Nikulas said suspiciously. "What do ya need us for? Why do ya not just use yer little magic tricks to do yer grunt work?"

"Nikulas---" Ragi started before Petamor cut him off.

"That's a fair enough question," the old wizard responded. "Nikulas, as I said earlier, I *could* use my magic powers to do the simple tasks in life like cooking, cleaning, and gathering supplies. But when this war begins I will need every ounce of my power to deal with the enemy. Even now, I prefer to do the daily chores by hand, although I have invented several mechanical contraptions to make those chores a little easier."

"We'll do it, sir! We'll come to your tower and help you," Ragi said. "It'll be an honor."

Nikulas stood up from the table and stared hard at his brother and then walked over to a large keg of ale that stood in one corner of the small cabin. "Speak fer yerself, brother," he said pouring himself another tankard.

"Come on, brother," Ragi urged. "If you won't do it for Mr. Petamor, do this for me. It'll be quite the adventure, just like when we were young lads."

"No," replied Nikulas. "I am quite happy where I am. Thank ye very much."

"Too bad," Petamor said, slowly shaking his head. "I suppose all of that Rockvorian rum will go to waste now."

Nikulas's eyes became as big as saucers and glittered like sunshine on the ocean waves. "Rockvorian rum? Did ya say Rockvorian rum?"

"Just the finest rum in all the land," Petamor said.

"Just how much Rockvorian rum are ya talking about?"

"Must be forty-five...fifty kegs," Petamor stated with just the slightest hint of a smile.

Nikulas slowly sank back into his chair as he silently

mouthed the words to himself. He was nearly in a state of shock.

"I'll do it," he said finally.

"Hoorah!" Ragi cried. "But, Mr. Petamor, sir, how are we going to get up there? Nikulas and I can't climb the escarpment wall."

"Why, we're gonna sprout wings and fly, brother. Ain't that right, Mr. Wizard," Nikulas spat sarcastically. Then he flapped his arms like a bird and ran around the room in mock flight.

"Something like that," Petamor said quietly.

Nikulas's smile evaporated as quickly as it had arrived, and his face paled considerably. "Wait a bloody minute! I'm not flying anywhere! I...I...I'm afraid of high places!"

"Too late, brother," Ragi laughed, "you have already accepted the position. You can't back out now."

Nikulas looked at his brother with bloodshot eyes and knew that he could not change his mind. "Fine, but tell me this, brother. Who's going ta take care of our business while we're away?"

"Our nephew, Tintin, can mind the shop," Ragi said. "After all, he's been helping us now for more than a year. He knows what to do and what not to do."

Nikulas nodded. "So it be, then," he said, chugging down half a tankard of ale. "Leave the lad a note then, and let's get this thing over with before I changes me mind again."

Petamor waited patiently while the two men packed a few personal belongings. Ragi was ready within two minutes. Nikulas tried to stall as long as possible.

Fifteen minutes later, Ragi finally announced, "We're ready, Mr. Petamor."

"Good," said the old wizard. "Now, would one of you be so kind as to open that window by the door?"

Ragi, eager to be on their way, quickly opened the window as instructed.

"Now," Petamor continued, "I want you both to stand in the middle of the cabin and close your eyes."

"Is dis gonna hurt?" Nikulas asked.

"Not if you do as you are told," Petamor responded.

Ragi and Nikulas went and stood in the middle of the floor.

"All right. Now stand very still and try not to move. This will only take a moment," Petamor added as he waved the tip of his staff over their heads. A brilliant blue flame swiftly encompassed the two men, flashed, and disappeared – all in the blink of an eye. Petamor bent down and gently scooped up the two mice that had once been men. One mouse was thin and had a tuft of white fur on top of its head, while the other mouse was fat with bulging red eyes. Next, he placed the two mice in the center of the table and then transformed himself back into an eagle. Carefully, he snatched up the two mice with his talons and with a flap of his powerful wings, flew out the open window. They flew up into the storm-darkened sky until they were far above the northern edge of the escarpment.

High above the enchanted plateau where the land was protected from most forms of inclement weather by Petamor's magic, the incoming snow had turned to a gentle rain in the warmer air. By the time they reached the tower keep, the rain had stopped completely, and the last stars of morning were peeking out from behind an array of whimsical clouds.

Petamor landed atop the tower and released the two mice. They quickly scurried to the center of the roof. A small flash of blue light erupted from the twig in the eagle's beak and once again, the wizard changed back into his human form. To return Ragi and Nikulas to their human forms, Petamor softly tapped the floor around the tiny rodents.

Ragi said, "Now that was rather exciting, wasn't it Nikulas? I could see our entire village from up there. But why is it so much warmer up here? Is that a bit of magic, too? Why, of course it is. You see, Nikulas. I told you this would be a great experience."

Nikulas just looked at his brother and said shakily, "Me needs a drink, me thinks."

"And you shall have one," Petamor said as he led them down the stone stairway to the main dining chamber.

For once, the great fireplace in the dining chamber was empty and cold. In fact, the entire tower felt unusually empty and cold despite the warm spring-like breeze that blew outside the walls of the tower.

"Mr. Petamor, sir, it's a bit chilly in here. Would you mind if I get a fire going to warm things up a bit?" Ragi asked.

"Be my guest," Petamor said. "Perhaps you two could also tidy up a little. I'm afraid the place has gotten a little dusty of late."

"Yes, sir, more than happy to oblige," Ragi replied.

"Now, about that Rockvorian rum," Nikulas said, eagerly licking his lips.

Petamor pointed towards the kitchen. "That way," he said. "There, through the kitchen, you will find a pantry containing enough food and drink provisions to feed a small army for an entire month. I think it will be sufficient for the five of us."

While Nikulas was busy in the pantry, Thoradal and Cinaran came down from their sleeping chambers in search of a cup of hot tea. A moment later, Nikulas returned from the kitchen carrying a pot of steaming hot coffee in one hand and a bottle of Rockvorian rum in the other. Ragi had managed to get a suitable fire started in the hearth, and the cold room was beginning to warm up again.

"Thoradal...Cinaran," Petamor began, "these are the two men I spoke to you about earlier. They will be staying here in the tower for the time being to help us out with the daily chores. This is Ragi---"

Ragi bowed slightly.

"---and this is his brother, Nikulas. Lads, allow me to introduce you to the wizards, Thoradal and Cinaran."

Both wizards nodded, "Welcome lads," Cinaran said with a warm smile, "it'll be nice to have a couple of new faces around here. This place can get awful lonely with just us stuffy old men hanging around."

"Yes, lads," Thoradal added. "I hope we can all get better acquainted. Nevertheless, you must excuse us for now. We have a lot of work to do up in the library. Just give us a few minutes to make some tea, and we will be out of your way."

"I'd be happy to make it for you, Mr. Thoradal, sir," Ragi said.

"No, no, lad. You've enough work to keep you busy for now. I can do it myself."

"Yes," Cinaran said, "perhaps we can talk later over lunch."

"Yes! I will prepare you both a wonderful lunch! I have so many questions to ask," Ragi said.

Thoradal and Cinaran smiled, nodded again, and then disappeared into the kitchen to brew their tea.

"A little while ago, you asked if it was my magic that kept the plateau warmer than the land below," Petamor began. "The answer to that question is, yes. It is magic that sustains the climate on the plateau, but the tower was built by the hands of my mentor and no amount of magic will trick it into believing that it's summer outside, when it knows good and well that it is really winter. That, gentlemen, is why these old stones refuse to submit to my magic. Only the magic of my long dead mentor could convince these walls to accept the enchantment. That is why every room in the tower has its own fireplace."

"Did ya here dat, brother," Nikulas said. "Even Petamor's magic tricks are defective."

Ragi smiled at Petamor and shook his head. "Even with enough rum to float a Rockvorian cargo vessel, he still isn't satisfied. He must find fault with something."

"Yes, well I hope you two do not mind sharing a room," Petamor said.

"We'll be fine," Ragi answered. "We've shared a cabin for over twenty years. Won't be much different here, I imagine."

"Very well, please make yourselves at home. I think you will be able to find everything you need. Not only is there a well-provisioned pantry, but there is a buttery stocked with wine, rum, and cider, as well as a chandlery full of candles, oil, and other lighting supplies. Your room is off the kitchen through that door over there. Once you have settled in, I'll give you a grand tour of the place. Until then, I will be in the library with Thoradal and Cinaran in the top of the tower. When you're ready, bring along a bottle of heart-berry wine and we will make a little toast to our agreement."

When Petamor left the room, Ragi turned to Nikulas and said, "I still can't get over that ride? Wasn't that remarkable?"

Nikulas lifted his shirt exposing his bruised ribs. "Aye," he said rubbing his sore abdomen where Petamor's eagle talons had left their marks, "if ya don't mind a few bruises."

"You didn't leave him very much choice, brother. You wiggled like a fat worm on a hook the entire time. Would you have preferred that he had dropped you on the rocks?"

"I couldn't help it. I told ya I was afraid of heights," Nikulas said, his face flushing red with shame.

"Hey, look here," Ragi said, picking up the small earthen jar that Petamor had left on the kitchen counter. "It's a jar of skin ointment made from heart-berries. You can rub some of this on your bruises. That and the Rockvorian rum should help ease your pain a bit."

Nikulas took the open jar and sniffed it. He shrugged. "I guess yer right," he said. "That old fart thinks of everything. Perchance it won't be so bad living here after all."

"By the way, Nikulas, how's that Rockvorian rum?"

"Divine, brother," answered Nikulas. "Simply bloody divine."

———•———

Nikulas spent the rest of the morning dusting the tower from top to bottom, while Ragi began preparing lunch for Petamor and his two guests. He really wanted to make a good first impression. During the meal, all three wizards, as well as Nikulas, praised Ragi's culinary creations. Later that evening, Ragi prepared a delicious chicken stew that included diced potatoes, carrots, celery, and fat noodles made from wheat flour, salt, and shortening. While they ate, they talked about the old race and the impending war with the Horrans. The old wizards even tried to answer as many of Ragi and Nikulas' questions about wizards and magic as they could. All in all, it was the most interesting and exhilarating conversation Ragi had ever had the pleasure of taking part in. Even Nikulas, as bleary-eyed as always, was fascinated by the wizards' incredible stories.

———•———

The following morning Petamor found Ragi and Nikulas on the tower roof admiring the panoramic view.

"Just look at it brother, it's just too beautiful to put into words," Ragi said as he looked out over the plateau. "I still can't get over it."

"It's all right, I reckon," Nikulas agreed with a shrug.

"I want you both to know," Petamor began, "that I am expecting several more of my colleagues to arrive today. And Nikulas, my friend, please try to keep in mind that some of them have a flair for the dramatic. They might arrive at any moment and in any place, so try not to have a heart attack," he added with a wink to Ragi.

"I'll not be waitin' round for 'em," Nikulas said, making a beeline for the open hatch. "I got me enough work ta do down below. I'll be seein' the two of ya later."

"Well, Ragi," Petamor said, "I guess it is up to us alone to greet our guests."

Ragi nodded nervously. "I am looking forward to it, sir."

Just then, a sparkling white cloud appeared out of the west. It hovered over the tower for a moment, condensed into a smaller cloud, and settled onto the roof. A second later, the water vapor consolidated into the form of the wizard, Eeowyn.

———•———

It was close to midnight when Rhiannon awoke from another dream of being trapped underground. The moons were in their full phase and silver moonbeams found their way through gaps in the jungle canopy. Topaz was standing a few feet away, watching over her like a faithful guard dog. Rhiannon would have preferred to sleep well into the morning; however, her demonic parasite was anxious to get moving and forced her out of her slumber.

Rhiannon now knew that the island was inhabited. The throbbing beat of drums and the faint sound of voices were drifting through the night air. The rock hopper, alert to the unusual noises, twitched his ears in different directions in an effort to locate the source of the sounds.

Despite the fact that the nighttime temperature was nearly as warm as that of the day, Rhiannon retrieved her robe, which she had left hanging on a tree. It was still a little damp, but she used it to cover herself anyway.

The music seemed to be coming from the western side of the island. Rhiannon decided to investigate.

The jungle vegetation was too dense for Topaz to negotiate safely in the dark with any stealth, so Rhiannon led him out of the trees and back to the beach. The moonlight lit the sand with a fierce blinding radiance, so they skirted the tree line and remained in the shadows.

As they neared the source of the primitive music, Rhiannon

could see the light of many brightly burning bonfires. After instructing Topaz to remain behind in the shadows where his dark coat would conceal him should anyone wander by, Rhiannon moved back into the jungle alone. She moved forward through the inky blackness towards the sound of the music. She did not encounter any jungle creatures, for they had all been frightened away by the noise. After several minutes, she came to the edge of a large circular clearing. On one side of the circle, a wide corridor had been cut through the jungle straight down to the beach. On the opposite side of the clearing, another narrower path had been cut leading back into the jungle. There were bonfires burning at various points around the edge of the clearing, while torches lined both corridors as far as the eye could see. In the center of the circle, several young native girls danced around a larger fire.

The clearing was filled with natives, most of whom were naked except for a string or two of seashells or similar ornaments. In the firelight, their skin appeared golden brown, their hair jet black. All of the young women in the center of the circle appeared to be about Rhiannon's age – sixteen or seventeen. Their arms and legs were heavily adorned with bracelets of tiny seashell and coral beads. Around their waists they wore skirts of grass while their breasts remained uncovered.

On the opposite side of the clearing, several young men watched the girls intently. Apparently, this was some sort of mating ceremony.

The rest of the natives in attendance, mostly older people and young children, appeared indifferent to the ceremony. They were more intent on the feasting and enjoying the music. While the older men lounged around on mats of woven grass, half-naked women served them food from a variety of beautifully crafted bowls and platters. The children played, as children do, and listened to their older siblings telling scary stories around the fires.

The unusual situation both excited and appealed to the demon within Rhiannon while it also had its enthralling effect on Rhiannon's own besieged bewildered mind.

As the three moons came into view at the open end of the corridor leading to the beach, the mesmerizing music began to intensify. Suddenly, the music stopped. The young men who had been watching the young women dance, now moved to form a semicircle and block the entrance to the corridor leading off into the jungle.

As the women added more wood to the fire in the center of the circle, the flames began to burn brighter. Everyone's attention was now focused on the twenty or so young women standing near the blaze. Then as abruptly as it had ended, the music began again. The beat of the drums was wilder than ever and even Rhiannon felt drawn to it. One of the native girls began to dance with uninhibited abandon. Rhiannon found her to be quite attractive and graceful, and she could not take her eyes off the dancing girl.

The golden-skinned girl could not have been more than sixteen or seventeen years old. Her raven black hair cascaded luxuriously about her shoulders and caressed her small naked breasts. Her wrists and ankles were covered with thick coils of hot-pink coral beads. Hanging low on her swaying hips, she wore a short skirt made from dried grasses which was cut on an angle to taper from her hip to her inner thigh. As she danced, she moved closer to the men waiting by the jungle corridor, their excitement evident in their nakedness.

Rhiannon could feel the heat from the fire as the girl danced closer and closer to the men, taunting them with her sensuous lips. The heat of the fire was pale by comparison to the heat generated by the uninhibited young woman. The music began to rise, pounding like a hundred anxious hearts. The young woman moved from man-to-man, swaying side-to-side like a snake. Then she made her choice and fell to her knees at the feet of her chosen one. Again the music stopped. The man bent down and scooped the girl up into his arms, turned and carried her off down the lighted corridor and into the dark jungle.

Rhiannon, her heart racing, found herself gasping for breath.

As soon as the young couple disappeared from view, the music started up again. In the heart of the circle, a second girl stood up and began to dance.

Rhiannon forced herself to turn away and quickly headed back to the spot where she had left Topaz.

On the beach, a cool breeze was flowing in along with the agitated waves as heat lightning flickered over the distant horizon like a candle flame in an unsteady breeze. Once again, Rhiannon found herself soaking wet with the perspiration from her own heat, so she quickly removed her sodden robe. For a long moment, Rhiannon supported herself against the strong shoulder of the rock hopper. She was breathing heavily from what she had just witnessed in the jungle clearing but soon forced herself to calm down.

First thing in the morning, she would make herself a staff. Then she would find the village and establish herself as sovereign over these simple child-like people.

Heavy storm clouds, infused with lightning, diminished the intensity of the moonlight, so Rhiannon led Topaz along the water's edge and back to the section of the beach where they had first arrived. Then they slipped back into the jungle and returned to the little pool. The flat rock upon which she had slept earlier had retained most of the heat from the day, but Rhiannon didn't mind. She curled up on the rock and went back to sleep only to dream of Breandan.

＊

It was early the next morning when Rhiannon awoke, awakened by Topaz as he contentedly munched away at some pear-like fruit he found on the ground near the pool.

Rhiannon stood and stretched her limbs, then dove head-first into the water. She swam to the waterfall and stood beneath it allowing the cascading water to cleanse her hair and refresh her body.

The morning sunshine filtering in through the lust jungle greenery made her feel warm and cozy. Rhiannon swam over to her rock, climbed out of the water, and began reviewing her plans for the day. *First, the staff,* she thought, grabbing a handful of sweet plump grapes. *The staff will enhance my powers and allow me to channel more energy straight from the sea itself.*

As soon as Rhiannon finished her breakfast, she began searching the jungle around the pool until she found a slender young teakwood tree with a reasonably straight trunk approximately two inches in diameter. She grabbed hold, yanked it out by its roots, and liked the way it felt in her hand. She cut the length to match that of her own height. Then she carefully examined every inch of the wood for flaws. She wanted her staff to be perfect.

Rhiannon could already feel the power building deep within the wood. Neraka was also satisfied with her choice. It was ready for the next step. She ran to the beach laughing delightedly.

Topaz had to trot just to keep up with the wizard girl. By the time he caught up, Rhiannon was already wading into the surf with staff in hand. When she was waist deep in the gently rolling waves, she stopped and lowered her right hand to the undulating surface of the water. She began by making a small circular pattern with her fingertips, creating in effect, a column of water. Slowly, the column grew until it was towering high above her like a waterspout. Then she held up her staff so that it was parallel to the swirling pillar of water and then thrust it forward until it was completely engulfed by the vortex. When Rhiannon released the staff, it remained suspended inside the waterspout. The young wizard girl then extended her arms and the swirling vortex began to move away from her and out to sea. It cut through the waves like a knife until it reached the coral reef that surrounded the island where it drilled straight down into the dense coral and disappeared.

Rhiannon stood frozen in place, eyes closed, arms outstretched towards the horizon. Minutes passed, and Topaz was becoming restless. Suddenly, at the exact spot where the staff had disappeared, the water began to boil and churn. The swirling column of water suddenly reappeared and rushed towards Rhiannon at tremendous speed. Just when it seemed that it would crash into the fragile looking girl, it stopped before her like a well-trained dog.

Rhiannon blinked and opened her eyes. Slowly, she reached into the spinning spout of water and took hold of her staff. The moment she withdrew her staff from the swirling spout, the water column collapsed back into the sea as if it had never existed. Rhiannon brought the staff to her lips and kissed it. At that moment, the ocean around her erupted with a bright flash that split the air with a thunderous clap, and she found herself surrounded by a thick fog filled with twinkling red, white, and pink lights.

The tremendous energy generated by Rhiannon's newly formed staff stunned Neraka. The power this wizard girl now controlled was far greater than anyone could ever have imagined.

Rhiannon turned and staggered out of the surf. When she reached the warm sand, she collapsed to the ground, exhausted. Her loyal companion approached and used his great wings to block the scorching sunlight from her unprotected body. She smiled. The sun could not hurt her, could not burn her skin, but Topaz was unaware of that fact. He was trying to protect her. As she lay there helpless, she realized that Topaz was the one true friend who would always love her regardless of what she had become. His love was unconditional. She rolled over in the sand and wept.

Neraka was impatient and he would not allow Rhiannon to rest. She sat up with a sigh and brushed the coarse sand off her body. Her strength was slowly returning. She picked up the staff and felt the raw power surging up through the ground into her arm.

Rhiannon inspected her staff for the first time since its re-birth from the sea. She was stunned to see that it was now encrusted with pearls and bits of red, white, and pink coral that formed rune-like patterns along its length. The top of the staff was crowned with a black pearl more than three inches in diameter. As she studied the priceless gem, it radiated with so much inner light that at first it seemed to be alive. As she stared at her own reflection in the pearl, she saw for the first time the eyes of Neraka staring back out at her, and her heart grew one more shade darker.

Rhiannon stood and pointed the staff out to sea. Instantly a thin black beam of light burst from the pearl and shot out over the waves. Seconds later, the ocean waves began to grow in size, accompanied by a loud rumble like thunder in a distant canyon. When she lowered the staff, the waves quickly returned to normal.

Neraka laughed and the salty sea air was filled with an unworldly sound.

Once again Rhiannon lifted her staff and pointed it out to sea. This time red, white, and pink flames shot into the waves. A few brief seconds later, hundreds of ocean fish of all descriptions began to jump out of the water to land at the wizard girl's feet. Again, the demon laughed, and all the creatures of the sea trembled with fear.

It was near midday when Rhiannon returned to the pool to freshen up. She rinsed out her wizard's robe and hung it up to dry in the bright sun while brushing the tangles out of her wet hair. She wanted to look like a queen when she walked into that village.

She was getting hungry again, but she was already tired of fruit. She had a craving for protein. *Perhaps the villagers can provide me with some fresh meat. I'd even settle for fish stew at this point.*

Rhiannon's robe dried quickly in the direct sunshine, so she slipped it on over her head and started back to the beach with Topaz following closely behind. Once clear of the trees, Rhiannon mounted Topaz, and together they flew out over the molten sea and into the azure blue sky of the Southern Reaches.

Rhiannon guided Topaz back to the western side of the island until they found the clearing she had visited the night before. They followed the narrow jungle corridor towards the interior of the island where the huge volcano awaited. Rhiannon wanted to take a closer look at the volcanic crater, so she encouraged Topaz to fly up above the cone-shaped mountain. They landed inside the crater, which was now full of water that had formed a shallow pool that reflected the color of the sky. She carefully examined the rocks and based on the information she had assimilated from Petamor's teachings, Rhiannon determined that the ancient volcano had been dormant for a very long time.

Neraka decided that if Rhiannon was to become the most powerful wizard that had ever existed, it was time for her to study the forbidden magic of earth and sea. Neraka laughed aloud again.

Returning to the path in the jungle, Rhiannon and Topaz glided low over the tropical foliage. The tree-lined path turned south and followed the southern slopes of the volcano until it came to another clearing that contained approximately thirty-five or forty bamboo huts. As the shadow of the rock hopper passed overhead, several of the villagers looked up in surprise and amazement. Topaz circled several times while looking for a convenient place to land.

Rhiannon recognized several of the villagers from the peculiar ceremony she had observed the night before. One of the villagers looked up just as Rhiannon and Topaz passed overhead and let out a warning cry. All of the natives scrambled for cover. Rhiannon readied her staff just in case any of them attempted to attack her, but by the time she landed, all of the villagers had disappeared. Slowly, she shook her head and smiled. "No wonder they're frightened," Rhiannon said to Topaz as she patted the beast on his shoulder, "these people have never seen a creature the likes of you before. Let's see if we can convince them that we mean them no harm."

Rhiannon swung her leg over Topaz's head and dropped silently to the ground. Although she could not see them, she could sense the villagers watching her from their hiding places. She walked several paces to the center of the village and closed her eyes. Although their language sounded strange to her ears, it was fairly simple. Using the language skills that Petamor had taught her, Rhiannon was able to absorb and learn the native tongue within a few seconds. She called out to them. When there was no response, she called out again. She waited a few more moments, and when there was still no response, she called them again, only this time her voice was that of a stern mother scolding a naughty child. She heard whispered voices around her. She could sense their uncertainty, but her uncanny ability to attract Mother Nature's more simple-minded creatures was still a part of her persona, and soon, the child-like faces of the uncertain villagers began to appear in doors and windows as well as from behind trees and rocks.

———•———

Rhiannon recognized one of the faces immediately. It was the face of the girl who had danced erotically by the fire the night before. She extended her hand to the wide-eyed girl and spoke to her in her native language. "Come here, I'm not going to hurt you. I only want us to be friends."

As the girl stepped out of the hut, Rhiannon could see that she was quite beautiful. She approached Rhiannon slowly, her eyes darting back-and-forth between Rhiannon and Topaz.

Rhiannon placed her hand on the rock hopper's neck and said, "Fear not. He won't harm you. He's actually very gentle."

When they stood face-to-face, Rhiannon reached out and stroked the pretty girl's long black hair. The girl's lovely almond-shaped eyes, so completely full of child-like innocence, captivated her. When Rhiannon leaned forward and kissed the frightened girl softly on the corner of her mouth, the girl's fear broke and she smiled back at Rhiannon. She reached up and gingerly touched Rhiannon's face in return. Rhiannon smiled back as she continued to talk and joke with the timid girl in an effort to entice the other natives out of hiding. Finally, the other villagers began to feel that it was safe, and they started to trickle out of their hiding places. Soon they had gathered around and were timidly touching Rhiannon's robe and staring wide-eyed at the winged beast.

Amazingly, Topaz did not seem at all disturbed by their attention. In fact, he seemed to be enjoying it. However, it was soon apparent that the heat was starting to get to him.

Before long, the entire community had turned out to meet her. All of the men wore simple loincloths, while the older women wore short skirts made of various materials. All of the younger children were naked. As their excitement at having a visitor grew, it became apparent that there was no leader among them. No one came forward to question her or greet her in any official capacity. This pleased Neraka greatly.

It was well past midday before anyone thought of offering Rhiannon food, and only then after Rhiannon had informed them that she was hungry. Word quickly spread and a grand feast was planned in her honor. Some of the younger men grabbed nets and headed for the beach to catch fish from their small dugout canoes. Others gathered up their crudely made spears, and headed into the jungle to hunt for fresh game. Some of the women began preparing a wide variety of wild fruits and nuts, while others carried cooking utensils down to the beach and began to build cooking fires. A few of the older men went into one of the caves in the base of the volcano and returned with several containers that were filled with a very strong and very potent beverage distilled from a mixture of fermented heart-berries and wild honey.

While the main dishes were being prepared, Rhiannon was offered fresh fruit and ice-cold pineapple juice. Her new friend, whose name was Melli, took her and Topaz to a shady spot where the men had hurriedly constructed a large lean-to where she could relax and be comfortable out of the sun while she watched the activities.

While the sun sank into an angry boil of blood on the western horizon, it dragged behind it a shade of tangerine twilight. Rhiannon relaxed in the shade as she watched the men return with fish, crabs, and a few wild pigs. They had also managed to snare three or four wild pheasants, seven wild chickens, and two tropical turkeys with brightly colored feathers.

Just before the sun disappeared altogether, Melli led Rhiannon and Topaz back to the beach where a wooden dais had been erected beneath a bamboo gazebo in Rhiannon's honor and Neraka could not have been happier.

As wild pigs roasted over the open fires, and fish baked on heated stones, the aroma of the roasting meat filled the night air causing Rhiannon's mouth to water in anticipation.

Although the sun had already disappeared below the horizon, it had left behind a sky painted with incredible shades of pink, orange, and crimson.

Melli brought Rhiannon a large hollowed out coconut filled with the fermented heart-berry drink she had seen earlier. The natives called the potent beverage 'nee'. Rhiannon found it to be delicious, and while she sipped her nee, Melli filled a large flat seashell platter with slices of roasted pork and a mixture of grilled vegetables, which Rhiannon ate native style using her fingers.

The demon was enjoying the banquet as much as Rhiannon, and could not foresee any problems taking control of these simple people. They were already treating her like a queen. Once she showed them the power she possessed, they would treat her like a god.

The feasting went on well into the early morning hours with Melli serving Rhiannon everything she demanded. The young wizard girl was drinking nee like if it were water, and she was becoming quite intoxicated.

Everyone was getting drunk; everyone was having a wonderful time.

Finally, as the three butter-yellow moons began their inevitable descent towards the western horizon, Rhiannon expected the music to change to the wild exciting beat as it had the night before. Try as she might, she could not force herself to stop thinking about the erotic ceremony, and for that reason, she asked Melli about it.

Melli exhibited no surprise at Rhiannon's request, and did her best to explain, in as much detail as possible, the purpose of the ritual. Melli told her that the ceremony only took place during the nights when all three moons were full. Only unwed girls between the ages of fourteen to sixteen were allowed to participate. At nightfall, they were taken to a specially prepared hut to prepare themselves for the ritual. There they waited until the three full moons were about to set. Then they were escorted into the circle of fire wearing only grass skirts, which were trimmed to be more revealing. They wore their prettiest jewelry and covered their bodies with perfumes made from exotic wild flowers. They were allowed to drink nee, often for the first time, until they lost all of their inhibitions and were ready to choose a mate.

Any unwed men that wished to participate in the ceremony were permitted, providing that there were an equal number of women to men. Once the women were ready to dance, they would dance before the waiting men until they were overcome with desire and picked a mate for the night.

The drinking of the nee explains a lot, Rhiannon thought. Her own body was heating up in more ways than one, thanks in part to the heady drink. Thoughts of Breandan began to run through her mind. But, Neraka didn't need or care about Breandan. Besides, Breandan was not here. The demon did not feel emotion, could not feel love or compassion, only need, and want, and greed. And pleasure, of course. Pleasure was, after all, pleasure. Pleasure was new. Neraka liked pleasure almost as much as he liked power. Power was one of the reasons he had left his own dark home far below the surface world in the first place. Now it was time to take advantage of Rhiannon's intoxication. Her body was ready; her mind had no choice but to follow suit.

Rhiannon told Melli that she wanted to watch her dance again, and ordered her to have the musicians play the same music they had played during the mating ritual. Within a few minutes, the native drums were pounding out an irresistible rhythm.

Melli took one more drink of nee, set aside her cup, and began to dance. She danced for almost an hour with Rhiannon's eyes on her the entire time.

Finally, Rhiannon stood up and walked to the center of the festivities. The demon inside her laughed, and the hollow laughter echoed out of her mouth. She held her staff in the air for all to see as she calmly recited an ancient incantation. A bright white shower of sparks erupted from the tip of her staff and harmlessly rained down upon the heads of the unsuspecting natives. Then, in a loud clear voice, Rhiannon said, "Get on your knees my people. Kneel before your queen and your god. From this moment on, I will command you, and you will worship and obey me."

One of the male villagers stood up. He was obviously drunk on nee and had no idea what was going on. He began to stagger towards Rhiannon talking rapidly and gesturing wildly with his hands, demanding an explanation as to what had just happened.

Rhiannon leveled her staff at him and said three words in the ancient language. Within seconds the man began to scream in agony as the flesh bubbled and melted off his bones. A few moments later, all that remained was a blackened smoking skeleton, which stood frozen in a puddle of steaming gore on the sand.

An overwhelming fear gripped the natives and they fell to the ground with their faces in the sand, pleading for mercy. Until that moment, they had not known real fear.

Rhiannon tapped the ground with her staff and the ground began to tremble. Off in the distance the dead volcano rumbled in response. The wizard-girl looked out over the prostrate figures at her feet and smiled wickedly.

When the shaking subsided, the wizard queen looked down at Melli, who was already on her knees kissing her feet. Neraka was pleased. *This is going to be even better than I thought.* "Stand up, Melli," she said sweetly.

Melli stood up, but was too frightened to raise her head.

Rhiannon put her arm around the native girl's waist.

"Lift your head and look at me," Rhiannon commanded.

Melli hesitated, but only for a moment. Then she looked up into Rhiannon's eyes trembling with a combination of fear and desire.

"Do not be afraid. As long as you obey me, you have nothing to fear," Rhiannon said as she kissed the girl softly on the forehead.

"Now, my friend," Rhiannon whispered, "help me find a place where I can rest in peace."

Rhiannon sat on a bamboo bench in one of the larger, dimly lighted natural chambers under the huge volcano. Several days had passed since the feast, and the villagers had grown to accept her as their queen without incident. After witnessing her powers, they had needed no further convincing. They truly believed that she was a god. For that reason, she had decided not to anymore unnecessary harm upon them. She would only do so if they left her no other choice. She wanted their love as well as their loyalty. They were a simple, childlike people, after all, and a good scolding from time-to-time seemed sufficient to keep them in line.

Rhiannon was turning out to be the perfect instrument for the demon, Neraka. Her innocence and gullibility had allowed him to invade her psyche before she understood how to use her extraordinary powers to evict it. Now, as her powers increased with every breath she took, she seemed capable of drawing power from almost everything around her. Yet Rhiannon remained a prisoner in her own body. For her there was no escape. Only death could release her, and death could only come from the hand of another wizard. Nevertheless, Neraka was convinced that even the old wizard, Thoradal, was not powerful enough to challenge her alone.

There were times when Rhiannon's mind *was* able to function separately from that of Neraka's. Yet even then, it was only when the intruder needed to direct Rhiannon's thoughts to suit his own purposes. For the demon, at least, things were going much better than expected.

Neraka had not been born evil; was not evil by nature; did not understand the difference between good and evil. He had always existed without physical form, and now that he possessed physical form, he had become obsessed with physical pleasure and the beautiful things of the surface world.

Rhiannon's body was the primary source of that pleasure and beauty – for she, herself, was beautiful, and just like any other healthy young woman – she desired sexual pleasure. Deep inside, Rhiannon was still deeply and hopelessly in love with Breandan, and despite the pressure from Neraka, Rhiannon would not allow another man to touch her. Instead, she had turned to Melli for friendship. Melli, who was both innocent and non-threatening, would make the perfect assistant, and help her take her mind off of Breandan.

Earth power, thought Neraka. *Through this female, I can already control the weather. I can make it rain, or snow, or even create a tornado or a typhoon out of thin air. Now the sea is my slave as well. I can create tidal waves or summon monsters from the murky deep; anything I desire is at my disposal. However, earth power is what I need to complete my collection. If I could only trick that old fool, Petamor, into giving up a few of his precious secrets, I would be unstoppable. I doubt if I can convince him to hand me the knowledge voluntarily. He and the others are already suspicious. I have no choice but to obtain the knowledge by other means.*

Melli sat at the wizard girl's feet waiting to do her bidding, but for the moment, the demon Neraka, was preoccupied with more important business.

Rhiannon sat with her eyes closed. In her mind's eye, she pictured Petamor's library chamber and the bookcases full of ancient books and scrolls. She focused her attention on the books she needed, the books of forbidden earth and sea lore. In her mind's eye, she reached out and took the books off their shelf. She watched them float in mid-air, dust motes falling around them like dandelion spores floating in a gentle breeze. She focused all of her energy onto the books and watched as they slowly separated into individual molecules, only to reassemble again a few minutes later on the floor of the cave at her feet.

Melli was shocked by the sudden materialization of the dusty old books beside her. When Rhiannon opened her eyes again, Melli was staring down at the books in awe. Melli gasped, and reached out to Rhiannon for reassurance and protection. Rhiannon lovingly stroked Melli's hair to calm the naïve girl. Melli tried hard to smile through trembling lips, but she feared Rhiannon as much as she loved her.

In the library at the tower, the sudden gap that had magically appeared on the shelf where the books once sat caused several neighboring books to tumble over, stirring up more dust. Petamor neither heard the noise nor saw the dust fly. He was sitting at one of the smaller tables in the dinning chamber eating a meager meal of roasted chicken, bread, and salt. He did not have much of an appetite. He ate alone because Ragi, Nikulas, and his other guests were still asleep.

He had been thinking about Rhiannon all day. Something was wrong, he could sense it. Exactly what it was he did not know. He could not put his finger on it no matter how hard he tried. He had a feeling, however, that it would not be long before whatever it was, was out in the open.

In the village of Ravenwood, the harsh winter was proving to be hard on everyone. Breandan did all he could to help his people, but privately he was growing more concerned about Rhiannon with every beat of his heart. Petamor had sent word that Rhiannon had finally left the escarpment and was planning to visit her parents before moving into the Southern Reaches. Breandan spoke with Rhiannon's father and mother about her brief visit and quickly realized that something truly was wrong. They told him about Rhiannon's promise to return soon, but he had seen the doubt in their eyes and felt the pain in their hearts.

Perhaps it's just that I miss her. I didn't expect to miss her this much, but now that she's really gone, I feel like a part of me is missing. Breandan's thoughts kept going back to that night in the council chamber when Petamor's old starship had turned red. On that night, Rhiannon's aura had also been intensely red, or so it had seemed. Maybe Rhiannon's subconscious mind *had* been trying to communicate a message. Perhaps she *was* in trouble, but just didn't know what to do about it.

He thought about those quiet days tending the sheep with Rhiannon in the glades and meadows around Ravenwood. *What a fool I was. All I could think about was wizards and magic, when the real magic was right there with me all along. Now Rhi is off in some other part of the world, out of touch and far away. And if she is in trouble, it may be too late to help her.*

On Rhiannon's island, deep down in the cave where she usually slept, she slipped out of bed. It was time to begin studying the books she had stolen from her mentor, Petamor. After brushing away the dust and cobwebs, she carefully opened the first of the two large tomes. The text had been written in the original language of Petamor's ancient star-faring race, and as such, it was interlaced with runes and other symbols of power. Rhiannon had no trouble deciphering the books, for Petamor had taught her how to read them.

Rhiannon read for hours, memorizing every bit of information in the stolen books, no matter how trivial or insignificant the material first seemed. Some of the text was small and had faded over the centuries, and Rhiannon's eyes were growing weary. However, Neraka was hungry for the earth knowledge, and he had no intention of allowing her to rest until she finished reading the entire text of the first volume.

Later that morning, when Melli awoke, she stretched lazily, turned onto her side, and watched Rhiannon as she studied her books. Her new queen was such a strange creature. She was a woman, of that Melli had no doubt, but she was much more than that. She could be demanding yet gentle, harsh yet kind. Many of the other young women were envious of her relationship with their new queen. Yet they were too fearful to say anything lest Rhiannon become angry and punish them as she had punished the drunken man on the beach the night of the great feast. But deep down, many of them were secretly hoping that Rhiannon would soon grow tired of Melli, so that they could have a chance at becoming the new queen's consort.

Rhiannon looked up and smiled. "You're awake," she said. "Good. I'm hungry. Go and bring me something to eat."

Melli brought Rhiannon baked fish, cold coconut milk, and bite-sized chunks of fresh mango and pineapple for dessert. She knelt at Rhiannon's feet and held up the platter of food. *An offering to the god,* Neraka gloated.

"Go now, Melli. Do not come again until I call for you. I have much work to do and I do not want to be disturbed."

The native girl left her queen alone, joining the other villagers in the afternoon heat where a major emergency had given rise to alarm. They were relieved when Melli came out of the cave and quickly crowded around her.

The woman who had been tending to the needs of the winged beast their queen called Topaz came running up to Melli in tears. She was obviously very frightened and in great distress. "Melli! Melli!" she cried. "It is the god-beast! He is very sick! He is dying. Please, Melli, you must do something! If the god-beast dies, she will kill me for certain!"

"Wh...wh...what's wrong with the god-beast?" Melli asked,

suddenly frightened herself. She knew how much Rhiannon loved the winged creature, and there was no telling what she might do if anything were to happen to it.

"I'm not sure. I think it's the heat. It lies on the ground with its tongue hanging out. It acts like it cannot breathe."

Melli nodded. She knew that if the god-creature was really dying, Rhiannon was the only one who could save it. She spun around and dashed back into the cave system calling out for Rhiannon.

At first, when Rhiannon heard Melli shouting her name, she became infuriated. She assumed that the natives had decided to attack her after all. She jumped up from the floor where she had been studying and grabbed her staff ready to strike.

Then Melli ran into the cave crying.

Rhiannon held her staff out in self-defense and demanded to know what was going on. Melli did her best to explain, but all Rhiannon heard was that Topaz was sick and might be dying. Guilt slammed into her like a cold ocean wave. Instead of attending to his needs personally, as she should have done, she had placed the burden of his care on a total stranger. Now it seemed that both she and Topaz might pay the ultimate price for her thoughtlessness.

Rhiannon ran to Topaz as quickly as her legs would carry her wondering what could possible be wrong. If left alone in their own environment, a rock hopper was capable of living for hundreds of years, free from illness and disease. But here, in this distant, sweltering land so different from his own world, Topaz was susceptible to the tropical heat.

The wizard-girl found Topaz lying on his side in the sand, panting like a dog. When he saw Rhiannon, he tried in vain to get on his feet, but he was too weak. All he could do was gaze up at her with rheumy red eyes. His black coat was covered in lather as if he had been flying in the tropical sun for hours.

Rhiannon turned angrily to the woman who was supposed to be taking care of him and grabbed her roughly by the shoulders. "What have you been doing?" she spat. "Have you been riding him? Can't you see that he is half dead from the heat?" Rhiannon pushed the terrified woman away. In her rage, she had forgotten that Topaz would never allow anyone but her to ride him alone.

Sobbing, the woman fell on the ground at Rhiannon's feet exclaiming, "No, no, no, my queen! I have not touched him, I swear! No one has been near him! He has been here, in the shade of these trees all along just as you commanded! But you are right, my queen! It is the heat! The heat is too much for him! He cannot take it!"

Rhiannon knelt down beside the weakened animal and gently brushed away the jungle flies that clustered around his sticky eyes. She realized that the woman was telling the truth. The rock hopper was a cold weather creature, preferring the snowcapped peaks of the Finger Mountains to the tropical climate of the island. His metabolism was not designed for the intense heat. The heat was going to kill him if she didn't think of something fast. "What have I done to you?" she whispered softly as her tears began to flow. Topaz didn't respond. Instead, his eyes rolled back in his head.

Rhiannon turned to Melli who had followed her out of the cave. "Quickly Melli, I need you to bring me some fresh water and a thin flat piece of obsidian, the sharper the better. I'll also need some of the soapstone I keep in my bag."

Melli stared at Rhiannon and shook her head. She did not understand. "What is obsidian?" she asked hesitantly.

Rhiannon searched for the native word, "Kaca!" she exclaimed. Find me a piece of thin, flat kaca gunung berapi. Do you understand? Kaca gunung berapi."

At last, Melli nodded. She understood that Rhiannon wanted a piece of the volcanic glass that could be found scattered around the island. Primitive people had often used obsidian to make arrowheads and knife blades because it was sharper than flint or any other material available to them. Melli turned and started to obey Rhiannon's command.

"Wait!" Rhiannon shouted.

Melli froze in place, expecting to be scolded for being too slow.

"I also want you to bring me a basket of heart-berries and a large bowl of nee. Have one of these wretched women help you. Now go! Hurry!"

Melli grabbed one of the women by her arm and pulled her along with her. She and the woman ran to the caves as fast as they could, knowing that the penalty for displeasing their queen would be severe. Melli found the box of soapstone in Rhiannon's pack and filled a handmade clay amphora with fresh water from a nearby spring. She sent the other woman to collect the heart-berries.

The other woman found a basket of heart-berries that were waiting to be crushed into juice to make wine, but she took them back to Rhiannon before anyone could question her.

Melli found everything Rhiannon had requested with the exception of the obsidian. For that, she would have to go to the jewelry maker's house at the other end of the village. She looked around and spotted the daughter of the bead maker standing in the shadows, so she commanded the child to run home as fast as possible and get a few pieces of obsidian for the queen. The child knew that Melli was the queen's favorite and obeyed the order without question.

By the time Melli returned, Topaz was eating heart-berries out of Rhiannon's hand.

Melli placed the bowl of water and the small box of soapstone on the ground next to Rhiannon.

"Where's the obsidian I asked for?" Rhiannon demanded harshly.

"It's coming, my Queen," Melli said. "I sent a child to fetch it for you. She's the daughter of the bead maker and she is also one of the fastest runners in the village. She'll know where to find it."

Rhiannon nodded and began mixing the soapstone and heart-berry juice into a rich soapy lather and gently applied the mixture to the upper surface of Topaz's left wing. By the time Rhiannon had completely covered the wing; the child arrived with several flat slivers of the black volcanic glass and handed them to Melli. Melli showed them to Rhiannon, and Rhiannon chose the one that had the finest thinnest edge.

Rhiannon used the obsidian like a razor blade and carefully began to shave the thick fur off of Topaz's wings. The membrane beneath the fur was very thin and laced with hundreds of tiny blood vessels and capillaries, and Rhiannon found it difficult to remove the fur without occasionally nicking the delicate skin. Melli helped Rhiannon by applying raw heart-berry juice to the tiny cuts, while another woman fed Topaz drops of nee with her fingers to help ease his suffering.

It took Rhiannon over three hours to shave all of the fur from Topaz's wings, but once relieved of the thick fur, Topaz began to recover. His furless wings began acting like a cooling system instead of a heater, dissipating much of his body heat and allowing his body to cool down much quicker than before. However, once the magnificent wings had lost their fur, it gave the poor mystical beast a decidedly sinister appearance. He now looked like the offspring of a horse and a giant vampire bat.

The heart-berries and the nee were starting to have their desired effect as well, for no sooner had Topaz finished eating, he gently nudged Rhiannon on the leg with his muzzle and then fell into a deep and healing sleep. A few minutes later his breathing returned to normal.

"He's going to be all right," Rhiannon said as her tears began to fall again. "He's going to make it, Melli."

Melli broke down and cried her own tears of joy and relief.

Neraka, indifferent to their relief, did not try to prevent Rhiannon's show of affection before the natives, because after all, she was a child among children. Melli held her weeping queen in her arms until they both fell asleep in the shade beside Topaz.

Nearly an entire month had passed since Rhiannon's arrival on the island, and the planet's three moons were once again entering into their full phase. Rhiannon had spent much of that time studying the forbidden spells and incantations in the purloined books of earth lore. She was hoping to have them committed to memory before the start of the next moon cycle.

Topaz had recovered from his bout with the tropical heat, but he would never be the same again. At first, Rhiannon tried to spend as much time with him as she could, but after a time, she began to lose interest in him again.

While studying the prohibited books, Rhiannon began to devise a scheme that could help her defeat the other wizards and conquer the world. First, however, she needed to find one very special magical ingredient.

The books of earth lore had explained how certain elements, such as gold and platinum, often contain more earth power than other less remarkable elements such as copper, nickel, and tin. However, any materials that came from deep inside the planet, no matter how simple they seemed, could contain an extraordinary amount of power. Therefore, Rhiannon began her search by scouring the island from top to bottom for the perfect power source of earth power.

Melli was constantly by her side, although she could not understand why they had to examine every rock they found.

At last, on the southern tip of the island, Rhiannon found what she was looking for – black volcanic sand. She could feel the earth power in the sand itself. Thousands of years in the past, when the ancient volcano was in its infancy, lava had flowed out of the very guts of the planet and into the sea where it then cooled and solidified. It had taken another thousand years for the ocean to pulverize the hardened lava into sand and deposit it here upon the beach at the foot of the volcano.

"Simple sand, Melli," Rhiannon laughed. "The sand that holds the power. It is the sand that is my key to both earth and sea power."

Rhiannon bent down, scooped up a handful of the ancient material, and sprinkled it generously over her staff. Then she and Melli watched in amazement as the staff began to glow from within as the black sand began to melt and imbed itself into the wood. When the process was completed, the staff was coated from tip-to-tip with a smooth, slightly opaque, black glass, beneath which shone white pearls and runes of pink, red, and white coral.

"It's beautiful," Melli said running her slender fingers along the glossy surface.

"Come," Rhiannon said, "let us celebrate this event. I just happen to know the perfect spot not far from here where we can celebrate in private."

Rhiannon took Melli by the hand and helped her climb up onto Topaz's back, and then she hopped up behind her.

Melli was thrilled, for she had never before been allowed to ride the god-beast. Her heart pounded against her ribs like a native drum as Topaz took to the sky and soared above the trees.

A few minutes later, they landed beside the lovely little pool that Rhiannon had found the first day that she had arrived on the island. They splashed and frolicked about in the refreshing water like children, until their stomachs began to growl. Then they sat upon Rhiannon's rock and fed each other tropical grapes while they watched the sun sink lower towards the horizon draped in robes of pink and peach.

With their appetites sated, Rhiannon told Melli the story of
how she had climbed the escarpment in search of Breandan
and ended up becoming an apprentice to a wizard. Melli was
fascinated and full of questions, especially where Breandan
was concerned.

"There's no need to be jealous," Rhiannon assured her,
when she saw the wounded look in Melli's eyes. Rhiannon
pulled her closer and held her gently. They quietly watched
the sun until it kissed the horizon, but before the light of day
had slipped completely away, Rhiannon and Melli were back
in the village.

Rhiannon, happy and relaxed for once, actually helped the
women prepare food for the monthly mating feast. While they
worked, the village women encouraged Rhiannon to take part
in the ceremony and chose a mate from one of the men on the
island. As tempting as it sounded, she rejected their offer to
participate in the ceremony and join the girls in the center
of the circle. For now she was perfectly content to wait for
Breandan.

Later that night, once the ceremony began, Rhiannon drank
nee as she listened to the hypnotic music. Her body wanted
to dance, move to the rhythm of the drums, but her intellect
would not cooperate. To do so would be lowering herself to
their level, and Neraka would not allow it. Besides, even back
in her home village of Ravenwood, she never danced, not even
at the wedding feasts given for her friends. She would have
to contend herself with watching the ceremony from her dais
and drinking her nee, even if it did make her lips feel a little
numb.

As the music filled the balmy night, the three moons of
Nox finally made their grand entrance, bathing the beach in a
cold, eerie light. Chaos, perfectly framed by Eden, the lovers'
moon, was in the foreground. Titan, as usual, loomed in the
background.

It was time for the ceremony to begin in earnest, and

Rhiannon noticed that Melli's original lover had returned to find a new mate. He did not have long to wait. The first of the dancing maidens selected him, just as Melli had. Rhiannon could not help but wonder how Melli would react, although she seemed as unconcerned as ever, and all of her attention remained focused on Rhiannon.

At times like this, Rhiannon could not prevent her thoughts from returning to Breandan. She wondered where he was and what he was doing. She wondered if he still thought about her. She wondered if she could persuade him to collaborate with her in her bid for world domination. After all, they still retained a strong emotional bond, and as unlikely as it seemed, it was not completely impossible that once he recognized the extent and magnitude of her power, he would realize the futility of opposing her. At the very least, he may inadvertently prevent the league from moving against her before she was ready to make her move against them.

In an instant Rhiannon made her decision. She would invite Breandan to visit her on the island. She would throw a great feast in his honor. During the feast she would provide him with entertainment and show him how much the people of her island loved and adored her. Then, once he was thoroughly impressed and full of admiration for her, she would rekindle their aborted love affair and use her physical charms to seduce him to her side. After all, beneath his wizardly robe he was still a man and subject to the desires of the flesh.

The following morning, Rhiannon and Melli went off into the jungle to search for an animal that Rhiannon could transform into a familiar. Familiars were typically animals that were bestowed with magical powers by one trained in sorcery and black magic. Rhiannon and Melli searched for hours until they found a beautiful multicolored parrot. The bird was healthy, alert, rambunctious, and took to Rhiannon as all wild creatures tended to do – without trepidation. Rhiannon was very pleased with her find and immediately began teaching the bird how to talk. The bird learned quickly but not quickly enough to satisfy Neraka. He forced Rhiannon to use her magic to provide the bird with a vocabulary superior to most human adults.

Later that evening, Rhiannon waited until Melli was asleep and penned a brief but passionate letter to Breandan. The letter was the invitation; the parrot was the messenger. The invitation included the exact location of the island and made it quite clear that he was to come alone. Since Rhiannon was no longer certain of Breandan's exact whereabouts at the moment, she sent the message to Breandan by way of Petamor. To keep the old wizard happy and prevent him from becoming suspicious, she added a brief but pleasant note describing her new home. She hoped that her note would be enough to prevent him from feeling ignored. He was, after all, a rather sensitive old fool.

Rhiannon attached her message to one of the parrot's legs and recited the proper incantation. Then she fed him a handful of heart-berries to help fuel his long arduous journey north. Her spell would ensure that he would have no trouble locating the tower on the escarpment. With any luck, Breandan would receive the letter within three or four days.

In the heart of the night, alone and unaccompanied, Rhiannon took her little envoy to the northern beach and released him. She then returned to her sleeping chamber in the caves beneath the ancient volcano and sat down at the small dressing table beside the bed. When she closed her eyes, she could see through the eyes of the bird and thereby make any necessary course corrections to help prevent him from going astray. Once she was satisfied that all was well, she returned to her private chambers deep within the volcano and climbed into bed.

Rhiannon's little messenger possessed neither the speed nor the strength of a rock hopper. It took him nearly three days just to reach the southern tip of Pega. He was so exhausted that he rested for an entire day before moving on. When he arrived at the tower the following day, he was weak and hungry.

Nikulas first found the weary bird perched atop a windowsill in the kitchen area. He recalled Petamor's pronouncement that some of the wizards would arrive in unusual ways, so he half expected the bird to transform itself into a wizard before his eyes, but the bird appeared to be just a bird after all.

"Here, would ya look at that?" Nikulas said. "I've never seen a bird like that one before in me whole life, have you?"

Instead of answering, Ragi ran to fetch Petamor.

The old wizard came at once. When he had finished reading Rhiannon's brief note, he smiled. He was both relieved and pleased to know that she had found a new home.

"I have to go for a short while, lads!" Petamor exclaimed with a big smile. "I have a letter to deliver to Breandan down in the village of Ravenwood, but I should be back before midday." Petamor rushed past Nikulas and Ragi. "Please take good care of our colorful little friend here. See that he is fed and find him a nice perch to rest upon."

As soon as Petamor left the room, Nikulas turned to Ragi and said, "What the devil is it, brother?"

"It's a bird, Nikulas," Ragi replied.

"I can see that. I not be blind. But I ain't never seen any bird like it before in me entire life. Have you?"

"Can't say that I have, but Mr. Petamor said to look after it, and look after it we will. It looks hungry. You wait here. I'm going to go have a look in the pantry. Maybe I can find something in there for it to eat."

As Ragi left the room, the parrot said, "Who the devil are you?"

Nikulas's jaw dropped open. "What the bloody hell!" he said incredulously as he stepped closer to the colorful bird.

"What the bloody hell," the parrot repeated.

"I must be losing me mind," Nikulas said, more to himself than to the bird. Narrowing his eyes, he leaned forward for a closer look. "What the devil are you?"

"I'm a parrot. What the devil are you?"

Nikulas took a step back and shook his head. "I don't believe me ears! A talkin' bird! If that don't beat all! Now I've seen everything!"

"I doubt that," said the bird.

"Here, what did ya just say?"

"I said, 'I doubt that you've seen everything.'"

"Blimey!" Nikulas exclaimed.

"Did you say something, brother?" Ragi asked as he returned from the pantry with a small sack of sunflower seeds.

"Didn't ya hear it? This bloody creature can talk!"

"What? Don't be silly."

"I heard it with me own ears, I tells ya."

"Really? Tell me, Nikulas, exactly how much Rockvorian rum have you had today?"

"It's not the rum talkin', I swear it! It's the bloody bird. Here, have a listen. Go on parrot, or whatever ya are," Nikulas said. "Come on now, I know ya can do it. Say something."

"What did you just call it?" Ragi asked with raised eyebrows.

"A parrot. At least that is what it said it was. I ain't never seen no parrot before, so I can't be sure it be tellin' the truth."

The parrot looked at Nikulas and cocked his head in silence sedition.

"Here," Ragi said handing the small sack over to Nikulas, "Give him some of these sunflower seeds. And don't let anything happen to him. I have too much work to do to be standing around listening to all this nonsense."

Ragi left the room shaking his head, rolling his eyes, and muttering to himself.

Nikulas's face turned red. He looked at the bird.

The bird looked at Nikulas, cackled like an old crone and said, "Maybe you should lay off the Rockvorian rum for a while, rummy."

Breandan sat alone in his parent's cottage drinking a mug of hot tea. He had grown fond of the beverage during his stay in the tower. In less than a month he had managed to alleviate most of the hardships in Ravenwood. Now, there was not much left to do. He was bored. He was restless. He missed Rhiannon. He wondered where she was and how she was doing. He wanted to continue his studies again and increase his wizardly powers. When he heard the tapping on the glass pane, he looked up and smiled. A lone eagle glared in at him from the sill outside the window. By the time Breandan opened the door, Petamor had already transformed back into his human form.

"Greetings, Grandfather," Breandan said with a grin.

"Greetings, Breandan. I have come with a message from Rhiannon," Petamor said with a grin of his own.

"Really! A message from Rhiannon? I certainly hope it's good news," Breandan said.

"I seriously doubt if anything that girl has to tell you can be good," said a hooded visitor who had been standing behind Petamor the entire time.

Startled, Petamor turned and asked, "Thoradal? Is that you?"

"Yes, it is I," Thoradal answered. "Ragi and Nikulas told me about the parrot and the message, and said that you left in quite the rush. Putting two-and-two together, I followed you here to Ravenwood."

"What is so important that you must follow me here?" Petamor asked.

"Someone has been using the forbidden earth lore, I can feel it. I think it may be Rhiannon."

"How is that possible, Thoradal? I have never taught her the forbidden knowledge," Petamor insisted.

"I believe you, old friend. Nevertheless, she has managed to learn it on her own somehow," Thoradal stated earnestly.

"What does Rhiannon's message say, Grandfather?" Breandan questioned.

"I do not know the exact contents of your part of the message, Breandan. You'll have to read it to find out. I am not in the habit of reading one's private communiqués," Petamor replied, handing the letter over to Breandan.

Breandan read the letter carefully, turning several shades of red in the process. Finally, he said, "It…it…it appears to be an invitation, Grandfather. Rhiannon claims that she's living on a tropical volcanic island somewhere in the Southern Reaches. She claims that it's one of the m…m…most beautiful islands in the world. She also says to tell you that it never snows there, whatever that is supposed to m…m…mean."

"Breandan, are you blushing?" asked Thoradal. "And I do not believe that I have ever heard you stutter before. That must be some letter you have there."

"It…it's nothing, really. Just Rhiannon's way of teasing me, I suppose. That's all."

"Of course," Thoradal said unconvincingly.

"Do you think I should accept the invitation, Grandfather?" Breandan asked, directing his question mostly to Petamor.

"I cannot think of any reason not to go. Can you, Thoradal?" asked Petamor.

"Let us not be too hasty, old friend. There is much more to this letter than meets the eye. Before we decide what to do, we should return to the tower at once and discuss this communication with the other members of the league."

The old keep had never been so brightly lit. Every room in the tower was ablaze with a combination of firelight, candlelight, and torchlight. Ragi was kept busy in the kitchen preparing enough food to feed everyone, while Nikulas transferred the finished creations from kitchen to dining hall.

The parrot, which Nikulas had named, Gabby, was perched on Nikulas's left shoulder, but the moment Breandan entered the room, he flew directly to him and began talking so rapidly, that no one could understand a single word he uttered. It was the first time the colorful bird had spoken to anyone other than Nikulas.

"Ah...ya see there, brother," Nikulas said to Ragi, "I told ya the bloody thing can talk, but ya wouldn't believe me."

"Well, I'll be...I promise that I will never doubt you again, Nikulas," Ragi said.

As the wizards turned their attention on Breandan, Breandan looked around befuddled while the bird rattled on about longitude, latitude, landmarks, and wind speeds.

Salaran was the first member of the league to interrupt. "Interesting," he said. "I have seen such creatures in my travels, and I've heard several of them mimic human speech. But this specimen is speaking in our own ancient language and in complete sentences at that. I think that it's safe to assume that Rhiannon is responsible."

"Yes, however, teaching an animal how to speak our language is not a crime," Petamor added quickly. "Our language may be uncommon, but it's not a secret."

"I never said that it was. I am merely pointing out the fact that we can now be certain that the bird was sent by Rhiannon," Salaran said.

"Very well," said Rimahorn. "Let's begin this discussion on

that note. Petamor, can you describe for us exactly when and how you received this... this correspondence from Rhiannon? We are assuming that this bird was the messenger. Is that correct?"

"Yes," Petamor replied. "Earlier this afternoon, Ragi came to inform me that this creature had arrived. Upon closer inspection, I discovered the communication addressed to Breandan. I also received a brief note from Rhiannon, although the greater part of the message was directed at Breandan."

"We already know the contents of the message directed to you, brother," Rimahorn said. "Now, if you don't mind, Breandan, we would like to know exactly what was in the other half of the message."

Once again, Breandan's face turned red. "It's just an invitation, Grandfather. Rhiannon has invited me to visit the island where she's taken up residence. It's somewhere in the Southern Reaches, just below the equator."

"That's it? Is that the entire message, Breandan?" Eeowyn asked.

"No, Grandmother," Breandan admitted, turning uncomfortably in his seat. "However, the rest of the message is rather...personal."

The wizards looked around at one another and nodded.

"Very well, Breandan," Rimahorn began. "We will not ask you to reveal anything that you do not feel is essential to this discussion. The bird, however, is another matter. I am afraid that my hearing is not as good as it once was. Can you tell us what it said to you a few moments ago when you first entered the hall?"

"Yes, Grandfather. The bird simply repeated the lines from the message, but included a more detailed description of the island, as well as directions on its exact location," Breandan replied.

"Directions?"

"Yes," Breandan admitted, "Longitude and latitude to be exact."

Rimahorn and the others nodded.

"Is there anything, anything at all unusual in the communication? Anything that may seem...unlike Rhiannon?" Cinaran asked.

"Well," Breandan began shifting in his chair again, "there is one thing."

"And what would that be?" Zalamar inquired.

"Well...the parrot did refer to Rhiannon as..." Breandan paused.

"As what, lad? Speak up. This is no time to be vague," Cinaran insisted.

Breandan turned to Petamor for support and then said, "The bird referred to Rhiannon as queen."

The League of Wizards turned and looked at one another. When they looked again at Breandan, their faces were grim.

Finally, Rimahorn said, "Breandan, may I see your staff for a moment, lad?"

"Of course, Grandfather. Please excuse me for a moment while I go to my room and get it." Breandan then stood and left the room. When he returned a few moments later, he held his staff out to Rimahorn.

Rimahorn took the staff and carefully examined it with his fingertips. "Red gold? You have ringed your staff with red gold. Red gold is one of the most powerful elements of earth magic," he said. "You have not been given permission to use this earth power."

"I made the staff for Breandan, myself," Petamor said. "And I *am* permitted to use the earth power. I chose red gold for its power, and because it is the perfect match for Breandan's abilities. I hope that someday he will learn how to master it."

"Yes, of course," Rimahorn said. "It is a beautiful staff. Bursting with power." He handed the staff to Thoradal. "What do you think?"

Thoradal also examined the staff. "Very nice. Strong. However, red gold or not, this is not the staff that was used to call forth the earth power. The staff that was used to call forth the earth power did not use red gold. The staff that called forth the earth power contained an element much more powerful than red gold. That element can only be found in the Southern Reaches. Once again, all of the evidence points to Rhiannon. I no longer harbor any doubts. Rhiannon is responsible." He handed the staff back to Breandan. "Perhaps this invitation to visit Rhiannon's island is a trap. She almost certainly intends to try and convince Breandan to join her in whatever little scheme she has cooked up."

"Scheme? What are you talking about? No! No way! I cannot believe that! Rhiannon would never turn against the league. Why would she? It doesn't make any sense. She knows it would be futile to challenge the league," Breandan protested.

"That is why you must accept her invitation and go visit her on this island of hers," Thoradal said. "We must try and find out what she is up to before it is too late."

"I'll go," Breandan said, "but I will not believe that Rhiannon would turn against the league of her own free will."

"No one here believes that Rhiannon is doing this of her own free will," Thoradal stated. "That is exactly why you must go to her, Breandan. We must find out whom or what is forcing her to use the earth lore before she unleashes these powers against us."

"You do realize that this mission will be a dangerous one. If Rhiannon discovers that you are there to gather intelligence, she may try to eliminate you," Rimahorn added.

"Rhiannon would never do anything to harm me intentionally, Grandfather. We've been friends since childhood. And I know that she would never turn her back on the league of her own choice," Breandan stated.

"Of course not," Rimahorn added. "But if Rhiannon is no longer in control of her own actions---"

Thoradal sighed, interrupting Rimahorn. "Again, no one here believes that she would turn against the league by choice, Breandan. Nevertheless, we all feel that something *has* interfered with her free will, and we need to find out what that something is as soon as possible," Thoradal insisted.

"I understand." Turning towards Petamor, Breandan asks, "What form should I use to travel, Grandfather?"

Before Petamor could answer, the parrot began to speak again. "Take the form of a bird and I will guide you. I know the way. I know the way. I will guide you!"

"Do you think it's possible that Rhiannon is using this bird as a familiar?" Eeowyn asked.

"Anything is possible," Thoradal agreed. "I do not sense that she is listening to us through this creature. However, I do sense that she can see through its eyes."

"Could this bird be recording our conversation to replay to her again later?" Cinaran questioned. "Perhaps it would be best if we keep this creature locked up here in the tower until we are certain."

"Yes," agreed Eeowyn, "Breandan doesn't need the bird to guide him. He can find the island on his own. He knows the exact location."

"I have a better idea," Thoradal said. "Why not use our little friend here to do a little spying for us?"

"Is that safe?" Eeowyn asked.

"Eeowyn is right. Let us not underestimate this girl. She has already proven herself very clever," Boradal added.

"Very well. I will make an exact duplicate of the creature," Thoradal continued. "It will be perfect in every detail. Even Rhiannon will not be able to tell them apart. Except, *our bird* will be working for us."

"A double agent?" Petamor pondered.

"Exactly," Thoradal answered. "We can keep the original

here in the tower. Nikulas can look after it. The bird seems attached to him already. I will transfer its ability to send visual images to Rhiannon into the duplicate. That way she will only see what we want her to see."

"Very well," said Rimahorn. "Make the duplicate and we will brief Breandan on his mission."

"Are you certain that you're not underestimating Rhiannon's powers?" Salaran asked. "I know that you are quite capable of making an exact copy of the bird, but wouldn't it be easier to alter the creatures programming and send the original bird back to her?"

"Perhaps, but sending back the original bird has risks of its own," Thoradal stated. "Let us play the game by *our* rules to start with and see what develops. We may learn more this way."

The decision was unanimous. Thoradal would make a copy of the parrot to act as a spy for the league, and Breandan would go to Rhiannon's island to try and discover what the rogue-wizard girl was planning. Then the league would determine which course of action to take.

Breandan wanted to leave immediately, but was forced to postpone his departure while Thoradal created an exact duplicate of Rhiannon's parrot. Once Thoradal had completed his project, Breandan and all of the wizards gathered on the roof to see him unveil his masterpiece. The duplicate was perfect in every detail except for one. Rhiannon would only be able to see what the league wanted her to see.

Rhiannon smiled. She knew that Breandan was on his way to her. She could see him through the eyes of her familiar – the parrot. Breandan was traveling in the form of a seagull.

"Excellent," she said. "Melli, we must plan a feast. Not just any feast, mind you, but the greatest, most spectacular feast in the history of your people. It must be ready three days from now."

"Yes, my Queen," Melli replied nervously. "May I ask, what is the occasion? Is it your birthday?"

"My birthday? No, no, it's not my birthday. I'm expecting a visitor, an old friend."

Melli's eyes widened in surprise. "A visitor, my Queen? One like you?"

"Yes, like me. Well...almost like me. But my visitor is a man. A special friend. I hope you will understand."

"Oh," said Melli, "is this the one you told me of? The one you once followed to the top of the sky?"

Rhiannon looked at Melli and saw the worry in her eyes. "Yes, Melli," she said softly. "It's the same man. But do not fear. I know what I am doing. You'll just have to trust me."

"Will...will he be staying long?" Melli asked.

"If all goes according to plan, he'll be staying for a long time. If he does choose to stay, he and I will rule this island together. We will be unstoppable. Do you understand? Unstoppable!"

Melli shook her head. She did not understand. She did not want to understand.

"Never mind," Rhiannon snapped. She was beginning to run out of patience. "Just do as you are told and all will be well."

It was nearing dawn on the third day of the journey, and Breandan was growing anxious. The trip had been much more strenuous than he had expected. Even in the form of a seagull, he was getting tired, although his parrot companion seemed undaunted by time or distance. In fact, the copy Thoradal had made could fly continuously for many weeks without resting, for it was not an actual living creature, but a small mechanical robot.

Just before sunrise, Breandan mentally checked his heading

with the current position of the stars and found it to be true. Now, as the morning starlight merged with the light of the sun, all he could do was rely on the parrot's sense of direction. He only hoped that Thoradal's facsimile would fool Rhiannon as the old wizard had claimed it would.

The sun was a brilliant orange ball on the eastern horizon. As Breandan watched, its golden rays seemed to lever it up and out of the ocean depths. He watched it ascend into the sky until the light hurt his eyes, then he turned and looked south again and saw Rhiannon's island, surrounded by a sea of turquoise-blue water, just a few miles ahead.

No wonder Rhiannon chose this place, he thought, *even Petamor's enchanted plateau pales by comparison. I wouldn't mind living here myself if the circumstances were different.*

Rhiannon awoke with the dawn and dressed quickly into a red silk kimono. The silk was light and only weighed a fraction of what her old woolen robe had weighed. Although she now preferred to go half-naked like the natives, she knew that Breandan would not be expecting such a radical change in her behavior.

Breandan followed the parrot down into the village and glided to a landing on top of one of the native huts. Immediately the parrot began squawking, demanding that someone go and get the queen.

"Hurry, hurry!" exclaimed the parrot. "He is here, he is here! I have brought him. He is here! Hurry, hurry!"

A small group of the young adolescent girls saw the parrot and dashed off in the direction of the volcano. Assuming that they were on their way to inform Rhiannon of his arrival, Breandan followed them as they ran up a well-worn path through the village. He paused on the edge of a hut, turned his head to the left, and saw Topaz for the first time since that day he had left the escarpment. He was shocked at the horrific condition of the mystical beast. Its wings, once beautiful and majestic, had been shaven clean of their fur and now resembled the wings of a giant bat. Topaz's dull, red-rimmed eyes were full of misery and sadness.

Within moments Rhiannon appeared and began stroking the winged beast's neck and speaking to him softly. Suddenly, as if beckoned, she glanced around and spotted Breandan in his seagull form perched on top of a nearby hut. She smiled.

She's looking right at me. She knows it's me. Her wizardly senses are keener than my own. Breandan spread his wings, launched himself off his perch and glided to a landing near Rhiannon's feet. He transformed himself back into a man before her eyes.

"Breandan!" she shouted happily, as she ran into his arms. "Welcome to my island!" she added, hugging him tightly. Once again, just for a brief moment, Neraka had lost control of his host. In that brief moment, her emotions had overpowered the demon's hold on her. But Neraka quickly regained that control and tightened his grip like a python.

Much like the rock hopper, Breandan was not used to the heat, and his heavy woolen robe was not helping the situation. Rhiannon, sensing his discomfort, took him by the hand. "Come, my love," she said, "let us find you something a little cooler to wear. I'll have your robe washed and dried so that it will be fresh when you are ready to return north to Ravenwood." Breandan did not protest. A cooler wardrobe sounded good to him.

Rhiannon took him to her suite of rooms in her subterranean lair far beneath the volcano. "I have had some heartberry wine chilling in my room, waiting for your arrival. It's already ice-cold. It will refresh you. I'll have one of my girls bring you food as well."

"Thank you," he said, a little dismayed by Rhiannon's amount of confidence.

Melli abruptly appeared at the entrance to the cave. Breandan glanced at her as they passed, and she looked at him. Rhiannon took his hand and pulled him along, making no attempt to introduce them. *So this is the one who holds her heart,* Melli thought. *He is handsome, but he seems so young.*

Breandan turned his head and smiled at Melli. It was not a mean smile. It was full of warmth and kindness. Melli tried to smile back but failed. She ran out of the village and through the jungle until she found the little pool where she and Rhiannon often came to play and relax together. She crawled onto Rhiannon's rock and wept. As much as she wanted to believe Rhiannon's explanation for Breandan's visit, she had seen that special look in her eyes whenever she spoke of him. Her heart knew the truth.

Breandan sat opposite Rhiannon in a large chair constructed of bamboo rattan. Soft candlelight illuminated the small shadowy cavern creating an eerie, salamander effect on the surrounding walls. It made Breandan very uncomfortable.

Neraka felt right at home.

Two young serving girls poured heart-berry wine into goblets fashioned from conch shells. The wine was cold and refreshing and went straight to Breandan's head.

"So, what do you think of my little island thus far?" Rhiannon asked, sipping her wine.

"It's exactly as you described it in your letter," Breandan admitted. "It is very beautiful."

Rhiannon smiled. "And the robe? Is it also to your liking?"

"Yes," Breandan answered. "It's very comfortable, very suited for the climate." The robe he wore was identical in style and color to the robe Rhiannon had made him on the escarpment, except that this one was made of the lightweight silk instead of heavy wool.

"Of course it is. I made it myself," she added with a smile. "Wool is not appropriate in this tropical heat."

"Yes, and speaking of the heat. I must ask, I am a little concerned about Topaz. He doesn't look well at all. It is the heat, is it not? What happened to his wings?"

"Yes, you are correct. The heat has proven to be too much for him," Rhiannon said sadly. "I had no choice. I had to shave the fur off of his wings to save him."

"Yes, I suppose. He also appears a little...disoriented. When he looked at me earlier, I saw no recognition in his eyes. Is it possible the heat may have affected his brain?"

"What? Affected his brain? No, now don't be silly, Breandan. Topaz is just fine. He just needs is a little more time to adjust to the new climate. You know me. I always take good care of my animal friends."

Before Breandan could ask for further explanation, the two serving girls returned with several bowls of fresh fruit. In spite of his hunger, he waited patiently for Rhiannon to make her selection first. Then he chose a small pear-shaped fruit with orange flesh. It tasted wonderful.

"Topaz will be fine," Rhiannon finally continued, wiping juice from her chin with the back of her hand, "as long as I keep him out of the heat. My servants attend to him day and night to help keep him comfortable. He gets everything he needs. He couldn't be happier."

He sure didn't look happy, Breandan thought, but said, "Yes, but don't you think it would be best for him if you sent him back home to the escarpment."

"You can't be serious," Rhiannon said. "Besides, Topaz would never leave me. *He* is my one *true* friend."

Breandan felt the jibe, but kept quiet. He hadn't come here to provoke an argument. Nevertheless, this was certainly not the same Rhiannon he had grown up with. He still found it difficult to believe that she would knowingly allow an animal suffer just to satisfy her own ego.

"I must go," Rhiannon said, standing up abruptly. "I have to attend to several important matters before the celebration later tonight. Please, make yourself at home. When you have eaten your fill, one of my girls will take you to a quiet chamber where you can rest until the feast tonight in your honor."

Breandan stood up, but before he could speak, Rhiannon disappeared into the darkness beyond the candlelight. He slowly sank back down into his chair, picked up a banana, and began to peel off the skin. Thanks to the heart-berry wine, the ache in his arms was easing, but the ache in his heart was just beginning.

Later that evening, Breandan was awakened by a lovely young native girl. She said, "Come, the queen is waiting. It's time for the feast."

Breandan sat up in bed and looked around. There was no sign of Rhiannon. A number of candles lighted the small sleeping chamber, although their combined light barely illuminated the walls of the cave.

"Come," the girl insisted. "We must hurry. It is not good to keep the queen waiting."

Breandan looked up into the native girl's face and saw fear in her eyes. *What is she afraid of?* he wondered. *Is it me, or is it Rhiannon?*

Sighing, Breandan turned and was just about to put his feet on the cavern floor when he froze. For a brief moment, he wasn't sure if there would be a floor to put his feet on. The surreal atmosphere of the underground world had left him feeling disconnected and isolated from reality. He felt as if he were actually floating in space.

Impatiently, the young girl reached down, took his hand and tried to pull him to his feet, but she was far too small to accomplish the task alone. "All right, all right, I'm coming,"

Breandan told her as he stood up under his own power. "Lead the way. Take me to your queen."

By the time Breandan and his escort reached the site where the villagers were preparing the feast, the sky had turned jet black in the east, deep purple overhead, and blood orange in the west. The delicious aromas of roasting meats filled the air, causing his mouth to water in anticipation.

Rhiannon was waiting. She was seated on a large dais beneath a bamboo gazebo with a canopy of bright green palm leaves. The bamboo supports were interwoven with streamers of brightly colored silk that represented every color of the rainbow. It reminded Breandan of the softly burning lamps in the wizard's council chamber back on the escarpment. The connection was not lost on him. Whether she realized it or not, Rhiannon was attempting to recreate the ambiance of the council chamber here on this island.

The outer perimeter of the dais was surrounded with a variety of tropical plants and wild flowers. The flowers added their perfume to the night air. At Rhiannon's right stood the serving girl she called Melli, looking tense and depressed.

"Did you get any rest, my love?" Rhiannon asked with a smile as she greeted him. "You look a little tense. Come here and relax with me for a while. We have much to catch up on."

Breandan sat beside Rhiannon and tried to smile. He said, "Well, the flight here was very stressful. And I am not used to this heat."

"Don't worry, my darling. You will adjust to the weather in no time. But for now, let us celebrate our reunion with a wonderful feast. I hope that you are as hungry as I am," Rhiannon added with a seductive glance.

"Well, to use the old adage, I could eat a horse."

Topaz, who was standing next to the dais, snorted from

beneath the shade of his tree and gave Breandan a mild look of reproach.

Rhiannon laughed. "Sorry, but horse is not on the menu this evening."

"In that case, I will eat whatever you recommend. Everything smells so wonderful."

"Ah, first try this wonderful drink. It's called nee. The natives make it from fermented heart-berries and wild honey."

Breandan took the cup and drank. The nee was truly delicious, and truly potent. The moment it hit his stomach, he could feel a warm pleasant sensation begin to spread throughout his body. "This is very good," he said. "However, if you don't mind, I think that I would prefer plain water flavored with a little lemon if you have it."

"Don't be silly," Rhiannon said. "This is a special occasion. We have earned the right to relax and enjoy ourselves. We must have a real celebration for once. And you need not worry. You're safe here with me. I won't bite you. Unless, of course...you want me to," she added with a seductive smile.

Breandan shrugged. "Perhaps you're right," he said deciding to go along with the game. "We should celebrate. We've been through a lot together this past year."

"This past year? Breandan, we've been through nearly every major event together since we first learned how to walk. Now we have come to a crossroads, and we have some very important decisions to make. So let the feasting begin. We can talk of these things after we satisfy our...other needs."

Breandan could not help but notice how stunningly beautiful Rhiannon looked on this balmy evening. She was perfect in face and form. She really looked like a goddess, and a true queen.

Instead of her usual red kimono, Rhiannon had decided to go native and worn a plain grass skirt modestly trimmed to fall several inches above her knees. Her arms and legs were adorned with dozens of bracelets made with delicate coral beads. Yet unlike Melli and the other native girls, Rhiannon was not topless. As an alternative, she wore a golden breastplate custom designed to fit her body like a second skin. On her head, she wore a simple golden tiara embellished with dozens of white pearls.

"Do you approve?" Rhiannon asked when she noticed Breandan's stare.

"You certainly do look lovely tonight," Breandan admitted.

Men, Rhiannon thought, *show them a little skin and they will forget their own names.*

Neraka laughed, but the sound that came out of Rhiannon's mouth was so alien, it startled Breandan enough to cause him to flinch. Rhiannon did not seem to notice.

What in the world was that? Breandan asked himself. *That wasn't Rhiannon. That was something else entirely. I'm starting to think that Thoradal and the others wizards might be right after all. Rhiannon is possessed.*

Rhiannon gave the order and her servants began to serve the food. While they ate, they discussed some of the interesting things they had learned from their mentor, Petamor. Breandan avoided all talk of the forbidden knowledge. That particular subject would have to wait until later, when they were alone and sober.

Throughout the evening the feasting was accompanied by native music and dancing, and Rhiannon was pleased to note that despite all of the beautiful half-naked dancing girls, Breandan did not take his eyes off her once during the festivities.

Breandan drank very little of the potent nee, nevertheless the spicy food made it difficult to avoid altogether. Between Rhiannon's strange behavior, the hypnotic music, and the nee, his head was beginning to spin.

Suddenly, Rhiannon turned to him and said, "Breandan, my love, why don't you stay here and live here with me on the island. We could wed right here on this beach, on this gazebo.

We could have a native-style ceremony. We would be so happy together, Breandan. Just like we always dreamed."

Breandan tried to smile, but thanks to the nee, he was beginning to see double. "I'd love to spend the night with you, Rhi," he said. "I have been thinking about it...about us, for a long time. Right now, at this moment, it is all I *can* think about."

"I'm not talking about one night, Breandan. I am talking about forever. You and me," she added kissing him passionately on the lips. "We were always meant to be together," she continued. "You know that as well as I do."

"Forever?" he responded trying to clear away the intoxicating effects of the nee. "I wish it was possible, Rhi. But we made our decisions when we accepted membership in the league." "There are no rules within the league that prevent us from uniting. There are no laws against us becoming man and wife. We may be wizards, but we are also man and woman. We can change the world to suit our needs and our desires. We can make it over any way we like."

"Rhi, what are you talking about? Make over the world to suit our needs? You can't be serious. What's gotten into you? We took an oath to protect the people of this world from the exact thing that you are contemplating. Don't be foolish."

"Foolish?" Rhiannon responded, her eyes narrowing. "You think I am a fool, do you?"

For a few seconds, Breandan actually caught a glimpse of the demon in Rhiannon's eyes. He froze as an invisible bony fingertip traced an icy path up his spine.

Neraka, too, had seen into Breandan's eyes and was both surprised and frightened by the power this mild-mannered wizard-boy was capable of wielding if provoked.

"I'm sorry you feel that way," Rhiannon said, although the words sounded hollow, as if they were coming from a well deep within the ground. "We were friends once, so I won't hurt you." She turned and whispered something into Melli's ear.

"What's happening to you, Rhi? Please...stop this nonsense and let me help you," Breandan pleaded.

Rhiannon calmly took another sip of nee. "Help me?" she said as more hollow laughter echoed out of her mouth. "I do not need or desire your help. I am the most powerful wizard that has ever lived, and soon I will have more power than you could ever imagine. And don't think that I don't know the real reason you came here, Breandan. I know you came here to spy on me, didn't you?"

"Rhi, please, you've had too much to drink. We both have. You're not thinking straight. Let's discuss this again in the morning when we're both in our right minds. I'm sure that once you think about it, you will come to your senses."

Rhiannon was furious. She took a long swallow of nee and grabbed hold of her staff. She stood. When the villagers saw Rhiannon's sudden rage, they fell on their knees with their faces in the sand simpering and begging for mercy.

Breandan finally used his powers to clear his mind of the effects of the nee. It was a frivolous use of power that Petamor would frown upon; however, under the present circumstances, he was sure his old mentor would understand. He stood and took a step back away from Rhiannon.

"Rhi, get a hold of yourself. Can't you see that you are frightening these poor people?"

"These *poor* people are my subjects, and they fear me because *they* have seen the power I possess. As for you, you are a traitor. I have waited for you to wed me all of my life so that we could start a family together. But no! You had to become a wizard – a simple, ordinary magician. Well, I can work magic, too, and I am a lot better at it than you. I am better at it than all of you put together!"

Rhiannon raised her staff above her head and blue-black lightning split the heavens. In an instant, dark clouds materialized out of nowhere, blocking out the stars and the moons. The land on which they stood began to tremble.

"Stop this, Rhi!" Breandan yelled in the ancient tongue of the wizards. "Please, don't do this! It isn't necessary! I believe that you are more powerful. You don't have to prove anything."

The villagers, with the exception of Melli, who remained on her knees at her mistress's feet, scattered into the dark jungle.

"I'm sorry, Rhi," Breandan said. "Put a stop to this before it's too late."

Rhiannon looked at Breandan, and then she lowered her staff. Within seconds, the trembling stopped and the mysterious clouds dissipated as rapidly as they had appeared. "Very well," she answered. "However, I can assure you that what you just beheld is but a small sample of my powers. I can control the sea, Breandan. I can control the land. I can move continents if I so choose. I can make this volcano come alive even though it has been dead for hundreds of years. I can do all these things and more."

"Rhiannon---" Breandan began, using her full name for the first time since they were children.

"Stop," she said. "Go! Go now. Leave my island before I change my mind and destroy you. Never come here again unless you have a change of heart." Then she turned away to hide her tears.

Sensing there was nothing he could do, Breandan walked away towards the gentle surf until he was completely cloaked by darkness. A moment later, a lone seagull flew through the night sky heading due north.

Back in Petamor's tower, the League of Wizards had seen all, heard all, and witnessed all. They were shocked and deeply disturbed.

"What now?" asked Eeowyn.

"We will wait for Breandan's report. Then we will decide," Rimahorn stated.

———•———

Breandan wasted no time returning to the escarpment. Once clear of Rhiannon's island, he transformed himself from a seagull into a bolt of lightning and flashed through the sky at the speed of light. However, the amount of energy required for this type of travel would drain nearly all of his strength, leaving him weak and vulnerable for several days.

When Breandan arrived at the tower, he exploded through the window of the council chamber where he transformed himself back into his human form. Weak and pale, he collapsed onto the floor at the feet of his mentor, who had been in an intense argument for several minutes with Cinaran and Thoradal.

The three old wizards squatted down beside Breandan and began checking his vital signs. Thoradal was the first to speak. "Breandan, did you take the forbidden books? Did you take them and give them to Rhiannon? Tell me, lad," he spat angrily. "Tell me now!"

Breandan was too shocked and exhausted to speak. *Is Thoradal accusing* me *of stealing?* he wondered silently. "Books? What books are you talking about, Grandfather?" he managed to say before blacking out.

"Answer me, Breandan!" Thoradal shouted, shaking the unconscious boy wizard. "You had no right to take those books! They are off limits to you. Now where are they? Did you give them to Rhiannon? Answer me, lad, before I box your ears!" he continued, uncharacteristically enraged.

Petamor placed a gentle restraining hand on Thoradal's shoulder. "I have already told you, old friend. Breandan did not take the books," he said gently. "He could not have taken them. Rhiannon does have them. But it was she who took them. Somehow she has been able to acquire powers that we did not think her capable of possessing. Somehow she has managed to use her powers to steal the books right out from under our noses."

Thoradal looked at Petamor astonished. "How can that be? Rhiannon is still a child...a...a little girl. Where...*how* could she have acquired such power in such a short time? It...it is impossible, is it not?"

"It's true that in some respects Rhiannon is still a child, but she is a very powerful child. A female child. You and I both know that females have always possessed a greater power over nature than men, especially when it comes to magic. Moreover brother, she is a wizard," Petamor reminded him. "Remember?"

"Yes! She is a wizard, thanks to you!" Thoradal responded gruffly.

"Yes, this *is* all my fault. I was blinded by Rhiannon's innocence and charming personality. I should have known that something was different about her from the start. If I had only seen the signs, maybe I could have helped her. If I had only turned her away, sent her back home to her village, the thing that now possesses her would have left her alone. She would be safe. It doesn't want Rhiannon. It wants her power. And I allowed it access to that power. Now, this thing, this... this...demon, has taken control of her mind and body. Unless we can stop it, it will most likely use Rhiannon's powers to do great evil. Rhiannon is a prisoner in her own body. Now we have no choice but to deal with this very unpleasant situation. But tell me, old friend. What has gotten into *you* lately? I have never seen you behave like this before. What has happened to upset you?"

Thoradal lowered his head and sighed. He slowly stood up.

Petamor also stood.

"You are right of course. I do apologize. I know the lad could not have taken the books." Thoradal sighed again, closed his eyes and lowered his head. "On the night of the lighting of the lamp ceremony, when I looked up and saw my own death in the face of our old starship, I knew that the ship had not malfunctioned. You see, I have learned how to communicate with the ship at will."

"But how? Certainly not one of us---" Cinaran started.

"I don't know, exactly. All I know for certain is that Rhiannon was somehow responsible. Perhaps it was a conscious effort by the parasite within her to challenge us, or perhaps it was a subconscious appeal for help."

Breandan, nearly forgotten on the floor, stirred and attempted to sit up.

"Come, my friend," Petamor said. "Help me get Breandan to his room. His ordeal with Rhiannon may help us learn something about this demon that possesses her."

Several hours later, when Breandan finally came to his senses, he found himself in his old room with Petamor, Cinaran, and Thoradal at his bedside.

"What happened?" he asked. "How did I get here?"

"Don't you remember?" Petamor asked softly.

Breandan closed his eyes and tried to focus his thoughts. "Wait, it's coming back to me now. Rhiannon...the island...the feast...the nee."

"Nee?" asked Thoradal. "What is nee?"

"It is a beverage. A very intoxicating drink made from a combination of fermented heart-berries and wild honey," Breandan said.

"Heart-berries? Well, at least it cannot be too damaging if it was made from heart-berries," Petamor said.

"Tell us what happened from your perspective, lad. Tell us everything, every single detail," Thoradal said. "Leave nothing out."

The telling took some time, and Breandan recounted every detail of his meeting with Rhiannon. He even read them her original letter in its entirety. When he was finished he said, "We have to help her, Grandfather. We can't let that thing, whatever it is, destroy her life."

"That thing, as you called it, Breandan, is a demon," Thoradal stated.

"Yes, I believe you're right, old friend. It certainly sounds like a demon," Petamor agreed.

"I saw it, Grandfather," Breandan stated. "I looked into Rhiannon's eyes, and I saw it. A demon like the old one they called Norack?"

"Yes, Norack. Exactly," said Thoradal.

"I'm afraid that this is all my fault, Breandan. I should have seen the warning signs. *I did* see the signs, but I chose to ignore them," Petamor said with a sigh. "Now it may be too late to save Rhiannon and send this demon back to where it came from."

"We're all at fault to one degree or the other. We all saw the signs," Thoradal admitted. "We allowed this problem to escalate unchecked. If only I had insisted that we addressed this issue on the night of the ceremony, we could have averted this problem. I should have pointed out the possibility that much of Rhiannon's amazing and unusual ability to retain such a vast amount of knowledge in so short a time might be coming from some other source. In this case, as we now know, a supernatural source. Maybe some of you would have listened."

"Well...we are listening now," Petamor assured them.

Thoradal nodded. "Breandan, you must get some rest because we are going to need your help most of all. Do you think you will be strong enough to make another trip to the island?"

"Yes, Grandfather. I'll go back to the island if there's any chance that we can save Rhiannon. I would give up my life for her. This is my fault. If I had only remained in our village and wedded her like she wanted, this never would've happened."

"We all make our own choices in this life, Breandan, be they good or bad, and we all have to learn to live with our mistakes," Cinaran said. "That is how we learn."

"All right," said Thoradal. "We must let Breandan rest for a time while we summon the other members of the league. We must be quick. Every moment counts."

———•———

Rhiannon stood alone on the beach. Five days had passed since Breandan's brief visit. She deeply regretted her little outburst and hoped that Breandan had been too intoxicated to remember most of the terrible things that she had said. Unfortunately, time was running out and she could not afford to wait any longer. It was now apparent that he had decided to side with the league. It was also a certainty that the league would respond to her proposal sooner rather than later.

Neraka was very excited. At last, it was time to show the league Rhiannon's extraordinary powers.

At the demon's bidding, Rhiannon raised her staff and closed her eyes in concentration. Blue-black lightning erupted from its black-pearl crown and blasted into the waves lapping at her feet. For one brief moment, the ocean itself seemed frozen in place as the waves shuddered and came to a complete stop. From under the motionless surface came a mighty rumbling, and then the water began to move again. Wave after wave surged away from the island, increasing in size and speed as they went.

Rhiannon, weakened by the effort, stumbled back and collapsed onto the sand.

Neraka laughed.

As the waves moved away from the island, they would continue to grow in size. By the time they reached the southern mainland of Pega, they would tower anywhere between two and three hundred feet high. They would slam into the unprotected coast like a battering ram, crushing everything before them for miles.

Neraka's laughter became a howl of satisfaction. His hatred for the wizards squirmed inside of Rhiannon's brain like a million greedy maggots eagerly devouring her sanity. *Soon, those pathetic creatures that call themselves wizards will crawl to me and beg for mercy. They will crawl to me on their bellies, and they will beg to worship me.*

Several hours later, just as the sun was about to retire for the night, the gigantic tidal waves began slamming into the southern half of the continent of Pega. There was little warning and no time to escape. By the time the sun had disappeared into the savage sea, every coastal village and town along the southern coastline had been completely wiped off the face of the planet. Nearly every living thing, including men, women, and children, was either drown or pulverized by the chain of tsunamis. And it was not over. Although the force of the waves diminished over distance, they continued to erase the hundreds of small communities along both the western and eastern seaboards until they eventually ran out of energy.

Thoradal suddenly rose from his chair clutching his chest. His face had turned a ghastly shade of gray and he grabbed desperately at the edge of the heavy oaken table before him.

The league had been in disagreement since they had been called to order. Some members wanted to destroy Rhiannon immediately together with the entity that now controlled her, but the remaining members of the league wanted to intervene and attempt to save Rhiannon and exorcise the demon that possessed her.

As Thoradal stood, all eyes turned towards him. Then the

old wizard slumped back down into his chair, his dark hazel eyes full of tears.

"Old friends," he began, his voice barely a whisper, "I'm afraid that I have some very bad news. We are too late. Rhiannon has struck the first blow. The planet cries out to me in pain. Thousands are dead. Many more are injured and dying. I can hear their screams. I can sense their terror. I can feel the weight of the destruction rushing up through the very foundations of this granite tower."

Salaran hurried over to the stricken wizard. "What are you talking about, Thoradal? Tell us! What is it? What has she done?"

"Rhiannon has gone insane! She must be stopped!" Thoradal stated. "Can't you feel it? Thousands of innocent people are dead or dying! I tell you, she is responsible. The demon that now possesses her has driven her mad! She must be destroyed, completely and utterly before she can inflict any more damage."

The other wizards were all wondering the same thing. They looked at each other and then back at Thoradal. However, Thoradal had buried his face in his hands in grief.

"Salaran, can you go out and have a look?" Rimahorn asked quietly. "Try and see if you can locate the site of this...disaster. If Thoradal is correct, there still may be time to help the victims."

"It's too late. She has deceived us all. She lured Breandan to her lair to distract us. The invitation for Breandan to join with her was only a scheme meant to lure us away from our people. She knew we would gather here at the tower to discuss the situation. She knew that by doing so, we would be leaving our people vulnerable. We fell right into her trap. If we had stayed where we belonged instead of coming here to bicker over how to handle this...this presumptuous child, we may have been able to prevent this disaster."

At that moment, Breandan walked into the council chamber on wobbly legs. When he saw all of their drawn faces, he asked, "What is it? What has happened?"

Petamor looked up. "Sit down, Breandan, please. I...I'm not sure how to tell you this. It appears that...it appears that Rhiannon has declared war on the citizens of Pega. She may have used the earth power to destroy a large number of innocent people."

"Yes," Breandan replied grimly, lowering his head, "I felt it too."

———•———

Rhiannon relaxed in the comfort of her cave retreat. Melli, as always, was at her feet ready to do her bidding. Both young women were drinking nee.

Neraka was relaxing too, enjoying the euphoric feeling of victory in the wake of the destruction it had instigated. *This will teach those meddling wizards a lesson. They will attempt to retaliate against me, but we are powerful enough to defend ourselves against any magic they wish to use against us.*

Suddenly Rhiannon jumped to her feet, accidentally knocking Melli to the stone floor. The deranged wizard-girl ran from the cave and into the warm tropical night. She climbed onto Topaz's back and urged the beast skyward. She guided him to the pinnacle of the dead rock.

A few moments later, Rhiannon and Topaz landed on the high rim of the volcanic crater. Rhiannon dismounted, closed her eyes, lifted her staff high into the air, and spoke the forbidden words of destruction. She used the ancient language of the wizard's race. The words she spoke had never been spoken aloud on her world before.

At her command, dark angry clouds began to gather over the far distant land of Pega. Tornados formed by the hundreds and began to etch their destruction across the countryside with pinpoint accuracy, while hurricanes raped and scoured what remained. To the north, titanic glaciers that covered the polar regions, began to split and fragment into icebergs that immediately began to melt as they began drifting south through the northern ocean.

***

Back in the council chamber, high in the tower keep, the urgency of the situation showed on the faces of the wizards huddled around the conference table.

Although Petamor's escarpment was protected from most climatic conditions by the enchantment, it too, could not survive if the dramatic earth changes that were happening all over the planet continued unchecked. As it were, sea levels were rising rapidly, and the continent of Pega was slowly sinking into the ocean. Nevertheless, Thoradal's latest plan was meeting with some strong resistance from some members of the league.

"I tell you all, it is a necessary risk," Thoradal insisted. "Individually, we cannot hope to defeat Rhiannon. She has grown much too powerful. However, if we remove the enchantment from the plateau, we'll be free to combining all of our powers into one and put an end to this destruction."

"If we remove the enchantment," Salaran began, "we'll be vulnerable to an attack. We'll be placing ourselves at her mercy."

"Not necessarily," Petamor admitted. "Rhiannon would not dare to attack us with earth power as long as the Allacor's original enchantment remains intact. She knows that he has placed a number of booby traps within the enchantment that will backfire upon her if she attacks the escarpment directly. Therefore, she will not be expecting us to remove the enchantment. It's very possible that she will not even realize that we have removed the enchantment until it is too late for her to use the earth power against us."

"She doesn't have to attack the escarpment directly,"

Salaran said. "If Pega sinks into the ocean, the escarpment, this keep and everything with it will also go into the sea."

"Petamor is right. We can only hope to defeat her if we attack her with our total combined strength, and maintaining the enchantment is draining far too much of our power," Thoradal added.

"We cannot simply kill Rhiannon as if she were nothing more than a rabid dog!" Breandan exclaimed angrily. "This is not her fault! She is being manipulated by that...that thing!"

"Are you completely certain of that?" Thoradal asked. "For all we know, she may have been in league with this entity from the start. She may even have invited it here."

"What! No! No, that's insane!" Breandan exclaimed. "Rhiannon would never do a thing like that."

"Really?" asked Thoradal. "It's a well known fact that many young girls Rhiannon's age like to dabble in sorcery. They play with witch boards, try to talk to the dead, burn black candles, have séances to summon ghosts. Perhaps she conjured up this demon of her own free will. We all know how powerful she has become. Where did all that power come from? Ordinarily it would take years and years of study and research to obtain that kind of power. Nevertheless Rhiannon managed to accomplish it in only one year, and not one of us bothered to question that extraordinary accomplishment."

"It no longer matters how or where Rhiannon acquired her powers. She has them. Now it is up to us to take them away from her by any means necessary," Rimahorn stated.

"Please...don't kill her," Breandan pleaded. "I know that she did not voluntarily agree to take part in this demon's scheme. She has a good heart...a...a pure heart!"

"I'm glad you feel so strongly, Breandan," Rimahorn said. "Because your role in our strategy is paramount to its success."

"I'll do anything you ask of me, but I will not harm Rhiannon," Breandan said.

"We're not asking you to hurt her," Petamor added. "But I trust you will do whatever you feel is necessary to stop her before she kills again."

Breandan looked into the sad face of his mentor. He saw the sorrow and grief there and understood how difficult this was for him. He loved Rhiannon, too. Breandan nodded, "Yes, Grandfather. I'll do whatever is necessary to stop her."

"Can we get on with this?" Cinaran insisted. "What is the rest of your plan, Thoradal?"

"Breandan must return to Rhiannon's island. The rest of us will remain here to concentrate our powers into one. That way, when the right moment comes, we will be able to channel all of our powers through Breandan," Thoradal said.

"You mean *if* the right moment comes," Rimahorn added.

"Correct," Thoradal granted, "*if* the right moment comes."

"If I go back, Rhiannon will automatically assume that I have changed my mind and have decided to collaborate with her," Breandan said. "I'm not a very good actor. She will see through my ruse quickly. Then what?"

"Rhiannon will believe you because she wants to believe you, Breandan," Rimahorn said. "And this demon of hers is too arrogant not to believe you."

"Not for long," Breandan said. "Rhiannon's not stupid."

"Hopefully, it will be long enough," Thoradal said. "All you'll have to do is touch her one time."

"That's it? That's all?" Breandan replied. "Just touch her?"

"One touch is all it should take," Petamor said.

"Yes. At that very moment, we will channel all of our energy into you. If we are lucky, we can catch her off guard. We can use our combined powers to stun her. She will feel as if she had been struck by lightning. It will temporarily drain her of her powers," Thoradal explained.

"It won't kill her, will it?" Breandan asked.

"No," Thoradal finished.

"It's too simple," Salaran concluded.

"That is exactly why it will succeed," Thoradal said. "Rhiannon has become so over confident, that she will not be expecting any danger from something as harmless as a mere touch of a hand. She believes that only extreme force can bring her down."

"All right," Breandan agreed. "Then what?"

"As I was saying, first we must use our combined powers to render her helpless. That one touch should be severe enough to result in her losing consciousness."

"Yes, but for how long?" Breandan asked.

"We cannot be sure, maybe only a matter of seconds. During that time, you will have to incapacitate her long enough to transport her back here to the keep before she has a chance to recover," Thoradal continued.

"Once she is within these walls," Petamor added, "we will have the upper hand. Her powers will be useless. We will have to keep her sedated, of course, until we exorcise the demon, but that should not pose a problem."

"And what if we cannot exorcise the demon?" Breandan questioned.

Neither Petamor nor Thoradal answered the question. They just looked at each other with grim expressions on their haggard old faces.

Breandan sighed. "When do I leave?" he asked.

"Just as soon as we remove the enchantment from the plateau," Thoradal answered.

———•———

On the roof of the keep, a warm breeze swirled gently around the feet of the wizards, filling the late-afternoon air with the scent of pine and wildflowers. Silvery fish jumped in the lake surrounding the tiny granite isle, while woodland birds sang their happy songs, unaware of the devastating changes that were about to take place in their perfect world.

Petamor's mentor had cast the original enchantment over

nine hundred years earlier. Petamor, Thoradal, and Rimahorn together had later enhanced the spell to restore it to its full integrity. However, constantly maintaining the enchantment took a great deal of energy.

As the three elderly wizards took their places around the tower roof, they were joined by their fellow wizards who were there to lend their emotional support. With one last look out over the lake at the enchanted land that had once been their crowning achievement, they took their positions like the numbers on a clock, and faced one another.

While the other wizards watched in reverent silence, Petamor, Thoradal, and Rimahorn held out their staffs. They closed their eyes, bowed their heads, and began to chant in unison. They spoke the ancient language of their home world. Slowly their voices grew in resonance until three identical rainbows shot skyward from the tips of their staffs, filling the heavens from horizon to horizon with a sea of color. The colors undulated and changed in the nearly cloudless sky like the wheel of a gigantic kaleidoscope. Then, from the center of the triangle, a dull white light erupted into the dome of color. The white light grew in intensity from its center until it totally obscured the rainbow sky and shrouded it like a foggy umbrella. The three wizards then leaned their staffs forward until the crowns of the staffs touched with a distinctive click. In that instant, the shroud of fog shattered like an old mirror, raining snowflake-sized ash down over the plateau. The enchantment was broken.

In the blink of an eye the wizard's plateau returned to its natural state. Where moments earlier the trees of the forests had been laden with the green of summer, they now stood barren of leaf with winter branch. Where the sky had been the blue of summer, it was now the slate-gray of deep winter. In that instant, the lake surrounding the tower froze over and snow now covered the land like a thick woolen blanket.

Rhiannon was busy preparing a defense of her island. She had discovered that her volcano contained a much more complex system of underground tunnels than she had originally estimated. She used her powers to open additional passageways and chambers until the entire complex resembled the empire of a giant queen ant. Rhiannon even opened several additional underground passages that connected to the ocean, creating large subterranean pools and harbors at strategic points beneath the island development.

From the very heart of the volcano in the deepest roots of the mountain, Rhiannon found a small deposit of extremely rare red-gold, Breandan's main power source. Neraka instantly devised a plan and passed it on to Rhiannon. If at any time Breandan returned to the island, she would use his own power source – the red-gold – to capture and imprison him. She could then hold him for ransom or as a bargaining tool should the need arise. First, however, she would need to fashion and mold a special red-gold ring. If necessary, this ring would become Breandan's prison. Although she could have easily created the ring using her magical powers, the books of earth lore demanded that it be forged by hand in the ancient tradition.

The wizards stood upon their tower gazing out in awe at the frozen wasteland that only moments ago had been a beautiful mid-summer wonderland. However, none of them was as unhappy with the desecration of the plateau as old Petamor. "Breandan," he said, "you'd better be on your way. We are all aware that you have not completely recovered from your first confrontation with Rhiannon. Unfortunately we do not have time to delay."

"Yes, Grandfather," Breandan replied, hugging Petamor

tightly. "I feel much better than I did when I first returned. You needn't worry about me. I'll be fine."

"I will always worry about you, Breandan," Petamor said. "I think of you as the grandson I never had," he added, embracing Breandan again briefly.

"This is all very touching," Thoradal began, "but you really do need to get moving, Breandan. Speed is of the essence."

Breandan nodded.

"Remember, lad," said Rimahorn, "it's not really Rhiannon with whom you will be dealing. She's merely the instrument of the demonic entity that is manipulating her. If you anger the demon, Rhiannon may not be strong enough to prevent it from killing you."

"I'll be careful, Grandfather."

"As like the last time, lad, we will be seeing through your eyes. We will be there with you, both in spirit and in power. Be ready and remember," Rimahorn said. "one touch is all you will need."

Breandan nodded and thanked each of the wizards as they wished him luck. Finally, they left him alone on the roof so that he could prepare himself mentally for the mission. He took a deep breath, closed his eyes, and rested his forehead against his staff. *Rhi, I love you. I have been such a fool to think otherwise. I know that you can fight this thing that possesses you. Together we will cast it out and destroy it. Then, if you are still willing, we can get married, just as you have dreamt all these years. To hell with wizards and their magic. You were right all along. I should have listened to you. I just hope that it's not too late.*

After a few moments, the red-gold bands on his staff began to glow and hum. Abruptly, both he and his staff transformed into a reddish-gold bolt of lightning and shot up into the sky until he was high above the tower. In the blink of an eye he was gone, jetting across the heavens to whatever fate awaited him in the Southern Reaches.

In the council chamber the League of Wizards prepared for their confrontation with Rhiannon and her demon. They moved the great table to one side and sat on the floor in a circle facing each other. Then they laid their staffs on the floor like the spokes of a great wheel with the crowns touching in the center. Each wizard sat at the base of their staff and waited in quiet contemplation for the critical encounter.

Moving at the speed of light, Breandan passed over the southern half of the continent and saw for himself some of the destruction brought about by Rhiannon's use of the earth and sea power. It was clear why the magic had been forbidden; however, it was far from clear why Rhiannon would commit such a crime, possessed or not.

As he channeled these images of the destruction back to the wizards in the tower, he could feel their shock as they reacted to the devastation. He heard the familiar voice of Rimahorn in his head say, "It's much worse than we thought! Hurry, lad! Hurry!"

Thoughts of Rhiannon began to race through his head again. *How could Rhiannon have become a pawn to such evil? Can we really save her after this? Do we really want to save her after all of this?* Breandan asked himself as he looked down at the ruins of the coastal villages and once prosperous river towns. *Is it possible to free her from this unknown entity? Will she be the same once she has learned what she has done? Will she ever be able to forgive herself knowing that her actions have taken the lives of thousands of men, women, and children?* Minutes passed and then Rhiannon's island came into view. It was past sunset in this part of the world as Breandan came to rest in the very same clearing where Rhiannon had first shown him a sample of her power. As soon as he returned to his human form, he started down the jungle corridor that led to the village and the rouge wizard. He should have been exhausted after his trip, but he had the strength and power of the league behind him. Yet he was afraid. Not for himself, but for what could happen to the world if the demon continued to have its way. Then he heard another voice in his head. This time it was Petamor. "You can do it, Breandan. Be brave!" He ran the rest of the way to the village.

———•———

Rhiannon was busy putting the final touches on the red-gold ring she had fashioned when she first became aware that Breandan had arrived on the island. The demon inside her was delighted, causing Rhiannon's face to twist into a hideously evil grin. She slid the ring onto her finger and closed her eyes. With her wizardly senses she could see Breandan entering the village on the western side of the complex, but she was too excited to sense his fear. Neraka was too arrogant to sense anything but impending victory.

Neraka's plan was simple. All Rhiannon needed to do was touch Breandan with the hand that displayed the ring. One touch, and Breandan's powers, as well as his life force, would be drawn into the ring, where he would be trapped and completely powerless.

Neraka laughed, and an unspeakable sound issued force from Rhiannon's mouth.

Breandan had come here to hurt her, of that Rhiannon had little doubt. But even if he had returned to the island to join her, she had no time to waste in establishing the truth, and she was not willing to take the risk. She could always free him later if she chose to; he would make a useful plaything. As for now, she would not allow him to interfere with her work.

Breandan was drawing closer, only a few steps away now.

Rhiannon removed her kimono. She thrust her hand into the open flame of a nearby torch. The fire could not hurt her;

she was protected by her magic. The harmless flames soon engulfed her beautiful, naked body. There was no pain, it only tickled. She laughed again and then stepped out of the flames, her body was undamaged by the fire. Then she stepped out into the night and into the presence of the boy-wizard.

Breandan had caught a glimpse of Rhiannon seconds before she had emerged from the fire. He had been astounded. The burning yellow and orange flames had licked her body like a thousand hungry tongues, but her powerful magic had protected her.

Rhiannon smiled and beckoned him forward. She extended her hand. The newly forged ring of red-gold glittering in the firelight. However, Breandan was not looking at her hand. It was her demonic eyes that had arrested his attention. The yellow eyes of the demon glared out at him.

"Come to me, my love," she said, "and we will rule this world together."

As Breandan stepped closer, Rhiannon's demonic eyes began to glow with the red-hot intensity of a blast furnace.

Far away in Petamor's tower, the stunned wizards prepared for the ultimate touch.

Breandan reached out to take Rhiannon's hand, desperately hoping that Thoradal's plan would work. "Rhi---" he began. It would be the last word he ever speak.

Unaware and unprepared for each other's plan, they touched hands.

In that unforgettable moment, most of Breandan's life force was instantly drawn out of him and into Rhiannon's ring, and his telepathic link with the league was immediately broken. His nearly lifeless body collapsed to the ground. Rhiannon, her powers temporarily checked, stumbled back in shock from the league's attempt to subdue her. She fell backwards into the flame of the torch. Again, the ravenous flames engulfed her body, only this time Rhiannon's weakened powers could not protect her. The merciless fire melted away her beauty in less than a heartbeat. Her ghastly screams could be heard across the island and into the very hearts of the wizards. In that moment of agony, Rhiannon and her demon were fused together as they had never been before. Her staff, now nothing more than a twisted blackened useless stick, lay on the ground beside her.

Far away in their lofty tower, the wizards were flung back onto the floor with such a tremendous force that they would lie comatose for hours before regaining consciousness.

Melli and the other natives, who had been hiding in the caves as Rhiannon had previously instructed, came running when they heard her scream. When they arrived they discovered Rhiannon's burnt and blackened body lying on her right side on the ground, smoldering. Most of her hair was gone, eaten away by the hungry flames. Her ears and nose had melted like candle wax.

Melli, believing that Breandan was responsible for killing her queen, picked up his staff and was about to use it to crush his skull when Rhiannon raised up and screamed. "No, Melli! Don't kill him! Leave him alone!" Melli jumped back, for she had been certain that Rhiannon, as badly burned as she had appeared, was dead.

"Take him---" Rhiannon gasped through clenched teeth, "---take him to the chamber I prepared for him. And I warn you. Do not harm him in any way."

For a moment, all the villagers could do was stare at Rhiannon's horribly burned body. Her burns would have killed an ordinary mortal, but Rhiannon was no ordinary mortal. Nevertheless, the pain was certainly real enough, and that she could not escape so easily.

Upon seeing their hesitation, Rhiannon growled, "I said, take him away!" Then she regained her composer, her voice suddenly calm and clear. "Give his staff to me," she commanded.

The grief stricken native girl obeyed.

Rhiannon pointed Breandan's staff at one of the innocent villagers. The young man's body exploded, showering the others in the entrance with blood and gore. "The next time I give you an order," Rhiannon screamed, "you will obey me at once or you will die. Now take him below!"

The terrified men picked up Breandan's limp body and carried him away into the bowels of the volcano.

Melli remained behind with Rhiannon.

Rhiannon looked at her for a long moment. "Go on now, Melli," she said softly. "Sound the alarm. I want you to get Topaz and everyone inside the caves as quickly as possible. I have work to do here."

Melli left the chamber immediately.

Rhiannon began to gather all of her remaining strength. With her own staff destroyed by the flames, Breandan's staff would have to suffice. It contained all of the power she needed for the task at hand. Slowly, she closed her eyes and spoke the forbidden words in the old language. Within seconds, the ground began to tremble at her feet. Fine dust and tiny pebbles began to rain down around her as all of the outer entrances to the cave system began to collapse. In less than five minutes, Rhiannon's underground lair was sealed off from the outside world. Then the island began to sink into the sea.

A short time later, Melli returned to the entrance chamber and helped Rhiannon to her bedchamber.

Rhiannon was in great agony, but she would never allow the pain to defeat her. *The League wants a war,* she thought, *so I will give them a war they will never forget.*

The sea surrounding Rhiannon's island churned and boiled for several more hours until the once peaceful tropical isle disappeared entirely beneath the waves. When the ocean surface finally returned to normal, it was as if the island had never existed.

Petamor and the other wizards gradually recovered from their confrontation with Rhiannon. All of their powers had been significantly weakened, and they still did not know for certain whether or not Rhiannon had been destroyed.

What they did know for certain, was that more than half of the population of Pega had died during the cataclysm, and many more were destined to die in the ensuing famine that was certain to follow in the wake of the catastrophe.

Petamor was the first of the league to check Rhiannon's Lamp of Life. The flame of her lamp spit and sputtered, but still burned, indicating that she was weak, but still alive.

"Rhiannon lives," he said astonished. "We have failed to destroy her." Carefully, he picked up Breandan's lamp. Although the flame had been extinguished for some time, the lamp remained warm to the touch. "Odd," he said, "I fear Breandan may be dead...or worse."

"He understood the risk," Thoradal said. "His sacrifice may have saved countless lives."

"Yet, if Rhiannon still lives, then so lives the demon," Rimahorn said.

"True," Eeowyn admitted. "It is also possible that the demon may have fled during the confrontation. It may already have found another host."

"That is a possibility," agreed Rimahorn. "It may also be that we miscalculated the strength of our assault. Rhiannon may be dying. That would explain why the flame in her lamp is sputtering."

"*If* she is dying," Eeowyn added. "She may yet recover."

"The problem is we won't know the answers to these questions. We must send someone down there to have a look at Rhiannon's island. Salaran? I know that this is the second time we've had to ask you, but you are the strongest and the fastest member of the league. Will you go and have a look?"

Salaran nodded saying, "I will go." He immediately walked to the window to prepare himself for the transformation.

To hide his pain and grief, Petamor turned his face away from his colleagues. He cradled Breandan's lamp for a few more seconds before returning it to its niche. When he turned around again, Salaran was gone.

"Salaran is quick and efficient, therefore we should have a report within the next few hours," Rimahorn said. "In the meantime, Petamor, why don't you try and get some rest? I know how hard this has been on you."

"I'll be fine. Besides, I won't be able to sleep until we learn what has happened to Breandan and Rhiannon."

Rimahorn picked up Breandan's lamp and held it between his own hands. His eyes widened. "Petamor! The lamp! It's still warm! Even though we were unconscious for hours, the lamp has not cooled. This can only mean one thing! Breandan must still be alive!"

"Is that possible?" Petamor asked.

"Here," Rimahorn said to Thoradal. "Take the lamp and tell us what *you* think."

Thoradal held the lamp. "I don't know what to say. The flame has died, but the lamp remains warm to the touch. What does it mean? Does anyone know?"

Eeowyn took the lamp. "*It is warm!* Perhaps Breandan is still alive, but in some sort of altered mental state or imposed hibernation. A coma perhaps."

"Perhaps Rhiannon has trapped him in some sort of enchanted prison...a...a... limbo of sorts...alive, yet helpless. He may be unable to contact us or use his powers to escape," Cinaran added.

"If that is the case, we must find a way to rescue him at once!" Petamor exclaimed. "We owe him that."

———•———

Four hours later, Salaran returned only to confirm the worst. Due to the melting polar icecaps, nearly a third of the continent of Pega had already been swallowed up by the rising floodwaters. Many of the survivors were now fleeing to the highlands in the north in a desperate attempt to escape the deluge. Some of those survivors, fearing that the waters were going to continue to rise, were attempting to climb the escarpment wall to the safety of the plateau. The rocks at the base of the escarpment were already littered with the bodies of those who had tried and failed to reach the top.

"And Rhiannon? Was there any sign of her?" Thoradal asked.

"I followed the coordinates that she gave Breandan, but there was nothing there, only empty ocean. Her island was nowhere to be found. I think perhaps the island may have been destroyed by her own hand, or perhaps it sank to the ocean bottom," Salaran said.

"Well, what do we do now?" Eeowyn asked.

"There is nothing more we can do but wait. In the meantime, I think the rest of you should return to your clans."

"What about the people who are trying to climb the escarpment wall?" Eeowyn asked.

"My powers have been weakened. There is nothing I can do to help them until they reach the safety of the plateau," Petamor said.

"Petamor is right," Rimahorn agreed. "We must return at once to what is left of our clans. Our powers may have been weakened, but there is still much we can do to help our people."

"What about Rhiannon?" Eeowyn asked. "If she still lives, she may attack again."

"I doubt if Rhiannon is strong enough to continue the offensive," said Rimahorn.

"Yes," Thoradal agreed, "I concur. If Rhiannon's power remained intact, she would have continued her attack. No, she will not attack us again anytime soon. Like us, she will need time to nurse her powers back to health. She has been seriously wounded. She used what was left of her strength to sink her island to the ocean floor. It will be some time before she can strike at us again."

"Here, we don't mean to interrupt your discussion, Mr. Thoradal, sir. But who's going to look out for our village?" Ragi asked, as he entered from the kitchen carrying a large decanter of wine. "I'm sorry. I didn't mean to eavesdrop. I was just bringing you all something to ease your nerves. It's not my fault if I overheard. But if Mr. Petamor goes back to Mr. Breandan's village, who's going protect our village on the northern side of the escarpment?"

Thoradal said. "Well, Ragi, since my entire clan was wiped out by one of Rhiannon's tidal waves, I have no one to protect. I would be honored if you and your clan would accept my protection."

Ragi put the decanter on the table. "Well, no offense, Mr. Thoradal, sir," he said, sticking his hands in his pockets, "but that doesn't sound very reassuring."

"You're right, Ragi," Thoradal admitted. "I should have been there to protect them. I let them down. However, I can promise you that it will not happen again."

"No," Petamor said. "It's not your fault, old friend. None of us could have anticipated Rhiannon's unprecedented attack on the innocent people of this land. If any of us are at fault here, it is me."

"Stop," Rimahorn said, "enough of this self pity. There's no need to go over it repeatedly. We're all to blame, here, not just Thoradal or Petamor. This just goes to prove that the demon has complete and total control over her. Ragi...Nikulas, you need not fear. From now on, your village and your clan will be protected by Thoradal. He is one of the wisest and most courageous members of this league. He will not fail you."

"You have my word on that, Ragi," Thoradal added.

"Alright then. I feel a little better now," Ragi admitted. "No offense, Mr. Thoradal, sir."

"None taken, lad."

At last, it was agreed. Despite their weakened powers, each member of the league left the Wizard's Escarpment in order to help the survivors of the holocaust as best they could.

Thoradal went to the village of Lorelei below the northern wall of the escarpment where the rising waters had already claimed more than two-thirds of the available land. He promised that someday, he would lead the people of that land to a new home where they would be safe.

Petamor went to Breandan's village of Ravenwood. Cinaran, Salaran, and the rest, returned home to help the survivors of their own clans.

And for a time there was peace in the world.

****

INTERLUDE

By THE TIME THE holocaust ended, the topography of Nox had been permanently and drastically altered forever.

Petamor managed to guide a few of the survivors, one hundred and fourteen to be exact, to the safety on the plateau. Most of them were women. All of them were young. Petamor gave them shelter from the remaining winter storms in his tower. When springtime arrived, they built a new settlement on the western shore of the lake using stone quarried from the Finger Mountains.

Occasionally, Petamor would venture into the lowlands where he had managed to collect enough stray herd animals to establish a good breeding stock for his new clan. Although most of his powers had returned, they were comparatively weaker than they had once been. From time to time, the old wizard would go on an expedition into the occupied lands of the south, often being away from the plateau for days at a time. Soon days turned into months, and months turned into years until, one day, old Petamor was nothing more to the people of the escarpment than a bedtime story told to young children late at night by their grandfathers while the wind howled in the eves.

As the years passed, the settlement on the escarpment grew in size and population. Gradually their social structure evolved and the settlers began to specialize in a variety of professions. There were leather workers, dressmakers, metalworkers, woodcutters, farmers, and shepherds, to name a few. And, of course, there were the warriors. These warriors quickly became the elite of their society. They were a very unorthodox group, for they were all women – and it all had begun on a dare.

Everyone who had lived on the escarpment in the early days knew the story of the wizard-girl named Rhiannon, who had tamed a wild rock hopper. One day, a young and very persistent shepherd girl named Shona was arguing with her friends. They did not believe the old stories, but Shona insisted that the stories were true. One of the other girls challenged her to prove it. As a result, Shona began spending most of her free time in the Finger Mountains letting the rock hoppers get accustomed to her presence. She stayed especially close to one in particular. After some time, the rock hopper became accustomed to her presence, and no longer regarded her with suspicion. One day, Shona reached out and gently stroked the animal's mane. The animal twitched his ears nervously but did not attempt to escape. She hand-fed him some fresh carrots she had brought with her from home. Day-after-day she returned, until at last, the winged creature allowed her to climb onto its back. It took months of love and patience, but eventually the two became inseparable. Later, other young women would follow Shona's example and domesticate more of the skittish creatures.

The village elders quickly recognized the strategic advantages that these unusual pairs could have in defending the settlement against enemies. They began training the young riders in the art of combat. Before long, entire aerial squadrons of the winged warriors could be seen flying above the countryside. In time, the people of the escarpment became known as the Pegazons.

Far to the west of Pega, the Horranian Empire flourished in the turmoil. When the Horranian emperor learned of the destruction on Pega, he quickly dispatched an invasion fleet to take advantage of the situation. Eventually, his bloodthirsty forces would gain control over all of the land south of the escarpment, enslaving more than eighty-five percent of the remaining human population.

Thoradal followed Nikulas and Ragi to their isolated village along the northern wall of the escarpment. This narrow strip of land had been left untouched by Rhiannon's initial assault on the land to the south; however, rising sea levels had swallowed up more than half of their territory.

Thoradal thought it best that they leave their ancient homeland behind and find a new home. Accordingly, he gathered the two-hundred and fifty-three men, women, and children who lived on the narrow strip of land and instructed them to build enough ships to carry the entire clan to a new land. He also ordered the ship builders to carve a dragon's head on the prow of every ship. The entire community worked day and night using pine, oak, and other wood from the local forest to construct their ships.

While the men were busy building the transports, the women and children collected hundreds of pine seedlings, as well as other types of important and valuable plants. Some of the older boys were given the task of capturing wild animals such as elk, deer, and rabbit. These animals were placed in temporary cages while they waited for the voyage to their new home, where they would be released to run free once again.

By the time spring had faded into summer, sixty-three long-ships had been constructed and loaded with enough raw materials to start a new colony. After a night of celebration, Thoradal and his new clan set sail and headed into the rising sun. For two and a half days, they sailed calm seas until at last they reached their destination.

Some of the men who had sailed these waters before were not very happy with Thoradal's choice of homes. The island was in the middle of nowhere, nothing more than a gigantic, barren rock approximately six miles in diameter. To make matters worse, the island was the legendary home of the huge and ferocious sea-dragons that lived in caves in and around the base of the island. These sea-dragons were known to be fearless and would attack anything that came too close to their territory. Sailors everywhere knew the place as the Dragon's Den.

As the long ships approached the titanic blue-tinged mountain of solid beryl, the water around the ships began to come alive. Apparently, the old legends were true.

For several minutes, the sea-dragons circled the long ships like hungry sharks, easily keeping pace with the swift moving vessels. Thoradal had given strict orders not to attack the creatures, but several of the men had set arrows in their crossbows, ready to fire at a moment's notice.

Meanwhile, the sea-dragons continued to circle the small fleet, eyeing the ships and the people on board intently. Still, they made no move to attack.

"What's this?" asked one of the old sailors. "We place our trust in you, and you lead us into the midst of these monsters."

"Fear not, my friend, for you are in no danger," the old wizard said. "As long as you do not attack them, you will be safe."

"And why is that?" asked the veteran sailor. "What makes

us any different from the other ships that have wandered too close to that useless rock?"

"Because the sea-dragons believe that these ships are simply other sea-dragons, and they are merely escorting us home."

The old man looked out across the water to the barren rock ahead. He said, "Supposin' we do fool these ugly buggers and make it over to the island in one piece. How are we supposed to live on that barren rock?"

"You'll just have to trust me," Thoradal said. "Now, have your ships wait here. Go no closer until I tell you. I'll need to use one of the dinghies to take me across to the island."

The old sea captain nodded and gave the orders to his men. By the time the dinghy was ready to go, the instructions Thoradal had given the old sailor had been passed along from ship to ship. The old Northman looked at his men and said, "All right, let's be about it, then. I need two volunteers to row us over to the island."

Two brave men, both veteran sailors, quickly stepped forward and climbed over the ship's rail into the small dinghy. They helped the captain and Thoradal climb aboard and then began to row towards the island.

One of the curious sea-dragons surfaced beside the dinghy and looked the old wizard in the eye. Thoradal gently patted him on his big gnarly head. The giant reptile snorted once, spraying the men in the boat with seawater, but otherwise did no harm.

When they reached the island, they could not find a place to tie-up. The rock walls along the shoreline were just too steep.

"There's no place to land," the old salt said. "It's solid rock and straight up. We can never hope to climb it without the proper equipment, which I might add, we don't have."

"Exactly," Thoradal agreed. "That is the main reason I chose it. This island is a natural fortress. It is the perfect place to build our new settlement. Now, Captain, if you will follow me. I must get to the center of the island as quickly as possible."

"Didn't ye hear what I just said?" the captain continued. "There's no place to land. No way to scale the---"

The wizard held up his hand to silence the worried sailor. "Please, Captain. You must learn to trust me. I did not bring you all this way for nothing. Now watch." Thoradal then inserted his staff in the hole normally reserved for a small sail-mast. Instantly, two beams of bright blue light shot up from the crown of the staff to the top of the cliff. The sailors watched in amazement as rungs of light sprouted between the two beams forming into what looked like a ladder of light.

Reluctantly, the captain followed Thoradal up the glowing ladder, while the other two men gratefully waited behind in the dinghy.

High above, millions of bright twinkling stars lighted the heavens like granules of salt spilled across a black tablecloth. Meanwhile, the three moons of Nox sat low on the horizon, barely more than silver crescents in the inky black sky.

Thoradal and the nervous captain could see the sea-dragons swimming lackadaisically around the long ships more than a mile to the west. "Come along, Captain," Thoradal said. "The center of the island is only about three miles away. If we hurry, we should reach there within the hour."

The trek was uneventful. Only the wind howling among the scattered rocks afforded any resistance. Once they reached the center of the island, the aging wizard lifted his arms and spoke aloud in the ancient language of his race. When the incantation was completed, he scratched a strange symbol into the stony soil with the tip of his staff.

"Now, Captain," Thoradal said. "We must return to the ship as quickly as possible."

"Then what?" the captain asked.

"Then we wait."

"Wait? Wait for what?" the bewildered man asked as he scratched his whiskered chin.

"You will see," Thoradal replied impatiently. "Now listen carefully. When we reach the ships, have your crews lower the sails, all of the sails mind you, and batten down the hatches and anything else you don't wish to lose. Make certain that the prows of all the ships are pointed directly towards the island. It's going to get a little choppy out here in a while, but tell your men not to fear. I will be here to protect you."

It took about forty-five minutes to return to the dinghy, and another twenty minutes to row back to the ship. "Is that it?" asked the irate captain. "Are we just going to sit out here and wait until these monsters decide to eat us for breakfast?"

Thoradal was not perturbed by the man's nagging. "Try and be a little patient, Captain," he said quietly as he gazed up at the stars shimmering between wispy clouds moving east across the early summer night sky. "It will not be much longer."

Mysteriously, the sea-dragons had disappeared. The captain shook his head and nervously paced the deck of his ship. "I don't like this," the captain stated nervously. "Where did the bloody beasts go off to?"

"Only a minute ago you were complaining about their presence. Now you are complaining that they have gone," Thoradal said with a kind smile.

The captain shrugged, looked down at his feet, but did not reply.

"The sea-dragons have temporarily returned to the safety of their caves beneath the island," Thoradal explained.

"Why? What are they afraid of?"

"The meteorite," Thoradal said calmly.

"Meteorite?" The old captain took off his cap and scratched his baldhead. "What's a meteorite?" he asked, looking out across the water as if he expected an even greater monster from the deep to appear.

"I believe that your people refer to it as a falling star," Thoradal replied.

The captain's eyes widened in surprise. Then he turned and looked up at the heavens. Seeing nothing out of the ordinary, he shrugged and walked away muttering to himself.

A half-hour passed and then another, until it seemed that dawn could not be far away. Suddenly the Northmen turned their faces to the sky and watched in amazement as a blazing star appeared to fall from the heavens, growing larger and brighter by the second. However, it was not really a star at all, but a large meteor, and it was headed straight for an impact with the massive island of rock.

The impact filled the night with a thunderous reverberation and showered the area around the island with dust and small fragments of rock.

The long ships rocked and rolled with the waves but remained afloat and did not capsize. Despite the shockwave of heat and dust, no one was injured.

By the time the sun appeared on the eastern horizon, most of the dust had settled and the refugees got a better look at their new island home.

The meteor had struck the island at the exact center, leaving a massive crater that extended from one side to the other. The wall of the crater varied in thickness from between fifty and three hundred and fifty feet within thinner ridge around the top. The intense heat created by the meteor strike had caused the outer surfaces of the crater wall to melt, giving the rock a smooth, glossy appearance similar to melted wax. The entire island had a blue-green tint due to the extremely high content of the bluish mineral called beryl, and shone like a jewel in the early morning sunshine.

Far below the island, in a honeycomb of subterranean caves, the dozing sea-dragons had also been shaken. Fortunately, none of the dragons in residence there had been harmed. One cave on the northern side of the island was now completely open to the sea, and large enough to allow Thoradal and his small fleet of long ships to enter to the interior of the island one by one. This new channel led to a shallow lake that was already forming in the center of the crater. It would make an ideal location for berthing their ships.

Thoradal guided the small armada to the northern side of the island and into the newly formed canal. They used their oars to row through the narrow channel, passing hundreds of watchful sea-dragons, both young and old, along the way. The dragons did not seem the least bit concerned that foreign dragons were invading their home.

"I don't understand. What is preventing them from tearing us apart?" asked the captain.

"Let's just say a little magic goes a long way," Thoradal replied with an almost imperceptible smile.

As they made their way through the crater wall, they saw natural springs of cold and hot water bubbling up out of the bedrock. Later, once settled in, they would be able to tap these springs to provide running water for their community. As they passed through the inner wall of the crater and back out into the open morning light, they discovered that the small lake that had started to form was already deep enough for the hulls of their ships to pass without scraping their keels on the bottom. In time, the lake would grow wider and deeper and eventually cover over a third of the crater floor.

The chieftains of the Northmen clan soon understood why Thoradal had insisted on bringing as many pine seedlings as they could carry, as well as the saplings of other useful trees. Eventually, these young saplings would be planted around the crater where they would grow into a new forest, providing valuable resources for future generations. The clan had also brought seeds to grow wheat, corn, and other vital food crops.

They began building their new settlement by constructing houses from materials they had brought with them. Then they converted several of their long ships into barges to ferry topsoil from some of the nearby islands. It was going to take time. It was going to take years. However, with dedication and hard work, the fruits of their labor would provide them with a self-sufficient community.

After several debates on home defense, the Northmen decided to create a fortress within a fortress by hollowing out the walls of their crater island. When the work was completed, the crater wall would be honeycombed with passages and chambers. In time, these man-made caves would ring the entire island. In time, the land surrounding the crater lake would contain both forest and farmland. In time, the sea-dragons would become their friends and protectors. Like their distant cousins, the Pegazons, they too, would evolve into a new culture that would later become known to the residence of this barbaric world as the Dragon Masters.

In the southern hemisphere, just below the equator, Rhiannon worked tirelessly within the confines of her sunken island. Although her fire-ravished body no longer caused her any pain, it was forever scarred, and no amount of magic could restore her former beauty. Her nose was now nothing more than a lump of melted cartilage; her mouth a twisted gash in her badly scarred face. Most of her hair was gone as well, burned away by the flames. What little was left, had grown back in thin scraggly patches. She no longer walked around half-naked like the native girls. Instead, she had gone back to wearing her heavy wizard's robe to which she had added a hood to better conceal her facial disfigurement.

Breandan, after having spent years imprisoned within the red-gold ring that Rhiannon had fashioned to hold his soul, finally gave up any hope of rescue and moved on to the spirit world. Yet, his body remained alive in a perpetual state of suspended animation inside a specially designed crystal vault, which Rhiannon visited from time-to-time. Despite the passage of time, his body did not age, for she had placed a spell on him that protected it from the ravages of the years.

Melli, who had been blinded by Rhiannon's own hand so that she would never have to look upon her queen's fire-scarred face, tended to Rhiannon's needs for as long as she could, often stumbling around the caverns in complete darkness. Eventually, she grew old and died in Rhiannon's twisted arms, never once regretting the love she had for her wizard-queen.

Neraka had experienced Rhiannon's pain, just as he had experienced Rhiannon's pleasures in the past. He now only wanted one thing – revenge.

For hundreds of years, Rhiannon and Neraka toiled as one in their undersea lair, but at last, they were ready to extract revenge and destroy what was left of the League of Wizards.

****

PART TWO

MACE, THE GOLDEN ROCK hopper, stood patiently beside Deena while she tightened the cinch straps on the small leather saddle. Deena was fourteen years old and apprenticed to Sylvee, who was both captain and group leader of her patrol squadron. Deena had been apprenticed to Sylvee since her tenth year, and she was fortunate to have been chosen from more than a dozen other young girls with the same dream.

Deena was short in stature, a trait common among the Pegazons, as well as a requirement to become a rider. Her hair was thick and black in contrast to her pale complexion. Her intelligent eyes were the color of the midnight sky.

She was just preparing her leader's riding gear, which included a short sword, a small round shield, a short bow, and a quiver full of arrows, when Sylvee entered the stable from her quarters above. Sylvee smiled her approval as she inspected her young apprentice's work.

"Excellent," she said before moving on to her other duties.

A good relationship between the rider and her apprentice

was essential, for if Sylvee were ever killed or severely wounded in battle, Deena would have to take her place. If both Sylvee and Mace were killed, Deena would have little choice but to seek apprenticeship with another rider. These days, however, few riders were lost in combat. Most of them lived long enough to retire and turn the reins of their rock hoppers over to their apprentices. All that was about to change.

Sylvee was wearing her winter patrol uniform, which consisted of a short cotton undergarment, a leather tunic, sheepskin leggings held in place with crisscrossing leather straps, and a heavy woolen coat. A leather harness that buckled around the waist and crossed over the shoulders served to hold various pieces of equipment. Lastly, she carried a steel helmet lined with sheepskin to keep the head warm.

Sylvee slipped her helmet on her head and adjusted the chin strap. Her hair stuck out from under the rim of the helmet about three inches. Like Deena, her hair was jet black. Her eyes, too, were dark, nearly as dark as her hair. Her complexion was also fair, only the cold of winter had added roses to her cheeks.

There were a total of twenty flight groups, and each flight group had a flight leader. Each flight group consisted of one leader and two wingers. Every rider, regardless of rank, had an apprentice on the ground whose only responsibility was to take care of her animals and equipment. In return, the rider taught the apprentice everything she needed to know about flying and fighting from the back of a rock hopper.

Every flight group was assigned to a squadron, and each squadron was made up of five groups. Each squadron was assigned to its own barracks. Each group leader and their wingers slept in separate rooms that were directly above the stables. Their rooms were plain but cozy, with a narrow window in the outer wall and a stone fireplace in the corner. Apprentices slept on cots in the stable to be near their charges.

The barracks were strategically spaced around the perimeter of the settlement to provide a faster response time in case of attack. Like other buildings in the settlement, they were built mainly of quarried stone with slate roofs. Each building or stable had a central hall where meals were served twice a day.

Sylvee led Mace down the corridor to the main assembly hall. The other riders in her group were already there waiting. They greeted her with a salute as they came to attention. She returned their salute and began her briefing on the morning's patrol.

"This morning we're sticking to visual recon," she said. "Let's try and avoid any unnecessary skirmishes with the enemy. Last night, Marta's patrol spotted a much larger contingent of human-slave soldiers than we spotted yesterday morning coming up from the south. I'm now certain that the Horrans are preparing to launch a massive assault on the escarpment utilizing their human-slave forces to absorb the brunt of our defenses. But today, we are not going to pick a fight. Are there any questions?"

Sylvee saw the excitement in her group's faces. It pleased her that they were so eager to do battle, but privately she wondered how long their enthusiasm would last once the real struggle began.

When no one raised their hand, Sylvee stifled a sigh and said, "Let's fly!" She turned and led them out of the hall and into the morning light. A thin layer of fresh snow had fallen during the pre-dawn hour, leaving the air smelling clean and crisp. The group mounted their animals and waited for Sylvee's order. When Sylvee gave the hand signal, the group took to the air in total synchronization.

Two minutes later they were flying high above the snow-covered lowlands of Pega. Sylvee led the patrol to the southwest, intending to make a sweep of the entire zone adjacent to the escarpment, but some low drifting cloud formations forced them to descend to an altitude just below four hundred feet, barely out of range of the Horran's latest killing machine. Nicknamed *the porcupine*, the new weapon could shoot up to fifty arrows at a time with deadly accuracy.

Far below, on the muddy well-trodden roads, marched column-after-column of human-slave soldiers heading for camps located near and around the base of the escarpment. Mingled among them were their merciless masters, the Horrans.

The Horranian guards were armed with crossbows and scimitars. As the riders passed overhead, they looked up brandishing their swords and shouting filthy curses. They despised the Pegazons and intended to annihilate them once and for all.

Sylvee's wingers fingered their bows anxiously, but the group leader kept them in tow and turning east, led them away from the temptation to engage the enemy.

When they reached the eastern coastline, the patrol spotted a small fleet of Horranian ships. The strange looking vessels had huge battering rams attached to their prows.

Whom do they intend to ram with those things? Sylvee wondered. *We don't employ ships of any kind, and the lowlanders have no warships of their own.*

Here, human slaves were forced to row the foreign galleys to the beat of a drum and the lash of the whip. For them there was no hope of escape, for their cruel masters had chained them to their seats.

Finishing their sweep of the valley, Sylvee's flight group headed back to the escarpment. Below, more enemy soldiers were busy making camp.

The snow was beginning to fall again as Sylvee's patrol made their routine pass over their settlement, but before landing near their barracks she led them out over the lake for a pass at the wizard's tower. The old abandoned tower was as dark and silent as ever, nothing more than a pile of old stones looming up out of the frozen lake like a cold dead finger. She had never seen a wizard, much less the one who had supposedly lived in the tower at one time. It was said that he had disappeared over a hundred years earlier. Most people believed that he was gone for good, but deep down in her heart, Sylvee knew that he would return again one day when they really needed him. Whatever the case, Sylvee understood that when the Horrans finally did attack the escarpment, they were going to need all the help they could get if their settlement was to survive.

Returning to the village, the patrol landed in the soft fresh snow outside their compound. The riders dismounted and led their animals inside to their stalls.

Sylvee helped Deena remove Mace's saddle and other flying gear and saw to it that he was dry and fed before retreating upstairs to change out of her own damp uniform. She revived the dying fire in her fireplace, kicked off her boots, and sat down to warm her feet. Flying in wintertime was a cold business.

Deena brought her a steaming-hot mug of tea and began preparing them a small meal of mutton and potatoes.

All the while Sylvee sat and stared into the fire. The build-up of enemy forces in the lowlands was constantly pressing on her mind, and tonight she had to try to convince the Village Elders of the seriousness of the situation. Elder Malachi had called the meeting, but only at her insistence, and many of the elders were not very pleased.

Malachi, one of the oldest and wisest of the elders, had listened attentively to all of the reports concerning the buildup of enemy forces, and he was in complete agreement with Sylvee. However, he appeared to be her only ally among the elders.

———•———

Far below the escarpment, in the valley of shadows, a small

group of human slaves was being forcibly marched along a road leading to the main encampment of the Horranian horde. The whip lashed at the heels of an old man causing him to cry out in pain. However, Petamor felt no pain, and the welts and blood were only an illusion to satisfy the cruel Horranian guard that was herding him and the others along like cattle.

Petamor had cloaked himself in the disguise of an old, half-crippled slave in order to try and learn as much as he could about the Horran's planned assault on the escarpment.

As soon as they reached the main encampment, Petamor was separated from the group and ushered into the compound of Ko-Kahn the IV, the most ruthless and bloodthirsty of all the Horranian emperors. One of Ko-Kahn's personal guards grabbed him roughly by the scrap of his neck and dragged him through the muddied snow towards a large brightly colored pavilion. Petamor pretended to be terrified although he was in no actual danger. He could easily disable or kill the guard if necessary.

"I hope for your sake you know how to cook, you miserable excuse for a human," the guard hissed.

"Yes, Master," Petamor whined. "I can cook. I can cook real good."

"You'd better not be lying, because if you fail to please our great emperor," he said twisting Petamor around to face him, "that will happen to you." He pointed to a spot near the entrance to the tent, where one of the other guards had just finished placing a freshly severed head on a pole. A few feet away lay the decapitated body of Ko-Kahn's last cook. Blood still ran fresh from the gaping stump where the head had once been. The gruesome sight had no real effect on the old wizard; nevertheless, he pretended to be shaken and quickly covered his eyes. The pitiless guards laughed aloud at the sight of the sniveling human.

"That's the third cook my lord has killed in less than five days," the guard spat joyfully. "When your turn comes," he said with a grin as he fingered his scimitar, "I hope that my lord and master will allow me the honor of cutting off your useless, empty head."

Petamor, continuing the ruse, fell to his knees. "Oh please, Master, please! Have mercy! I can cook, Master! I can! I really can!"

"Get up, vermin," the guard said, well pleased with himself.

Petamor stood and was pushed towards another opening in the large pavilion where he almost slipped in the blood of the dead cook. The guard laughed again as he shoved him through the aperture.

The inside of Ko-Kahn's private tent was lighted by several lamps that were suspended from the ceiling on chains. It had been divided into several rooms by huge tapestries and other wall hangings. Expensive antique furniture adorned each room while the floor was covered from wall-to-wall with plush hand-woven carpets.

At one end of the largest room, upon a high dais, was a throne that appeared to have been gilded in gold leaf. Upon the throne sat the great and terrible Ko-Kahn the IV, the latest descendent of Ko-Kahn the Terrible. He was a large Horran, the biggest Petamor had ever seen. He wore a heavy robe made from a polar bear skin, dyed royal blue, and trimmed with black sable fur. With the exception of several golden armbands around his huge biceps, he wore no other jewelry, not even a crown. However, there was no mistaking his authority.

Six of the emperor's personal guards stood at rest behind the throne, watching the comings and goings of Ko-Kahn's personal staff. Beside him on the floor knelt two human women, completely naked except for the iron chains fastened around their ankles. Their bodies were covered with dozens of ugly, purple-black bruises; their once pretty faces were drawn and haggard as they awaited the emperor's next command.

Ko-Kahn was drinking wine from a large golden goblet embedded with a fortune in emeralds and sapphires. When he looked up and saw Petamor trembling before him, he smiled, if you wish to call it a smile. The guard pushed the old man forward to the foot of the dais.

"Lord and Master," said the guard with a salute, "I bring you a fresh slave who has begged to be your new cook."

Ko-Kahn hissed through his pointed teeth and emptied his wine goblet in one gulp. Instantly the slave girl on his left refilled his cup from a large vessel sitting near her feet. The girl on the right proffered him a large platter heaped with chunks of grilled meat.

Petamor wisely dropped to the floor whimpering in fear as any half-witted creature would be expected to do.

Ko-Kahn selected a large chunk of the rare meat and said, "I hope this feeble old man can perform the duties I require of him. Tonight, slave," he continued, addressing Petamor directly, "I will be dining with my chieftains, and I want the feastings to be perfect." He leaned forward, his claws on the arms of his throne. "Do you think you can prepare a great feast by nightfall?"

Petamor did not answer at first. And while he understood the question perfectly, no normal human being would have understood Ko-Kahn's question the first time due to the emperor's tangible hiss.

"Did you not hear what I said, slave?" Ko-Kahn asked, as his guard reached for his sword with a half-hidden grin.

"Yes, Master!" Petamor pleaded. "I can cook real good! I can prepare a feast for you and your guests by tonight."

Ko-Kahn shook his head. "Take him away," he said, "and put him to work in the kitchen. If he fails to prepare a delectable feast, I can always use him to entertain my chieftains after we dine."

"Yes, my Lord, I will see to it personally," said the guard, as he roughly shoved Petamor back out through the flap in the tent wall.

"Guard," called Ko-Kahn. "Find that vermin more suitable clothing before he stinks up my tent. I don't want the sight and smell of him to ruin my guests' appetites. And be sure to burn that rag he's wearing. I don't want any of his filth in my food."

"Yes, my Lord," the guard said with a slight bow as he followed Petamor out of the pavilion.

Before Petamor could retrieve his staff, which he had reduced to the size of a twig and hidden in the hem of his old robe, the guard ripped the dirty clothes off his body. Then he dragged Petamor into the cooking tent by his hair.

Although Petamor could not be harmed or killed by anyone other than another wizard, he could still be imprisoned, and without his staff, he would be incapable of escape by any magical means. Somehow, he would have to retrieve his staff from his old robe before it was lost.

Outside the kitchen tent, a small campfire burned dully. As they passed the fire the guard tossed Petamor's robe into the flames. There were several Horranian soldiers standing around the fire, and they all laughed at the sight of the old man being dragged naked through the muddy snow.

One of the soldiers called out to the guard, "I hope you don't plan on roasting that shriveled up old toad. It would be a shame to waste a good fire on that scrawny piece of gristle. Why don't you butcher one of those ugly human females that our lord and master keeps around him? Now one of them would make a much tastier meal."

"Yes," shouted another soldier, "I wouldn't mind a nice juicy thigh right about now."

"And I could really go for some breast meat," called another soldier, laughing.

The guard stopped at the entrance to the kitchen tent, "Yes, I'm sure you would," he answered with an amused snarl, "and all of our heads would end up decorating the emperor's pavilion by nightfall." Then he turned and dragged the old man into the tent behind him.

The guard deposited Petamor in the center of the cooking tent and searched around until he found a heavily stained white tunic and a greasy apron. "Put these on, human, while I see if I can find something for your feet." Then he turned and stomped back out of the tent.

There were several large cooking pits at the opposite end of the tent, but they had been left unattended for so long the fires had gone out. At the other end of the tent hung the butchered and bloody carcasses of a dozen or more cows, pigs, and sheep. There were also the slain bodies of several human women hanging from meat hooks. However, there was no time for mourning; Petamor had to recover his staff and quickly. He carefully peered out of the tent. The soldiers were still gathered around the fire. The flames had already consumed his old robe, but his staff could not be destroyed by natural fire. Nevertheless, he had to get to the staff before it was lost or discovered by one of the guards, and he had to get it without attracting too much attention from the soldiers.

Suddenly the tent flap flew open again and the Horranian guard stalked in, almost knocking the old wizard off his feet. "Oh, trying to escape are you, you ungrateful---"

"No, Master, no!" Petamor whined. "I was just going to get some hot coals from the fire. The cooking pits have cooled. See there!" he exclaimed, pointing. "The fires have gone out."

The guard eyed him suspiciously and then handed him a worn out pair of leather sandals with woolen leggings. They looked oddly familiar. "Here, put these on," he said gruffly. "The slave who last wore them doesn't need them any longer. I don't want you dying on me just yet. However, if you try to escape from me again, I'll have your head on the end of my spear before your puny heart stops beating. Do you understand me?"

"Yes, Master. Thank you, Master," Petamor said, convincingly sincere. He took the sandals and the leggings and strapped them on as quickly as he could and then searched the tent until he found a bucket and a small shovel. He pointed to the fire outside the tent and the guard nodded. He hurriedly crossed the yard to the campfire under the watchful eye of his keeper and began scooping hot coals into the bucket.

Fortunately, the soldiers had gone off to perform their own duties elsewhere, and he was able to search through the ashes alone. It took several trips to fill the cooking pits with enough coals to rekindle the fires, but finally, on his seventh trip, he located his staff. He waited until the guard turned his head and snatched up the twig-sized staff as covertly as possible.

After some time, the kitchen tent was ablaze with light from the cooking fires. The wood smoke drifted up and out through several vents cut into the top of the tent. Petamor worked the rest of the morning and the early part of the afternoon preparing the emperor's feast while the guard watched his every move.

Petamor roasted meat in great chunks and slabs, but avoided using any human remains. The idea of roasting human flesh truly sickened him. There was absolutely no need to prepare any vegetables or fruit, because these pureblooded Horrans ate only meat, and lots of it. Nevertheless, he wanted this feast to be perfect, not for fear of his life, but so that he might be allowed in the dining tent while the feast was being served. Then, with any luck, he might overhear the Horranian's conversation, which most assuredly would be focused on the pending invasion of the escarpment.

The old wizard had temporarily hidden his twig-sized staff in his dirty matted hair. Now, as he realized that he might have to bathe before serving the feast, he prudently transformed the staff into a narrow strip of leather and tied it around his waist like a belt to hold up his breeches.

Everything was going according to plan; nevertheless, he had to be certain that he would be present in the dining tent during the feasting without drawing suspicion. "Master," he said, crawling on his knees over to the Horranian's scaly feet, "you look thirsty. Would you care for a flagon of wine?"

For a moment, the guard hesitated. Drinking on duty was strictly forbidden, but what the hell. He was thirsty, and one flagon of wine couldn't hurt. "Yes, slave. Bring me a flagon of wine, and be quick about it." Then, after a moment's thought, he added, "And bring me a chunk or two of that roasted pork as well."

"Yes, Master," Petamor replied as he hurriedly fetched the wine. "Here you are, Master. Now I will get you your meal." He hurried back to the roasting pits and sliced off several huge slabs of pork belly. He placed the half-raw meat on a platter and set it on a table before the guard.

The greedy guard had already polished off his wine, so Petamor refilled his flagon without seeking permission. The hungry guard picked up one of the chunks of meat and began to eat. "Good," he mumbled as grease and pork juice dripped down his jaw onto his uniform. "Perhaps you really do know how to cook, slave. Here, fill my flagon again."

As soon as the wine began to have its anesthetizing effects on his overseer, Petamor asked for permission to assist in serving the feast. The guard agreed, providing of course, that Petamor clean himself up first. The old wizard wanted to use his powers to save time, but he could not risk being seen. He would just have to wait until the guard's back was turned. In the meantime, he would continue tending to the cooking pits.

After refilling the guard's flagon six more times, he started to ask him for permission to go and bathe, only to discover that the guard had fallen asleep at the table. Petamor decided that it would be safe to use his powers after all, and in a heartbeat both he and his robe were as clean as would be expected under the circumstances.

It was getting late. Outside the sun was starting to set, and the shadows were becoming as one. The chieftains were in their tents, dressing in their finest uniforms for the feast with their emperor.

The Horranian guard was beginning to snore, so Petamor woke him up. "I'm ready, Master," he said. "I hope you didn't have to wait too long."

The sleepy guard lifted his reptilian-like head from the table and opened his thick-lidded eyes. "What? Huh...you, you what?" he grumbled groggily. He looked around slowly. "It's a good thing you returned when you did. I was just about to come looking for you."

At that moment the outer tent flap was flung open as a dozen naked serving girls entered, escorted by two of Ko-Kahn's personal guards. "We've come for the food," said the first guard looking around at all the meat still roasting on their spits. "Why is the feast not ready? You dare expect our lord and master to wait."

Petamor's guard stood up rather clumsily, but somehow managed to keep his wits despite his drunken condition. "No, no, not at all," he replied. "We were just keeping the meat warm until our lord and master was ready to eat. I'll have the cook put the roasted meats on serving platters. It will only take a minute. In the meantime, have these serving wenches fill these flagons with wine and begin serving them to the emperor and his guests. By the time they return for the meat, it will be ready to serve."

"It had better be," the emperor's guard replied. "All right, you lazy wenches, do as he said. Fill these flagons with wine and serve them to the emperor and his guests, and be quick about it. Then return here for the meat at once. And I warn you," he continued with a hideous grin. "Serve well and you will be rewarded. But if you fail to please our emperor and his guests, and you will suffer the consequences."

The slave girls did not need to be reminded of the consequences of displeasing Ko-Kahn. They could see the dead women hanging from meat hooks at the other end of the cooking tent. Despite their misery, they were not yet ready for that eventuality. They complied as swiftly as they could, filling the large flagons to their brims. Then the guards led them back to the emperor's pavilion to begin the feast.

Once the emperor's guards had left the tent, the frightened guard turned towards Petamor. "What have you been doing?" he demanded angrily. "Why is the meat not on the serving platters? Do you want me to serve your lily liver as an appetizer?"

"I was waiting for your orders, Master. But I'll have the food ready to serve in less than two minutes, Master," Petamor whined convincingly.

Abruptly, the guard reached out and steadied himself against a tent pole. His head was spinning from the effects of all the wine he had consumed. "It had better be ready when I get back, or I will cut out your spleen with a dull knife," the guard said gruffly. Then he turned and half walked, half staggered outside the tent for a breath of fresh air.

Reacting quickly, Petamor cast a spell over the roasted meats, insuring that every morsel would taste better than the last and satisfy all who partook of the feast. He was hoping that a good meal and a belly full of wine would help loosen the tongues of Ko-Kahn's warlords.

Having cleared his head, the drunken guard returned before Petamor could place the meat on the serving platters. He had been too busy thinking about his escape plan.

"I thought I told you to have the food ready to be served," the guard said angrily, looking around anxiously at the empty platters. "What have you been doing all this time? The serving wenches will be back shortly."

"They *are* prepared, Master," the crafty old wizard replied. And in the blink of an eye, the succulent meats were displayed and arranged on the serving platters in such a way to please the eye of any meat-eating warlord.

The Horran rubbed his eyes in disbelief and looked again. "I must be drunker than I thought," he mumbled to himself.

At that moment, the other guards returned with the serving girls to collect the food. "Excellent," said one of the guards, obviously impressed. "I am sure that our lord and master will be quite pleased," he added as he ordered the girls to gather up the platters.

"This slave is the one who prepared the feast," the guard said, grabbing Petamor by the back of his neck. "It is only fair that he be present when the great Ko-Kahn tastes the food. If for any reason the emperor is not pleased, he can deal with this slave personally."

Ko-Kahn's guards grunted their approval and led the slaves back to the pavilion carrying the platters of roasted meat. It took Petamor and the twelve serving girls five trips to move all of the feastings to the dining area.

Far to the east of Pega, in the blue-gray northern sea, sat the crater island of Dragon's Den. It was the home of the clan known as the Dragon Masters. They were not called Dragon Masters because of any genetic affiliation with reptiles; they were not reptilian in any way. They were, in fact, completely human. They were the descendents of the Northmen who had migrated to the island from the northern coast of Pega at the end of the holocaust two thousand years earlier.

The Northmen had not always been a seafaring people. The name, Dragon Masters, originated long after they had settled their island home, which also happened to be the home of a species of giant reptiles known as the Northern Sea-Dragon.

Their island, which had once been nothing more than a huge chunk of rock in the middle of the northern sea, had been struck by a meteor. The meteor had left a shallow crater nearly six miles wide. The ancestors of the Dragomen had then created a new home by hollowing out the narrow wall of the crater into enough living space for the entire clan. They had also transported thousands of tons of topsoil, one barge at a time, from the surrounding islands, spreading it across the crater floor. They had transplanted an entire small, pine forest so that their heirs would have a renewable source of building materials.

The highest point on the island was the section of the crater wall that towered over the only entrance to the interior of the island. Here, lookouts could watch the comings and goings of the long-ships, as well as the approach of any unwelcome visitors. Far below the watchtower was a narrow channel entrance that led through the crater wall to a shallow lake in the center of the crater.

Rolf, the highest-ranking chieftain of the clan, stood gazing quietly out of one of the narrow viewing slits that had been cut into the outer sea wall. He was a big man, as strong as an ox and highly intelligent. He was tugging unconsciously at his thick red beard with his rough and calloused hands.

Beside Rolf stood his younger brother, Neff, who also stared out the window in anticipation. Like his older brother, Neff was a big man, although not nearly as bright. However, whatever Neff may have lacked in intelligence, was more than made up for by his devotion to his family and the clan.

On Rolf's right-hand side stood the wizard, Thoradal. His physical appearance had not changed at all in two thousand years, although he was much more cautious than he had been in the days of the demon-wizard, Rhiannon. He placed a reassuring hand on Rolf's shoulder, "Be patient, my old friend. Your brother will return soon."

"Kile should have been back days ago," the big man replied. "I should never have let him go out on his own. He's too young and inexperienced to be poking around in the Southern Reaches."

"If I recall correctly," Thoradal said, "you were about the

same age when the adventurous spirit first lured you out to sea."

"That's true," admitted Rolf, "but many things have changed since those days. Back then, we didn't have to worry so much about the bloody Horrans. But you and I both know they're out there again prowling around. They're up to something."

"Don't worry, brother," Neff said trying to sound less worried than he was. "Kile's dragon ship can outrun those Horranian tugs any day."

"Yes, my brother," Rolf replied smiling, "I know you're right."

Minutes later a reddish-orange sail appeared on the western horizon. Thoradal's keen eyes saw it first, and pointed it out for Rolf and Neff. No one said another word until the ship's prow, with its distinctive red dragon's head, was close enough to identify.

"It is Kile," Rolf shouted joyfully as he good-naturedly slapped Neff on the back. "He's returned at last."

It was true. Kile's dragon ship sailed gracefully over the waves escorted by a pod of happy frolicking sea-dragons.

The three men waited until Kile's ship passed under the arch that marked the open passage, and then hurried down the carved-stone stairs to the canal that led to the crater lake where Kile would beach his long ship. Despite their haste, they were too slow, for Kile's swift vessel was already entering the lake by the time they reached the inner wall of the crater.

"All of a sudden, little brother is in a big hurry to get home," Neff said, slightly puzzled.

Kile's crew were hastily stowing the sail as the three men approached. Thoradal could also sense that something was awry.

Kile was standing on the deck of his ship, his long blond hair blowing in the cool breeze. As Rolf and the others neared the beach, Kile and several members of his crew jumped into the shallow water and pulled the strong-keeled ship up onto the pebbly sand. Kile's face was pale and grim; his normally bright eyes were dull and troubled. He was unaware that the three men were approaching, and started at the sound of Rolf's voice.

"Kile! You're more than a week late. What have you been doing all this time? I let you talk me in to letting you go out to patrol the Southern Reaches and---" Rolf stopped short. The crewmen still aboard Kile's ship were passing down the bodies of three men wrapped in sealskins. Kile's eyes were brimming with tears as he laid the still body of the first man down in the sand. He carefully wiped the salt away from the dead man's face. The salt had been used to help preserve the body during the sea voyage.

Rolf and Neff were shocked to see that the dead man's face was ruined. It looked as if it had melted away. The nose and part of his left cheek were completely gone, burned away by something that had left a star-shaped wound. The dead man's name was Tor, Kile's first mate and best friend.

The other two dead crewmembers also bore similar wounds, one on the throat, and one on the back of the head where the gaping, five-pointed hole had exposed part of the man's brain.

Upon seeing the grief-stricken brothers, the old wizard left them alone to mourn. He quietly returned to his suite in the crater wall. He wanted to know what had happened to these men, but he had seen enough grief in all his years that death no longer affected him as it once did. Nevertheless, he felt a powerful sense of impending doom, and the image of a red moon abruptly pushed into his thoughts again for the first time in years.

"What happened to these men?" Rolf asked as he watched Thoradal walk away.

"We were attacked by some strange creatures. They came up out of the water so fast! There was no time to react! They threw these fat ugly slug-like things at us," Kile answered, apparently still in a mild state of shock.

"Creatures? What kind of creatures, Kile? Tell me exactly what happened," Rolf insisted.

"I don't know what they are," Kile began. "We were sailing along in the southern ocean. It was a beautiful clear late-afternoon day, everything appeared normal. The ocean was empty. We hadn't seen another ship in days, so I decided that it was time to return home. Then, just as we were coming about, we saw these large dark shapes moving below the surface of the water and under the ship."

"What were they, Kile? Sharks? Whales?" asked Neff.

"No, not sharks or whales," Kile answered, shaking his head. "Although that's what we thought they were at first. We tried to outrun them, whatever they were, but they were able to keep pace with us easily. They were everywhere, like shadows on a sunny day. They were huge too. Whatever they were... they were huge. We were terrified. We thought that maybe it was the end of the world.

"Far to the south, just over the horizon, we could see a plume of thick gray smoke. I mean, one minute the sky was clear and the next thing we knew it was full of smoke, which smelled of rotten eggs. Then there was a tremendous rumbling from beneath the water. Rolf, it...it sounded like the very planet was tearing itself apart right under our ship. Then it stopped just as suddenly as it had started, and everything was calm again.

"All that was left was the smoke rising above the horizon. Accordingly we turned south again to investigate," Kile continued, gripping his brother by the shoulder. "Rolf, when we reached the area where the smoke was coming from...there was an island there. A dead, black, smoldering island with a huge stinking volcano sitting right in the center of it." Kile took a deep breath as he shook his head.

"Are you telling me that the island had not been there before?" Rolf asked.

"Rolf, I swear, we had just sailed over that area earlier in the day and there was no island there at that time. I don't know where it came from. It...it must have risen up out of the sea."

"You must report this to Thoradal at once. I'm sure that he will know what to make of it," Rolf said. "Now, Kile, tell me what happened to these men."

"I decided that we needed to investigate the island more closely," Kile said, shaking his head sadly, "but Tor, there," he added, pointing to his dead mate, "wanted to leave the area immediately. I should've listened to him, Rolf. I should've listened. Now he's dead, and it's all my fault."

"No, Kile, you did the right thing," Rolf insisted. "That's why you were out there in the first place."

Kile nodded and continued with his report. "The smell, that ungodly smell, got worse by the hour. It stank to high heaven. It reminded me of that time those whales swam in through the channel and ended up beaching themselves on the shore of the lake. Do you remember, Rolf?"

"Yes, I remember," Rolf replied. "For some reason, a pod of narwhales found their way into the canal and swam up into the lake. We were just children at the time. I was twelve, Neff was about ten...and you were...what...around four or five, I think?"

"Yeah, that's right. It was exactly one week before my fifth birthday. I'll never forget it. Do you remember that smell? When they died there on the beach. They were too big for us to move, so all we could do was leave them there to rot in the sun."

"Yes, it was terrible. I wasn't able to keep my food down for a week."

"Well, this stench was a hundred times worse."

Rolf and Neff nodded.

Kile continued. "As I was saying, we circled the island twice. All that time, black smoke pored out of the volcano. But there was nothing more to see, just a dead, black island covered from one end to the other with rotting vegetation. So I gave the order to turn the ship around and head back here to Dragon's Den. Not long after that...it happened.

"At first, we thought they were just a school of fish, until they broke the surface. At first, I thought they were some kind of ray. But they were monstrous. Their wingspan was easily thirty-five or forty feet."

"Forty feet? I have never heard of a ray that size. Have you Rolf?" asked Neff.

Rolf shook his head.

"That's not the worst of it," Kile continued. "These...these monsters were being ridden by some other kind of...creatures. They looked human...well...almost, but if you had seen them with your own eyes, you would agree that whatever they were, they weren't human. They had arms and legs like men, but their hands and feet were twice as large and their fingers were webbed. Their skin was as black as pitch and hairless, too. They looked emaciated and hungry."

"My god," Neff said.

"But it was their eyes that really sent shivers up my spine. Their eyes were cold and predatory, like those of a shark. I have never seen anything like it in my life, and I hope I never see it again."

One of Kile's men handed him a mug of wine, which he accepted with shaky hands. "Why don't you go back to your quarters and get some rest, Captain," the crewman said. "We'll see that these men are properly buried."

"Thank you, but no. These men are my responsibility. I must go and see their families personally to arrange for their burial."

"Aye, aye, Captain," replied the crewmember.

"These men can wait another hour or two," Rolf said. "First we must go and talk to Thoradal."

"I don't think Thoradal wants to hear about it, brother," Kile said. "Didn't you see the look on his face when he first saw my dead crewmen?"

"Well, like it or not, he's going to *have* to listen," Rolf said. "He's the only one of us that will know what we must do next."

Kile nodded and started for the main entrance to the crater wall. Seven of his crew followed: six carrying the dead bodies of his fallen crewmembers, and the last carrying a large wooden bucket fitted with a lid.

"Is there anything else you can tell us about these creatures that attacked your ship?" Rolf asked as they walked together.

"The creatures...the riders, that is, were naked, except for some sort of bag or pouch they had strapped around their waists," Kile answered after taking a sip of wine from his mug. "They came up out of the sea all around us. Five of them. Maybe six. It was hard to tell because they kept diving and resurfacing all over the place. Every time they resurfaced, they would throw another one of those things at us."

"What kind of thing?" Neff asked, totally fascinated by the drama of the story.

"I don't know what they are. Some kind of starfish, I suppose. As you can see from the wounds on my men, they are shaped like a five-pointed star."

"I think you're right. Must be some species of starfish," Rolf agreed.

"These riders carry them in pouches strapped around their waists," Kile continued. "Every time they get close enough, they'd pick a target and throw. Once the *starfish* makes contact with the target, it attaches itself to the flesh with round suckers, like those on an octopus. We tried to pull them off, but it's very difficult because they're covered in some kind of acidic slime. It starts by searing the flesh, and then the flesh begins to dissolve. We tried to wash them off with seawater, but it didn't help. The ones that ended up on the deck, left burn scars in the wood."

"How long did the attack last?" Neff asked.

"It seemed like a long time, but in reality maybe...five minutes. The creatures retreated once we started shooting arrows at them. But it was too late to save Tor and my other two crewmen."

"What happened to the ones that landed on the deck?" Rolf asked.

"We threw most of them overboard after we crushed them and made sure they were dead. However, I saved one to show the wizard. Maybe he will know what it is," Kile said.

"Where is it? I want to see it," Rolf said.

Kile stopped outside the door to Thoradal's private chamber and took the bucket from the crewmember before sending him on his way. "Can we go inside? I think Thoradal should see this, too. I believe this is his door."

Rolf knocked twice, but there was no answer. When he tried the door, he found it unlocked, so they all went inside. The three brothers found Thoradal in the watchtower lost deep in thought.

"I apologize for the intrusion, Thoradal, but I thought that you would want to see this for yourself. This is what killed my men," Kile said as he dumped the dead creature on the floor. "Do you have any idea what it is?"

The star-shaped creature was covered in slime that glistened in the torchlight. It was approximately six inches in diameter. The top of the creature was black, with dark and light gray mottling around the edges, while the bottom half, or belly of the miniature beast, was a pale pink. It had a soft, plump body like that of a slug or snail, but no protective shell. It had five arms radiating from its center, as well as round, puckered mouth full of long, needle-like teeth.

"I believe it's called a soul-leech," Thoradal said, "although I have never seen or heard of one this large. They usually get no bigger than your fingernail, and they tend to live on the ocean floor eating anything they can find. They digest their food by dissolving it with a strong acid. That, I believe, is how it managed to kill your men, Kile."

"Get that thing out of here," Rolf told his man, "and make sure you burn it to ash."

"Wait," Neff said. "Can I have it? I want to study it more closely."

Rolf looked at Neff and shrugged. "Take it if you want, brother, but make sure that you destroy it when you are finished examining it."

"I will," Neff replied.

"All right, Kile. Tell me exactly what happened. And don't leave out any details," the old wizard said.

In the southern hemisphere just below the equator, Rhiannon's blackened, fetid island had finally resurrected itself from the seabed. The once beautiful tropical paradise had become a cesspool of rotting waste regurgitated out of hell itself. Thick gray smoke billowed from the cone of the volcano blocking out most of the sunlight for miles around, but the smoke did not originate in the molten bowels of the planet. Instead, it came from the subterranean chambers in the very roots of the volcano. It was in those deep dark and dank chambers were the demon-wizard, Rhiannon, worked day and night to create her horde of ghastly sea-monsters.

Rhiannon's face and body had been horribly disfigured during her first confrontation with the League of Wizards. So had her mind. Yet she was no more insane than was Neraka, her demon tormentor. Once Neraka had wanted to *rule* the world. Now, he only wanted to *destroy* it, and the time had finally come.

Deep in the cold black core of the island, Rhiannon gazed at the red-gold ring upon her withered finger. She had no way of knowing that Breandan's soul had moved on to the spirit world, for that knowledge belonged only to the creator. She still believed that his life essence was trapped within the ring. Breandan's body still lived, however, unaffected by the passage of time. It remained in the same state of suspended animation that had claimed it two thousand years earlier – nothing more than an empty shell.

The smile on Rhiannon's face was just as ugly as it had once been beautiful. Her lips twisted grotesquely as she gave orders to the servants waiting before her. Her hoarse bark-like commands caused the servants to jump. They would carry out their queen's orders to the letter or face the consequences, and that was a prospect no mortal creature wanted to face. "Take a patrol north until you find a Horranian ship. Bring her and her captain here to me, and try to leave enough of the crew alive to sail their own vessel."

"Yes, my Queen," responded one of the black creatures, thumping its claw-like fist against its thin chest. It turned to leave and shuffled out, followed closely by the others who had been lurking in the shadows.

Rhiannon's mouth twisted into another evil grin as she contemplated her revenge. She had spent hundreds of years creating her monstrous army. She had started the project by combining the DNA of various sea creatures with the DNA of the gentle natives that had inhabited her island. She had also crossbred one species of sea-life with another, mixing, matching species after species, year after year, century after century. Experimentation. Manipulation. Abomination. After two thousand years, she had nearly perfected her menagerie of beasts. She had turned them all into killers – and there were thousands of them inhabiting the caves and catacombs of her demonic lair. At last she was ready to unleash them upon the world.

With uncanny swiftness, Rhiannon's servants moved through the caverns until they reached the vast chamber where the sea-bats were being corralled. Although there were intermittent torches placed at key locations along the walls of the caverns, Rhiannon's troops didn't need them. They could see in the dark.

The sea-bats were anxious and ready to go; they were getting hungry. As their riders approached, they extended the tips of their wing-like appendages to the shoreline to allow them to mount their backs. There were two riders per sea-bat, one to guide the creature in the desired direction, the other to toss soul-leaches at their targets.

When the patrols were ready, the sea-bats swam out to the open sea through one of the channels Rhiannon had added to the complex. The riders paused only long enough at the start of the mission to allow the hungry sea-bats to feed on a passing school of tuna.

In the southern ocean just a few degrees below the equator, one of Rhiannon's sea-bat patrols skimmed the waves, while another patrol flew high above searching the horizon for signs of a Horranian galley.

While beneath the waves a sea-bat can use its sonar to help it locate its prey or search for enemies; above the waves it switched on its built in radar to help find the enemy.

Suddenly, one of the sea-bats became extremely agitated. Based on this elevated state of their anxiety, the riders instinctively knew that the sea-bat's biological receptors had made contact with something bigger than a whale. The flat broad-winged creature immediately sent out a telepathic signal to its companions to follow and abruptly turned east. Several minutes later their contact appeared on the horizon. As expected, it was a large Horranian galley under full sail heading west at about six knots.

On board the galley, the human slaves who staffed the oars were being given a brief respite. It was not concern for the slaves' welfare that motivated the captain of the Horranian vessel, but his own comfort. After all, it was much more agreeable to simply relax and enjoy the warm sun of the tropical ocean, compared to the frigid temperatures of the northern sea. Both the captain and his crew had grown lax in the absence of any hostilities. They were not prepared for the swift and sudden attack.

The first sea-bat plunged straight out of the cloud-filled sky. As its shadow expanded over the deck of the ship, the Horranian sailors looked up in surprise, just as the riders knew they would. It would prove to be a fatal mistake for some.

Soul-leeches rained down upon the crew, as they were caught off guard. The Horranian archers scrambled for their bows, but they were too slow. Suddenly, a second sea-bat erupted out of the waves on the portside of the galley. Again, soul-leeches rained down on the crew. By the time the attack had abated, all of the Horranian crewmen on board the ship were dead or dying. Only the captain and his human slaves remained unharmed. The shrieks of the dying lizard-men could be heard for miles across the open sea.

Unexpectedly, the entire galley was lifted out of the water on the back of one of the giant sea-bats.

The human slaves began to scream, for they were still chained to their seats inside the hull of the ship. If the wooden ship were to break apart and sink, they would have little hope of survival.

The Horranian captain was knocked to the deck where he hung on for dear life.

Abruptly, the sea-bat dove back into the water, nearly capsizing the wooden galley.

For several minutes, things quieted down. The sea-bats were no longer attacking. Then, just as the frightened captain found his feet, sea-bats appeared on both sides of the ship.

They gently nudged the galley with their wing tips until its prow was turned south.

The hideous black riders grinned menacingly and pointed towards the horizon. The stunned captain just nodded his head and waved back. He had little choice. He was going south whether he liked it or not.

Ko-Kahn sat on a golden chair at the head of a low, rectangular table over thirty feet long. Twenty of his most important chieftains were seated at the table, each being attended by a human slave girl. They were all wearing their dress uniforms, which oddly enough, did not include any weapons, as it was the Horranian custom to dine unarmed in the presence of the emperor.

Petamor recognized many of the warlords from his earlier missions of espionage deep inside the Horranian Empire. Most of the chieftains were full-blooded Horrans, while some were half-breeds, part human, part Horranian. Each had risen through the military ranks the Horranian way, by treachery and murder.

At the sight of the old half-crippled slave, Ko-Kahn ordered one of his men to bring him forward. Petamor was quick to fall to the floor at the emperor's feet.

"Here it is, my Lord," said the guard, kicking Petamor hard in the ribs.

"Well, well," hissed Ko-Kahn through a mouthful of meat, "it seems that you can cook after all. Too bad. I was looking forward to...entertaining you this evening. On the contrary, it is about time we had a decent cook around here, isn't it men?"

The Horranian chieftains responded with grunts and hisses of approval as they enthusiastically stuffed their ugly, battle-scarred faces with chunks of dripping meat.

"I've been known to be very generous with my slaves from

time to time," Ko-Kahn stated drunkenly. "I always reward my slaves in one way or the other. Therefore, I will allow you to work in my kitchen for now, at least until you start to bore me. Tonight however, in honor of this glorious feast you have created, I will reward you in any manner you desire."

"Thank you, Master," Petamor answered, pretending to grovel at the emperor's feet. "All I want, my Lord, is to serve the great Ko-Kahn."

Suddenly, the emperor was less drunk than he had first appeared. He looked at Petamor with the cold, unemotional eyes of a venomous snake. "I'm not so sure you are the fool you pretend to be, old man. But, very well. I will allow you to serve me and my distinguished guests tonight. Just remember, give me a reason to kill you and I will not hesitate, good cook or not."

"Yes, my Lord," Petamor replied.

On that note, Ko-Kahn waved the old man away and whispered to the captain of his personal guard, "Keep a close eye on that one. There is something about him I do not trust. He's much cleverer than he appears. Do not allow him out of your sight, or you will suffer the same unpleasant fate as he."

"Yes, my Lord," the guard replied, a cold chill running up his reptilian spine. "I will not let this human out of my sight."

While the Horrans continued to gorge themselves with meat, they began discussing their planned assault on the Pegazonian settlement.

Petamor was permitted to stay and serve the wine along side the slave girls. As the wine flowed, so did the details of the forthcoming invasion.

At the end of the conference, Ko-Kahn's chieftains returned to their quarters, each accompanied by a couple of slave girls of their own choosing.

Petamor was ordered to stay behind to clean up the mess the feasters had made, but he had other plans.

When his guard's back was turned, Petamor slipped quietly out of the tent and into the night air. Instantly the guard responded and followed him outside, shouting, "Hey! Where do you think you're going, you spawn of a slime-bol? Get back here before I---" he stopped short. The old man's footprints came to an abrupt halt in the fresh snow. He searched the compound in vain, but the old man had disappeared into thin air.

The next morning, the guard's head decorated the entrance to Ko-Kahn's pavilion. The expression on the reptilian-like face was one of disbelief.

As the sea-bats pushed his ship towards the slimy stinking beach, the Horranian captain looked with disbelief at the abominable black island dead ahead. The hull of the galley creaked and groaned as the sand kissed and scraped its keel, stopping thirty-feet past the water's edge.

The black riders dismounted and beckoned him to follow them up a path lined with broken, rotting vegetation. He obeyed and followed them up the slippery path towards the volcano. He noticed that the creatures had webbed feet and hands and seemed as out of place on land as his would be in the water. And what he had first assumed was hair, was actually jelly-fish-like tentacles hanging down around their scrawny shoulders. They led him to the base of the volcano and stopped. They seemed to be waiting for something, then a narrow slit in the side of the mountain began to widen. A putrid odor assaulted him like a hard punch to the stomach, and he vomited all over his uniform. When he looked up again, he saw her.

Rhiannon was standing just inside the cave entrance. She was even more grotesque and malicious looking than the black riders. She glared out at him from the darkness with glowing yellow eyes. She smiled, delighted that a creature as physically intimidating as a Horran, would be frightened of her petite self. She said, "There's no need to be afraid, Captain. I will not keep you long. Please allow me to introduce myself. I am the wizard, Rhiannon. I have brought you here to my island so that we can have a little chat. Now, if you will be good enough to accompany me to my council chamber, I will inform you why you are here."

Rhiannon spun around and disappeared into the deeper darkness.

The Horranian captain followed, but only because he was being prodded along with a pike point at his back.

Rhiannon led him into a dimly lighted cave and ordered him to sit on one of the hand-carved coral chairs before a low thrown constructed completely out of pearls. One of her servants offered the Horran captain a goblet of seaweed wine, which he reluctantly accepted with a trembling claw.

"First, let me apologize for this tiny little misunderstanding," she said. "I am afraid that my servants were a little rough with you and your ship. They do try so very hard to please me. Certainly you can understand that, can't you?"

The Horranian captain just nodded numbly.

"Good...very, very good! Because, you see, I want you to do me a little favor. You will do me a little favor, won't you, Captain?"

The Horran sailor nodded again, too frightened to speak.

"Good. Now, here's what I want you to do. I want you to deliver a message for me. I want you to deliver the message to your emperor, Ko-Khan. Can you do that? Can you?" Rhiannon smiled, causing the Horran to lose control of his bladder.

Rhiannon ignored this and continued. "I have it all written down for you, and I expect you to deliver it to Ko-Kahn personally," she said, handing a letter to one of her servants, who then handed it to the Horran. "That is all. You see. Now that wasn't so bad, was it? You may return to your ship now. Oh, and remember, Captain," she said with a gruesome and most unforgettable smile, "take my message directly to your emperor personally, or we will meet again." With that, Rhiannon turned and left the chamber, disappearing behind a wall of human skulls.

The big Horranian Captain was escorted out of the caverns by two black creatures that kept making a strange smacking sound with their mouths. Once outside, the Horran turned around just as the mouth of the cave snapped shut like the jaws of a giant crocodile.

The next thing the Horranian captain remembered, he was back on his ship sailing north with Rhiannon's message gripped tightly in his claw-tipped fingers.

———•———

Ko-Kahn sat on his throne and glared angrily at the veteran sea captain before him. "Wizard!" he screamed. "I thought all of those meddling bastards were dead and gone."

The sailor shivered in his reptilian skin. "Yes, my Lord. She is a wizard. I am certain of it."

The expression on the emperor's face changed instantly. "Did you say, she?" he asked disbelievingly.

"Yes, my Lord."

"Rhiannon!" Ko-Kahn growled as he jumped up off his throne. "It can't be! She disappeared ages ago!" He looked again at the crumpled piece of paper he was holding with renewed interest. Then he returned his terrible gaze to the petrified messenger. "Get this sniveling sack of worthless garbage out of my sight and put him in chains. I will deal with him later."

As the Horranian galley captain was being dragged away begging for mercy, Ko-Kahn reread Rhiannon's communication. He walked over to examine a map of the world hanging from one of the tent supports. He neither needed nor desired an ally, and he did not intent to share his empire with anyone, wizard, or not. Nevertheless, if everything the captain of the galley said was true, he would be a fool not to entertain Rhiannon's wishes. Besides, these bat-like sea creatures intrigued him immensely. Being a warlord, he was always interested in new effective weapons.

Rhiannon was demanding that Ko-Kahn send her a large number of transport galleys to help her ferry her mutant army to Pega. She insisted on taking part in the assault on the Pegazonian settlement for reasons of her own. *Perhaps this wizard can be of some use, after all.* Ko-Kahn considered. *Her flying creatures can certainly help defend my troops against those annoying Pegazonian warriors on their winged horses. I can always find a way to dispose of her afterward. Very well. I will send her fifty transports. Each galley can carry five thousand men. That should be enough to suit her needs. However, I will not postpone the assault on the escarpment to wait for her.*

The Horranian transport galleys were nearing Rhiannon's island. The sky and ocean were full of sea-bats escorting the twin-hulled ships to the hastily built piers. The Horrans were not too thrilled at the sight of the monstrous creatures with their black riders, but at the same time, they were relieved that they were to be on the same team.

In order to accommodate as many of Rhiannon's bizarre soldiers as possible, each galley carried only a skeleton crew. When the galleys reached the island, they were guided to the eastern side where Rhiannon's soldiers were waiting beside the piers.

Thoradal was in his chambers when he made the telepathic contact with his colorful little spy. Although the little robotic parrot was over two-thousand years old, it still functioned perfectly. At the moment, it was perched atop the spar of a Horranian transport galley sitting at anchor. Below, spread out between the coral reef and Rhiannon's island, fifty galleys bobbed like corks on the ocean waves. The beach was over-crowded with thousands of Rhiannon's mutant horde, waiting for the order to begin boarding the ships.

Thoradal sighed heavily. "Time to talk to Rolf," he said to himself.

———•———

Rhiannon's troops boarded the galleys in perfect order. They carried all the normal gear of a foot soldier, with the exception of one of Rhiannon's latest weapon – the soul leeches. Unlike sea-bats, soul-leeches could not live long enough out of water to be a useful weapon on dry land.

Despite the speed and efficiency with which the loading process was carried out, it still took several hours to complete. When the heavily loaded galleys finally headed back out to sea, they were escorted by a ten squadrons of sea-bats.

———•———

High Elder Malachi called the late-evening meeting to order. In attendance were all the group leaders, Captain Sylvee, and about a hundred other concerned settlers, including Sylvee's main antagonist – High Elder Budoc.

Malachi began, "I have called this meeting tonight, as most of you already know, for the explicit purpose of discussing the threat facing our small community. Based on the daily reports from our patrol leaders, we feel that the Horrans are going to scale the escarpment wall and attack our settlement. We're not sure how they plan to do it, but we believe that they have discovered a way to get up the escarpment wall."

"Wait just one minute, Malachi," interrupted Budoc, High Elder of the High Elders, who adamantly opposed any preparation for an invasion that would never come. "We've heard these reports before, and we all agreed that there's no way that---"

"You are out of order, Budoc," cautioned Malachi. "Kindly take your seat and wait your turn to speak."

Budoc's face turned a bright shade of red. Nevertheless, he sat down to wait his turn.

"It is my considered opinion," Malachi continued, "that we must set up a defensive line along the rim of the escarpment immediately, just in case the Horrans do manage to climb the escarpment wall. However, before we put it to a vote, I've asked Captain Sylvee to fill us in on the latest activity below."

Sylvee was wearing a dark blue dress uniform that fit her like a glove. She quickly rose from her seat and walked confidently to the speaker's podium.

Elder Budoc twisted uncomfortably in his chair as he watched her walk past. Several years earlier, he had attempted to convince Sylvee to become his mate; however, she had rejected him and chosen the life of a warrior instead. He had never forgiven her and had grown bitter at the memory.

She nodded her head slightly to Elder Malachi as he turned the podium over to her, and then she turned to face the audience. "As a flight leader, I have seen with my own eyes the build-up of enemy troops now entrenched along the base of the escarpment, and that number is increasing everyday. We must ask ourselves why. Why are the Horrans amassing such a large force at our very doorstep? A harmless military exercise? No, I think not. The answer is simple. Somehow, someway, they have discovered a way to get their soldiers up the escarpment wall."

Again, Budoc interrupted. "That's impossible. You know as well as I do that no one has managed to climb the escarpment in two-thousand years. Now you want us all to believe that the entire Horranian army is going to scale that wall. I am sorry Captain, but the Horrans are lucky if they can mount their horses, much less climb the escarpment wall. And do not tell me that they intend to use their human slave army to scale the wall. They can't even tie their own bootstraps. So tell me Captain Sylvee. Who, exactly, is going to do the climbing? Can you answer me that?"

"I don't know. Maybe they plan to build some towers beside the escarpment wall," Sylvee said, feeling somewhat foolish.

"Build towers? A thousand feet tall?" asked one of the settlers. "Impossible. We all know that the tallest structure ever built is the Great Lighthouse at Southpoint, and it's only one hundred and eighty-seven feet high."

"That's true," admitted Sylvee. "However, you must keep in mind that the Horrans are very clever. If they believe that they can reach the top of the escarpment by building towers, they'll find a way to do it."

"Don't be absurd," Budoc laughed.

"Elder Budoc," Malachi said, "I have already cautioned you once for speaking out of turn."

"It's all right, Elder Malachi," Sylvee said holding up her hand. "Elder Budoc makes a good point."

"As I was saying," Budoc continued, ignoring Elder Malachi's threat, "just read your history. No one has managed to attack our settlement because they cannot and will never be able to reach us simply by climbing the escarpment wall."

"Yes, Elder Budoc, I am aware of our history," said Sylvee. "All I'm asking the Elders to do is prepare a defense *just in case* the Horrans *have* figured out a way to reach us. You must keep in mind how much they hate us. They have amassed a huge army down there. They have enough workers to build a tower all the way to Titan if they wanted to."

"Captain Sylvee, with all due respect, it would take years to build any type of structure high enough to reach our settlement," said the same settler. "Not to mention the construction materials it would require."

"Have you seen any signs of building materials during any of your patrols, Captain Sylvee?" Budoc asked.

"The Horrans have several hundred wagons parked along the base of the escarpment at various intervals," she replied. "It's difficult to say what's on those wagons because they are covered with tarps."

"Just how big are these wagons?"

"Oh...they vary in size, but most of them are about the size of your average supply wagon."

"That doesn't mean that they are loaded with building materials," said Dillon.

"What else could it be?" Sylvee asked.

Budoc shrugged, "Food, clothing...weapons---"

"Or building materials," Sylvee finished.

"All right, Captain Sylvee. Let's suppose for a moment that the Horrans really are planning to build a tower high enough to reach the top of the escarpment. It's your job to make sure that they never reach the top," Budoc said.

"Yes, I know, Elder Budoc, but my riders are few in number by comparison to the enemy soldiers, and it's unrealistic to assume that none of us will be killed in the course of action. The Horrans literally have thousands of soldiers down below, and more arriving everyday. How long do you think we can hold them off? Two months? Six? Maybe an entire year at the most. We could kill them by the thousands, but more would come to take their places. Eventually they would build their tower and then what?"

"All right," began the settler, "let's say for a moment that the Horrans do manage to construct a tower, or two towers, or even a dozen towers. So what? How many soldiers would be able to climb those towers all at once? Not very many. Our riders and our ground archers would pick them off like flies. At the very least, they would need a hundred towers or more if they wanted to overwhelm us by superior force, and even that is questionable."

Dillon, the chief metalworker, did not care for all this talk of war. He wasn't a lazy man by nature, but the thought of having to manufacture all of the materials needed to wage a full-scale war on the Horrans turned his well-padded stomach into a vat of acid. "I agree with Elder Budoc," he said from the floor. "Even if everything you say turns out to be true, Captain

Sylvee, we don't need to rush into anything. If the Horrans do intend to construct some type of tower, it would be physically impossible to complete it within a few weeks or even in a few months. I say we wait and see what they intend to do before we decide on a course of action."

"Dillon has a point," Budoc was quick to point out. "This entire discussion is unwarranted. There's no need to panic. We have plenty of time."

"I still think that we should begin preparing our defenses now. The longer we prepare, the better prepared we'll be," Sylvee stated.

"Captain Sylvee, we're a small community. We simply can't spare all of the manpower needed to set up a permanent defensive line just so we can sit around and wait for a hypothetical attack. Besides, it's your job to protect this community. Try and remember that." Dillon said harshly.

"Enough of this," Budoc said. "You've already wasted enough of our time, Captain Sylvee. I say we take a vote right now."

Sylvee looked at Elder Malachi and nodded.

Malachi shrugged. "Very well then," he said. "Let's vote now. Will all of you who agree with Captain Sylvee please hold up your right hand."

All of the riders and a few of the settlers held up their hands. Malachi took a count.

"All right. Now, all of you who are opposed to Captain Sylvee's proposal, please hold up your hand."

Budoc and the majority of the settlers in attendance raised their hands. Malachi did not need to count; the majority had gone against Sylvee.

"I'm sorry, Captain," he said as he turned to Sylvee, "but it appears that we'll have to wait and see what happens."

The crowd stood up from the wooden benches they had been sitting on and began to file towards the big oaken doors at the front of the lodge. Outside, the snow had finally given way to a clear sky, and the heavens were ablaze with stars. The night air was fresh and crisp. When the first group of settlers reached the doors, they were struck with a sense of awe and wonder. For there, directly across from the lodge in the middle of the frozen lake stood the Wizard's Tower, brightly lighted from top to bottom. For a long time, no one spoke. They just stood and stared. Then elder Malachi said, "I believe that our wizard has returned to us at last."

Thoradal sipped wine at Neff's dinner table. Leecy, Neff's wife, was busy clearing away the empty plates, bowls and eating utensils. Rolf was watching Kile, and Kile was lost in thought as if miles away.

Leecy called their six children around so that Neff could kiss them goodnight. She was a heavyset woman with a pleasant face and a joyous spirit. She was a good wife and a great mother. She loved Neff and it was obvious that he loved her too.

It was late evening and Thoradal was contemplating the strange events that had occurred during Kile's voyage in the Southern Reaches. If what Kile had said was true, and there was no reason not to believe him, then Rhiannon had resurrected her island from the ocean deep. *After all these years, she has returned. This can only mean one thing. She wants revenge.*

"Wizard," Kile said, changing the course of the old wizard's thoughts. "It is a certainty that we will have to fight the Horrans, but they outnumber us more than a thousand to one. How can we possibly win against such odds?"

"We don't have to win," Thoradal said plainly. "We just have to make it too difficult for them to defeat us."

"I don't get it," Kile admitted.

"Try and look at it like this. We are a small fish in a big pond, while the Horrans are the big fish."

Kile nodded. "The Horrans could eat us in one gulp," he said.

"Exactly," Thoradal agreed. "But if they end up with a bellyache every time they try to eat us, after some time, they may decide that we're not worth the trouble, and leave us alone."

Kile just looked at him.

Thoradal sighed. "Do you like bellyaches, Kile?" he asked.

"No, of course not," Kile answered.

"Well...my guess is that the Horrans don't like bellyaches, either."

Kyle nodded. "Okay, I get it now, I think."

"Yes, but bellyache or not," Thoradal continued, "eventually they *will* come here to try and destroy us."

This time it was Rolf's turn to nod. "You should also keep in mind, little brother, that over ninety-percent of their army is made up of human slaves. Those slaves have no real desire to fight us or anyone else for that matter. If they are given the opportunity to escape, they would do it in a heartbeat," he said.

"That's another thing I don't understand. If their human slaves outnumber them ten-to-one, why don't they simply rise up and fight the Horrans themselves?" Kile asked.

"If you ask me, they're all cowards," Neff answered.

"Don't be quick to judge them, brother," Rolf said. "When they're hungry, the Horrans give them food. When they're thirsty, the Horrans give them water. When they're cold, the Horrans give them a fire to warm themselves. That's why they obey their masters. They have become like well-trained dogs. The Horrans have brainwashed them into thinking that they cannot be defeated."

"That's true, but even dogs can turn against their masters," Thoradal added. "My primary concern right now is not the Horrans, but---" he stopped in mid-sentence and cocked his head as if he were listening to something far away.

Rolf was curious, but knew better than to interrupt Thoradal when he was behaving strangely.

Suddenly, Thoradal rose from the bench mumbling to himself. "My friends, you must forgive me, but I have to leave you for a short time," he said.

"What? Leave us?" Rolf asked, jumping up from his seat. "How can you leave us at a time like this?"

"An old friend has summoned me to his tower to discuss the Horranian issue. I must leave at once. After all these years, I have been hoping that he was still alive. Now, don't worry. I will return as quickly as possible. You must trust me. It's in our best interest if I go to see him. He may be able to help us."

"Who is this old friend?" Rolf asked.

"His name is Petamor. He is a wizard like me," Thoradal said. "But I haven't seen or spoken to him in nearly two thousand years. It will be good to see him again. He lives on the escarpment high above the land once inhabited by your ancestors. Now, please. You must excuse me. I must take my leave at once."

"Wait a moment," Rolf said. "Why would he summon you after all these years?"

"It all is starting to make sense now, don't you see? We know that Ko-Kahn has sent transports to Rhiannon's island, but until now, we did not know why. Now, I believe I know the answer. The Horrans are going to attack the people living on the plateau above the escarpment. Petamor has been looking after them, as I have been looking after you. So you see...we are not alone. We have an ally."

"Then let me take you there," Kile said. "You shouldn't travel alone."

There was a moment or two of silence, as the absurdity of what Kile had said sank in.

"Thank you, Kile, your offer is greatly appreciated," the old wizard said sincerely, "but I can travel alone much faster."

Kile nodded. "I keep forgetting that you don't need a ship to travel."

"That's true. Nevertheless, your offer is still appreciated. And do not worry about me, my friends. I will return as quickly as I can."

Thoradal turned and left Neff's quarters. He hurried along the passageway inside the wall of the crater to the watchtower above the north gate. There he transformed himself into a bolt of lightning and shot out through the narrow window and on through the night to the continent of Pega.

Petamor gazed over the parapet into the late evening mist rising off the surface of the lake. Just beyond the western edge of the frozen lake, the settlement was brimming with activity. He was home again. He watched as a patrol of riders flew south towards the edge of the escarpment on the backs of their rock hoppers. He recalled the first time he had seen Rhiannon riding on Topaz.

Suddenly there was a bright flash, followed by a clap of thunder directly behind him. It caused him to jump.

"Greetings, old friend," Thoradal said, after transforming back into his human form.

"Thoradal!" Petamor exclaimed, embracing the old wizard. "It has been a long time. How have you been? It has been too long since we stood here together. Many things have changed. I hope all is well with you."

"I have been better."

"Thank you for coming on such short notice, but I'm afraid that I have a serious problem on my hands. The Horrans are camped out along the base of the escarpment. They are preparing to climb the escarpment and invade the settlement here, and I'm afraid that my powers alone are not enough to stop them. I could really use your help," Petamor admitted.

"Then we must help each other, old friend, for I too am the

bearer of unpleasant news. Our worst fears have come true at last. Rhiannon has arisen from the bottom of the sea. Even as we speak, she is joining forces with the Horranian emperor. Ko-Kahn has already sent transport galleys to her island to ferry her army here to help defeat you."

"That is bad news."

"Have you tried to summon any other members of the league?"

"I was afraid you were going to ask me that, old friend. Aside from Breandan, you and I are all that's left. The others have chosen to move on."

"All of them? Well...I'm not surprised. I have thought about it myself many times."

"Are you serious?"

"Yes, but don't worry. I will not desert you during this crisis. You mentioned Breandan. Is he still alive?" Thoradal asked incredulously.

"He lives, I am sure of it. Although the flame of his lamp does not burn, the lamp itself remains warm to the touch. However, I don't think he can help us. He is still under Rhiannon's enchantment."

"Nevertheless, we must try and rescue him," Thoradal said.

"Rescue him? Is that even possible after all this time?" Petamor asked.

"We must try," Thoradal said flatly. "We owe him that. We have waited far too long as it is."

"We had no choice. There was nothing we could do, imprisoned as he was on Rhiannon's island beneath the sea."

"Well, Rhiannon's island isn't on the ocean floor any longer."

"Then I will go," Petamor said. "There's still a chance that Rhiannon might listen to reason."

Thoradal thought it over for a few minutes. "No, my friend, I will go. I can take a few members of my clan for support. Your people are already under siege. You must remain here and help them. If anything happens to me, you will just have to carry on without me."

"Very well, but if you are successful, you must bring Breandan back here to the tower. Perhaps we can revive him before we are completely overwhelmed. But we must work fast."

"Yes, let us hope it is not too late," Thoradal said embracing Petamor once again. "Now I must return to my people to begin the mission at once."

"Here," Petamor said, holding out Breandan's small clay lamp, "Take this with you. It might help you find him."

"Thank you, old friend."

"So long, my brother," Petamor said. After he turned away, an overwhelming feeling of dread came over him. He turned around to warn Thoradal, but he was already gone.

At Dragon's Den, Thoradal sat in conference with Rolf, Kile, and the other chieftains and sea captains of their island home.

"So it's all settled then," Rolf was saying. "Kile will take Thoradal to the black island and attempt to rescue Breandan. I will take the rest of our fleet out to sea to hunt down and destroy the Horranian transports before they can reach Pega."

"Right," Neff agreed, "and I will remain here to organize our defenses just in case the Horrans attack us while you're gone."

"Not much chance of that happening," said one of the minor chieftains, "the sea-dragons would tear them apart in minutes."

"I hope you're right," said Thoradal. "Just remember, the Horrans are part reptilian. I hope that our dragons don't decide to join with them."

"I seriously doubt that," Rolf said.

"Don't be so certain. Remember how your ancestors first arrived here."

"I'm as aware of our history as you are, Thoradal, but these dragons have become our friends as well as our guardians. I cannot believe that they would ever betray us. Still...it would be best to be prepared just in case they do," Rolf admitted although he only said it because he wanted to avoid arguing with the old wizard. "Is there anything else bothering you, Thoradal? You don't seem like yourself."

"I'm sorry, Rolf," Thoradal admitted. "Perhaps I am getting too old for all this drama. Maybe when this is all over, I will follow my fellow wizards into the next world."

"Don't say that!" Neff said. "You belong here with us, Thoradal. You've been like a father to all of us."

"Thank you, Neff. Those are kind words. However, let's get on with this discussion, shall we? Exactly how many ships do you plan on sending, Rolf?" Thoradal asked, picking up where the original conversation had left off.

"We can send thirty ships," Rolf said. "I know it doesn't sound like much when compared to the Horranian fleet, but it's the best we can do. I must leave a few behind to help guard the island. As for the rest of our fleet, they're all in need of repairs, too dangerous to take to sea. They would only be a liability. Does anyone else have any thoughts or ideas they would like to put forth?"

"I was thinking that maybe, if you attach your rams to the prows of your ships before you put out to sea, it could save you time when you finally encounter the Horranian galleys," Neff said.

"That is true. If we attach the battering rams before we put out to sea, we would be ready to fight when we encounter the enemy," replied one of the captains.

"You're right, Captain. And I realize that it can take a little time to attach the rams properly when we are at sea. However, since we already know where the Horranian armada is headed, all we have to do is get there ahead of them. We can attach the rams and shear blades while we wait for them to arrive," Rolf explained.

"Right," agreed Kile, "we'll attach the rams after we reach the rendezvous point."

A quick show of hands proved that most captains agreed.

"Now, are there any other issues we need to discuss before we depart?" Rolf asked.

"I...I have something," Neff said, slightly embarrassed as he held up a strange looking headpiece. "Leecy came up with the idea," he continued, "after what happened to Kile's men." He looked apologetically towards Kile.

"What on earth is it?" asked one of the captains.

"Uh...well, I don't have a name for it yet, but it can help protect you and your men from those squishy things that killed Kile's men."

"The soul leeches?" Kile asked.

"Yeah, yeah...the soul leeches. You put it over your head like this," he added as he fitted the contraption over his head and shoulders. "See...it covers your head and shoulders, but still lets you move around. It's made of thin leather, with a layer of over-lapping seashells. I don't know why, but that slimy stuff won't eat through the seashells like it will wood or metal."

"How do you know that, Neff?" Kile asked.

"I took the soul leech home with me and did some little experiments on it. I squeezed all of the slime out of it and tried it on different materials to see if there was anything it couldn't eat through. Sea shells were the only thing that the slime didn't burn."

"Interesting," Kile admitted.

"Leecy and some of the other wives have been working night and day to finish them, but they ran out of time. I'm afraid that there's not enough for everyone."

"Thank you, Neff. That was very considerate of Leecy. Please tell her and the other wives thank you from all of us. I'll see that they are distributed fairly among the crews. Now, the rest of us have jobs to do as well, and I suggest we get started. The sooner we get out to sea, the better our chances of taking the enemy by surprise."

———◆———

Sylvee, Malachi, Deena, and four other brave settlers cautiously walked across the surface of the frozen lake to the Wizard's Tower. When they reached the small island of rock upon which stood the tower, they paused, looking curiously at the heavy oaken door.

"Where did that door come from?" Sylvee asked. "I've been out here dozens of times and I've never noticed it before."

Malachi raised his eyebrows and shrugged his shoulders in response to her question.

Deena said, "You're right, Captain. When I was a little girl, I used to come out here all the time to play with my friends. That door wasn't there then."

A few of the settlers smiled. To them, Deena still was a little girl.

"Well, what are you waiting for?" asked one of the settlers. "Go ahead and open it."

"Perhaps we should knock first," Malachi suggested drawing looks from Sylvee and Deena. "You know...just in case."

Sylvee reached out and tapped meekly on the door. "Hello," she called softly. "Is anyone there?"

"Geez!" said Deena, "I don't believe this! Let me do it!" Sylvee's young apprentice boldly walked up to the door and pounded with her fist. "Hey, in there! Answer the door, will you! We don't have all darn night!"

"Deena!" Sylvee exclaimed, trying to stifle a laugh.

However, Deena was not in the mood for jokes. She was getting angry. With no further ado, she turned the handle and pushed the door inward as hard as she could. The big oaken door opened slowly on protesting hinges. Deena smiled victoriously at Sylvee.

"Show off," Sylvee said, smiling back at the girl.

With the door now wide open, there was no longer any doubt that someone was inside. There was a roaring fire in the hearth, and the thick coat of dust covering the floor had been disturbed by footprints. They were everywhere, but the room itself appeared to be empty.

"Wow!" Deena said unable to conceal the wonder in her voice. "Get a load of this place. Is it just me, or does it look bigger on the inside than it does on the outside?"

Sylvee had noticed the odd difference in dimensions, too. She could feel her excitement building. "Never mind that now," Sylvee answered as she slipped her slender dagger from its sheath and pointed to the winding staircase that lead to the upper levels. "Whoever is in here went upstairs. See the footprints on the risers?"

Everyone nodded.

Deena was about to speak again, but Sylvee put a finger to her lips.

"We'd better be quite," Sylvee said. "Maybe our guest isn't friendly."

Malachi and the others nodded in agreement.

Sylvee led them up the winding stairs, stopping to check each level in turn.

The intruder, whoever it was, had lit oil lamps and built fires in nearly every hearth they encountered. Whoever it was, was very industrious. Not exactly the type of behavior one would expect from a prospective burglar. However, the footprints continued to climb higher into the tower, and every step took them closer to a confrontation with the mysterious visitor.

At last, they reached the door outside a chamber where the footprints entered but did not exit. The door was closed.

Whoever had entered the chamber had closed the door and not come out again.

Malachi pointed to the dusty runes engraved into the stone lintel above the door. Although he studied ancient runes as a hobby, he was unfamiliar with these. But he could recall most of the stories his grandfather had once told him, and if there was any truth in those old tales, this door opened to the room where the Lamps of Life were supposed to be stored.

Sylvee gripped the handle of her dagger tightly as she pushed the door open. For a moment, the figure standing across the room was difficult to see due to the bright light from the fireplace. However, as their eyes adjusted to the light, they were shocked to see a strange, half-crippled elderly man dressed in grease-stained rags, staring back at them. He smiled and nodded in greeting.

Elder Budoc, who had been lagging behind the group out of fear, suddenly found his courage. He pushed forward and said, "Who are you, sir? And just what the devil do you think you're doing here?"

The old man's eyes widened in surprise. "What am I doing here? Why I belong here," he replied. "And who the devil might you be?"

"I am Budoc, Head Elder of the Pegazons."

"I see," said the old man. "My name is Petamor and this tower is my home."

"Petamor? The wizard? Ha! You sir, are no wizard! You're just an old beggar...a thief by the look of you...or a spy perhaps. Yes...that's it, isn't it? You're a bloody spy sent here by those bloodthirsty Horrans."

"Shut up, Budoc," Sylvee said angrily. Then, as she moved between Budoc and the old man, she slipped her dagger safely back into its sheath.

"Yes, well...I guess that I have been away longer than I thought," the old man said more to himself.

Sylvee looked him up and down doubtfully. *Budoc's right*

about one thing, she thought. *This old man sure doesn't look like the wizard I've always pictured.*

"Oh," he said, as he realized for the first time that he was still in disguise, "no wonder." He closed his eyes and mumbled something in a strange language. Suddenly, his grease-stained wardrobe morphed into an old brown robe, and he was Petamor again, just as in the old days. "My apologies," he said. "I forgot that I was in disguise."

Every mouth in the room hung open in amazement.

"If you ask me," Deena began, "you don't look much different."

Ignoring Deena's comment, Petamor smiled and bowed slightly. "Please allow me to begin again. My name is Petamor, and this is my tower – my home. I have returned because I have urgent news for all of you concerning Ko-Kahn's plan to invade your settlement."

"Then it *is* true," Budoc said. "I have been such a fool."

"There is yet time to prepare," Petamor replied. "If Ko-Kahn's plan goes according to schedule, it will only take them a few weeks to reach the top of the escarpment. But I think that we can delay their progress somewhat with a little strategy of our own."

"What exactly do you suggest we do?"

"Harass the ladder builders as much as possible. Keep them on their toes, so to speak. We may not stop them completely, but we can certainly slow them down."

"What can you do to help us?" asked Malachi.

"I'm only one old man, and my powers alone cannot protect you for very long. There are just too many of them."

"Perhaps it would be best if we abandon the settlement and find a new home," Budoc said.

"Where would we go?" asked Malachi.

"We could scale down the northern side of the escarpment.

Climbing down is much easier than climbing up," Budoc stated.

"All right," said Malachi, "let's suppose we move everyone to the northern side of the escarpment. How many would die in the move? Then where would we go? We have no ships. As soon the Horrans figure out where we are, they would come after us. We would be sitting ducks, trapped between the escarpment and the sea."

"We're sitting ducks if we stay *here*," Budoc insisted.

"One of the reasons our ancestors built this settlement in the first place was to escape from the Horrans," said Malachi. "I say we stay and fight. We have Sylvee's riders to defend us, and we have a wizard to help us with a little extra magic."

"We're not completely alone in this war," Petamor said, gesturing at one of the lamps burning in its wall niche. "My friend, the wizard Thoradal and his clan live on an isolated island far to the east. The Horrans are their enemies, too."

"Is that his lamp?" Deena asked, pointing to the lamp with a bright red flame. "No, that is Rhiannon's lamp. And she may prove to be our worst enemy before this war is over."

"What?" Asked Sylvee startled. "Are you serious? I thought that she was just a legend, an old wives' tale. Are you telling us she really exists?"

"Yes, I'm afraid so," Petamor replied. "Rhiannon still lives, and she is out for revenge."

"Then Thoradal and his people are the only ones who can help us."

"At the moment, yes," Petamor replied.

"Is there any way we can contact them. At the very least we can exchange information on the Horrans," said Sylvee.

"I've already spoken with Thoradal. His people are going to try to rescue Breandan, who has been Rhiannon's prisoner for two thousand years. If Thoradal and his clan are successful, they will bring Breandan back here so that we can try to revive him."

"Who is Breandan?" Sylvee asked.

"Breandan is a wizard. Unfortunately, he has been imprisoned on Rhiannon's island for two thousand years. However, if Thoradal and his clan are able to rescue him, he may be able to help us if we can revive him."

"Revive him?" Deena asked. "Revive him from what? Is he sick or something?"

"In a manner of speaking, yes. But it would take too long to explain it to you now. However, if we do manage to revive him in time, it is possible that we can use our combined powers to defeat the Horrans."

"What about Rhiannon? What does she have to do with this?" Sylvee asked.

"The Horranian emperor has sent transport galleys to Rhiannon's lair, so that they can ferry her army here to help defeat us," Petamor answered.

"What!" Budoc exclaimed. "As if things weren't bad enough, now we have to fight a rogue-wizard as well?"

"All is not lost," Petamor added. "Even as we speak, Thoradal's clan is preparing to go to sea to attack the transports and stop them before they can reach Pega. For now, all we can do is defend the escarpment and pray that Thoradal's people are successful."

Dagar was one of Rolf's most experienced sea captains. He steered his ship on a southwest heading, running several miles ahead of Rolf's fleet. He was scouting for any sign of the Horranian transports and was the first to spot the armada of slow moving galleys heading northeast away from Rhiannon's island.

Dagar was preparing to signal Rolf, when one of his men cried out. High above the ship, several sea-bats were spiraling down to attack. Dagar and his crew had been briefed on the monsters and knew what to expect. He quickly ordered his men to battle stations where they put on their specially designed headgear that would protect their faces, necks, and shoulders from the soul-leeches. His archers took up their prearranged positions on the deck and were all set to fire.

The sea-bats soaring above Dagar's ship were riderless tag-alongs, too small to accommodate the weight of a rider. There were also a few young and inexperienced adolescent sea-bats in the flock. They had been flying along with the Horranian fleet searching for food. At first, they had been confused by the dragon ships, mistaking them for the real thing. Normally, they feared dragons. Sea-dragons were their only natural enemy. Today, however, they were too hungry to be afraid of anything. They attacked.

Kreel's dragon ship was only two miles behind Dagar's ship. He and his men had also seen the sea-bats circling Dagar's ship. Kreel ordered his men to man the oars and steer for Dagar's aid. This maneuver brought attention to the fact that they had an escort of their own. Apparently, a pod of sea-dragons had followed them all the way from Dragon's Den and was currently escorting their ship.

Back on Dagar's ship, his archers fired their arrows, fatally striking the soft, unprotected underbellies of several sea-bats. One of the younger sea-bats crashed into Dagar's ship, breaking it in half, and smashing it into pieces.

Kreel hoped to reach Dagar and his men before the sea-bats could devour them, but the sea was rough and the going was slow. Several of the wounded creatures were floundering in the water around Dagar's broken ship.

Suddenly, the sea-dragons escorting Kreel's ship peeled off and hurried towards the wreckage. When they reached the broken ship, they attacked the dying sea-bats and dragged them to the bottom of the ocean where they could do no more damage. Then they gently slipped beneath Dagar and his crew, lifted them upon their backs, and proceeded to deliver them to Kreel's ship.

Most of Dagar's crew had survived the attack unharmed, although two were killed when the sea-bat crashed into the ship. Dagar, himself was also injured, but not seriously.

"They destroyed my ship, Krccl," Dagar moaned.

"I know, but don't worry, Dagar," Kreel said. "We're on our way to rejoin the rest of the fleet. Then we'll hunt down those bloody Horrans and teach them a lesson or two."

Sylvee looked at Flight Leader Jana. "Are you certain that they've started building the ladders?" she asked anxiously.

"Yes," replied Jana, who had led the afternoon patrol over the escarpment, "there's no doubt about it. They appear to be hammering iron rods directly into the rock wall."

"How high have they managed to get?"

"It looks as if they've just started. However, I'd estimate that they've already reached a hundred feet or so. And they are beginning to construct scaffolding between the siege towers."

"That's not good. How many of these iron-rung ladders are they building?"

"Again, I don't know the exact number," Jana said. "There were too many to count. Every time we tried to get in for a closer look, they would fire off one of those porcupines. But a rough estimate would be about a fifty or sixty."

"Fifty or sixty," Sylvee repeated. "That's not so bad. However, the scaffolding is another story. That presents a serious problem. Very well. Thank you, Flight Leader Jana. Please inform the other flight leaders that I want to see everyone in the briefing room in one hour. You're dismissed."

"Thank you, Captain," Jana said with a sharp salute.

Sylvee buttoned her jacket and went outside. *I have to find Shane right away,* she thought as she ran down the narrow street. She found Shane in the blacksmith shop where he was busy examining some newly fashioned arrowheads and swords.

Dillon was busy ordering his men around, while Shane hounded his every step. "Your men will have to work faster than this, Dillon, if you expect---"

"Get out of my way, Shane. I don't have time for this. You go and do your job and leave me alone so I can do mine," Dillon spat as he pushed past Shane. "Seff, get these points to the woodshop now, chop-chop. Jac, get the lead out of your ass and oil the blades of these swords before they start to rust. Shane, I thought I told you to get out of here," Dillon said harshly. "We have a lot of work to do here," he added.

"Dillon, I'm not leaving until you hear me out. I've been trying to tell you that you will have to do better than this," Shane insisted. "These arrowheads are useless. They're not properly balanced."

Dillon grabbed Shane by his collar and shoved him up against the wall. "That's because these arrowheads have not been filed yet," he said. "Once they have been filed down, they will be balanced. Damn it, Shane, can't you see that we're working as fast as we can. Please, stop pestering me, will you?"

Sylvee smiled at Shane who was obviously flustered. He was not used to being ignored. But Iron Master Dillon had his own way of doing things, and nothing Shane said or did was going to make any difference.

"Shane, I have to talk to you," Sylvee said.

Shane turned and looked at the pretty woman warrior and wondered what it was that she found so amusing. For a moment, he just stared at her, and then a wry smile crept onto his face. "Well, I'm glad that someone wants to talk to me," he said as he strolled over to Sylvee. "Let's get out of here. This heat is starting to get to me."

"From the look of things," Sylvee laughed, "the heat's not the only thing that's getting to you."

Shane smiled warmly at the young woman. "Tell me Sylvee, how can you be so cheerful at a time like this?"

"What's not to be cheerful about? There's only twenty-five thousand bloodthirsty psychotic maniacs running around at the base of the escarpment intent on cutting the throats of every man, woman, and child in the settlement."

"Oh, please," he replied teasingly, "all you have to do is hop onto the back of that rock hopper of yours and fly away."

The smile on Sylvee's face vanished instantly. Her eyes narrowed.

The moment it came out of his mouth, Shane was already sorry he'd said it. It was meant to be a joke, but it came out all sounding like an accusation. He knew how seriously Sylvee took in her duty. "Sorry," he said. "I suppose the pressure's getting to me, too. I know that you'd never abandon the settlement."

Sylvee was not one to hold a grudge. Her smile returned. Besides, she really liked Shane. "It's all right. We're all a little edgy."

Shane took her by the arm and led her out into the open air. "So what is it you want to see me about?"

"The Horrans have started building their ladders up the escarpment wall. Just like the wizard said they would."

"I'm already aware of that," he said.

"And that's not all," she continued. "They have also started constructing scaffolding between the towers."

"Oh. Now that *is* a problem. If they manage to connect all of the towers together, it will be very stable structure. They'll be able to continue right up the escarpment wall to the top. Of course, constructing all of that additional scaffolding is going to take time. They can't do *that* in a week or two, no matter what Petamor says. Exactly how many siege towers have they built so far?"

"They've built about fifty of them along the base of the escarpment to protect the ladder builders, and they've mounted porcupines on top of all of them."

"Ouch. Well, the first thing you must remember is not to panic. There are ways of dealing with the scaffolding."

"What about the ladder builders. They're moving a lot faster than even Petamor expected. At the rate they're going, they might reach the top of the escarpment within the week."

Shane nodded. "Yes...well the first five hundred feet of the escarpment is not very difficult to scale. Even my grandmother could do it. It's that last five hundred feet that's difficult," Shane said. "If your riders can keep the workers looking over their shoulders while they are building the scaffolding, it can slow them down considerably."

"I hope you're right," Sylvee said.

"So do I. Also, keep in mind how big and clumsy the Horrans are."

Sylvee started to speak but Shane held up his hand.

"I already know what you are going to say, the Horrans will send their human slaves up the ladders first to bare the brunt of our defense."

Sylvee nodded.

"Nevertheless, the Horrans will have to climb the ladders eventually, won't they? After all, they're not about to allow their slave army to go unsupervised. That would be a big mistake."

"Not necessarily," Sylvee said. "Once they've completed the scaffolding---"

"*If* they complete the scaffolding," Shane interrupted.

"Okay...*if* they complete the scaffolding, the Horrans won't have any problems climbing up the ladders," Sylvee said.

"True, but until then, they have little choice but to rely on their human slaves to do most of the fighting. And once the slave soldiers reach the top of the escarpment, they will have to decide whether to fight us...or fight their masters. And the Horran's won't be able to do very much about it."

"Until they complete the scaffolding."

"Exactly. So I guess that we will just have to make sure that they never get the chance to complete the scaffolding."

Sylvee sighed. "Do you have any more ideas?"

"At the moment I have every able-bodied man working day and night hauling rocks and stones down from the mountains. The women and children can help by tossing the rubble over the ridge of the escarpment onto the heads of the ladder builders. That should slow them down a bit, don't you think?"

"But will it be enough?"

"No, but at least the women and children will not be in any jeopardy while they do it."

"Well...it's a start at least," Sylvee said with a slight frown. "Got anything else?"

"Some of my men have started boiling caldrons of oil near the edge of the escarpment. Of course, it won't do much good now. We'll have to wait until they get close enough for it to be effective, but it'll definitely slow them down when we start pouring hot oil down on top of their heads."

"That's it? That's all you're going to do?"

"What else can we do but wait?"

"If I were you, I'd pour some of that oil down the face of the escarpment wall directly above the locations where the ladder builders are working. That'll make the wall so slippery, the ladder builders will have a tough time just hanging on, much less pounding iron rods into the rock face."

"Great idea. "I'll have my men start on it immediately. Any other ideas?"

"What about the Wizard's Pass. Is it still open?" Sylvee asked.

"I don't think so. Besides, no one had tried to use it in two thousand years. But you're right. I can have some of my men take another look and make sure that no one can get through it."

"It's a shame. The Wizard's Pass has always been a landmark and a symbol of hope for our people."

"I know. Without it, none of our ancestors could have climbed the escarpment wall. None of us would be here today."

"What about ammunition? Has Dillon's crew made enough arrows to handle the enemy once they reach the top?"

"We should have enough to last us for a few days, depending on the intensity of the assault. Our archers are ready, but all they can do now is sit and wait for the enemy to begin climbing up over the top of the ridge."

Sylvee nodded. "Sounds like you and your men are ready."

Shane looked at Sylvee. "I do have another idea. Although it'll put your riders in a great deal of danger," he said.

"What is it?"

"Set fire to their siege towers. Burn them to the ground. I know it'll be risky. But if your riders can get close enough with a few burning arrows---"

"I have thought about it, too. But you do know how squeamish our rock hoppers are around fire."

"Then train them first. Get them accustomed to being near the flames. We can build some practice towers and set them on fire. What do you think?"

"It's worth a try. You build the towers and I will get my riders ready for the training."

"Okay."

"But one of us needs to go and see Petamor and tell him about the scaffolding," Sylvee reminded him.

"You're right. As soon as I get my men started building the training towers, I'll go and see him," Shane promised.

The night sky was carpeted with thick clouds. Comet, Jana's

rock hopper, spread his great gray wings, and flew confidently out over the escarpment. Below, clinging to the escarpment wall like tiny army ants, the enemy continued to build their ladders despite the constant air attacks from the Pegazonian riders.

Working in shifts to avoid fatigue, Ko-Kahn's slave army was working night and day to build their ladders. They did so by hammering strong iron rods, one rung at a time, directly into the face of the rock wall.

The Horran's siege towers, protected by their deadly arrays of porcupines, were well lit, so Captain Jana gave her flight group the signal to attack. Swooping down out of the dark sky, they managed to take the first tower by surprise. Their arrows fatally wounded the Horranian gunner, as well as the four human slaves needed to operate the porcupine.

Reacting quickly, the crew on top of the next tower leveled their porcupine at the interlopers.

At that exact same moment, just as Shane had planned, thousands of small rocks and stones began to rain down upon the heads of the ladder builders, causing many of the ladder builders to lose their balance and fall, their plummeting bodies in turn knocked more workers off their precarious perches, creating a sort of domino effect. This tactic distracted the other crews operating porcupines long enough for Captain Jana and her wingers to reel in for a second attack. This time they fired burning arrows into the towers, setting three of them ablaze before any of the porcupine crews could fire back.

After the attack, Jana pulled Comet into a steep climb away from the deadly towers. She was followed closely by her wingers, but before they could get out of range, the click of a porcupine echoed off the escarpment wall, followed seconds later by the sickening sound as two dozen arrows hit their target in the belly and hindquarters of the rock hopper to Jana's left. Although the winger had not been hit, she refused to abandon her beloved animal. A few heartbeats later, the fatally wounded rock hopper veered helplessly into the escarpment wall killing the winger instantly. Their bodies plunged and bounced six-hundred feet to the rocks below.

Kreel's long ship joined up with the rest of Rolf's fleet and headed south to intercept the Horranian galleys transporting Rhiannon's legions. The wind was in their favor.

Rolf stood at the prow of the lead ship. He had divided his fleet into two separate columns, each with a specific job to do. The enemy's estimated position was just over the horizon. Within a short time, they would become involved in the biggest sea battle in the history of the planet.

At Rolf's signal, his first column adjusted their course and headed southeast to outflank the enemy. He ordered the remainder of his fleet to reduce speed by one-half. If his plan worked, they would lure the Horranian vessels into a trap. When Rolf saw the masts and sails of the Horranian armada on the horizon, he realized that they were heading right down the throat of the enemy. He smiled.

By now, Rolf was sure that they had been spotted, but the Horranian armada made no attempt to change course. Obviously, the sight of his puny ships did not intimidate the Horranian commander. He was confident that his gigantic, double-hulled galleys could run right over top of Rolf's long ships smashing them to bits. Again, Rolf smiled.

Norgus, the commander of the Horranian armada watched the slow approach of the dragon ships through his spyglass and wondered. *Don't those fools realize that we will crush them like bugs beneath our feet if they attempt to fight us? Their commander must be desperate or insane.* So confident was he of their invulnerability, and so arrogant in his supremacy, he did not even bother to set up a defense. If the dragon ships attacked, he would simply ram straight into them, sending them all to a watery grave.

Undaunted by the size of the lumbering galleys, Rolf's column headed straight into the armada. Once they were almost
on top of the Horranian fleet, Rolf's men would retract their
oars and attempt to maneuver their tiny ships in between the
huge galleys. As they passed between the gigantic ships, they
would use their port and starboard shear blades to destroy
the enemy's oars, while showering their decks with burning
arrows. It was a daring plan, one that seemed suicidal, but if
it worked, the Horranian ships would be left crippled.

As the Horranian vessels had lost their forward momentum, the other half of his fleet would strike the enemy from
the east. The battering rams built into the prows of their long
ships would rupture the hulls of the enemy ships just below
the waterline. The idea was to come in as fast as they could,
and hit the big ships before they had a chance to raise their
sails and sail away to safety. If necessary, Rolf's column would
swing about and race in for another attack, until the Horranian
armada was completely destroyed.

When Commander Norgus saw the shear blades fastened
to the prows of the dragon ships, he began wishing that he had
not sent the sea-bats on ahead to the escarpment. At the last
moment, he ordered his ships to raise oars and come together,
but it was too late.

Rolf nodded with satisfaction as his ships slid in between
the giant galleys like minnows swimming between catfish.
Their well-sharpened shear blades sliced through the enemy's
oars with ease. The slaves, chained to their seats inside the
galleys, began to scream in stark terror, and Rolf's archers and
crossbowmen went to work firing burning arrows and bolts,
one after the other, into the crowded decks. Then, as Rolf's
column, slipped out from behind the badly crippled armada,
his second column of long ships began ramming into the galleys from the east.

The overcrowded decks of the galleys left little room for
standing, much less hand-to-hand combat, and Rhiannon's

great and undefeatable army was helpless to do anything but watch their comrades being slaughtered. In the midst of all the confusion, Rhiannon's troops fumbled uselessly with their bows. The few arrows that they did manage to use bounced harmlessly off the raised shields of Rolf's crew. In an effort to escape the carnage, many of Rhiannon's soldiers jumped into the sea and began to swim away from the battle.

In the course of the fighting, dozens of enemy troops – some alive, some dead – fell into the water. The sea-dragons, who had been circling the battle, moved in and finished off the enemy soldiers. They could smell the difference between Rolf's men and Rhiannon's minions. Anyone could. Nevertheless, there were far too many of them for the sea-dragons to dispatch and many managed to get away. Those that did escape the scene swam for the mainland of Pega.

As Rolf's column turned back for another assault, he quickly realized that his plan had succeeded. The battering rams of his second column had completely devastated the Horranian armada.

A few of the less-damaged galleys tried to escape by maneuvering around the burning hulks of their comrades. Some had raised their sails, but without their oars, they were sitting ducks for Rolf's fast moving long ships. One-by-one, Rolf's ships rammed the fleeing Horranian galleys until they were all destroyed.

Rolf's fleet did not come out of the battle completely unscathed. Many of his ships had been damaged, and he had lost several of his men as well. Nevertheless, he had won a great victory, one that neither the Horrans nor the demon wizard, Rhiannon, would ever forget.

Petamor waited in the tower for Shane. He was already aware of how much progress the Horrans had made building their steel-rung ladder up the escarpment wall. He also knew that they would reach the settlement much sooner than he had anticipated.

"Sit down, Shane," Petamor said when the man arrived. "Tell me, what is the latest news?"

"One of our wingers was killed last night," Shane replied.

"I'm sorry to hear that. How is Captain Sylvee taking it?"

Shane sighed. "She's taking it hard. But she's tough. She'll be okay," he replied.

Petamor nodded. He did not have to tell Shane that many more of Sylvee's wingers would die before it was over.

"I have other bad news as well," Shane continued. "The Horrans have started linking their siege towers together into one massive unit."

"This is a new development," Petamor admitted. "This was not part of their original plan."

"Perhaps not, but you have to admit, it's pretty clever. With all of their siege towers linked together, the structure will be very stable."

"That's true," Petamor agreed. "So, how do you plan to deal with the problem?"

"Captain Sylvee and I have decided that we should try and burn down the towers," Shane answered.

"Yes, burning down the siege towers will certainly slow them down. But it will not stop them for long. They are committed to destroying the settlement at all costs."

"How can you help us?"

Petamor poured some heated wine into a mug and handed it to Shane. He said, "I have decided to place an invisible barrier along the edge of the escarpment. A force field. When the enemy troops finally reach the top, they will not be able to cross over the protective barrier."

"A force field. That's very interesting. But why didn't you think of this sooner? It could have saved us all a lot of hard work," Shane said angrily.

"It's not that simple," Petamor replied wearily. "This force field will tax all of my strength. I will not be able to maintain it for very long. Perhaps a week or two at best."

"I guess I had it all wrong," Shane began, sipping his wine. "I always believed that a wizard could do anything. I remember my grandfather telling me a story about the wizard who had once lived here in this tower. He told me how that mighty wizard had placed an enchantment over the entire plateau. Because of that enchantment, the plateau remained summer-like all year round. If I remember correctly, my grandfather said that the wizard's name was Petamor. I would think that such a powerful wizard could do just about anything."

"Your grandfather was right about one thing, Shane. For many hundreds of years, there was an enchantment over the plateau. But I was not the one who put it there. That distinction belongs to my mentor, the wizard Allacor, who first placed the original enchantment over three thousand years ago. All I did was use my powers to help maintain the enchantment. Many things have changed since those days, especially the magic. The magic has been fading from this world for ages. Soon, it will be gone forever."

"If your magic force field isn't strong enough to hold back the Horrans, why are you even bothering to try?"

"I am hoping that once Ko-Kahn realizes that the plateau is being protected with magic, he will see the pointlessness of his invasion and withdraw."

"And if he doesn't?"

"If he doesn't, then you and the rest of the settlers will have to fight them the old fashioned way," Petamor said. "Yet all is not lost, for even as we speak, the wizard, Thoradal, is on his way to Rhiannon's island to rescue Breandan. If he succeeds, and we are able to revive Breandan in time, we can combine our wizardly powers to defeat Ko-Kahn and annihilate his army."

In the southern ocean, a lone dragon ship sailed cautiously towards Rhiannon's island. The ship had been painted black to help it blend in with the terrain. Aside from Kile and Thoradal, there were sixty highly trained and fearless warriors aboard the ship. They were all volunteers, and they understood the dangers of the mission.

Thoradal's plan was simple. First, he would help Kile and his men locate Breandan, then, while Kile and his men helped Breandan back to the ship, he would hunt Rhiannon down and destroy her. Failure was not an option.

They waited until well after midnight and then approached the island under the cover of darkness. Thoradal carried Breandan's Lamp of Life, and as he had hoped, it grew steadily warmer as they neared the island. He was also hoping that the lamp would help them locate Breandan once they were inside the labyrinth of caves and passageways deep below the volcano.

"What will we do if we're spotted before we find the entrance?" Kile asked.

"We need only be concerned with Rhiannon's personal guard. The rest of her servants, as she likes to call them, were either destroyed by your brother's fleet or are on their way to join Ko-Kahn's forces on Pega," Thoradal answered.

"Rolf's fleet has destroyed Rhiannon's transports?"

"Yes, but many of Rhiannon's mutants escaped by jumping into the sea."

"Excuse me, Wizard, but how do you know this?" Kile asked.

"A little bird told me," Thoradal replied with a slight smile.

Scratching his head, Kile looked up and saw a colorful little parrot perched atop the mainsail looking back down at him with inquisitive eyes. He looked at Thoradal. "A little bird?"

The old wizard nodded. "It is not a real living bird. It is a robotic device I made two thousand years ago to deceive Rhiannon. It saw everything. Rolf's long ships. The sea-dragons. The fierce battle. And most importantly, Rhiannon saw it all, too."

"So Rhiannon knows that her transports were destroyed?"

"Yes, she knows."

"Then she also knows that we're here?"

"No, the bird only allows her to see what I want her to see."

"Nevertheless, I think she's going to be in a really bad mood," Kile said. "Will you be able to handle her alone?"

"Don't worry about me, Kile. No matter what happens, you must stick to the plan," Thoradal replied. "Do you understand?"

"Yes, Wizard. I understand."

The festering, blackened island loomed ahead like a gangrenous sore on the face of the planet, a nightmarish landscape arisen out of hell itself. Kile and his men donned black cloaks to blend in with the surroundings. Camouflage, Thoradal had called it, whatever that meant. Their weapons had also been carefully wrapped in dark cloth to minimize the noise. Stealthily they made their way through the phantasmagoric wasteland to the base of the volcano.

Half-rodent, half-cockroach like creatures scurried about in the shadows, while fat maggots – the color of puss – and slimy slugs – some as big as a newborn pig – were gathering in reeking cesspools of filth and muck.

"Wizard," Kile said, pointing to one of the oily looking palm trees, "if this island has been underwater for two thousand years, how come these plants and trees are still here? Shouldn't they have all rotted away by now?"

"They still live," Thoradal said.

Kile looked at him bewildered. "How can they still be alive after spending two thousand years under water, and salt water at that?"

"Rhiannon is a powerful wizard. She taught herself the forbidden knowledge of these things. They live, because she wills them to live."

Kile looked up into a banana tree and saw that the blacken fruit was dripping with rancid yellow puss. "Disgusting," he said. "I don't think I'll ever be able to eat a banana again."

The entrance to Rhiannon's underground realm may have been easily hidden from mortal eyes, but Thoradal had no problem finding it. He made a pass over the spot with his staff and the door opened without a sound. The passageway was darker than death. The vile odor that assailed them made many of Kile's men sick to their stomachs.

Thoradal lit the way with his staff, its eerie blue light created bewitching patterns of shadow on the cave walls. Nevertheless, Kile and the five men who had volunteered to follow him into the labyrinth, stayed close behind the wizard.

They were all wondering where Rhiannon's guards were, when suddenly, out of the eerie silence, came the sound of soft padded footsteps echoing along the corridor ahead. Suddenly, one of Rhiannon lumbering troglobites came around a bend in the tunnel. Its luminous green eyes were too busy watching its own feet, and it did not see its enemies until it was too late. As it looked up, its ugly glowing eyes widened in shock. It attempted to call out a warning, but its warbled siren voice was quickly cut short as a bolt from Kile's crossbow smacked it right between its eyes. It was thrown back against the slimy rock wall. The long pike it had been carrying dropped from its dead webbed fingers and fell to the floor with a loud clang.

Within minutes, the sound of running feet filled the cavern. Several of Rhiannon's guards came rushing around the corner like mad demons, but they were ill prepared for the ensuing battle. Their pikes were basically useless in the narrow passageway, and Kile's men clove them into fish-food with their broad swords.

Although shouts and alarms could be heard coming from deep within the catacombs, the corridor ahead was deserted.

Once again, the old wizard led the way with his lighted staff, deeper and deeper into the bowels of the ancient volcano.

After some time, they came to a large cavern containing a vast underground lake. The water was so still, it first appeared to be made of glass. The only sound they heard was the steady---

...plink...*pause*...plink...*pause*...plink...*pause*...

---of water dripping somewhere in the gloom.

Thoradal and the other men began to edge their way along the shore of the grotto, when a sudden ripple disturbed the serene surface of the water.

Cahir was between Kile and the wizard, when a giant eel-like raised its slimy head up out of the lake.

The sea monster was unlike any creature the men had ever seen. It towered more than thirty feet above the lake surface, which meant that its total length was somewhere close to one hundred feet. It had a row of needle-like spikes running the length of its spine that were eight to ten feet long, and created its own bioluminescent light, which was alternating in constantly changing shades of pink, violet, and cobalt blue.

It looked down at the trespassers with the cold deadly eyes of a merciless predator and abruptly snatched Cahir up between its massive jaws. Before Kile or any of the others could react, the eel tossed back its head and swallowed Cahir whole.

Before Kile and his men could react, a bolt of blue lightening shot out of Thoradal's staff, but missed the creature as it dodged to the right. A second bolt also missed its target as the creature darted left. Somehow, the monster was anticipating Thoradal's every move.

Then a bolt from Kile's crossbow caught the giant eel-like creature in the throat, and it reared back screeching in pain and rage.

While the monster was distracted, Thoradal fired off another lightening bolt from his staff and the eel's head exploded into a pinkish-purple cloud of blood and gore. As the creature sank back into the lake, dozens of extremely large piranha-like fish began to devour the carcass.

Undaunted, the determined men walked on for nearly two hours, slowly inching their way through one winding passage after the other. With each step, Breandan's lamp grew warmer until the wick began to flicker with a pale blue flame. Every time they wondered too far in the wrong direction, the flame would begin to sputter and die again, and they would have to turn back to search for a new path. At last, they came to a bend in the tunnel. The area beyond was brightly lighted. Kile gave the signal and his men drew their swords once more. Together they rounded the corner and found themselves in another large cavernous chamber.

On the far side of the room stood fifty of Rhiannon's personal guards, with pointy teeth and large green eyes like those of ravenous jungle cats. Unlike the earlier guards, these creatures were properly armed with swords and battle-axes. Just beyond the guard's position was another smaller chamber where Breandan's body was being kept in a crystal vault. Apparently, they had assembled their forces to protect Rhiannon. Abruptly, they rushed across the room towards Kile's small company.

Although they were outnumbered by more than ten-to-one, Kile and his men fought like berserkers. Rhiannon's guards were fast and agile, but they were no match for the well-trained and experienced Dragon Masters, whose broad swords dealt out death like the scythe used by Death himself harvesting two and three deserving souls at a time. When the skirmish was over, the floor was strewn with the shattered corpses of Rhiannon's elite guard. Among the dead were three of Kile's own men.

When Kile and the other surviving warrior regained their wits, they found Thoradal standing in front of the closed door of the chamber where Breandan's unconscious body laid in state.

"Breandan's body is in here," the old wizard said sadly. Unlike the demon wizard, Thoradal could sense that something had gone wrong with Rhiannon's plan. He was certain that Breandan's body was alive, but he was not yet aware that Breandan's life essence had moved on into the spiritual plane.

"Do you want us to break it down?" Kile asked.

"No," Thoradal answered gloomily. "You'll need all of your remaining energy to get Breandan out of this place. I will open the door." Thoradal placed the palm of his wrinkled hand against the entry and spoke so softly that Kile could not understand the words. A moment later, the door vanished into smoke that dissipated along the empty corridor.

There, in the middle of the small chamber, lay the body of the boy-wizard, Breandan. He was resting inside a crystal sarcophagus from which the lid had been removed. The body was alive but in a state of suspended animation. His hands were crossed over his chest; his staff had been placed at his side.

Beside him, as if in silent prayer, knelt Rhiannon. She seemed either unaware or unconcerned of their presence. With her scarred and twisted hand, she lovingly stroked the boy wizard's hair.

For a long moment no one spoke, then Thoradal quietly carried Breandan's lamp into the room.

In that instant, Rhiannon jumped to her feet and began to howl in pain. The red-gold ring on her finger had burst into flames. Although fire was not supposed to be able to hurt a protected wizard; however, these were no ordinary flames. Frantically she grabbed and clawed at the burning gold, but it was too late. The melting metal had burned completely through her finger, leaving a blackened, smoldering stump.

"Fools!" she screamed in agony. "You will all pay for this,

especially you, Thoradal, you meddling old fool. How dare you come here to my island and challenge me!"

This was the opportunity that Thoradal had been counting on. He looked at Rhiannon and asked, "Who are you, demon? Tell me your name so that I can cast you back into the abyss from which you escaped."

"My name is Neraka!" Rhiannon hissed through clenched teeth. "And you do not have the power to cast me anywhere, old man. It is I who will cast you out of that stinking skin you're in!"

"Well, if you want me, demon, come and get me. With that, Thoradal bounded out of the room and headed through one of the natural passages that led to the upper levels of the volcano.

Howling with rage, Rhiannon flew after him intent upon murder. In her blind fury, she left her staff behind near Breandan's vault.

Kile's man was starting out the door in pursuit, but Kile called him back, "No! Let them go! Thoradal can handle her."

"But, Captain," he replied, "she intends to kill him surely."

"Our orders are to move Breandan's body to the ship as fast as we can," Kile said reluctantly, "and that's exactly what we're going to do. Now help me get him out of this vault."

They moved quickly back the way they had come, using one of the torches that had been inside Breandan's chamber to light the way. While they had been searching for Breandan, Kile had scratched a series of marks on the walls of the passageways with a piece of chalk. These marks now led them back to the tunnel entrance, saving them a great deal of time.

They were cautious at first, expecting to be ambushed along the way by more guards, but they met no further resistance until they exited the labyrinth and were spotted but some seabats circling overhead. Since they had discarded their dark cloaks earlier after fighting the guards outside of Breandan's chamber, they were easy to spot from the sky. One of the creatures dove down and snatched Kile's last man away before he could fire off a bolt from his crossbow.

The sea-bat flew out over the ocean where it dropped its struggling victim to its hungry mate waiting in the water. Its cries of delight soon attracted the attention of other sea-bats. Before long, the sky was filled with the hungry, circling beasts.

Some of the men who had remained behind to look after Kile's ship came running to assist him. Fortunately, the sea-bats were too busy feeding to bother with them, at least for the moment.

On the highest peak of that ancient volcano, the northernmost edge of the crater, Thoradal waited patiently for Rhiannon to catch up with him. He could hear her coming, stumbling through the darkness and the rage. His heart felt sick. At last, he had come to the realization that the league had failed. They had not only failed Breandan and the people of Pega; they had failed Rhiannon as well. When she had needed their help, they had turned their backs on her, allowing her to become the tool of a demon. And now, it had come to this.

Above, in the night sky, a billion stars twinkled and sparkled in an endless universe of swirling galaxies and colorful gases. It was more beautiful than he could ever recall. He searched and quickly found the star system from which he and his fellow wizards had come all those years ago.

He looked down and scanned the beach until he found Kile's long ship. Kile and his men were lifting Breandan's still body onto the deck of the ship. He sighed. He waited until Kile's men had pushed the ship off the sand and were heading back out to sea before raising his staff to the sky.

It had been over two thousand years since he had used this kind of magic. This would be the last time. Then he spoke the words in the ancient tongue of his ancestors and lowered his staff to wait.

Kile ordered his crew to put as much distance between them and the island as possible. When he turned, he caught a glimpse of Thoradal standing on the peak of the volcano with his staff raised in the air. Before he could analyze the situation; however, he was distracted by a sudden change in the sea around his ship. At first, he thought that more of Rhiannon's mutated creatures had surrounded them from below and were about to surface and attack again. He was preparing to order the men to raise the oars when one of his men pointed to the night sky.

Chaos, the tiny, chameleon moon, had turned a bright red and it appeared to be growing larger. Then Kile understood. Thoradal had called the moon down to destroy Rhiannon's island, just as he had once called a meteorite down to create Dragon's Den.

At last, Rhiannon clamored out of a crack in the crater wall and faced Thoradal. He saw for the first time just how horribly burned she had been all those years ago. She looked up into the sky and saw Chaos descending upon them. For one brief moment, their eyes met. Rhiannon – the real Rhiannon – tried to smile in spite of her pain. The yellowish light in her eyes suddenly went out and Thoradal found himself looking once again into the kind and innocent eyes of the young shepherd girl.

Neraka had vacated the premises, leaving behind yet another victim. Then, in a blinding flash, the little moon called Chaos, which had once been a starship from another world thousands of light-years away, struck Rhiannon's island. The collision shook the entire planet. Millions of tons of dust and debris showered down around the island for miles. A wall of water twenty-feet high began to move away from the point of impact growing larger by the second as it threatened to capsize Kile's ship. Nevertheless, Kile had an experienced crew, and they managed to turn the prow of the ship into the wave in time to avoid destruction.

By the time most of the dust had settled, the sun was breaking into a dusty morning sky the color of muddied urine. There was no trace of Rhiannon's island or the moon once called Chaos. Rhiannon was gone.

Thoradal was gone.

On the deck of Kile's dragon ship, out of harms way, rested the body of the boy-wizard, Breandan. The flame in his lamp, which had once been a lovely shade of blue, now burned a bright red, having burst to life only seconds before the explosion. It now burned brighter than ever. One could say that it burned like the fires of hell.

Kile and his crew were too busy trying to avoid debris floating on the surface of the ocean to pay attention to the unconscious boy-wizard, so no one witnessed the wicked smile that crossed Breandan's face when he opened his eyes for the first time in two thousand years. No one saw the cold yellow gleam deep within those eyes that shone brighter and hotter than the rising sun.

TO BE CONTINUED